304 MONSTERS

STEPHEN BIAS

The Henlo Press

Printed in the United States of America
First Printing, 2024
Paperback isbn-978-1-962019-08-8
Hardcover isbn- 978-1-962019-07-1

The Henlo Press
P.O. Box 1694Ashland, KY 41105
www.thehenlopress.com

For My Family

A NOTE FROM THE AUTHOR

My father died yesterday. I know that is a hell of a way to start a dedication and introduction, but it's true. I am writing this on January 3rd, 2024, sitting on the floor in my pajamas and drinking a Diet Coke. I am trying to find the right words to say to all of you. I had completed the original version of this the day before he passed, talking about how I thought he was out of the woods, which turned out to be completely wrong.

I am less than two months away from the release of the book you now hold in your hands. The past year has been littered with loss for me. I've tried to put on a brave face and smile. I've done it for my wife, daughter, and mother. It's been hard trying to hold myself together; I've gotten used to telling people the little white lie, "I'm fine."

First and foremost, to those of you who kickstarted this project to life, I appreciate your patience. We were close to release in May of 2023, and I was on the downslope of editing and preparing to go into advertising 304. I was having t-shirts made, and posters. I would contact the town's mayor, where I was raised, and have my release party there. I had the highest of hopes for this book. The thrill of Afterwords and the positive response I had to it was fueling me.

That's when June hit; our target date was my 50th birthday in August. I was ready for all of it. We (The Henlo Press) geared up to launch, and it was all smiles. On June 9th, 2023, ironically, my father's 70th birthday, my son passed away at only twenty-seven years old. I was extremely close to Andrew and talked to him nightly. The spiral a parent takes when their child dies was something I never thought I would deal with. To say I was devastated was an understatement.

The number one thing I heard over this entire process, especially from other parents, was the phrase, "I couldn't imagine." There is no more accurate statement. There is nothing like the pain and something I wouldn't wish on anyone. It's like someone tears a hole through you that you know deep down nothing can fill. The Henlo Press and I met at the end of June and decided to push the release back till the holiday of the year to give me time to at least try and put the pieces back together.

My father went to the hospital in the final week of June and didn't come home till November. We were told on numerous occasions that he wouldn't be coming home. He kept fighting, primarily for my mother, whom he'd been married to for 52 years. When he was healthy, they had a relationship people only dream about. I watched as she never left his side and as a part of her drained away.

It was bad enough to lose Andrew, but now we were losing my father, too. In October, my dog, at the ripe age of 15, had developed cancer throughout her stomach and esophagus, and I had to have her euthanized. I held her while she went and asked no one in particular on my way out the door.

"Is there a place I can just pay the fine and things get better?"

The family gathered for Thanksgiving, and it was fantastic. Dad was his usual self, minus a leg they had to remove while he was ill. I had a bunch of hoodies made for the book, commissioned some art, and off we went. We locked down the date of February 25th, 2024, and again, I started the final rush to release.

The thing about 304 Monsters is that while it is meant to be a horror story, the underlying theme in this book is and always has been about family. West Virginia is not your typical place; I am sure most people who read this are from here. I am hoping to get those who aren't to understand.

So, the point I am trying to make is I don't think my family had to cook a meal till September. My phone and doorbell never stopped going off, even when I asked to be alone. On June 22nd, the day I laid him to rest when I sat down at the end of the day and glanced at my phone, I had almost two hundred text messages, two from people I hadn't talked to in over twenty-five years.

I'm not trying to darken your mood or bring you down. What I want to do is set the stage. West Virginia and its people prop you up. They won't let you fall as they brace themselves against your back. When I would tell that little white lie of "I'm fine." the people around me were saying with their actions, "You will be."

For the love of God, someone was texting me hydration reminders. They made sure I drank water, and if I told them I was having coffee, they would chastise me. Now I know what you are thinking. *Family and friends do these things. That's what they are for.* That's just it; this wasn't just family and friends. Someone I hated throughout high school and into adulthood reached out to me. People who hadn't seen me in decades got my phone number and called in support. I still don't know who the family that sent me the Long John Silvers is. I got hugged by a woman I had never met and social media messages from a few people who heard what happened to me through the West Virginia grapevine.

I decided then and there to go back through this book and change names as a tribute to people who were there when I needed them. Those who listened to me lash out at the world, those who made me laugh, and those who made me cry. The characters don't look like them or act the way they do, but I wanted to give them a nod. To let them know I loved them and that I heard them. I felt all the warmth they sent my way.

To the people who backed this book, I couldn't do this without you. I shattered Afterword's original funding and have continued to grow, and it's a beautiful feeling knowing people like what I place on the page. To everyone who comes to the booth at shows I am at, take time to listen to my spiel. I thank you. I love nothing more than going to book festivals and conventions. They brighten my day.

Now, for the hard part, this book is dedicated to two people; the first is Andrew. My son left the world way too soon. I am a better man for knowing you, and I will always ache when midnight rolls around. I would call him most nights just to argue about things. He is the real reason this book exists. After my first novel, he called me up once he finished it and said, "Dad, I liked it, but it wasn't what I expected. I thought you'd do more of a horror comedy. That's so up your alley."

That's precisely what I did, Andrew, and I think it is a fantastic story. I hope everyone else does, too. I think you'd be proud of this one. I hope wherever you are in the After, you get a chance to read it.

The second is my father, David. You were sick for a long time but tried to force a smile. I was proud to be your son. I am honored to carry your last name, and I am happy that I got to tell you how I felt about you before the end. On the day he passed, that morning, my mother was wearing a 304 Monsters hoodie, and my dad told her. "I hope he hits it with this one. He's worked hard." Six hours away from leaving the world, he was still thinking about his children. That was David in a nutshell. I couldn't dedicate this to two better people.

Stephen

1

Veronica Carter was teetering on the edge of her shift, ready for the start of a well-deserved weekend. An excited smile spread across her face, reflected in the terminal in front of her—reading just after three o'clock. The day had been dull; Veronica wrote one ticket to a man speeding through downtown—driving twenty-two miles over the limit with no valid excuse. Though he had been respectful, Veronica still elected not to let him off the hook. An elementary school was less than a block away, and she wanted him to learn his lesson.

It was a stroke of luck and had been a welcome respite from the rest of the week. On Monday, she'd entered a home where an elderly woman had passed away in bed three weeks prior. The son had contacted her department from Las Vegas, concerned when his mother stopped answering her phone. When Veronica arrived at the house, the body had begun to liquefy. It had been brutally hot at the start of September, and the only air circulating in the entire home was from a fan pointed toward the bed. Even now, the odor lingered in her nostrils.

Other than the excitement from the occasional high-speed chase or drunken brawl, her first two years on the force had been relatively peaceful. In the past six months, however, Veronica noted a dramatic increase in violence and hostility, leaving her drained and worried about what could come next. Veronica caught herself wondering if she had time to walk away and find something else. She was still young, after all. The pay wasn't great, and the constant swinging from day to evening shift took a toll. The mere thought of it depressed her. But she would put the negativity on hold until Monday.

She had big plans for this Saturday. She was throwing her grandmother a surprise birthday party, and then she had a date with someone she'd been talking to for months. It was supposed to rain in the evening, but she'd be indulging in a beautiful dinner at The Blennerhassett by then. She'd hoped the dinner would charm the pants off her date, Skylar, and in the most literal way.

She glanced up to the rearview mirror and smiled. She loved her eyes. Her grandmother had always told her she could get away with murder because of her "baby browns." Veronica always chuckled at that; she'd heard the phrase used for blue eyes but never anything else.

Veronica didn't pride herself on her appearance. There wasn't time to worry about how her makeup looked when she was chasing down bad guys. She *could* be pretty when she wanted, and over the years she had grown to appreciate her looks. She was tall, and on the thicker side, but her assets were in her intelligence and her competence. She had always joked with her grandmother that she could take over the world if she'd been born in a different body—and her grandmother had tutted at her every single time. "It's your mind and your heart that matter, sugar," she'd always said.

She waved at some children on bicycles that passed by her, before her eyes drifted back to her reflection. She made a face of disgust. She was going to have to do something about her hair, it was getting way too long and it never made it through the day without feeling gross and greasy. She would try and make an appointment tomorrow morning and get it done before her big day kicked off.

Veronica decided to end her day out in the nicer neighborhoods. She had the driver and passenger windows down, liking the feel of warm air on her face instead of air conditioning. The sun peeked out from behind batches of pearly clouds. The radio had been silent for a few miles, and she was enjoying the drive. She looked down at the panel of her terminal again, it was blank.

Oh shit, did I knock the connector out?

She pulled to the side of the street next to a yellow home with sharp, angular lines. Tall pillars lined the generous porch and brickwork fenced in a large yard. Two slender sycamores led the way up to the house, which stood out against the greenery like a sunflower among the grass. Veronica put the car in park and lightly tapped the darkened display. Dead. She ran her finger down the cables that lead into the dash and felt where their plugs attached.

No issue there.

That was as far as her technical expertise went on the matter. It was best to call Metro and let them know her system was down. She grabbed her phone from the center console and pressed the bottom's center button, but the tiny device only displayed darkness.

Shit.

She had just put the cruiser in reverse when she saw it. Her heart froze, and her stomach tightened. A woman was lying halfway between her patrol car and the house at the end of the driveway. Even at this distance, Veronica could see the blood.

"What the hell?" Veronica cursed under her breath. She opened the door, peering intently at the unmoving person in the center of the road before getting out of the car.

"Ma'am?" Veronica called out cautiously.

Complete silence filled the air around her, a tense stillness broken only by the low hum of her cruiser. Taking a deep breath, she slipped her keys into her pocket and closed her fingers around the grip of her sidearm.

"Ma'am, Parkersburg Police Department, do you need assistance?" Veronica called out.

She was startled by how meek her voice sounded. She scanned the area again as a slight breeze rustled through the trees. There were only three homes on Greystone Lane: the one she parked in front of, the one to the right of the person she approached, and the one at the end of the street. There weren't very many places for an individual to ambush her. She would see them coming.

"I am coming over to you," she called out again. She reached up and pressed the handle button on the police radio on her chest. "78 Metro," she said, tilting her head in. She waited for a response.

Shit. Shit. Shit. First the terminal. Then the phone. And now the radio? Great.

Veronica quickened her pace as she approached the lady lying motionless on the asphalt in a pool of blood so large it seemed impossible to be one person's. The woman was facing Veronica. A look of terror was etched across the brow and gaping mouth, the world a glass reflection in hollow eyes.

The woman was clearly dead, but there were protocols, expected steps that had to be taken.Veronica knelt, placing the front of her hand near the woman's nose and mouth, and felt nothing. She gripped the wrist with two fingers and a thumb to check for a pulse.

Nothing. No surprise there. What the hell happened?

Veronica swallowed hard and examined the body. She moved to the left, examining the wounds on her back. Veronica could see the shredded fabric of her shirt around the collar. Deep gashes spread in jagged lines, and the dead woman's flesh was torn open and bloody. The rips deeper near the top of her shoulders. The attacker had swung down and into her repeatedly before she fell.

Her arms were out to her sides and adorned with cuts that ran deep across her forearms where she had defended herself from the blows. She had faced her attacker before he turned her around. One hand was deeply lacerated, torn through the skin and muscle tissue, indicating she brought it up in an attempt to grab the weapon. She had been stabbed with something pointed and sharp. It had to be a knife.

Mail was scattered across the ground, and Veronica looked up at the open mailbox a few feet away. The side of it read *Dunlap #2*. Veronica noticed a young girl crouched behind a bush, near the door with her hands covering her mouth. Her eyes were wide and full of terror, The little girl couldn't have been older than six.Veronica held her left hand out, palm down.

"Are you okay?"

The little girl took her hands away from her mouth and shook her head. This child was hiding from someone.Veronica, staying low, rushed over to the porch where the girl was, trying to block her view from the dead woman at the yard's edge.

"I'm Officer Carter; I'm here to help. Are you hurt?" Veronica whispered as she held her hand out.

"I don't want him to find me." Her voice shook as she gasped in air.

"Who?" Veronica asked.

"He's got Chris! He hurt Mommy!" the girl responded hysterically, her voice hoarse from crying.

Veronica knelt and grabbed the little girl's hand. "I need you to tell me who hurt them so I can help."

"The man next door." The girl jerked away and pushed herself up to her knees.

"What's your name?" Veronica spoke slowly and backed away a step to appear non-threatening.

"Grace," she answered, wiping tears from her cheeks.

"Okay, Grace, do you know where he is now?" Veronica peered behind her and to both sides. "Does he live in the yellow house?"

She shook her head. "No. That's Mr. Ray and Ms. Lori. They went to the beach. Shane lives in the brown house."

"Do you know why he did this, Grace?"

"No," she sobbed.

"Do you know where Shane went?"

"He took Chris into his house." Grace pointed to the end of the road.

"Okay, how old is Chris?"

"Eleven." Grace placed her hands on her head and looked around frantically. Veronica paused and glimpsed around the bush to the house at the end of the street. She had to act quickly.

"Is anyone else home?"

"No, Daddy doesn't live with us anymore." Grace pushed her blonde hair away from her face. Veronica noticed a set of keys on the ground near them both.

"Is the door unlocked?"

Grace turned toward it. "I think so. Mommy was getting the mail. Is she okay?"

"POLICEMAN!" a man's voice echoed throughout the street. Grace rushed forward and clutched at Veronica's waist. The door of the brown brick house was now ajar and Veronica could hear the man yelling from inside.

"I SEE YOU POLICEMAN! YOU GOT THREE MINUTES TO GET IN HERE BEFORE I KILL HIM!" he screamed again, followed by a loud slam.

"He's going to kill him," Grace bawled.

"He's not going to kill him," Veronica said.

Shit, he's going to kill him.

Veronica put her hands on Grace's shoulders and focused on her tiny blue eyes. "Check the door." Grace spun around, turned the handle, and it opened. "Great, you are doing great. Is there a phone inside the house?" Veronica sped up her cadence. She knew the clock was ticking. Grace crept low and snuck toward the end of the porch, out of Veronica's sight, before rushing back with a cell phone.

"I got Mommy's, but I don't know how to use it."

"Thanks, honey." Veronica pressed the home button, slid her finger across the phone's screen, and tapped Emergency Call before bringing it to her ear. She reached out and hugged Grace. She needed it as much as she felt Grace did. "It's going to be alright. I promise," Veronica told her.

"9-1-1, what's your emergency?" the voice on the other end came through.

"This is Officer Veronica Carter, unit 78 of the Parkersburg Police Department. I am on Greystone Lane, off Red Hill Road. I need an ambulance and as many officers as can be sent. I have a hostage situation and a middle-aged woman injured in the street."

"How many hostages?" the woman asked.

"One, an eleven-year-old boy, is being held by one suspect I know only as Shane. He's in the house at the end of the street. I am here with– How old are you, Grace?" Veronica asked as she looked down at her.

"Five."

"I have a five-year-old that I am sending inside her house. It's the one with the woman in front of it. The house has a mailbox in front. It is number 2. She will be– Hey Grace, do you play hide and go seek inside?"

Grace nodded.

"Where did you like to hide?" Veronica smiled, trying to console the frightened child.

"Under my bed."

"She will be hiding under her bed, but I am giving the phone to her. I need you to keep her calm and make sure she stays hidden. Suspect has demanded I come out in the open, or he will harm the boy," Veronica said into the device before handing the phone to Grace. She began to wonder how much time she'd already wasted.

"But what about Mommy?" Grace tried to look around Veronica at the street, but Veronica guided her shoulders, turning her back from viewing it.

"I'll help her," Veronica lied. "The person on the phone will keep you company until my friends get here." Veronica nodded at the phone Grace was gripping. You talk to them, and you hide. Got it?"

"O-okay," Grace stammered.

"Go," Veronica told her, patting her back and standing upright. Grace went through the door and closed it behind her.

She drew her pistol from its holster, and she felt a rush of anger overcome her. Shane murdered this woman in front of her children and took one of them into his house. Why? What would cause a person to do something so heinous? A child Grace's age should never have to witness anything like that, and who knew what shape the boy was in?

Don't think.

She marched toward the house at a quickened pace. She didn't have a watch and had wasted too much time already. She had the upper hand if he only had a knife, but Shane had a home-field advantage. He could be waiting by the door to—

Don't think.

Veronica knew the protocol and understood what she was supposed to do in a hostage situation, but he was dictating her actions. If Shane meant what he said, he'd murder the boy while she set up a perimeter or held off till someone could watch her back. She was already charging across the yard and toward the front entrance. Grace had just watched her mother die, and now there was a chance her brother might join her. Veronica wasn't the type to be a hero, but she was running on pure adrenaline. She had to do something; she just didn't know what.

Don't think.

Veronica didn't pause as she reached the door. Her foot was already on the way up and connected hard against the white wood near the door handle. She charged through the open doorway with her pistol raised, ready to put anyone who showed an ounce of hostility down.

The voice from before called out from off to her left. "MAKE SURE YOU SHUT THE DOOR! DON'T LEAVE IT OPEN!"

Veronica crossed the house's threshold, her senses firing on all cylinders. She was now in a small entranceway with walls on both sides of her that, after a step-down, opened up into a much larger room. The problem was she couldn't see around the corners to the left and right.

"Sir? Parkersburg Po-" she began.

"HURRY UP AND SHUT THE DOOR!" the man screamed. Veronica stepped back and attempted to close the door, but she'd broken the frame, and it wouldn't latch.

"IS IT SHUT?" he asked.

"Yes," Veronica lied. She leaned up against the left wall and peeked around the side. Someone, she assumed Shane, had covered the entire living room in strange symbols. Uncapped black Sharpies lay strewn across the carpet. They were written all over the furniture, the walls, and scraps of paper across the floor. She glanced into the dining room and noticed more drawings. The first thought that popped into her head was hieroglyphics, but this was something darker. One looked like an upside-down *A* with a line through it next to something that resembled a shark.

She looked around the corner and noticed that the glyphs went to the ceiling, which explained the ladder leaning against the room's far corner. The writing was across the trim and even the light bulbs of the fan. It was everywhere, and none of it made sense. She looked for one recognizable letter but couldn't find one.

A young boy sat in a brown dining chair on the far side of the room. Sweat dripped from his face, and his eyes swelled. Blood poured from his mouth and nose. This must be Chris. The child wasn't looking at her; his eyes were floating from place to place. He was showing signs of a concussion. A shirtless man stood behind him, the tip of a kitchen knife pressed into the boy's throat. He was thin and not very muscular. His jeans were bloody. He was wearing a West Virginia University ball cap turned slightly to the side. He was filthy, covered in dirt and grime, unshaven. It looked as if he hadn't bathed in weeks, and smelled just as ripe.

He was too far to close the gap and try to wrestle the knife from his hands. His eyes were glassy and, from this distance, seemed red. They were wide, exposing too much white around his pupils, and his cheekbones were wet as if he'd been sobbing. His face flushed almost purple. The veins in his neck showed as if he was straining.

This has to be bath salts.

Bath salts were ravaging the state at the moment as a cheap alternative to cocaine and methamphetamines. And with a bit of know-how, anyone could make it at home. She stepped out with her gun raised and walked to the center of the room.

"That's far enough," he warned as he tilted the knife, and a little blood ran down Chris's neck onto the collar of his shirt.

"Sir—the ambulance is on the way. No one else has to die. You've done enough," she said as calmly as possible.

"Don't do that," he said between heavy breaths.

"Do what?"

"Patronize me. I'm not stupid," he mocked. "And I'm not no sir. Just Shane. Always just been Shane."

"I never called you stupid, Shane," she nodded at Chris, "I'm just trying to get that boy out of danger."

He glared down at the boy and then back to her. "Well, give me what I want, and you can have him."

"And what is it you want?"

His eyes darted around the room, but he didn't answer.

Veronica felt her hands starting to sweat. Something about the man's eyes unnerved her. She tried to remember her training and control her breathing. She inhaled deeply through her nose and let it out through her mouth. She was afraid she'd start trembling, and that would be disastrous. She didn't want to give off any semblance of fear, but inside, she screamed. Veronica's gut told her this would end badly, no matter what she did.

Just breathe. If you need to shoot him, it needs to be perfect, Veronica told herself.

She'd never noticed how heavy her Glock 19 was until now. It had felt comfortable and solid in her hands for the past two years. But here it felt twenty pounds heavier and like she might drop it. Aiming at paper targets or dummies was one thing, but pointing the barrel directly at a man's face was entirely different.

It wasn't just the gun that felt off. Veronica's uniform felt cumbersome, like the fabric was restricting her movements. She was trying to concentrate on anything else, but her mind wouldn't let the feeling of discomfort fade. She needed to be strong; she didn't want to die here today and certainly didn't want to lose the eleven-year-old hostage.

"Where is the girl?" Shane questioned.

"Girl?" she asked. She had to keep him talking. Another officer might arrive, come through the back door, and subdue him. Something, anything, would be better than a standoff.

"The little bitch– Grace. Where is she? You bring her here, and I let the boy go." His voice rose when he said the child's name. Veronica felt her stomach flip. There was no way in Hell she was letting him anywhere near Grace.

"She's at the end of the street. She's the one who flagged me down. Lori has her," Veronica lied, using one of the names Grace had mentioned earlier.

"No," he muttered, "No, no, no." Shane smacked his forehead with his right hand each time he said it, making a loud slapping sound.

"Calm down. It's going to be okay," she wanted his attention off Grace, so she changed course. "Did you draw all this?" she asked as she drifted to some of the larger pieces.

He nodded violently. Chris moaned with each movement, the knife tip still firmly pressed into his neck.

"What does it mean?" Veronica stalled, and even though she had an ulterior motive, she was curious. The writing wasn't something someone could accomplish in a day; he'd been working on this for weeks, maybe months.

He looked away from her, and his mouth opened slightly. He seemed lost in the question. After what seemed like an eternity, he snapped out of it, angrier than before.

"It keeps her out!" he snarled

"Keeps who out?" Veronica took a step forward.

"The girl!" Shane raised his eyebrow and tightened his lips. "She's evil. I almost had her. I... I could have saved all of us. You have to bring her here. ALONE! We have to stop her!" His eyes met hers, and he was spitting as he spoke. He took his right hand, gripped the boy's shoulder, and squeezed. The boy cried out.

Veronica shook her head. "That's not happening, Shane. She's scared to death. You just killed her mother in front of her and took her brother."

"Her mother and brother? You idiot, she just..." he trailed off.

"Shane, have you slept?" Veronica steered the conversation away from Grace. "Have you eaten? You look like you could use a little of both. I just want to help. I don't want to hurt you. I just want to help." Veronica lowered her sidearm a few inches. "Please, no one has to die."

"She does," he whispered.

He's gone. At this rate it is him or the boy.

"Shane, do you live here alone?" she pried. She realized she wasn't just stalling anymore. She was delaying the inevitable. She was afraid.

Veronica had never taken a life. A sergeant who had taken her under his wing told her this had happened twice in his career, haunting him every so often.She thought for a moment about aiming for his shoulder, and if he was tweaking as she suspected, there was a good chance a bullet wouldn't stop him. No, this would end with either him lying dead or a young boy losing his life too soon.

"No... Well, yes. I live here with my mother... Well, I did," he started to cry.

"Did?" she asked, already knowing the answer.

"She's in the garage," he confessed, his voice filled with sorrow.

"Dead?"

"About a month now," he said.

"Did you do that?" she asked, not meaning for it to come out sounding as disgusted as she did.

"Because *Grace* infected her," his voice dropped to a low growl. "Same with the boy's mother. She is infecting them all," he bellowed.

I can't take the shot. He's jerking way too much. I could miss and hit the kid instead. "And if I don't do what—" she began.

Wait for an opening.

"Ten," he said through gritted teeth.

Oh shit.

"Nine."

No, please, no.

This was it. She was going to have to stop him. He had to die. She had no idea if this was drugs or suicide by a cop. It didn't matter. She wasn't about to let a boy get murdered in front of her. She raised her gun and exhaled. Shane had moved past reason and Veronica believed he would finish what he started when he arrived at one.

She felt her heartbeat, and the world seemed to melt away around her. She could only see him and nothing else. She blinked hard and steadied her aim. She braced for him to continue his count. He didn't.

Shane's face slowly turned pale white as his mouth opened in shock. His eyes widened, and he muttered something under his breath.

Is he second-guessing himself? Does he finally see that he is about to die?

"You didn't close the door. I told you to close it."

He was staring at something behind her. Veronica lost her concentration; the man was *afraid*. His demeanor, even though he'd run a gambit of emotions in front of her, was different. His shoulders slumped, and the viciousness he displayed throughout was utterly gone.

Veronica felt something against her right leg, and it caused her to jump. Veronica wasn't about to take her eyes off him, her nerves were frayed enough. She felt it again before a small black cat came into her field of vision sniffing the ground in front of her, its tail twitching back and forth. Shane's face locked in dread. He was completely focused on the animal.

"The cat?" she questioned, confused.

His voice raised several octaves.

"Yes, the cat! Oh my God, what have you done?" He was stuttering and had begun to shiver.

"Shane, I need you to step away from the boy, drop the knife, and place your hands on your head," she commanded.

He pulled the knife from Chris's neck and pointed it at her. "You don't understand. That's her familiar; it's he—"

Veronica squeezed the trigger, and the gunshot was deafening. The bullet left the barrel and hit Shane in the right eye, his hand instantly released the knife. He fell backward against an entertainment center and sideways onto the floor. Veronica rushed forward to the boy as he slumped forward. She caught him gently and laid him on his back. She held her hand under his nose as she'd done for his mother.

Still breathing. Good.

"Help will be here soon. Just relax. Can you speak?" she asked as she ran her fingers through his brown hair.

He grunted, his eyes glassy and unfocused.

My God, he's hurt bad. What did he do to this kid?

She stood and walked around the chair to where Shane was lying. Blood had started pooling under his head. She'd shot through his eye and out the back. She checked the wall beside the entertainment center, and found the bullet hole, in a splatter of blood and what she could only assume was the man's brain matter.

She glanced down at the body. "Crazy bastard."

She returned to Chris and held his hand until the sirens pierced the air in the distance. Veronica sprinted back to the front door and out into the yard as both an ambulance and the Sheriff's cars turned onto the street. She waved her arms over her head and slowly approached as they came to a complete stop.

"Here!"

She continued across the yard until she stood before Eric, a young man from emergency medical services for Camden Clark Medical Center. She'd worked with him on several accidents and injuries before. He was in his early twenties and a raging ball of energy. He was friendly, though, and fantastic at his job.

"E, I got an eleven-year-old boy in there that's been hurt pretty bad. The kid's name is Chris, and I think it's a concussion. He can't speak," Veronica said.

"Anything else?" Eric looked over her shoulder to the home as he asked.

"Dead body..." She took a breath and gained her composure. "He had a knife to the kid's neck. I shot him through the eye." Veronica nodded.

"I'll let the coroner know." Eric turned around in the direction of the ambulance. "Gaby! Hurry up, get the kit, and let's go!"

A young woman came sprinting toward them. She had green highlights on her dark hair, and her uniform seemed too big for her small frame. She was carrying an orange bag over her shoulder and holding her glasses in place with her right hand.

"Who's that? Where's Chase?" Veronica asked. A feeling of unease crept over her. She wanted people she could trust to handle this.

"He moved to Morgantown, running the whole department up there," Eric explained, waving at his partner to move faster.

"Shit. I think you might need him," Veronica responded.

"Don't sell her short. She's good, or I'd have already asked for someone else."

Eric and Gaby took off for the front door, leaving Veronica standing at the edge of the street. She started to tremble. The adrenaline was wearing off. She jogged toward the house she'd left Grace in. An officer called out to her, but she held up her hand and screamed back at him that she had to check on the little girl.

She passed the porch and went straight through the door. The house was much smaller than she anticipated. The outside had given it a much grander scope. Veronica scanned the living room and called out, "Grace!"

"I'm in here!" She heard the little girl cry out from down the hall, off to her right.

Veronica moved without hesitation down the hallway to the last room on the right. Grace was climbing out from under the bed, still clutching the phone that Veronica handed her. She was still gasping for air from crying so hard. Veronica knelt and helped her to her feet.

"Is my brother okay?" Grace asked, hugging Veronica around the neck.

"He has to go to the hospital, but he will be just fine. Are you alright?" Veronica asked, holding onto Grace's shoulders.

"Yes." She nodded forcefully. "What happened to the man?"

Veronica paused. "I took care of it."

"Did you shoot him?" Grace asked.

Veronica wasn't ready for that. It wasn't that she asked the question. It was the way Grace had done it. It seemed as if the little girl was hoping that she had. Veronica stammered slightly. "Um, I —"

"I heard the pop. Daddy used to shoot guns before he died." The girl looked away out the window.

"Oh, when did that happen?" Veronica changed the subject.

"Right when school ended," Grace said sadly.

Oh my God, her dad and now her mother. This is terrible.

Veronica had no idea how to comfort this child. She'd been through so much trauma; nothing she could say to her would wipe it away. Veronica finally took a second to look around the room. It was a simple white with the only thing on the walls being a "Live, Laugh, Love" plaque. There was an oak dresser with a mirror. The bed was a queen-sized mattress with no sheet or comforter, and the pillow had no pillowcase. A rocking chair was in the far corner with a doll that looked dirty and old, like something from the 1940s. It was missing one eye and covered in stains. The room looked unlived in.

"Grace..." Veronica turned her head to both sides, retaking note of the contents.

"Hmm?" Grace asked, still staring toward the window.

"Is this your room?" Veronica was concerned; this wasn't acceptable in her eyes.

"It was going to be. Mommy said I could have a big girl room now. That's what we were going to do tonight. I was getting my own room." Grace began to tear up again.

I should just shut up. Everything I do is making it worse.

"Grace, honey, I need to go outside. I have to check on everyone. There are a lot of police officers out there, and they need my help. Can I turn the TV on in the living room for you, and you stay on the couch?" Veronica asked softly

Grace squeezed her hand. "Do you have to?"

"I do. They need to know what's happening, and I need to tell them you're safe," Veronica reassured.

"Alright, but don't leave. You promise you won't leave me?" Grace begged.

"I promise."

Veronica took her hand and guided the little girl to the light gray couch in the living room. This room was slightly dusty, unlike the room they'd just left. This looked lived in. Veronica went to the stand beside the sofa, found the TV remote, and hit the power button. It sprang to life, and the familiar face of Spongebob Squarepants came into view. She sat the remote beside Grace, whose hands were on her lap.

"I'll be back," Veronica said as she patted her shoulder.

"Okay," Grace said.

"Are you hungry?" Veronica asked with her hands on her hips.

Grace shook her head, and Veronica walked back to the front door. "I will leave the door open, but you stay in here, okay?"

Veronica didn't wait for a response; she walked out to what looked like the entire Parkersburg and Wood County police force. Two Parkersburg squad cars had blocked the front of the street, and now two ambulances were parked in front of her. Several officers surrounded Grace's mother's body, taking pictures and drawing an outline around her.

"Carter!" Eric yelled.

She followed the voice and saw him standing in the yard of Shane's house. He was jogging in her direction, his eyes wide with concern.

"Everything okay?" she asked as he got to her.

"No, the second ambulance will take the kid to the ER, but he's already coded twice. I don't think he's going to make it."

"Coded twice? Did that maniac crack the boy's skull?" Veronica whispered in shock. This was a disaster. She had told Grace that her brother would be okay. She thought he was just loopy from a head injury.

"It's not his head. His sternum is floating around in his chest. His ribs are in splinters, his heartbeat is all over the place, and he isn't getting enough air. Impact to the chest; maybe he stomped on him or threw him against something," Eric growled through gritted teeth.

"Shit," Veronica muttered.

"I know. You should have shot the son of a bitch in the stomach and let him bleed out."

The ambulance closest to her came alive as the lights began to flash, and the siren wailed over the rest of the commotion. The driver went straight through the yard and onto Red Hill Road, leaving the two staring after it.

"Be straight with me. How much of a chance are you giving the kid?" Veronica asked.

Eric glanced away, and shrugged. He looked back to her eyes, and shook his head.

"I should have shot the bastard when I came into the room. I fucking hesitated." She paced back and forth. "I should have—"

"This ain't on you. That prick did this—" Eric stopped abruptly as another Parkersburg officer stepped beside him. "I'll talk to you later, okay?" Eric said to Veronica and walked away.

She recognized Officer Webb immediately. He'd been instrumental in her training. He'd been with the department for fifteen years when she was hired. He knew everything and didn't mind sharing any advice he could. There weren't many people in their field that you would consider friendly, but he was one of them.

He was a burly man with a thick beard and bushy eyebrows. He'd put on a few pounds in the last year after his marriage ended, but was still trying to stuff himself into his older uniform. It looked as if he would burst out of it at any moment. "Well, this is a mess."

"Yeah."

Officer Webb patted her upper arm. "Want to let me in on everything before you fill out paperwork for the rest of the night?"

Veronica recounted the story, and he said nothing for a long moment. He looked down the street toward the yellow house and her cruiser. He sighed before turning back to her.

"The house here belongs to Bruce and Karrisa Marsden. Bruce passed away recently. I was the one who took the report, so I know this house."

"Grace told me about him dying. What happened?"

"Suicide. Shotgun, terrible scene. Room at the end of the house." He pointed toward the window where Grace had been hiding. "The boy found him. I couldn't calm the kid down. I had to send him to the hospital. I can't say I blame him, after what he saw."

"How much tragedy can one family take?" Veronica might have been asking for herself as well.

"You know why this happened?" Webb pointed at the body now covered, in the street.

"Not really," Veronica admitted.

"You have a good rapport with the little girl, right? Why don't we go in there? I'll take notes while it's still fresh," Webb suggested.

"Did you meet her when you were here last time? She's a sweetheart. I hate that she's all alone now." Veronica felt her heart breaking.

"No, I never met her. I don't remember a girl being here at all," Webb answered.

Veronica dismissed what he said. Maybe she wasn't home, or the mother had put her in another room away from the commotion. She would be sure to ask. Veronica led Officer Webb into the house to where Grace was still sitting. Grace's face beamed when she saw Veronica.

"Grace, this is my friend, Officer Webb." She saw him wave politely out of the corner of her vision. "I'm going to ask you a few questions about what happened today, and he is just going to listen. Do you think you can give us some answers?"

Grace nodded. "I'll try."

"Grace, why did the man attack your mother?" Veronica queried.

"I was with her at the mailbox. I wanted her to get a pizza. Chris went to the door. He always grabs Mommy's keys. Then the man, Shane, came running out of his house screaming. He grabbed my shirt, and Mommy started punching him. That's when he hurt her. She told me to run, and I did. I went around back and down by the creek. I could hear screaming." She started to tear up again. "I was so scared."

"What happened next?" Veronica sat down beside Grace.

"I waited, and he never came around the house after me. So I ran back to where Mommy was, but she wouldn't answer me. I got her phone and hid by the door. I prayed that someone would come, and then you showed up." Grace was crying again.

"It's okay, honey." Veronica put her arm around her and hugged her tight. She held her until the tears slowed.

"Are you sure he's your friend?" Grace asked, her eyes lifting to Officer Webb.

"Yes, he was here when your daddy got hurt. Do you remember him?" Veronica questioned as she wiped tears from Grace's cheeks.

She shook her head. "I was with my aunts. They were supposed to be here tonight to help me move into my room."

This was the first good news she'd heard throughout this ordeal. At least Grace would have family with her, and the way the little girl's eyes lit up when she said the word *aunts* she could tell she liked them.

"Yes, they live in Inky-man. It's a long drive." Grace smiled.

"Inkerman?" Webb interjected.

"That's it!"

Veronica looked at Webb, confused. She'd never heard of it. "Where is Inkerman?"

"Hardy County. It's on the other side of the state in the eastern panhandle," Webb explained.

"Alright, if they were on their way, there is a good chance they might show up." Veronica looked at Webb. "Let the officers know they might arrive. They can come get us when they do." She turned back to Grace. "What are their names?"

"Babby and Ariel," Grace said.

"Bobby?" Veronica attempted to correct her.

"No, Babby," Grace said with a shake of her head.

Veronica chuckled slightly and looked at Webb. "You heard her."

Webb started toward the door. "What are you going to do?"

Veronica patted Grace's leg. "I will sit here with my friend and watch cartoons while we wait for her aunts. If you don't care, can you get her a pizza?"

Webb nodded at her and left through the front door. Grace and Veronica continued to watch Spongebob together, with Veronica commenting every so often that this wasn't funny and Grace arguing that it was hilarious. Webb eventually returned with a pepperoni pizza from Dominos and Grace ate a slice while Veronica observed her. She began to wonder if something was off with the little girl. Her emotions would go from one extreme to the next, and right now, Grace was humming and eating pizza while kicking her feet. She didn't act like someone who'd just gone through a life-or-death experience. Veronica tried to remind herself that Grace was only five, but she hadn't even asked about her brother.

She wasn't begging to see her mother. She wasn't asking for her favorite toy. She was sitting here without a care in the world. Veronica didn't want to press her, but she started to suspect the family wasn't very kind to Grace. Maybe she was abused or ignored. Her father had died a few months ago, and who knows how the other family members dealt with it.

Veronica watched the wall clock after a while, the show droning on in the background. The time seemed to crawl as it did earlier in her patrol car. Five turned to six, and by six-thirty, Webb had come in and told her the coroner was finished, and most of the officers had left.

"I'm on shift till eleven. I'll stick around the front of the road for when her aunts come," he said.

As it passed seven, Veronica was concerned that she might have to call child protective services to come out and help her. She couldn't stay here all night, and she certainly couldn't just leave Grace alone. She was hoping it wouldn't come to that.

A few minutes after eight, Officer Webb walked through the door. "The aunts are outside."

Grace excitedly jumped up, knocked the empty pizza box off the couch, and ran toward the door. Veronica stood and stretched. She had grown tired and was thankful she would be able to get out of there soon. Veronica picked up the remote and pushed the button, cutting a Bob Saget monologue short from a rerun of Full House. She picked up the pizza box from the floor and sat it back on the cushions.

As Veronica exited the house, she noticed how the cloudless sky had darkened and how empty this little area felt. No lights were on in the three homes, giving off an unsettling feeling. She stepped forward off the porch, and Webb called out to Veronica.

"Look at this thing. I haven't seen one of these in this condition ever."

She looked forward and saw Grace being embraced by two women. The first had to be around six feet tall. She was slender and wearing a Janis Joplin t-shirt, blue jeans, and sandals. She had light brown hair, was well-tanned, and wore horn-rimmed glasses with transparent frames. She was bent over, holding Grace against her. She looked as if she might cry.

The other woman couldn't have been more different. She was much shorter. Her frame was filled with muscle; even her neck looked as if it had been sculpted from ivory. Her forearms were covered in tattoos of skulls and flames, and her hair was as black as could be. She wore a shirt that said, "I fuck on the first date," that was low cut and showed off her abdomen. She was extremely pale. Veronica initially assumed it was makeup, but once she noticed her arms and stomach, she knew this woman never went out in the sun.

Veronica stepped over to them and noticed that Webb was looking at their car. The black antique shined in what was left of the light. Veronica smiled. "I don't know anything about cars."

"This is a 1967 Ford Fairlane. I mean, this thing looks brand new!" Webb exclaimed.

"It belonged to the father," the dark-haired one said.

"*Our* father, it belonged to our father," the taller one interjected, standing upright and pushing her glasses up her nose.

Grace lunged forward and grabbed Veronica's hand. "This is the woman who saved me! She stopped Shane from getting me. We had pizza and watched cartoons."

"What does she mean 'saved' her? What the hell is going on? " Again, it was the muscular one that spoke, much ruder this time.

"Ariel, behave," the tall one hissed.

"You must be Babby?" Veronica asked, chuckling at the absurdity of how it sounded.

"Babette, my name is Babette. Grace here," she reached out and tousled the little girl's hair, "gave me that nickname."

"So, what happened?" Ariel asked again, not hiding her disrespect.

"Grace, do you have a bag or something you need to take with you? Are you forgetting anything at all?" Veronica asked.

Grace's face brightened as she nodded and ran off to the house.

"Are you on her father's or mother's side of the family?" Veronica whispered.

"Father's," Babette answered.

Ariel rolled her eyes, which Veronica ignored. She was glad to hear it. She didn't want to be the one to tell her that Shane killed her sister. Veronica leaned in and quickly reviewed the events of the afternoon. Babette's hand covered her mouth, and she shed a few tears as Ariel shook her head.

"I'm sorry about Chris," Veronica said. "I don't know anything about his current status."

"He belonged to Karissa. He wasn't our family," Ariel spat.

Veronica was about to ask Ariel what her problem was when Babette said, "Mind your manners. This woman saved Grace's life." Ariel rolled her eyes, but before she could say anything, Babette added, "A young boy is hurt and you're being a shit."

Ariel's lip curled in, but she nodded slowly in defeat. "You're right."

Babette huffed, then turned back to Veronica. "Forgive my sister, Officer; she doesn't like being around people and hates being so far from home. We will check on the boy when we leave."

Grace came up behind them, holding the same cat that Veronica had seen earlier in Shane's home.

"Wait, that's your cat?" she asked.

"Ah, yes, we can't forget Mumbles," Babette said, taking the feline and stroking its face.

"That cat distracted him. He was nervous about it."

"Well, it is Grace's cat, and you said he was delirious and fixated on her. It makes sense, I suppose," Babette said.

"Maybe," Veronica muttered as she furrowed her brows. Something was under her skin about this situation; these women didn't seem upset about the brother, just like Grace had not been.

"We will stay the night in town. I'm sure we will need to speak to a detective or something tomorrow?"

"Yes." Veronica came back to her senses. "Detective JT Bradley. He'll want some information from you."

Ariel threw her hands up. "We didn't bring any clothes, and we don't have a lot of money to—"

Babette shook her head disapprovingly, and Ariel grunted low before walking around the car, entering the driver's side, and slamming the door.

"Again, I'm sorry about her." Babette rubbed her forehead.

"It's alright. I'm just glad Grace has someone to help her through this." Veronica smiled.

"I just thank the heavens and Gaia you were here to protect her," Babette said.

Oh my God, this is one of those crazy hippies. What's next? Is she going to try and sell me rocks to heal my aura?

Grace was being led to the car by the hand when she stopped and looked back at Veronica. She let go of Babette and slowly walked back to her. She put her hand out, and when Veronica took it, Grace took her finger and began drawing things on the back.

"Oh, baby, are you sure?" Babette asked, concerned.

"Um, hm," Grace nodded.

Veronica looked over to Webb, who shrugged.

It didn't take long. Grace traced her finger along her knuckles like she was spelling something. Once she finished, Grace smiled. "I hope it helps."

"Thanks?" Veronica said, not hiding her bewilderment from Babette, who clutched Mumbles tightly.

"Ok, I'm ready now," Grace said, and ran to the back door on the passenger side. Babette opened it for her, gently tossed Mumbles in, and began buckling Grace up. Once she finished, she shut it gently, and as she entered the passenger side, said, "Thank you again, Officer. I hope we see you again."

Veronica waved and scratched the back of her hand. It was a reflex. It wasn't itching, but Grace's odd action had made her uncomfortable. The car came to life and rolled slowly down the driveway.

Veronica stepped beside the street to catch a final glimpse of Grace as they passed. All three were laughing hysterically; she could see a strange joy on their faces just as they went by. The little girl looked out the window, meeting Veronica's gaze and her lips curled in a knowing smirk. The innocence she'd seen earlier in the eyes of the child was no longer there. It was replaced by something sinister and conniving. Veronica felt a chill go down her spine and into her legs. Grace turned her attention forward and began laughing again as the car accelerated and pulled away.

Veronica was frozen in place when Webb called from across the street. "Well, if they get to raise her, I can't wait to see the tie-dye shirts she makes for her their flea market stall."

"Come on," Veronica ordered as she returned to the house.

"Why?" Webb asked.

"Humor me," Veronica said without looking at him.

They entered the house together, and Veronica went straight for the kitchen. A few questions popped into the front of her thoughts, and she struggled to prioritize what she should do first. There was so much *wrong* here; she felt it in her bones.

"What the heck are you doing, Carter?"

"Do me a favor; check the living room for toys. Also, there are a few shelves; look for pictures of Grace and the family together.

"What's wrong?"

Veronica was already at the refrigerator. There were magnets from the Newport Aquarium and King's Island, and pictures of Chris in a soccer uniform. There were no happy drawings hung with love, no colorful letters to learn ABCs, and no images of the girl in the few pictures. She looked over at the kitchen table and saw only three chairs, and the hairs on the back of her neck stood up.

No, the father passed, remember? Three is right.

She walked through the living room past Webb, who mentioned as she went by, "I've found pictures of the mom, dad, and the boy together, but no girl."

She went into the hallway and turned on the light. There were school photos of Chris up and down the wall, showing his childhood pass in the same pose year after year. She stopped at the family picture at the far end of the hall and noticed only Karissa, Chris, and the dad.

"There are none," she whispered.

"Nothing," Webb answered from beside her.

"Check the bedrooms for girl clothes, toys, anything."

She entered the first door on the left, which was a bathroom adorned with an awful lavender and purple duck shower curtain with matching rugs. She walked straight to the medicine cabinet and opened it. In the toothbrush holder sat two lone brushes, orange and blue. Veronica closed it slowly and exited the bathroom.

"I found a boy's room, tons of toys," Webb called from across the hall.

"Anything for a girl?" Veronica yelled back. She already knew what he would say.

She heard him rummaging. "No."

She trotted to the end of the hall and went into the left room this time. It was the master bedroom and was a cluttered mess. Women's clothing lay strewn across the floor. The bed wasn't made, and some empty bottles of wine were at the foot of the bed. She walked over to the dresser and started opening the drawers. They were filled with items only for Karissa. There wasn't any sign of anything belonging to Grace.

She left the master bedroom and finally entered the one she found Grace hiding in. She opened the drawers on that dresser only to find that they were all empty. None of this made sense. How can you have a five-year-old girl and not have any items for her? It was like she wasn't even a member of the family. Veronica stormed into the hallway where Webb was waiting, and they walked outside together.

"So, what are you going to do?" he asked as he closed the front door.

"Did you take their license plate or their IDs?" she asked.

Officer Webb raised his hands and stepped back before uttering, "Who?"

Veronica looked at him in shock, "Those women. The ones who took Grace. You know who I mean."

She tried to remember the aunt's name. The one with the nickname she found humorous, but it just wouldn't come. She found herself having a hard time concentrating and couldn't place the woman's face.

Webb opened his mouth slightly, shook his head.

"Oh, come on! They just took... they just left... They just..."

She scanned her memory. Her thoughts flooded with the boy in the chair and how she shot Shane through the eye. He was babbling about his mother, and wanting Veronica to bring him something. It was all gibberish, convoluted and running together in her head. Everyone was concerned for her after what had happened, but she had sat in the boy's house and watched television for some reason. There had been a reason, hadn't there?

Officer Webb stepped in front of her, his eyebrows lowered, his face concerned. "Listen, this has been hard on all of us. It's always worse when there are children involved. I don't even know why you waited around. Let's head to the hospital and see if the kid made it. Then you turn the car in and head home. Take the weekend to clear your head."

Veronica stood there glaring at him. What was she doing? A minute ago she was furious about something. Now, she couldn't recall it. She dug at the back of her hand as she watched Webb go to his cruiser. There was nothing more to do here. Shane was dead, the mother didn't make it, and she knew when she stopped by Camden Medical, the boy would be gone, too.

With her hands on her hips, she shuffled to her patrol car and got in. It had seemed like a lifetime since she exited the vehicle and saw the woman dead in the street. She turned the keys in the ignition, the engine started, and her terminal instantly appeared.

"Are you serious?" She smacked the steering wheel. She picked up her phone and hit the tiny button at the bottom of the screen, and her lock screen flashed in front of her. "I hate these things," she muttered, noticing that she only had 19 percent of the battery left. Maybe that's why it didn't come on before.

She had a notification from Skylar, so she tapped the screen and read the text message.

> Hey, I gave it some thought, and I am not looking for a relationship right now. I should have contacted you sooner, but I need to cancel for tomorrow. Sorry.
>
> — S

Veronica leaned forward and let her forehead rest against the warm leather. This weekend was bordering on fantastic, and now it was ruined. She sighed, exited her messages, and went to her contacts. Veronica selected Maw Maw, hit the speaker icon, and waited.

It rang three times before the familiar voice greeted her. "Hi, sweetie."

"Hey."

A small pause. "What's wrong? You alright?"

Veronica fought back tears and gulped. "Not really. I just had to fire my gun at someone."

"Oh, goodness. What are you doing right now? Do you need me to come to you?" The old woman asked.

Veronica laughed at the absurdity of her Maw Maw getting out to retrieve her police officer granddaughter. "No. I was going to call the hospital to check on someone, take the car back, and then I was going to come over. Are you going to be up?"

"I will make cocoa," Maw Maw said.

"Maw Maw, I'm a little too old for cocoa."

"You don't want me to make it?"

Veronica looked at the phone in disbelief. "Of course I do."

"Well, call me when you are coming."

"Will do." Veronica closed her eyes as she said it. She wiped the tears from her eyes as she ended the call, put the car in reverse, and headed for the station. Later, when the report was done, her equipment checked in, and she could sign off for some much-needed rest, she spent the rest of her night crying in her grandmother's arms.

2

*

A Decade Later

The door to the trailer was open. Veronica didn't want to go in. It was closing in on seven, and the sun was starting to set. A faint whiff of sun-baked garbage tickled her nose, and she dreaded what might wash over her once she crossed the threshold. The mobile home had been abandoned for quite some time, and judging by the outside, what awaited her inside would be much worse. Add to that it was a scorching West Virginia September day, it would be like walking into an oven. She felt nauseous at the thought.

At least the body was gone. The coroner carted it away two days ago. The corpse of Jeff Browning, a man at the spry age of thirty-two, had been found inside. He'd been missing for two weeks, and his ex-wife and sister had called Veronica daily, wondering if there had been any leads. She heard them losing hope with each call.

Her investigation into Jeff's life turned up surprisingly little. She felt sorry for him after she'd gone through his apartment. Outside of high fantasy books and Nintendo games, he had nothing to call his own. It would have been boring if she didn't suspect the supernatural. The coroner in Huntington had ruled his death was of natural causes. His heart just gave out. The fingerprints matched, and the DNA she'd

29

taken from his toothbrush was dead on. The problem was the photos she'd received. They looked nothing like the pictures his sister had given her. The man lying on the slab in the basement of Cabell Huntington Hospital was in his nineties.

They couldn't match dental records; there were no teeth. The autopsy technician told her this had to be a mistake, a computer glitch, or a paperwork error. Veronica knew better. She knew the body was Jeff, so she made the trip to prove it.

She placed her hand on the badge attached to her hip. She'd gotten the detective's shield in late 2016. Veronica hoped no one would pay her enough attention to notice that it was for Parkersburg, not the local area. She hadn't gotten permission to come down here. What would be her explanation for showing up? She couldn't just call West Virginia State Police and tell them she suspected a ghost was involved. She'd lose everything she'd worked for.

Veronica glanced around the small trailer park. A few people watched her, but they stayed away. They didn't want to talk to her; she knew that much. No one liked speaking to the police. She closed her eyes and felt his presence inside. She didn't know how, but Jeff was in there. The problem would be convincing her partner to help her speak with him.

Jeff was dead, and Veronica had a nagging feeling he'd been murdered. She pulled the police tape off the right side of the doorway and stepped into the living room. There was the stink of stale cigarettes, garbage, and sick. She felt her stomach lurch and held her breath momentarily. She closed her eyes, counted in her head to three, and took tiny breaths through her mouth.

"I'm gonna burn these clothes after I get out of here," she muttered.

The air was thick, and it was unbelievably hot inside the trailer. The place was the definition of a mess. Wadded up papers were everywhere, and cheap patio furniture damaged beyond repair sat against the wall. There was a rug covered in shit. God only knew if it was from a human, canine, or something else.

As she went farther in, the overpowering odor of dirt wafted around her. It was a musty smell coming from either the ripped-up clothing in the corner or the stains on the carpet. She wondered if any of it was blood. She glanced around the room in disgust.

This place needs to be torn down.

Jeff had been found completely naked in a bathtub in a place known for methamphetamine and heroin overdoses. They were shocked to find nothing of the sort in his system.

She couldn't recall the name of the doctor she'd spoken to. Veronica had gotten what she needed from him anyway. He'd told her Jeff hadn't been moved. He had died in that tub, with the way the blood coagulated and the pattern of bruising. He had quite a few bed sores. The medical examiner couldn't tell her much besides that. He was as dumbfounded as she was. Someone had left him there to die.

Veronica suspected something supernatural. Just a few years ago, she would have scoffed at the idea. Now? Nothing was off the table. She'd dealt with a ghost already, but kidnapping someone would be new. Usually, it was a violent exchange because someone wouldn't heed the warnings to stay away from their territory.

She had little experience in such matters. The simple truth was she'd only known of three such instances of a ghost killing an individual, and they were all committed by the same entity. It was why she wanted nothing to do with North Bend Rail Trail Tunnel 19. She walked past the small island that separated the living room and kitchen. She was going to take a deep breath, but the stink of her surroundings made her think twice.

"Ethel?" Veronica called out.

There was silence, except for the sound of a tiny scurrying down the hall, which Veronica assumed was a mouse. At least, she hoped that was all it was. She waited a few more moments and called out again.

"I know you're here. Let's just get this over with."

It was sudden, but she felt the familiar chill, as if someone rubbed ice across her bones. She shivered and rubbed her forehead. She dreaded this part, but she couldn't do anything without Ethel's help.

She felt her condescending gaze on her back.. Veronica turned around slowly and smiled.

"Hello, Ethel."

Ethel Carter was seated in one of the plastic chairs with her legs crossed. Her blue flowered dress was still pristine, and her gray curled hair flowed all around her shoulders. Not a bead of sweat glistened on her face, and her makeup was as glorious as the day it was put on. Veronica could barely stand the sweltering heat, but Ethel showed no signs of it affecting her.

She was a thin woman, almost frail. Her glasses were halfway down her nose, and her brown eyes were staring a hole through Veronica. The scowl on her face didn't hide anything. She wasn't happy.

"What do you want?" Ethel huffed.

"Now, don't be that way. I just want to talk," Veronica said, walking toward her and trying her best forced smile.

"Let me guess, a murder?" Ethel glared. "Did you kill them too?"

Veronica took a deep breath.

"Are we ever going to move past that?" Veronica leaned against the wall.

"Absolutely not," Ethel hissed.

Veronica rubbed her eyes. She felt the stress giving way to a headache. "There should be a man in here. Something weird went down, and I'm curious. It's right up our alley."

"Don't care," Ethel mocked.

"Yes, you do," Veronica whispered.

She stood silently for a moment as Veronica thought of her next move. There was no handbook or guideline for this. Probably no one in history had ever dealt with what she was doing at this very moment. She would feel honored if it wasn't so eerie.

"So... did a ghost kill him?" Ethel asked.

"Mmm..." Veronica was caught off guard by the question.

"This seems like a terrible place for a haunt. Why here?" Ethel pushed her glasses up.

"I don't know, honestly. The cause of death is strange. The whole situation is confusing. He celebrated his thirty-second birthday a few weeks ago, but the body they found is old and decrepit," Veronica explained.

Ethel's right eyebrow arched, and Veronica knew she couldn't resist the puzzle.

"I've never heard of that—"

"Me either," Veronica interrupted. "I've looked over previous cases and unsolved crimes—nothing. Not that a medical examiner would sign off on a guy magically aging fifty years overnight, though."

Ethel's eyebrows relaxed, and her eyes widened; Veronica had scored a minor victory. Ethel wanted to know just as badly as she did.

"There's no ghost in this room." Ethel folded her arms defensively.

"He was found in the bathtub down the hall. His name is Jeff. If he freaks out with you, tell him Annie sent us to find him." Veronica wiped her forehead and looked at the sweat on her hand.

"Is that his wife?" Ethel asked, concerned.

"Yes, she is. Well, she was. I need to know where he went and where he's been."

Ethel didn't speak. She stood still, not hiding an ounce of her contempt, while Veronica continued.

"Listen, I know you're angry with me. I get it, I do, and you know what, I don't blame you," Veronica pointed her index finger at her, "but you are the only person that can give this family closure. You can help me ensure what happened to this guy doesn't happen to anyone else."

"You ain't being sincere," Ethel said through clenched teeth.

"Actually, I am. And when we finish this, we can finally sit down and talk," Veronica finished.

Ethel seemed to mull over Veronica's plea.

"What's in it for you? Lord knows you aren't doing this out of the kindness of your heart," Ethel spat.

Veronica kept her voice steady, trying to convey that it didn't bother her as much as it did. "I just want to help. Can we just... Please? It's bad enough you make me call you by your first name."

She wasn't looking to get a rise out of Ethel. She'd hoped to keep things friendly and cordial, but every word from Ethel's mouth burned her more than the last.

Ethel slapped the arm of the chair with the palm of her hands in anger, and the strangest thing happened: it moved. Slightly, but it *moved*.

Veronica kept her composure. She placed her hand over her mouth to try and disguise her shock. *Where did she learn that? Did she realize she'd even done it? Was it because she was upset?*

"Stop lying to me!" Ethel raised her voice.

"I'm not," Veronica quipped back.

"You were one of our own, raised with love," Ethel sneered. "We didn't rear you this way. We taught you to respect the Word. We gave you everything we had and then some. We cared for you, and look at what you've become! You killed a man in cold blood. I saw it! You don't deserve our last name." Ethel waved her hand dismissively. "Thank God your grandfather isn't here to see you."

Veronica felt the hairs on the back of her neck stand up. If she bit her lip any harder, there would be blood. Veronica hadn't meant for Ethel to see her that night. She wished she'd been more careful. But Ethel was right about one thing: she'd led a man to a secluded area and killed him while he was on his knees begging for mercy. She'd tried, in the beginning, to explain herself, but Ethel wouldn't listen. She'd shut parts of herself off long ago, but to see the revulsion in Ethel's eyes bothered her.

"I can't stand to look at you." Ethel pointed at her. "You're going to wind up in Hell."

Veronica ground her teeth but decided to switch tactics. She smirked at Ethel. She had to; she'd have started screaming if she didn't.

"Don't mock me, girl." Ethel's lips curled into a snarl.

"Hell?" She chuckled as Ethel's face flushed, something else that surprised Veronica. Veronica walked straight toward her and got in her face. "You died in 2020, Maw Maw," Veronica jeered. "It's been three years! Where is your door? Why are you still here?"

Ethel stared at her in silence.

"No? You're here with me. I am the only living person you can talk to," Veronica said.

"God has a plan for me," Ethel retorted, her abhorrence oozing in every syllable.

"That's not the point I'm trying to make, Ethel. You were an honest woman. I mean, church every Sunday. You were married only once. You're a mother who raised her son and then his daughter. A little far down the line from a piece of shit."

"Which is more than I can say for you," she barked.

"Right, so if God has a plan," Veronica continued. "You ever thought this is it? This is what you are supposed to do? Maybe, just maybe, we're still meant to be together."

She saw the shift briefly in Ethel's face, in her eyes. Veronica had placed doubt into Ethel's mind. She scored her victory this round and left Ethel speechless. Veronica relished in the accomplishment as Ethel stood and walked past her.

"What are you doing?"

Ethel shot a look back toward Veronica, her eyes narrowing.

"Going to see if he's here."

Veronica shook her head and followed Ethel down the hall.

***

The bathroom wasn't any better than the rest of the place. The toilet was stained in a barrage of different colors, half of the walls were missing, and the bathtub was smeared with mold. There was no sink, just rusted pipes sticking out of the ground.

Ethel was standing in the middle of the bathroom on the white, cracked vinyl tile, staring directly at the tub. Veronica approached and cleared her throat.

"Is he in here?" she asked. She looked out the broken bathroom window at the falling rain.

"An old man is sitting in the tub," Ethel whispered. "He's crying."

"Old man? How old are we talking?" Veronica asked, confused.

"My age," Ethel answered.

"No, Jeff was a young man." Veronica rubbed her nose. Somehow the smell was worse in here.

"He looked over when you said that name," Ethel walked to the tub and bent slightly. "Jeff?"

Veronica watched as Ethel jerked back.

"Yes, I can see you. Relax. It's going to be alright." Ethel smiled at the empty tub. "We're here to help you.".

Veronica stood beside Ethel and gazed at the same spot her grandmother was looking toward. "Hello, Jeff. I need you to understand that I can't see or hear you, but I need to talk to you. My partner, Ethel, is going to tell me what you say."

Ethel looked at Veronica and shook her head; it was evident that Jeff wasn't taking this so well. Veronica reached into her back jeans pocket and produced a 5x7 photo of Jeff and Annie from a cookout the summer before their divorce. She held it out to the tub, showing it.

"Annie sent me to find you, Jeff."

"You can't take the picture," Ethel explained. "He's reaching for it." Veronica tossed it into the bathtub.

"There you go, Jeff, it's yours. But we need to know what happened to you."

"He's hysterical," Ethel noted.

"Jeff," Veronica held out her hand, "tell me who did this to you."

Ethel's brow lowered. "Nadine did this. He's cursing up a storm. He's screaming about a Nadine."

This isn't a ghost; he wouldn't have seen her. He certainly wouldn't have gotten a name, Veronica thought.

"Alright, Nadine. Do you have a last name?"

"That can't be right," Ethel said.

"What can't be right?" Veronica asked, trying to hide her excitement.

"He said he didn't know her last name but that she is a witch," Ethel said skeptically.

"Witch?" Veronica was confused.

"I thought he was saying the b-word. But no, he's saying, witch."

Veronica took a moment to process. She waited until Ethel nodded.

"How do you know she's a witch?" she asked the empty bathtub.

Ethel didn't say anything for what seemed like forever, then finally said, "He met her at the gas station. She invited him to her house. She kissed him, and he got ill."

"A sick ghost doesn't invite people anywhere. They just kill you outright," Veronica said.

"Sick" was the word Veronica used for the dead who wandered in anger. It was the only thing that was fitting. Ethel had described them to her once. Said they had black gunk coming from their eyes, nose, and mouth. The only one they ever ran into was the ghost at Tunnel 19. Ethel had tried to reason with her. It might as well have been deaf. The spirit was singularly focused, repeatedly spitting the name Gary, each time more hateful than the last. If it disturbed Ethel, Veronica wanted no part of it, so they left well enough alone.

"He says she did some sort of ritual, and then he woke up on a bed, unable to move. He says every time she'd kiss him..." Ethel paused and glared at Veronica.

"Go on," Veronica wanted her to continue.

"He grew older while she got younger."

Veronica gasped before gagging. The combination of heat and smells from the dilapidated trailer finally got to her. She was on the verge of vomiting. She asked Ethel to continue talking to Jeff while she walked outside.

This was something new, something different. The supernatural deaths they had encountered were mostly violent affairs from ancient specters, but here? It wasn't the same old story. Maybe it was a witch? Did those even exist? Until her grandmother's death, Veronica had no idea that some of the dead stayed behind as ghosts. She often wondered how many people attended their funerals, crying out that they were still here, though none of their loved ones could hear them. The idea always made her nervous.

A drunk driver killed Ethel in January 2020. She was in the

passenger side of Veronica's car, and they were going to dinner. Ethel never wore her seatbelt. She always made excuses that it choked her. Even though the warning sound would ding every twenty seconds, she refused to put it on. They were at a four-way stop sign, and Veronica didn't see him coming. It wouldn't have mattered if she had. He never even touched his brakes when he T-boned the passenger side of her car and killed Ethel instantly.

Veronica's ribs punctured her right lung, and she lost several teeth from Ethel flying sideways and slamming into her. Veronica was in the hospital for a week and a half and was drugged out of her mind from pain medication. They held the funeral for Ethel while she was still admitted, and she attended through Facetime by connecting with her cousin's phone. It killed her because she wasn't there. Very few things mattered to her, but her Maw Maw was one of them.

She first saw her grandmother after her passing when she got home from the hospital. She walked in through her door, and there Ethel was, depressed and sitting on the couch. Veronica thought she was having a psychotic episode and began to cry. It took everything in Ethel's power to prove to her that she was real. They couldn't touch, but they could talk to one another, and as the hours went on, Veronica finally calmed down.

Veronica had concluded that it was pleasant, even if it was because of a brain injury or emotional breakdown. Being able to talk to a figment of her imagination that represented her grandmother wasn't the worst thing that could happen. It was after Veronica returned to work she received proof that all of it was real.

A supernatural case landed on her desk the day she returned to work, though she didn't know that's what it was at first. A young man named Brandon had been found dead on the outskirts of town in the front seat of his car. He had enough alcohol in his system to kill three people. Brandon had been a drinker and was a large man, but there was no possible way he'd consumed that much without vomiting or passing out first. The bruising patterns and other physical evidence showed that Brandon had been moved to the front seat of his car and had most certainly not been the one driving on the night of his death.

Through Ethel, who could see and interact with his spirit, Brandon revealed that he'd been given a sedative and an enema of pure grain alcohol. A man he thought was his friend was sleeping with his girlfriend behind his back and had concocted a plan to rid himself of Brandon and make it look like alcohol poisoning. They had no motive to kill him at first glance. Not really. He was planning on breaking it off with her soon anyway. Maybe it was fear? Perhaps it was the thrill? But thanks to Ethel's ability to converse with Brandon's ghost, she told Veronica.

She leaned on both the friend, Shawn, and the girlfriend hard.Veronica confronted them with things she couldn't have found out alone. Who drove his car out there, how they moved his body, even the meal they had in celebration after they'd finished. Veronica knew it all. After all, Brandon had witnessed the whole thing and was devastated by their betrayal.

The girlfriend flipped on Shawn. A quick confession later and Veronica was able to bring them to justice for Brandon and his family. There hadn't been much evidence to rely on, and they might not have been able to make the case if it wasn't for their combined effort. It is how they found out about the doors to the other side too. "Great shining doors to paradise," Ethel told Veronica. Swore she saw Brandon get his and walk into the unknown.

Veronica and Ethel were delighted to work together like this. For a while, it brought them closer. Ethel could sit in a room with a suspect while they were with their lawyer. Of course, it was illegal for Veronica to know what was said, but there was a thrill in breaking the rules. No one else could see Ethel, so it was their little secret.

Ethel would leave now and then to search for answers, only to return and tell Veronica that the others she encountered knew as little as she did, if not less. The only thing she had learned for sure was that every death did not produce a ghost. They both assumed those were the ones that went on to the other side.

Veronica tried to help as best she could. She looked through every corner of the internet, looking for signs of someone who could converse with the dead. YouTube was flooded with them, and she had reached out to a handful under anonymity. She was trying to find out why and or how this had happened to her. All of them turned out to be scam artists wanting money.

So, they stopped trying to figure it out and accepted things. Veronica could see her grandmother, and Ethel was ecstatic to see her granddaughter. The two of them were able to give many loved ones closure and help bring justice to the dead, whether by telling the victim's family or dropping a clue that led to the capture of their killer.

Veronica found herself lost in those memories as the rain beat down all around her. The awning wasn't much help, and she was wet, but at least she was out of the nastiness of that place. She didn't want to be in there anymore and didn't want to deal with Ethel's judgmental tone.

Lacy's face came to the forefront of her mind. Veronica had thought she'd found love and would have done anything for Lacy. Her relationship with her had lasted two years, but it ended in a whirlwind of hate and bitterness. Veronica had been depressed about Lacy finding someone else and honestly thought that Lacy would reach out after her accident. It never happened.

Veronica had stayed in contact with the family, though. Lacy's brother Jimmy was a career criminal. He was involved in all kinds of messes that Veronica had found herself getting him out of. She liked Jimmy. He'd helped her out several times before when she needed to find out about someone or something before Ethel came into her life in a new way. They had a good rapport, and Jimmy always told Veronica that his sister had made a mistake leaving her, which stroked her ego quite a bit.

Jimmy wasn't an evil man by any stretch. He just couldn't keep his hands off things that didn't belong to him. He'd reach out to her sometimes to get out of trouble, but always managed to keep things light and easy. So when he called her in tears, she knew it was severe. His step-daughter had been hurt by an uncle, in a way that no child should ever experience. Veronica had been around this child for a third of her life—birthday parties, holidays—and the rage that took her was uncontrollable.

She took the man out on an old back road to a worn down building and pulled the trigger. There was no way to prosecute the man, and he would never be punished for his crime. She'd tried every way to do it by the book, but he had been meticulous in covering his tracks, and the young girl was terrified to speak against him.

Veronica had seen enough of these situations and acted on them. In her mind, this man was evil, and the world would be much safer without him. So, she murdered him. At the time, it felt like the right thing to do. One of Jimmy's friends disposed of the body—the less she knew about where they'd dumped it the better.

She could call upon Ethel whenever needed, but getting her to stay posed a problem. She had no control over when Ethel would just pop in, which brought her into this mess. Ethel had watched the whole thing. It was a downward spiral from there. Ethel chastised her every chance she got, and Veronica fell into a depression. The promiscuity and the drinking all started the night she thought she was doing the right thing. Ethel wouldn't let her forget; she'd watched her from the shadows. The guilt Veronica felt was soul-crushing.

Even though they were at odds, they could push it to the side to be civil with one another. Most of the time, Ethel spouted nothing but insults. But in the end, they always tried to do what was best for the situation.

At least today she isn't talking about how 'crowded' her world is getting. Maybe Heaven and Hell are full?

Veronica felt cold suddenly. She shuddered, and waited for Ethel to speak.

"I'm going to sit with him for a little while. That man is a mess right now," Ethel said.

"That's fine. I'm going back. I need to figure out how to talk to the sister and convince her that the body is his."

"How in the world are you going to do that?" Ethel questioned.

"I have no idea."

"What about Nadine?" Ethel asked.

"What about her? Ghosts are one thing, and we didn't do anything about the one on the trail."

"Yes, but..." Ethel started.

"But what? We couldn't do anything about that, and now you want to go searching for a witch? I'm curious, Ethel, not stupid. She's something... different," Veronica explained dismissively.

"What if she does this to someone else? I know the house he went to, he told..."

"What do you think we should do?" Veronica turned around and interrupted Ethel again.

"Stop her," Ethel said matter-of-factly.

Veronica chuckled and shook her head. "I don't think she'll be afraid of my badge." They looked at each other briefly before Veronica broke the silence. "I'm out. Do you think he'll be okay?"

"You don't care about him," Ethel sighed.

"Jesus, Ethel... Just one time, can we not?" Veronica sighed.

"Don't say the Lord's name in vain, girl," Ethel warned.

Veronica shook her head. "I'm sorry." Veronica could feel a wave of sadness overcoming her. "I didn't... I'm just sorry, okay?" She left before Ethel had a chance to respond.

<hr>

Veronica was soaked by the time she returned to her Nissan Sentra and shut the door.

"I swear I'd kill her if she weren't already..." Veronica muttered. The cold feeling was still there, but not from the rain. Unnatural, bitter, and intense. The same feeling when Ethel was close, and it made her uncomfortable. She wouldn't say it was painful, but it was almost unbearable.

What else could Ethel possibly want? Hadn't she said enough?

She looked at the passenger seat, which was empty, before glancing out her window. She expected to see Ethel, but she wasn't there. She clicked the button on the overhead light. Veronica saw nothing until she happened to catch a glimpse in her rearview mirror at him sitting there. He was entirely still, with his eyes focused on the back of her head. He was directly in the center of the backseat. His head almost touched the roof.

He was a large man in a Cincinnati Reds t-shirt and blue jeans; his left hand was on his lap, gripping a pen, and in his right, he was holding index cards. His hair was thinning, and his goatee was showing signs of age. He didn't look as if he was breathing, but their eyes met when she turned her head to look at him.

Veronica reached for her gun and felt a ping of panic. She had never seen this man before and had no idea what he could want with her. *Is he here to kill me?* She started thinking of the people who hated her—it was an extensive list—and she racked her brain trying to place him. He hadn't made any moves, and his expression showed no anger. He was blank. If he were going to strangle Veronica or shoot her, he'd had his chance.

He slowly took the pen and began writing on one of the index cards. His movements were slow as his large hand traced across the card. A chill went all through Veronica; she shivered, and her teeth chattered. She knew this man was dead. She would have been excited if he hadn't startled her. It proved she could see more than just her grandmother. He finished writing on one of the cards and placed the pen back down in his lap. He flipped it around, and Veronica read it slowly.

Help my daughter. Please.

3

*

Jennifer placed her ID card up against the glass just as he asked. She finally caught her breath after climbing five flights of stairs just to reach the tiny security room. The elevator was being serviced, so Jennifer had no other options. There were many days she regretted smoking, and this one would join that list. Her throat burned, and she felt her pulse in her throat. She didn't know if that was from her being in this place or her body telling her the cigarettes were killing her.

Jennifer had parked directly in front of the building and cursed the rain as she got out of her car and hurried to the door. She should have known to bring her umbrella with her, but in her rush to get here it had just slipped her mind. West Virginia was always a weather mystery in September. One minute, it could hit ninety degrees and the next, you'd wonder why it was so cold. It was one of a litany of reasons she used for staying away.

She collected her bearings and took a look around the room. There were three worn-down brown leather chairs, along with the heavy wooden door she came through. It was all very cramped and unsettling. The plexiglass in front of her was yellow with age.

The walls were a light green that reminded her of the vomit scene in

The Exorcist. A small monitor mounted to the back wall showed an image of the hallway through its static. She'd had anxiety since childhood, and it clawed toward the surface. She took a deep breath and hoped that it would pass quickly. She let the sound of the ocean fill her mind. It was the one thing that relaxed her. She'd only been twice, but it stuck. She let the sound engulf her and took another deep breath. She swore she could almost smell the surf. The mind is powerful, and in Jennifer's previous line of work, she never took anything it did for granted.

A loud crash startled her back to reality. She felt her body jerk as thunder reverberated around her. The storm must have begun to pick up. She made eye contact with the orderly.

"I hate storms," she smiled feebly.

He grinned back. "It's okay, Doctor Simmons. I just want to know why you're here. I wasn't told to expect visitors."

Okay, here we go.

"Doctor Morgan and I go a long way back. Is she in her office?" Jennifer knew she wasn't in her office because her car wasn't parked out front. If it had been, she'd have driven around and returned when it was finally gone.

"You just missed her. Maybe twenty minutes or so, I can call her back if it is an emergency."

Jennifer rubbed her left eye, "No, she's got enough going on right now. I wasn't even supposed to show up till next week."

"Well, is there anything I can help you with, Doctor Simmons?" he asked.

He was still grinning at her, and she relaxed. He was attractive and looked to be in his early thirties, but she was never good at guessing a person's age. He needed to trim his beard a little; it was a deep brown with no signs of gray yet. He leaned toward the glass, his brown eyes shot back to the laminated card and then to her face.

She was supposed to turn in the identification months ago after the board revoked her license. She hadn't been called Doctor Simmons since that day, which crushed her every time the realization hit. She felt the board had been too harsh to suspend her, but she didn't put up much of a fight. She would apply for reinstatement after the year was up and probably get turned down.

It was her fault—she should have covered her tracks better, and she certainly shouldn't have pushed Michelle as hard as she had. The young girl was dead, and if Jennifer was being honest, it was her fault. She tried to push memories of the teenager out of her mind. Those blue eyes pleaded with her for help, but Jennifer was so close she never stopped to think about the repercussions of her actions.

That won't happen this time.

She pulled her phone from her pocket and unlocked it with her face. She opened the photos app and clicked the first picture of her and Tina. They were at a Mexican restaurant, and both had sombreros and fried ice cream in front of them. She couldn't recall the place's name, but it was in downtown Baltimore, and Tina had come up for her birthday. She turned the screen to face the glass.

"She's my best friend," Jennifer said, smiling.

He looked at the screen and smirked. "I've never seen her like that."

"Like what?"

"Happy."

Jennifer's brow furrowed at that. Sure, Tina could be a hardass about some things, but she was also funny, easygoing, and a real party animal when the time was right.

"Are you here to sample the local cuisine?" he asked, nodding to the picture.

"Not exactly. I don't get a chance to get down here often, but she asked for a second opinion on one of her patients," Jennifer lied.

"Ah, well, like I said, you just missed her."

Jennifer had planned for this moment and was thankful only the one guard was dealing with her. "Maybe it would be a good idea if I spoke to him without her. That way, there would be no interference. I don't know much about him and can give my unbiased opinion."

His smile faded. "Right now?"

"I mean, that wouldn't be too much of an issue, would it? I can leave Tina a note that I spoke to him in her office. Leave her my findings, and then head on my way."

Maybe she would be able to pull this off. She was halfway there already. She was so confident when she'd left Maryland, but her mood changed completely after the drive. The West Virginia turnpike was still terrible after all this time. She hadn't made that trip in years. With the twists and turns on top of the storm she had driven through, Jennifer's stomach was still nauseous.

She didn't want to be here. Too many memories. She'd never again grace the Mountain State with her presence if she could help it. She contemplated turning around and going home several times during the drive, but now that she was in the building, there was no turning back.

"Well, you're the doctor. If you're ready to see the patient, that's between you and Doctor Morgan."

"Fair enough," Jennifer said. She tried to keep her tone level, but couldn't stop the smile spreading across her face.

"I hate to ask this, Doctor Simmons, but they make me do this." He pointed his thumb back toward the camera she hadn't noticed looming over the both of them.

Here it comes, she thought. *A bunch of bullshit. Don't shut me out now.* She knew the camera system didn't work. Tina had mentioned it on a phone call a few months back, and that the hospital had zero plans to fix them. So he'd done that for show.

"Do you have any firearms on your person?"

"Umm, no," she shook her head and laughed. "I didn't even bring my purse in."

He shrugged. "They never told me what to do if a doctor had one. Maybe you could tell me the procedure for that?" He chuckled, looked down, and marked something with a pen. "No gun, so I'm going to go ahead and say no knives or any other instruments of destruction on you?"

"I leave the grenades at home when I visit psychiatric hospitals," she joked. She caught a glimpse of his nametag—Corey Thompson. He looked nothing like the picture on his badge. He had much more hair then and wasn't smiling in the photo. But his brown eyes were the same. He had a permanent squint almost like the star of those old westerns her father used to gush over.

"Hell of a storm you drove through to get here."

"I had no idea it would do this, or I would have waited till tomorrow."

"I'm sure," he said as he reached under the desk.

"I'm gonna buzz you through the door to your right, Doctor Simmons. Once you're in, I will leave my cage here and lead you to the office. We've just started dinner. You never told me who I am bringing for evaluation."

"Oh," she paused to give the impression she was trying to recall the name. "Dylan Jeffery."

Corey winced. "Oh, okay, I didn't realize it was him."

"Problem?" She could feel the hairs on the back of her neck stand up.

"It's just, because of his crime, he's handled a specific way. He isn't like most of the adolescents in this section," Corey said, looking away from her. "They're going to want you to be on the schedule, when there's more security available in case..."

She could tell he was growing uncomfortable, and she only had a small window to put him at ease. "I am well aware of what he did. Look, I'm sorry to be a burden, but since I am already here, I'd like to see him."

Corey hesitated. Slowly, he said, "I understand."

Jennifer held her phone up. "I can call Tina—I'm sorry, Doctor Morgan—and get her back here if that will help. I just worry that if she's in the room the boy will repeat everything he's already said to her and I won't get a fresh review. It would taint my analysis."

She was bluffing, and hoping he wouldn't call her on it. If he did, how was she going to get by with faking a call to Tina? She was surprised she'd gotten this far. Normally an orderly would be extremely protective of the rules in a situation like this. She wasn't a good liar, and never had been. What made her think this would work?

The loud buzz reverberated through the room. As he waved his hand at her, Jennifer smiled and nodded. She pushed the metal door with the large handle to her right. It was heavier than it looked, and she had to strain to open it wide enough to slide through. After she released the handle and was clear, it swung back with a monstrous clang.

"You seem a little on edge tonight, if you don't mind me saying so," Corey said from behind her.

She turned to face him and noticed again how he was smiling at her. She was used to orderlies being large, underpaid, and overbearing. This man was goofy. He certainly didn't seem to fit in with his surroundings, too bright for the misery he was swimming in.

"I'm used to a cushy office with couches and plants. This is so..."

"Soul sucking, I know," he responded.

The hallway was the same ghastly color as the room she'd just left and was lined with metal doors. The only difference was that these doors had tiny windows to peer in to check on the patients. The hall was longer than she anticipated, and she wondered how many of those rooms were occupied. She wasn't a fan of state-run facilities and wondered if the water ran adequately in these *modern* cells.

Stay focused.

Corey stepped to the side and put his hand out for her to go first. "We're going to the end, the last door on the right. Doctor Morgan's office."

She placed her card in the front pocket of her jeans and pushed her glasses up. She wished she'd dressed more professionally, but in her experience, children responded better when dressed casually. So, denim and a Ravens t-shirt it was. She'd hoped Dylan was a football fan, anything to get him to open up. She had to know what had happened and prove she was right. She'd followed his case from the day after his arrest. It was all anyone talked about for months in the West Virginia media.

She'd become convinced that he was just like her, that his situation and hers intertwined. She'd called his lawyer, Craig Robbins, a public defender, claiming she was writing a book about Dylan.

Jennifer was, up to a few months ago, a fairly respected children's psychologist. She hoped the lawyer would give her anything to confirm her suspicions. She'd only briefly talked to the man but remembered him saying, "He hasn't spoken much since his mother's death. He hardly talked to me, his doctors, hell, anyone."

A conversation with Tina a month ago set this plan into motion. It was late, and she was going on and on about work when she mentioned that Dylan had told her he didn't kill his mother. That a monster had done it. She poured over the internet about his case and the death of his mother. She was positive that she had found another. Just like she'd found with Michelle Still, two years ago, she killed herself after Jennifer talked to her.

"So, I got to ask," Corey said, yanking her out of her fog as they walked down the hallway together. "Why would Doctor Morgan want a second opinion on a patient? I've been at this job for a few years, and she's never done anything like this."

"I study violent crimes in children. I travel all over speaking to them about what led to their actions," she lied.

"Oh, alright. Are you, like, a big deal?"

"Big deal?" she asked.

"Yeah, like some kind of celebrity? You write books or journals? Have some technique named after you?"

"No," she laughed. "I'm lucky to be employed." The words stung as they left her mouth. She wasn't employed and probably would never get a job in her field again.

"Me too! That's why I'm out of here in nine days."

"Oh, is that so?"

"The fiance and I are off to Georgia," he proclaimed triumphantly.

"Moving?"

"No, we're walking the Appalachian Trail. Georgia to Maine. Over 2000 miles. I can't wait. You gotta get out and see the world. Be one with nature before it becomes housing." He paused as if in deep thought. "Or golf courses."

"Not for me." She smiled, impressed by his enthusiasm.

This is why he was so lackadaisical with the rules, he's leaving.

"No car, no cell phone, no television—"

"No deodorant, shower, or expensive mattress I'm still paying for," she interrupted.

He walked backward in front of her, his arms outstretched. "I get it. It's not for everyone."

"Corey, I don't think it's actually for *anyone*. Except maybe that guy who drinks his piss."

"Hey, now," he turned back around, leading her, "I love Bear Grylls."

Jennifer felt herself relax. She was getting close and it was both exciting and terrifying. Dylan could be the key to everything. She was digging for the truth to put the mystery to rest after decades. She needed this, so maybe she could move on and have a life or something that at least resembled one. That was why she was here.

"How long have you known Doctor Morgan?" he asked as he shifted through the keys on the massive keyring he held in his left hand.

"We were roommates at the University of Maryland. One of my oldest friends. She's the best."

Corey dropped the keys and scrambled to pick them up while turning to look at her in shock.

"What's wrong?" she asked.

"Nothing," he said, retrieving the set and looking through them again.

"No," Jennifer began, "what is it?"

"It's just—" he said as he found the key he was looking for and reached for the knob on the wooden door. "I'm stunned she has friends."

Jennifer mulled over what he had just said for a moment before asking, "Why's that?"

"Well, it's just that she's a bit of, and excuse my French, a bit of a bitch," he said.

"Is that so?" Jennifer asked flatly.

Corey turned to her, his face red from embarrassment. "I didn't mean to insult your frie—"

"Oh, that's not it at all," she said, waving her hand at him. "There's no bit about it. She is a bitch. Doesn't keep her from having friends. Or getting married."

"No way." Corey's mouth hung open.

Jennifer nodded. "Two children, too. They always go on trips together. They went to Japan before the pandemic. Real great mom. I love her kids."

"You're lying. She's constantly berating us. She makes us stand when she enters the room. The guy who quit just last month told me that if he didn't leave, he would strangle her in the parking lot."

"Seriously? She's an absolute sweetheart. When my cat died, she came to Baltimore to help me spread its ashes."

He shook his head and unlocked the door. "The woman I know is evil in human form."

"Maybe she just hates it here?"

He stood in the doorway and laughed loudly. "You aren't like other doctors."

Jennifer's anxiety spiked. "Are you saying I lack professionalism?"

"No, not at all. I was just thinking if more therapists were like you. I might have gone more than twice in my life."

Dr. Morgan's office was as barebones as it got. A simple espresso-colored, L-shaped desk sat in the back corner, with a somewhat uncomfortable-looking brown leather couch against the right wall. A tiny monitor and an outdated computer sat alone on the desk. There were no pens, no nameplates, just those two items.

A degree from Maryland and a Baltimore Orioles schedule from 2017 hung on the walls. There was nothing else of note, nothing in the way of personal items, no photo of the children or her husband. She walked across the room to a black filing cabinet and opened the top drawer. Jennifer had helped Tina file papers in Maryland years ago before Tina moved down here to take this job. She knew her system. She flipped to the one that said *Jeffrey, Dylan* in marker across the top and removed it. She slid the drawer closed, returned to the desk, and sat in the executive chair. It was the only thing in the room of any quality. She opened the folder and looked up at Corey.

"You want me to see if he is done with his dinner, Doctor Simmons?" Corey asked her.

"Jennifer," she said as he was leaving.

"Excuse me?" He paused at the door.

"Call me Jennifer. No need to be so formal."

"If I weren't quitting, I would beg you to work here," he smiled.

She smiled back. "You hardly know me."

"I know enough. Not getting called stupid is an upgrade," he said, and was out the door.

Jennifer let everything Corey said sink in.

Why was Tina like that to these people? Was she harsh to the kids here as well? Sure, they were violent criminals, but they were still children and needed help. Jennifer loved her job. It had been emotionally draining, but she cared for her patients and wanted to see them do well.

It was kind of Corey to want her here, but she hated everything about this state. She would never return to this area. She always felt that something was off about this place and its people, even though she began her life as one of them.

She looked down at the open folder on the desk and was instantly sickened by the photos of Dylan's mother. She also had the autopsy photos underneath, but these in front of her were from the crime scene. She wasn't expecting them to be awaiting her inside. She found herself wondering why these graphic images were in there at all. Her stomach twisted into a knot as she glanced at the top picture.

It was a top-down view of Dylan's mother. She was face down, missing her right arm, and her back was completely open, exposing her insides. It was as if an animal had torn through her to the floor. Bits of bone and most of her organs lay strewn beside her. Without thinking, Jennifer turned the pictures over and pushed them away. She picked up the police report on top of the other papers.

Tina had made several notes, along with her preliminary care findings and current treatments, which, at first glance, were to medicate him. Tina had been under the impression that the child had rage issues and was now suffering from post-traumatic stress disorder for what he'd done. She started reading the police report and noticed nothing she hadn't already known. Jennifer had made it halfway through when she heard someone clear their throat from the doorway. She flipped the folder closed and pivoted in the chair.

Corey was standing in the doorway with a young boy in front of him. He was short for eleven years old, with unkempt red hair. His face was littered with freckles, his eyes a piercing blue. He wore a white uniform resembling hospital scrubs, with black numbers over the right side chest: 7361119266. She did her best to smile.

"Hello, Dylan. It's a pleasure to meet you." She stood and gestured toward the couch beside her. "My name is Doctor Jennifer Simmons, and I've come a long way to see you. I'm a close friend of Doctor Morgan, and she thought that you and I should spend some time together."

Dylan started toward the couch; he barely looked at her. She could tell he didn't want to be there by his body language. His shoulders slumped, avoiding eye contact, down to how he trudged along. This child was miserable and in pain, and she knew why. She was just going to have to play this perfectly. He sat down and stared at his lap. Corey walked over and sat on the other side away from them.

"I can't leave him. You know the rules. However..." he said as he pulled his AirPods case out of his breast pocket and flipped them open. "I will be enjoying an evening of Stevie Nicks and a round of hearts on my phone. So, you will have as much privacy as I can give you."

"Did they pluck you out of 1969, Corey?" Jennifer joked.

He put his earbuds in and shrugged before looking down at his phone.

Jennifer sat back down and wheeled the chair over in front of

Dylan. She paused for a few moments to see if Dylan would acknowledge her. He didn't. She peeped at Corey quickly, who seemed lost in his music and game. It was time. She had rehearsed this for the past week, and she was ready. She just prayed it worked.

"I believe you," she said to Dylan. "I know you haven't said it yet; you haven't told a soul, but I believe you." She inched forward. "I am going to tell you a story, Dylan. A story I have never told anyone. A story I think is very similar to yours. "

Dylan didn't look up. He seemed not to be paying any attention to her. If this was going to work, she needed him all in.

"I know you didn't kill your mother Dylan."

No response.

"But I know what did."

He glanced at her, then back down.

"I named it the Nothing. Because there was nothing there."

His eyes raised slowly and locked onto hers. His bottom lip started to quiver.

Oh my God. Am I right? After all this time, did I finally find someone else?

It was the summer of 1994, and Jennifer Simmons was eleven. Her school had just let out for summer break, and Oak Hill, West Virginia, was in the middle of a heat wave. Jennifer thought about going inside for the day, but it was still early, and she didn't want to waste a second of her vacation. This year had been rough on her. Her grandmother had died; it was her first natural brush with death. She walked two houses down almost every day to see her, but that was before. Jennifer had difficulty accepting the fact that she wouldn't be here anymore.

This summer would be something new, something different. Her parents talked about spending a week in Florida during July. She'd not seen the ocean in person, only in movies and pictures. She couldn't wait to see the waves, to feel the sand. The family had spent time at

Summersville Lake, but her dad had told her several times that it wasn't the same.

She was riding the purple bicycle her parents had gotten her for Christmas. They tried to pass it off as a gift from Santa even though she knew he didn't exist. She played along though, for her parents' sake.

Jennifer thought she was ready to grow up. She read well beyond her grade level, and she adored art. She would tell anyone who listened that she would be a painter. Her father always had the same response: *"Like houses and shit?"*

She'd roll her eyes and sometimes punch his arm. The joke lost its luster after the tenth time. She wanted them to treat her like a teenager; she would be twelve in December and wasn't a baby anymore. She wanted to watch the Simpsons and Seinfeld. She knew she could handle scary movies and music with the big black parental advisory stickers didn't frighten her. Jennifer couldn't wait to grow up.

The wind was at her back as she rode down Old Minden Road. Circle Drive and Harvey Avenue were the limits, and anything past that was forbidden. There were a lot of blind curves on Old Minden —and uphill, too. Her mother had told her she was worried she'd get struck by "some asshole flying out that road."

Her uncle Joe had an accident out Old Minden. He was prone to seizures and went through a guard rail, over the hillside, and into the creek below. It was a miracle that he survived. He'd been in the hospital for months learning to walk again after countless surgeries. She'd visited Joe several times with her mother, but they weren't all that close.

She was coming up the hill right by where Joe had crashed through the railing. The state hadn't sent anyone to put one back up. Her dad had said it was because Governor Gaston Caperton had let the state go to hell, and the road workers laid on their asses all day. As she closed in on the spot, she noticed someone leaning against where the break started.

It was Neil Dunkle. She knew it from his wild, brown hair. He wasn't wearing a shirt, and his jeans were filthy, like he had rolled around in mud all day. He looked at her with a toothy grin, his arms folded across his chest. They were in the same grade, but Jennifer had no idea how he kept passing. He never did his schoolwork and was in constant trouble. She hated Neil. He was cruel and lewd. She asked her father about something he had said to her once, and her dad told Neil's father if he ever spoke to her that way again, he'd thump him. That didn't matter anymore. Neil's dad was arrested for beating his mother when he caught her with someone else. The whole town knew about it, and it only made Neil worse.

"Hey, Tits!" he called out to her.

"Shut up," she said back to him, pedaling faster. The sooner she got by him, the better.

"Aww, don't be that way! You come to look at your uncle's fuck up?"

"He had a seizure." She slowed down a few feet away from Neil and the curve. Neil shook his head and snickered.

"I heard he was drunk."

"He wasn't. He's had them since he was a kid." She stopped her bike and sat there staring him up and down. She knew she should just move along, but he had struck a nerve with her, and she wouldn't let him get away with it.

"Well, then, he shouldn't have been driving. What a bag of shit." He put his left index finger to his left nostril and blew snot onto the ground.

"You are so gross," Jennifer said, not hiding her contempt.

"Whatever, Tits."

"Stop calling me that!"

"Or what? You'll tell your daddy? You'll cry again? You're a fucking baby."

She got off her bike and sat the kickstand down. Neil stopped leaning and stood up tall.

"What? What are you going to do, bitch? Just run on along and cry some more."

She saw the rock right beside the road where she stood. An almost perfectly round stone. In one sweeping motion, she bent down, scooped it up with her right hand, and threw it as hard as she could. It left her hand and arced toward Neil, careening off his forehead just above his left eye.

His head tilted backward, and he cried out in pain as his hands shot up to his forehead. Neil stumbled through the open guard rail, and before she could call his name, he fell over the embankment. Her stomach dropped. She was stunned; her emotions had gone from pure joy to terror almost immediately. He was out of sight, and it was a long way down. "Neil?" she called out weakly. Before gathering her thoughts, Jennifer said louder. "Neil?"

She forced her legs to move and slowly made her way over. She peered down and saw him face down on the grass below. He wasn't moving. She couldn't tell if he was breathing. "Neil? Are you okay?" she whispered. He didn't respond or move. The air was still. "Neil? Quit screwing around. Get up!" she shouted.

Panic overwhelmed her. *He's hurt*, she thought. *He's hurt bad*. She backed away from the hillside and paced back and forth on the road. *I didn't mean to. He wouldn't shut up*. She paced faster. Her heart pounded in her chest, and she felt like she would be sick.

I'll go to jail. Mom will hate me. I didn't mean to. She looked around. There was no one coming or going on the road. She was alone, and her mind wouldn't stop. *God, tell me what to do*. She was overcome with fear, and tears streamed down her cheeks. She bit her lip hard and took a breath. *I'm in so much trouble. He's going to tell*. And then Jennifer did something that would haunt her for the rest of her life. *I need to get out of here*. She rushed to her bike, mounted it, and began peddling for home.

"I left him to die." Jennifer put her right hand to her lip. "I didn't know the extent of his injuries. I left him because I was afraid. I thought he'd get up after a while, or someone would find him with a broken arm or leg." Jennifer shook her head slowly and let the impact of what she'd said weigh heavily in the room.

Dylan was watching her face now, his eyes wide, his mouth slightly open. She hadn't noticed how frail he was until now. The dark circles under his eyes were profound, as if he didn't sleep. After Nothing had visited her, she'd woken up screaming for years. She had been lucky. She still had her mother, but this boy had no one. She waited for a visual cue to continue. Dylan looked away from her and closed his eyes. He shuddered, and she wondered if he was reliving what happened to him. His mouth opened slowly.

"Was it under your bed?" he asked her.

He'd spoken. Dylan had not uttered a word to anyone in months. They knew he could talk. The state had assumed it was because of what he was: a monster hiding in a tiny body, a killer with no remorse, much less a soul. Jennifer knew differently; she knew the real reason Dylan hadn't let out as much as a peep. Fear.

"Under my bed?" she responded too quickly. *Calm down.*

"The Nothing," his eyes met hers, "was it under your bed?"

She took a deep breath. "Do you want me to continue? We can get you a soda. We can take a small break."

He shook his head. "No, I want to know."

Jennifer looked up; the thunder she'd just heard was nowhere near as loud as before. The storm was moving on. She rubbed the collar of her t-shirt. It felt as if it was suffocating her.

"I'll tell you, but you have to make me a promise."

"What?" he asked. She took notice of how thick his accent was.

"You tell me what happened the night your mother died," she said. He nodded.

Jennifer rode into her front yard and leaped from her seat. She didn't put the kickstand down and let the bike fall over. Her mother, who was watering her plants on the porch, instantly piped up.

"We told you to be careful with that! You break it, you don't get another one."

Jennifer bounded up the wooden steps and almost reached the screen door when her mother took her by the arm.

"Are you listening to m—are you alright?" Her tone instantly changed to that of concern.

"I think I'm going to throw up," Jennifer gasped. Jennifer's mother opened the screen door.

"Go on, baby."

Jennifer rushed through the living room and turned right into the hallway toward the bathroom. Her stomach was on fire, and she felt faint. She'd barely reached the bathroom before she could taste the acid in the back of her throat. She hit her knees and lifted the toilet seat.

Jennifer's mother clicked the light switch and stood in the doorway.

"It's going to be alright. You probably got too hot." Jennifer nodded and braced for the worst. Her mind was reeling at the image of Neil lying at the bottom of the hillside. She wanted to tell her mother; they were close, and she might understand. The fear came rushing back over her. She didn't want to hurt or disappoint her mother. She didn't want to let her down. She was so afraid of being sent away; it was the only thought at the forefront of her mind. *You'll never see your mother again.* She said nothing. The illness took hold.

"Patrick!" her mother called down the hall before looking back at Jennifer. "Patrick, come here!"

Jennifer braced herself as she felt her insides doing flips. Her father came into view out of the corner of her eye as she dry-heaved.

"Damn it, Andrea. I'm eating. I don't need to see that," he yelled.

"She's sick. Maybe I should stay home tonight. I could get Mike to cover."

Jennifer dry-heaved again.

"Why? I'm not an idiot. I know how to take care of a sick kid."

Jennifer heard her father respond, but she couldn't see him anymore. He had walked away from the door.

"I didn't call you an idiot. It's just if she's sick—"

"If she's sick, I put a bucket beside her bed, give her some Pepto, and let her sleep it off," he said.

"You won't check on her."

"Of course I will. I've got nothing else to do. The Reds are on this evening."

Finally, she vomited. She didn't have much on her stomach. She spat and flushed the commode.

"Could you guys do that in the living room?" she asked before gagging again.

"When you're done, brush your teeth, and I'll lay your pajamas on your bed," her mother said calmly before leaving Jennifer's sight.

"See, you upset her," she heard her mother say.

"Are you serious?"

Jennifer stayed on her knees for a few minutes after she was finished. She couldn't stop wondering if Neil was alive or dead. He was a tough boy. He was always in fights at school. *It wasn't that far down*, she lied to herself. She began to relax. Maybe she should go back. He'd be gone when she got there. That brought on another set of worries.

What if he broke his arm? Would the Florida trip be canceled? Would she be grounded for the rest of the summer?

A fierce chill came over her; she almost expected to see her breath in front of her. The hair on her arms stood up, and she began to shake.

He just died.

She jerked away from the sound of the voice. Hollow, metallic, and deep. She was positive someone had spoken to her. She sat on the bathroom floor, staring at the shower curtain's beige color and ugly flower pattern. The voice had come from that direction.

Something was on the other side of the shower curtain, and it was watching her. It had spoken to her. She felt it. She could sense it there. She slowly got to her feet and, without thinking, took a step forward. *What are you doing?*

Then another step.

Jennifer reached for the shower curtain. She wanted to prove to her mind that what was in front of her was the truth. She pulled the curtain back slowly and scanned every stain and every crack in the white tile leading up to the wall. "Did you need a shower?" her mother called from the doorway.

Jennifer let out a hoarse scream, her throat already raw from vomiting. She'd jumped and landed facing her mother. Andrea's hand shot up to her chest, and her eyes widened.

"What the hell, Jennifer!" Andrea exclaimed, obviously startled.

"I'm sorry, Mom. I thought I heard something," Jennifer said.

Andrea frowned, walked over to Jennifer with her hand outstretched, and felt her forehead. "Well, you are clammy, but there's no fever."

"I'm feeling better already," Jennifer fibbed.

"Oh no, you brush your teeth. I can smell your breath, and your clothes are on your bed. Rest, and listen to your radio, but keep it down. You know how your father is."

Andrea turned to leave the bathroom.

"Are you still going to work tonight?" Jennifer asked.

"Oh, honey, you know I have to. But I wish I could stay here with you," Andrea answered.

Jennifer shuffled her feet. She wanted her mother to stay home to tell her what happened. "If I feel better tomorrow, can we go to the park together?"

"Depends on how tired I am. Now, brush your teeth. We can talk about that in the morning."

Jennifer watched her leave and looked back toward the tub. She didn't feel anything there anymore. She brushed her teeth quickly, and when she finished, she rushed down the hallway to her room and changed her clothes. Her mother came in with a small bucket and some newspaper and set it on the floor next to her bed.

"It's early. I don't want to go to bed," Jennifer whined.

"Well, you need to rest. Maybe you can sit here and color?" Andrea tried to compromise.

"I'm not four. This is why I need a TV."

"And that is why you need a job to pay for that TV," Andrea grinned.

"Mom, what time is it?" Jennifer asked.

"A little after four. I go in at eight, so I am here till seven-thirty if you need something." Andrea explained. Her mother tucked her in and kissed her forehead. "Well, you don't smell like puke anymore."

"Thanks."

Andrea stood and walked across the room and turned on her shelf stereo. "Bump n' Grind" by R. Kelly started blaring out of the tiny speakers. Andrea looked back at her, made a face feigning disgust, and began turning the dial until "My Love" from Little Texas popped in.

"I don't know how you can stomach that other stuff. It's just filthy," Andrea complained.

"It's not all like that," Jennifer said.

"Whatever you say." She turned the volume down till it was barely audible. "Get some sleep." She crossed the room and walked out the door, leaving it cracked open.

Jennifer turned to her pillow and started to cry. *It was an accident.* She wished she hadn't picked up that rock. She wished she'd obeyed her mother and stayed on the streets she was allowed to ride on. She wanted the headache to go away and her stomach to ease up.

The incident replayed so many times in her mind that she couldn't stop crying. Her pillow was covered in tears, and the back of her hand was wet from wiping her nose. She hadn't moved from her bed; she felt stiff. She wished her mother would come back in and check on her. Her thoughts were foggy, and her little body trembled. The voice she heard from behind the shower curtain had terrified her.

She listened to the music for a while and felt her limbs grow heavy. She closed her eyes with her last few thoughts of Neil not moving.

Her father opened the door and called out to her. "Jenn?"

She sat up in her bed and noticed that night had fallen out her window. She rubbed her eyes. Had she drifted off?

"Yeah?"

He walked into the room. The only light source coming behind him was the hall light, but it was enough for her to see his face. Something was off.

"Jenn honey, did you see Neil today?"

She felt a pounding in her chest. She glared at Patrick. He was standing there with his arms folded and one eyebrow raised. He didn't seem himself. He looked a little bit shaken. She shook her head slowly.

"Well," he cleared his throat. "He was involved in an accident on Old Minden. They think he was hit by a car."

She was shaking. "Is he okay?"

Patrick looked away, saying nothing, and she knew. Jennifer began to cry again, this time harder than ever. She wanted to tell her father it was her. She tried to confess, but it just wouldn't come.

"I know he could be rough on you, baby girl." He ran his fingers through what hair he had left. Patrick was never one for Jennifer to lean on. He wasn't very good with his emotions or great for advice. Her dad had two speeds: jovial, loveable fool and a hot head.

Jennifer was shivering now, and she shook her head no again.

"Oh," Patrick paused. "I should have waited till morning to tell you this. I know you're sick." He turned and was out the door before she could say anything to him, not that she could have.

He's dead, and you just lied. She went to get out of bed, but her legs wouldn't move. She flopped back down hard and put her face in her pillow. She gripped the pillow tighter and was wailing when she heard it. A slow creak. She looked toward her bedroom door to see if her father was coming in. The door was still cracked. It wasn't coming from over there.

She sat up in her bed and watched as the closet door swung wide. She squinted, her eyes adjusting to the dark, but the moon was new that night. The room was practically pitch black.

"Dad!" she called out.

A sense of dread came over her. She felt eyes on her, just as she had earlier that day. It wasn't long before Patrick opened the door.

"You throw up again?" he asked.

"Can you turn on the light?" she asked.

The switch clicked and she held her hand up to cover her eyes. The headache from earlier was still there. Her closet was wide open.

"You okay?" Patrick asked, stepping into her line of sight. He turned his large frame in the direction she was staring. "Oh, I get it." He walked forward and closed the closet door. "I can't stand when mine is open either."

"It came open. I heard it." She tried to hide the panic in her voice but failed as her voice cracked.

"Honey," he said, smirking. He walked back and opened the closet door. He put his head inside, waved his arms, and then moved some hangers across the bar. "Nothing here." He closed the door tight, bumped his backside against it, and knelt in front of her bed. He bent out of her sight. "There's nothing under here either." He stood back up and gave a small chuckle. "You're becoming more like your mother every day."

Jennifer let herself breathe a little deeper; her dad was here, and he was a huge man. If something had been in that closet, it would be foolish to mess with him. After all, he was a miner, and his forearms were bigger than her head. Her mother always made Popeye jokes about him. He was tall; she didn't know his exact height, but he was the biggest based on the other fathers in town.

"Sorry, Dad."

"It's fine. Have you had anything to drink since you've been sick?" he asked before walking over and placing his hand on her head.

She shook her head.

"I'm going to get you a glass of water. You're gonna take a few sips and go back to sleep."

"Alright."

He strode out of the room, leaving the light on and the door wide open. Jennifer sat in bed. Maybe she could convince him to let her sleep on the couch. He always fell asleep in the recliner watching television. That way, she wouldn't be alone. She wouldn't be worried about–

Her closet door opened again. The room felt cold. Her skin tingled. Something was in there, and it was staring at her.

"My dad is coming back," she whispered. "My dad is tough." She let the words hang in the air. She was trying her hardest to seem brave for whatever was watching her. She almost bolted out of her bed and rushed down the hall, but she sat there, afraid.

You killed him.

The same voice as before. This time, it was coming from the closet.

You're going to get away with it. Do you know that? No one saw you. His mother will kill herself while you play in the ocean. But at least you won't be in trouble.

"It was an accident."

Then why not get someone to help? Maybe he would have survived.

"You aren't real. I'm sick," she said as she threw the covers off herself onto the floor.

Oh, Jennifer, I'm real.

Jennifer got out of bed, the hardwood cold on her bare feet. She faced the closet, using every ounce of courage to talk to whatever awaited her in the dark.

I don't think it's fair.

"If you know what happened, you know I didn't want that," Jennifer whispered.

What do you say, Jennifer, an eye for an eye?

"My grandma used to say that. Vengeance is mine, sayeth the Lord," she said in defiance, the fear consuming her.

God isn't here, but I am.

It wants to kill me, Jennifer thought and she ran. Her bare feet pounded against the wood as she bolted away. She almost missed her doorway as she turned her body to keep from slamming into the wall. She was in the hallway and sprinting toward the kitchen. It was right on her heels and biting at her ankles. She tried to yell out for her father, but her voice escaped her.

She'd never run so fast in her life. She exited at the end of the hall, banging her shoulder on the wood frame. She fell forward onto the cold, tan linoleum of the kitchen, her father dropping the plastic cup back into the sink as he jerked in surprise. Quickly, Jennifer rose to her feet and grabbed her father around the waist. Tears streamed down her face, stinging her eyes, and she could barely catch her breath.

"What in the hell is wrong with you?" he barked at her.

"Daddy, it's going to kill me!" she wheezed through the tears.

He looked past her shoulder into the hallway. "Goddamnit, Jennifer, there's nothing here!"

She only gripped him tighter, shaking her head. She gazed back into the hall and then back toward him and pleaded. "We have to go. We have to go now!" She pulled him toward the door past the cabinets. Her mother called it the back door, but it led to the left side of the house, facing their neighbors, the Pullens.

"You're acting crazy. There's nothing in this fucking house!" he yelled.

She pulled away from him and, with one swift motion, unlocked the door and turned the knob. The night air was a welcome feeling to her flushed face. She stepped onto the wooden stoop and looked back at her father. How silly she must look to him, ranting about an invisible boogeyman in her bedroom. There she was in her bare feet and her nightgown in the middle of the night, crying uncontrollably.

But her father stood in the doorway, looking at her as if she had lost her mind.

"Daddy, I can hear it. It talked to me." She begged him to believe her and come outside. His expression changed, and he turned his back to her and walked away into the house.

"No!" she yelled out, but it was too late. He was already out of her view. *What are you doing? It's going to kill you.*

She gathered the nerve to enter the house when her father stepped back into the doorway, causing her to almost fall off the stoop.

"Will you calm down?" He was angry, eyes bulging, and his face was a sharp red.

"I can't. You didn't hear it!" She started to sob again.

"I checked your bedroom, the closet, my room, the bathroom,

under the bed, even behind the couch. Jennifer, you are acting like a fool. THERE IS NOTHING IN THIS HOUSE!" he yelled.

"An eye for an eye, it said" she stated weakly. "It's going to kill me."

It came over his back, a darkness, a shadow. Jennifer could see it behind him as it rose. He hadn't noticed it. He was fixated on her. It was almost blocking out all the light behind him.

I wasn't talking about you.

It made a *thunk*, and something warm splashed across her face. Her father groaned and fell forward, knocking her off the stoop. She landed almost face first on the ground, her hand outstretched, taking some of the impact. She rolled over on her back and heard a loud banging but her vision was blurry.

"Jennifer, run!"

Jennifer sat up, rubbed her head, and looked at where her father's voice, wet and gurgling, was coming from. He was against the Pullen's house, covered in blood. Wounds opening up on him left and right. He swung wildly, but another massive gash formed across his midsection and across his arm.

There's nothing there.

She couldn't see anything. He was fighting for his life against nothing.

"Baby girl, run!" Patrick screamed before the bottom of his jaw was ripped clean off and discarded onto the grass near her. Jennifer scooted backward away from it, screaming.

"What the hell is going on back here?" Jennifer recognized the voice instantly.

"Mister Pullen! Help my daddy, it's got my daddy!" she screamed, closing her eyes tight and curling up into a ball."Oh my... Oh my God," he gagged. "Gwen, get the dog! Get back inside! Call the police, there's a wild animal on the loose!"

Jennifer felt someone touch her, and she opened her eyes to see her neighbor, Mr. Pullen. She could barely make him out because they weren't in the light of the open side door.

She cried as he scooped her off the ground to carry her. "Did you see it? Jennifer, is it a wolf or bear? Where did it go?" he asked nervously.

Jennifer could see her father slumped against the white house, the light shone on him perfectly. His neck was torn apart, and his jaw was missing. His eyes were lifelessly looking at the ground, and every inch of him was soaked in blood. Jennifer screamed into Mr. Pullen's chest.

"Don't look. Don't look at him, honey. Let's get you out of here," he whispered and trotted toward his front door.

As he whisked her away, she heard its voice one last time.

Now we're even.

Jennifer could barely speak to the police once they arrived. The shock of everything that happened was too much. She had to stand with a female officer in the bathroom while they took pictures of her naked body. Then she had to wait for a detective before they would allow her to clean the blood from her face. They swabbed her cheeks, took her tiny nightgown, and placed it in a paper bag. She'd asked several times if her father was all right, but she already knew the answer.

She caught glimpses of her mother as they led her around the house. They didn't make eye contact or speak. Jennifer wouldn't have wanted to anyway. The detective asked her several times what she remembered, what she saw, and how it attacked. Each time, her answer was the same. *I saw nothing.* No one pressed her on the issue. They kept calling her *honey* and *sweetheart,* which just made it worse.

She didn't remember when she fell asleep; the sun was up in the sky. The fear had finally dissipated, and somehow, deep down, she knew that *Nothing* was satisfied. It had gotten what it wanted. It took her father as penance for her actions.

They never entered the house again. She never saw that bedroom after that night. They left everything intact and purchased all new items. Her mother couldn't stomach even looking at their home, and with that, the family moved to a small town outside of Beckley, West

Virginia, named Mount Hope. Her mother never really recovered. She began drinking heavily and shut herself away from her child.

Jennifer never told anyone about the voice, Neil's death, or the *Nothing*. She let it sit deep in her soul, allowing it to fester.

On her graduation day, she left the state with her flavor-of-the-week boyfriend and moved to Baltimore. She had to leave if she was going to have some semblance of normalcy. She packed in the middle of the night and left a note on her bed. Jennifer had hoped the dark cloud hanging over her would stay behind. She couldn't put up with her mother anymore. She was tired of cleaning up after her and making excuses. The feeling that she was constantly being punished for Neil's death would not follow her hours north across the state line.

Maybe her mother could move on and heal herself without Jennifer doing everything for her. Tough love and whatnot wasn't to be the case. Her mother was lost to cirrhosis in the early 2000s. Jennifer, however, outside of her personal life, was quite successful in College Park. After spending three months in Baltimore, she decided to study child psychology at the University. She was very successful in school, and her grades were top-tier. She surrounded herself with every facet of her school work, studying meticulously every detail of childhood trauma.

University was a wonderful distraction, but she couldn't shake her nightmares. She thought that trying to explain Nothing would help her recover somehow. So, in her free time from working at a mental institution specializing in troubled teens, she started studying textbooks on the occult. After that, she moved on to the spirit world and read all she could about ghosts. None of it even remotely resembled what happened to her. She spent many sleepless nights pouring over as much information as she could get her hands on, but Nothing wasn't in any of the works she studied.

Jennifer had begun to question if an overactive imagination had heard something that wasn't there. Had she created Nothing to explain away something so painful? Maybe her guilt of Neil coincided with an animal attack on her father. Could she have meshed them together in some macabre story in the furthest reaches of her subconscious?

What if it was her fault? What if she had an episode and had done something horrible? The damage to her father was too extreme; she knew she wasn't strong enough to do something like that. Still, the thought hid in the back of her mind, constantly scratching its way to the surface. If she was ever to find peace, she had to prove to herself that Nothing was real, no matter the cost.

Jennifer sat across from a scared little boy. He had to be the same age she was when Nothing had taken her father away. She knew this was the story she'd spent her life searching for, the one that would help it all make sense.

"There was nothing there, am I right?" Jennifer leaned in. Her palms were drenched, and her throat was dry. "It spoke to you."

Dylan looked into her eyes, nodding slowly.

"Why, Dylan? Why did it do this to you?"

Jennifer felt her stomach doing flips. *Nothing* was real.

"Miss Addis. I killed Miss Addis," he said.

"Who is that, Dylan?"

"My teacher. She was so mean. I didn't know she'd die," his voice broke.

"Slow down, Dylan, take a breath. If you need a break, even if you feel like talking tomorrow, that's okay," she said, reaching out to him.

"Miss Addis used to be with my daddy. He left her for my momma. She hated me."

"Was she mean to you?" Jennifer placed her hand on his knee.

He nodded his head and closed his eyes tight. "She poked fun at me all the time. Called me white trash, said I was stupid."

"And you killed her?" Jennifer asked, confused.

"It was an accident. I just wanted her to leave again." He wrung his hands to the point they turned red.

Corey looked at Dylan, who was squirming uncomfortably in his seat. He caught Jennifer's eye, and she nodded at him. Corey glanced at Dylan once more and frowned. Still, he went back to his phone.

"Dylan, look at me. You are safe here. I know you're afraid. I'm here to help you." She put her hand out and took his. "I promise you, Dylan. I'm going to get to the bottom of all of this. I have searched for a long time for someone else who's been hurt by the Nothing."

"So, what happens now?"

"Now?" Jennifer leaned back in the chair. She smiled. "Now, you tell me everything that happened. I want to find the Nothing," Jennifer leaned forward and whispered, "so I can kill it."

4

Veronica had the accelerator pushed to the floorboard. Now seated in the passenger seat, the ghost had her wholly unnerved. He ran his fingers through his hair, fidgeted, and looked at the clock on her dash. She tried to dismiss him and focus on the task at hand, but the slightest movement from him was enough to startle her every time.

She was doing well over ninety on the interstate heading for Hurricane, where he had directed her to go. She wasn't far from it, but the index cards he had shoved in her face had urged her that time was of the essence. She thought that if they went any faster, they would take flight.

"Listen," Veronica looked behind her at a car that blared its horn as she passed. "How the hell am I supposed to convince her I'm not crazy?"

The specter scribbled furiously, reached over, and held the card above the steering wheel.

She'll listen to you.

"Yeah? But I wouldn't," Veronica explained, flying past the semi on her right when a thought cropped up in her head. "Wait, how the hell did you find me?"

He held up another card.

Heard you could see Grandma.

He dropped the card, and it vanished on the way down. She looked at him and then back to the road as she almost rear-ended a Chevy Silverado. She jerked the wheel to go around and nearly lost control, but turned toward the skid and got the car back under her command. Her heartbeat thrummed in her palms against the wheel.

"I could only see Ethel, and now, suddenly, I see you. How is that possible?"

He smiled at her and produced his next card. *I wanted you to.*

"Are you shitting me? You have to know more than that." She was livid at the absurdity. He shrugged and looked down at the clock again.

"I'm going as fast as I can. We'll make it," Veronica said.

She swerved onto exit ramp 34 and let off the gas. He had written to her when he was in the backseat that this was where they needed to go. Everything had happened so fast from the moment they met that she barely had time to process any of it. Veronica had always been self-centered and selfish, but her curiosity was the one thing that was her weakness. It had gotten her in way more trouble than not.

The current situation was proof enough of that. Here Veronica was with the ghost of this man without a good reason, trusting him and believing the words he'd jotted down. He insisted that she help him and that his daughter was in grave danger. He had written that she would perish if she didn't leave right then.

She hadn't the foggiest idea of what she was getting into, nor did she think at the time to ask. It was the ghost's face that pushed her on. She could see the desperation in his wide eyes and how he obsessively expressed one word: *please*. A dead father looking after his baby girl from beyond the grave. She was the only one who could help him, the only one that she knew of that could see him. She was the only option this man had, and she didn't even know his name.

Veronica was not one to just up and help anyone. She lost a part of herself the day she tried to save a young boy and failed. Something was never quite right inside her after that. Lacy left her, and then Ethel died, and even though the accident wasn't her fault, she still bore the blame. Everything had been teetering on edge and finally tipped over when she decided to help Jimmy and kill at his behest.

It was why this whole day had been out of character for her. First, she searched for Jeff, and the only reason she'd done that was curiosity and the chance to try and speak to Ethel. She hated admitting it to herself, but her heart leaped whenever she saw her grandmother. Their conversations were few and far between.

Veronica was wondering how many spirits she could see. This was the first one besides her grandmother, and she was rolling everything around in her mind, wondering what the criteria were for her to see them. Ethel was right to question her motives earlier. She thought about calling out for Ethel but decided against it. She didn't want Ethel speaking negatively about her to this ghost and didn't like the headache that arose from arguing with her.

"Do you know where we are going?" She took a deep breath and shifted her weight in her seat. She had been so tense during the drive on the interstate that she hadn't realized she was shaking. She needed to catch her bearings.

She stopped at the light and waited till he showed her the little card he had written on.

Sam's Fork. Back road. He motioned for her to turn right.

"Ninety percent of our roads are back roads," she complained.

He nodded in agreement.

She turned the wheel and headed in the direction he had pointed.

"Why can't you talk? Could you not speak when you were alive? If not, that's... Well, that's some bullshit."

He started writing again and flipped it over to show her.

I try. Doesn't work. He dropped the card, and it disappeared on the way down. *It took forever to learn how to do this.* Again, it vanished when he released it.

"I can't get used to that. It's creepy." She nodded toward where the card had disappeared.

He rubbed his temples. She could only imagine how frustrating it was to not only be dead but unable to communicate efficiently. She had so many questions for him. How much of the other side did he know that Ethel did not? Could he tell when people were about to die, or maybe that was only for his daughter? She would help him with this and then bombard him with questions after retrieving her and getting her safely away.

When they first got on the interstate, he had written that her name was Jennifer, and to get her across the state line into either Kentucky or Ohio, he was adamant that she get out of West Virginia. She could not stay here, no matter what. Veronica agreed to everything he asked and had been on a collision course with whatever awaited them ever since.

"Are we in danger?" she questioned abruptly.

It had just popped into her head; she wasn't going to say it, but it was out of her mouth before she could stop it. Whatever was at the end of this car ride, could it harm her too?

He pointed at her, then to himself, and shook his head no. She had an uneasy feeling that he was lying, but she kept quiet.

"But she is?"

He nodded slowly.

"So, she's in danger from a ghost? A spirit?"

Would she be able to see the danger at all? If a ghost had to want her to see them, wouldn't this assailant be invisible to her? Could Jennifer see ghosts, too?

The look he gave her at that moment wasn't encouraging. His lips parted, he gritted his teeth, and he gazed away. It caused the hairs on the back of her neck to stand up.

He held the pen to his card and paused for what seemed like forever. She slowed the car, and he wrote steadily and held it out to her.

Worse.

"Well, that makes me feel better."

She sighed. Why was she rushing headlong into this and not stopping? Her mind was reeling from everything churning through it. She needed to clear her head and focus on getting Jennifer and getting out of the sticks. She would take her back toward Huntington and into Ohio, Chesapeake maybe, or go up the road and cross into Ashland,

Kentucky. She looked down at the clock and noted that it was 8:55. There was no night sky; the clouds from the storm earlier had decided to stick around. It made the dark even more imposing.

She hadn't noticed, but he had written something else and held it to her. She could barely make it out and had to reach up and activate the dome light. He had pressed hard, considering the hue of the ink, and had gone over the letters several times. It was one word, and if being around the dead wasn't enough to chill her to the bone, this froze her down to the soul.

CURSE.

5

Jennifer wasn't prepared for him to answer the door. She'd been under the impression that the house was empty since Dylan's mother died. As Jennifer approached the two-story, blue house from the long gravel driveway, she noticed the light in the front window. She panicked and thought about turning around. The curtains were drawn, and she couldn't see inside when she came up the stairs to the wooden door. She moved quickly so her nerves wouldn't get the better of her, and as she raised her hand to knock, it swung open. A middle-aged man was standing in front of her. He was wearing black shorts and a white T-shirt stained with God knew what, with his belly barely protruding out from the bottom of it. The left side of his jaw was swollen with chewing tobacco. If that didn't give it away, the plastic see-through spitter in his left hand did. His salt and pepper hair was thinning across the top. He wasn't bald yet, but it wouldn't be long.

He hadn't shaved in a few days, a thick stubble crossed his face and neck. He had the faint whiff of hops, a smell she knew well, and she realized she'd interrupted an evening of beer and television. The scowl across his face showed he was already annoyed with her. She had to tread carefully here.

"Can I help you?" he asked, studying her.

"Hi, I hate to bother you. I know it's such a late hour. My name is Jennifer Simmons."

She smiled at him as she fumbled in her purse for her card. She finally found it and thrust it out in front of her. He took it slowly in his right hand and looked at it before their eyes met.

"Late hour? Lady, it's nighttime."

"I know, and believe me, I wouldn't be here unless it was imperative. I don't know if you know about the incident here a few months ago."

"The murder, I am *aware.*"

"Oh, okay, I'm sorry. I am Dylan's doctor." She smiled, trying to sound as professional as possible.

"That so?" He sat the spit cup down, along with her card, out of her sight on the other side of the door and folded his arms.

I'm losing him. She felt fear growing inside her. She needed to keep talking and get through this.

"We had a breakthrough tonight. A fairly substantial one, and I was wondering if it would be possible to see Dylan's room." She kept her tone firm and hoped she didn't sound as crazy out loud as she did in her head.

He unfolded his arms, and his face couldn't hide how stunned he was by the request. "You a shrink?" His eyebrow rose.

She hated that word, but nodded and said, "I am a child psychologist."

"Dylan killed my sister. He doesn't need a doctor. You ask me, that boy needs put down." He leaned over and reproduced his cup before spitting in it. "He stabbed her with a kitchen knife; even after she was gone, he kept going. Piece of shit."

"I know I'm bothering you, and I apologize for your loss. I honestly didn't expect anyone to be here. I only get to come down from Baltimore occasionally, and Dylan isn't very high on our priorities. My boss forced me to come down here through the storm," she lied, changing tactics

He leaned against the door frame, listening to her. "You out of Maryland?"

She nodded. "So, here I am. I was supposed to do a whole workup on Dylan, but I haven't finished any of it. I hadn't even spoken to the boy before today. I haven't been to the crime scene; there are a million things I should have done before now, and you know how it is—I'm so behind, and the boss is a hard ass. I just need a few minutes in his room, and I'll be on my way back to Baltimore."

He smiled slightly then, showing his discolored teeth. Clearly he sympathized with the asshole boss narrative.

"What's so important about his room?"

She leaned forward a little, drawing him with the promise of a secret. "I mean, does any of this make any sense to you? He didn't have a history of anything remotely concerning, yet this crime was so violent. I couldn't get a bearing on any of it. And Dylan hasn't said a word about any of it." She lowered her voice conspiratorially and added, "Until today."

"He spoke about it?" The man jerked upright.

"To me, yes."

He shook his head. "I knew he hadn't talked about Beth. Probably out of shame. What kind of animal does that to his mom?"

Jennifer started to feel antsy. She needed in the room, and this asshole was standing in her way.

"I just want to ensure we have all the facts and that he gets the treatment he deserves, if you catch my drift. I'll be quick. I just have to take a few photos with my phone and make some voice recordings. It'll be ten minutes, probably less."

He glared at her, then spit the whole wad of tobacco into the plastic cup. She never broke away from his stare. She didn't want him to perceive her as weak, but kept her smile so she seemed non-threatening.

"You're one of those, huh? Always trying to figure out *why*. Well, I'll tell you why: some people just aren't good. They were just born bad. His dad was a scumbag, and the little shit is a scumbag too."

He spit again, getting the last bits of the tobacco out of his mouth, and shook his head as he sat the cup out of sight again. Jennifer decided to go for it; she was running out of options with this man, and she could tell his patience was thin. If she needed to play the role, she would.

"I want to make sure there's no chance of this happening again. If there is something deep inside that boy, and I can prove that, then he isn't released back into the wild the day he turns eighteen. What if there is more to all of this like I suspect? What if I can get him to talk about the *why*? And maybe those words will prove to everyone that he was born bad, like you said. It could save someone down the road from ending up like your poor sister."

The man looked away for a second before looking back into her eyes. He sighed, took another step back, and put his arm out.

"Thank you," she said, stepping in, and he closed the door behind her.

"If you think it'll help. I loved my sister. She had her demons..." He looked at the ground. "This place belonged to our parents. She lived here with Dylan and his sister. I live a little up the holler. I come down here sometimes after work and stay, just to keep her memory going. I was going to sell it, but..." He pointed to the stairs to her right. "The room is up there, on the right. I don't go up there. I... Well, I can't. I don't want to. His sister came by and got her stuff a few months back. I haven't seen her since."

"Isn't she a teenager?" Jennifer asked him as a sickening feeling crept up her back.

"Yeah. She ran off with some forty-one-year-old." His face looked as if he might be sick. "I know—It's this family, Doc. Something's wrong with all of us."

"Oh yeah, so what's wrong with you?" she asked him in jest in a horrible attempt to lighten the mood.

"I keep trying to hold us all together," he whispered, sadness clear in his tone.

"I'm sorry," Jennifer finally came to a realization. "I didn't catch your name. It wasn't in my notes at all."

"Quentin."

"Forgive me, Quentin. You've been through a lot, and you have my condolences."

She was being sincere and she felt pity for this family. Quentin didn't seem like an evil man. When he spoke of his sister, she could see how his shoulders dropped, and the lines around his mouth sagged; he hurt. He cared deeply for her, and he hadn't remotely come to terms with any of this.

He gave her a quick nod. "Like I said, no one has touched anything. The last people inside were the police. I couldn't bring myself to go up there and clean... I don't go in till ten tomorrow, so I wasn't going to bed till after my movie. Take your time, Doc."

"I won't be long." She could barely contain her relief.

He waved at her and walked back through an open area, past a rather old grandfather clock, and through an archway, leaving her alone. She took note of the pine smell and the wooden floors. The area she could see was immaculately clean and, from the look of the white on the walls, freshly painted. He was honest with her and was taking care of this old home. He wasn't letting it fall into disarray, and he probably spent several nights torturing himself over his loss.

She'd seen many of these cases when she was studying. Sometimes, it was best to rip off the band-aid and move on. Easier said than done, of course, but when you hang on to something, you aren't holding onto a memory; you're holding onto pain. You don't want to let the person go. Even though you think you're keeping their memory alive, all you seem to do is drive yourself further down a spiral of depression.

Jennifer tried for years to convince herself that was what she was doing, that holding onto her father this way was the same. Yet as time passed, it wasn't the things she kept that fed that pain. It was sorrow. She questioned every day why she wasn't closer to her father, why she took their moments for granted, and how she blamed herself for his death. She knew that was bad; she'd learned as much in her chosen profession. She'd spent countless hours telling people to move on and deal with their trauma head-on.

It was one thing for you to lose a loved one to another person, but a malevolent being had killed her father and placed the blame on her young mind. Yes, she should have paid for hurting Neil, but for it to brutalize her dad that way? There was no rational reason for it. Nothing was evil; she would try to find and stop this monster tonight. What it had done to Dylan was just as vile as what it had done to her. Two people were left broken by the destruction it left in its wake. No one else was going to hurt like this. No one else would bear this scar.

She would scour Dylan's room; she hoped to find a clue, something to prove its existence. It couldn't be completely invisible, as she thought. It had to leave something behind, maybe under the bed or in the closet. She would go to priests, mediums, anything, but she would find a way to end its reign of terror. She'd wondered if Beth fought the way her father did. Maybe she hurt it? A blood stain, a fingernail, or something out of the ordinary. She had a gut feeling there would be something, and she would find it. After she finished, she would make the trek home to see who lived in her old house and look there. Maybe she'd forgotten something, and being there would bring those memories flooding back.

She hated lying to Quentin. She knew what she was doing was wrong. She had broken so many laws, and once Tina found out what she'd done, she'd be throwing away a friendship that started more than a decade ago. Maybe she could tell her about all of this one day; maybe she'd understand. She doubted it.

She put her hand on the banister and stood on the first step. She gazed up into the dark at the top of the stairs, and her heart fluttered. *Don't you do this. Don't you quit now. It was here,* she told herself, and went up one step. Quentin thought Dylan was a monster. The entire state thought he stabbed his mother repeatedly. Everyone who could remember her story thought a rabid animal tore her father to pieces. She pushed the fear away and took another step.

She reminded herself how her mother drank herself to death. Nothing took so much from her; she would be damned if she didn't get something back. She went up one more. She thought of Neil and how he went over the hillside. How long was he conscious? Did he know he was going to die? Was he afraid? She hated herself for allowing that to happen to him. It was tragic and terrible. She had come to terms with the fact that she meant to hurt him. She was so pleased to see the rock strike his forehead when she threw it. She never hid the fact that she disliked the boy, but she didn't want him dead. It was an accident, and her heart ached at the knowledge that she had left him to perish. It was wrong, but Nothing had no right to kill her father in retaliation. She fought back the tears and climbed another step.

Dylan told her of his crime a little over an hour ago. He had killed Miss Addis, and just like her situation, it wasn't something he'd meant to do. He'd told her how awful this woman had been toward him. Miss Addis didn't just have antipathy for the young boy. She outright hated him. When he told her what the woman had said to him, it stung her as much as it did him. She was atrocious, from scoring him low on papers to belittling him in class in front of the other students and his friends. Why did no one step in? How could this have possibly gone on in a public school?

Why Dylan's mother never went to that elementary school and got Miss Addis away from that child is a mystery. Why didn't Beth confront that woman? Why didn't a student speak up in defense of Dylan or tell their parents so someone could bring it to the authority's attention? This couldn't have been over Dylan's father, could it? Jennifer would never have an answer since Miss Addis was gone.

Dylan had explained that Miss Addis had gotten sick. One day, he'd gone to school, and his principal greeted their class in the morning to tell them she wouldn't be back for a while and introduced their substitute, Mr. Floyd. Dylan voiced his fondness for Mr. Floyd, and his eyes would light up when he mentioned him.

While Dylan spoke, Jennifer glanced through Dylan's file to where his grade cards resided, and sure enough, they had improved dramatically. The notes on the next page from the interview with the principal also claimed that Dylan's behavior was a complete one-eighty. He'd gone from always being in some sort of trouble to practically a model student. It's why none of the staff at the school could believe he'd snapped and committed the crime.

Miss Addis was gone for months; Dylan had mentioned that several students claimed she had developed cancer, which made sense for her to be away for so long. If she had to have surgery from it, the timeline fit. She was speculating, of course, that maybe the woman just needed time away, but the cancer theory was more than plausible. She made a mental note to look more into that later.

Dylan told Jennifer he enjoyed attending school after Miss Addis was gone and that it all came crashing down when he saw her the morning she returned. There had been no announcement that she was returning, so Jennifer could only imagine his surprise. He recalled how she spoke to the class about how much she missed them and thought about them daily. Dylan was hopeful that things would be different, that what happened between them would stay in the past.

"She jumped on me right after lunch. I'd gotten some words wrong on the spelling test, and she told me I was the one thing that made her think about staying away." This was the one that burned into Jennifer's memory the most. What kind of person would say that to a small child, especially one involved in teaching?

Jennifer took another step.

She became unbearable over the next few days, and Dylan wanted her gone. Miss Addis was making up for the lost time by humiliating the boy. From the memories Dylan recanted, it sounded as if Miss Addis wasn't hiding her disdain for him. All the child wanted was for her to leave so he could move on to the next grade and be done with her forever. He prayed every night that Miss Addis would get sick again so she couldn't come to school.

Jennifer paused halfway up the stairs, her emotions over Dylan overcoming her. She felt such sympathy for him.. But, what happened next no one deserved, and it was Dylan's youth and lack of awareness that caused the death of Miss Addis.

Every morning, Miss Addis would make a shake of some kind and drink it while she taught. She told the class that her stomach always hurt, and the mixture made her feel better. She claimed it kept her from throwing up and confessed to them that she couldn't stand it.

She told them she'd spent the last few months nauseous daily, and the thought of vomiting was terrifying. Dylan realized that she would leave on the days she got sick,so he formulated a plan to rid himself of her for a while.

Dylan's mother was a drug addict. It was in his file. She was on the verge of losing her kids right before she died. She was to have a hearing the next week, but as far as Jennifer could tell, Dylan had no idea. All he knew was that she kept a sandwich bag under her bed, and inside were little white pills shaped like skulls. He'd almost taken one once, but thought it was a bad idea since his mother would crush them at the kitchen table and snort them up her nose. She would dance, laugh, and sometimes even wrestle with him after taking them. But within a few hours, she was extremely sick. He told Jennifer about all the times he would get up at night and have to pee but couldn't because she was asleep in front of the toilet, with vomit all around her.

When those pills were crushed, they looked almost identical to the powder Miss Addis used in her drink. So, Dylan thought that if he took some of his mother's "medicine" and put it in with Miss Addis' powder, she would drink it and go home daily. It sounded ludicrous coming from his lips as he explained it. Dylan was a child, and in her profession, children, especially when emotionally broken, rationalized almost anything. To Dylan, this made sense, and he knew it would be easy to accomplish. So, he wasted no time.

He snuck into his mother's room and took a handful of the pills, then headed to the kitchen to get another sandwich bag, placed the pills inside, and crushed them at the table with a salt shaker. He told Jennifer it was harder than it looked but spent hours getting them into a fine powder resembling Miss Addis's medicine.

He was supposed to be in class early the following day for morning detention that Miss Addis had leveled on him for supposedly talking back to her. He was to place papers in folders and wipe down desks. Miss Addis left the room briefly, and Dylan hurried and opened her bottom desk drawer. He couldn't believe his luck that it wasn't locked. He pulled out the container that housed the powder and remembered it was almost empty. He poured the contents of his sandwich bag inside, shook it once, and left. Jennifer had scoured Dylan's file as he spoke, but nothing was there about the teacher. How could something so vital be missing? Why did no one mention that his teacher died the same as his mother?

Miss Addis mixed her shake as the day began, and Dylan couldn't wait for her to leave. She had already started in on him and mentioned that he had scored an F on his math test the day before. She told him that if he didn't straighten up, he'd be the only kid in America who would be able to drive to elementary school.

She made a face of disgust as she took her first drink. Dylan thought he would get caught, or she might throw it out. But he said she shook her head and kept drinking as she started talking about the capital cities of each state.

"It wasn't long before she started laughing," Dylan told Jennifer. "She was laughing so much it made us laugh. She came around her desk, and her face wasn't happy even though she was laughing. She was scared." Dylan explained while rubbing his hands on his legs. "I knew something was wrong—really wrong."

She suddenly stopped laughing, and spit flew everywhere from her mouth, her hands twisted into a weird shape. Dylan tried his hardest to mimic it. He held his hands up and stiffened them into a claw pattern.

Neurological damage, Jennifer thought to herself. She recognized it instantly. *She was having a seizure.*

Jennifer's mind raced to things that could cause that kind of damage in such a high dosage, and she settled on ecstasy. It probably wasn't just a high dosage either; this was an insane amount. The face she made was likely because of the bitter taste. If Miss Addis had stopped after that one drink, that was probably enough to get her extremely high, but for her to drink the entire mixture? Even if a medical team was on site, Miss Addis had zero chance of survival.

Her whole body went stiff, and she fell straight back. Her head made a nasty thud on the floor and split open.

"Who went and got help?" Jennifer asked.

"I did," Dylan confessed.

Dylan had retrieved the principal, and when they returned, he sent their entire class to the gym. They stayed there all day playing basketball and jumping rope. Dylan hoped Miss Addis wasn't hurt too badly and she'd be alright. He just hoped that his plan had succeeded and she would be out for a few days but that her head was fine.

It was when he got to the bus he found out the truth. Dylan liked to sit in the front of the bus; he didn't have any friends that rode home with him, and it was primarily kids from Hurricane Middle School. They were loud, nasty, and made him nervous.

"They picked on me because my momma worked at the club," he told Jennifer, wiping tears from his cheeks.

So he sat close to the bus driver, a man whose name he couldn't recall. Jennifer hoped the bus driver was at least decent to him because it seemed like every person who came into contact with Dylan was just an awful person. He had no hope of being a success in that environment. He was destined to fail. She wanted to hold him but couldn't. Corey would have gotten suspicious; but if anyone needed love, it was this boy.

Another teacher boarded the bus before they departed, and Dylan recalled the driver asking her quietly if Barbara was okay. She tried to keep her voice down so no one would hear as she told him Miss Addis had died on the way to the hospital. Dylan had killed her; he started crying, and the teacher realized he'd heard, and she sat beside him. She put her arm around him and told him it would be okay and that she was sorry.

Jennifer stood at the top of the stairs, a few feet away from a door with a poster of a pro wrestler on it. It was fading and crooked from the tape falling from the left corner. Beyond was where Nothing had claimed another victim, and she would come face to face with the emotions and feelings that defined her teen and adult life. She had to steel herself. She'd come this far. What was she looking for, and what if this was a dead end?

"I'll cross that bridge when I get there," she said out loud.

She thought of her father and how everything changed the day she lost him, the day he was taken from her. Everything in her life was ruined in a flash. Her sadness and despair turned to anger. Would Dylan's life become a replica of hers?

She turned the handle, slowly opened the door, and entered Dylan's room.

6

eronica was on the gravel driveway and almost to the blue house at the end of the drive when the ghost began pointing frantically at the car parked in front of them.

"Is that her car?" She leaned forward to get a look at the Maryland plates.

He nodded quickly.

"Alright." Veronica put the car in park and turned to face him. "I'm going to go in there and get her out. You stay behind me, and if this curse or whatever is waiting for us pops up, you get my attention, okay?"

He stared blankly at her momentarily, his tongue protruded as he licked his lips.

"What? What's the matter?"

He shook his head no.

"What the hell do you mean no? I came all this way just to save your 'baby girl,' I could use your eyes and ears for the shit around the corner I can't see."

He shook his head slowly again.

"Are you kidding me?" she scoffed. "That is some ungrateful shit you got going on here. I ought to turn around and say to hell with you both." She'd have punched him in the face if she could.

He took up his pen and began scribbling again.

"Oh, this better be good."

He held it up, his eyes softening, growing wet.

I made a deal.

"What are you talking about?" She was confused, and the mood in the car had changed entirely.

He already had the card prepared.

To save her, I made a deal.

"Like what kind of deal? You mean the devil? You better not mean the devil." She almost chuckled. Her sense of excitement was morphing into something else entirely.

He wrote slowly and turned it around.

Something like that.

Veronica felt her heart sink. She had a feeling when she came back to this car that the man wouldn't be here. It didn't take much deduction to figure out that he'd leveraged a lot to guide her here, and she could see a hint of fear in his eyes. He was doing a fantastic job of keeping his face still, but his brow was raised, and in her line of work, she could read a person's features. This man had a lot of trouble heading his way.

"So, what's the plan?"

He pointed his finger toward the house's second story and shook it.

Veronica let out a sigh. "Right, I got this. You stay here. I'll be right back." She opened the door and stood beside the vehicle. She paused for a moment and leaned back in. "I got her, don't worry." She tapped the roof of the car, and he smiled at her.

He held out a card. *You are a nice person. Thank you.*

"Well, make sure you tell that to whoever you're going to see. I could use a good word."

She shut the car door and started toward the house, not wanting to look back at him. Veronica knew his time was up—she could *feel* it. She checked her Glock 19, then placed it back in its holster and shook her head. She didn't know why she decided to take her gun. The thing would be useless if this were a ghost, but it added a sliver of courage to her resolve.

Veronica stepped in front of her white Sentra and looked back toward the windshield. She gave in to the urge and looked for him, even though every fiber told her not to. She placed her hands over her eyes to cast a slight shadow where she'd left the engine running and the headlights on. If there was trouble and they needed to escape quickly, they could see coming out of the house. The man wasn't in her front seat anymore; there was no trace of him ever being there.

"Shit," she spat as she turned back toward the house and started inching in its direction.

Veronica took her badge out of her hip pocket. Jennifer may be more receptive to a police officer than some crazy woman ranting about seeing the dead and telling her she was in grave peril. She began rehearsing in her head how she was going to deal with Jennifer when she saw her. Would she be overly friendly, or would she be the hard ass? She was leaning toward the latter. It made more sense.

She could feel her hands starting to sweat and her pulse rising. A feeling of dread overcame her. Something was wrong with this entire situation. Not that receiving a warning from the woman's dead father was right to begin with.

Veronica had been in danger before. She stared down a man holding a knife to a young boy's throat; she'd crashed her car during a high-speed chase; she'd even had a drug dealer turn his pitbull loose on her. So, high-pressure situations were nothing new to her.

This was different; the specter had written that they were dealing with *a curse*. Veronica had no idea what that even meant. Did that still have something to do with the undead or something supernatural? Her eyes focused on the second floor; no lights were on upstairs, and no sounds came from the house. Veronica could only hear the fan from the home's air conditioning unit, and the silence was maddening. She'd never felt so alone in her entire life.

"Get it together," she said under her breath as she drew nearer to the house.

Her chest began to tighten. What if she couldn't save this woman?

What if whatever was in there killed them both? She gripped her badge tightly, and even though her mind kept screaming to stop, she kept moving forward. She had reached the bottom of the porch steps when an overwhelming feeling to flee overcame her. She'd even taken a step backward.

"What the hell is wrong with you?" she muttered to herself.

Veronica had always been level-headed, but something had set her almost into a full-on panic attack. She kept thinking of Jennifer's father pleading with her through index cards to help his child. Yet the fear that death awaited her in the house gnawed at her nerves. She started to tremble and found herself flabbergasted at how quickly this emotion had overtaken her.

Was the thought of the unknown to blame? This could be another one of her gifts. After all, she could see the dead, and this could be a perk of the set, a warning system telling her this was a terrible idea. This had never happened to her before, but her mind was buzzing. If she continued in this state, she would fail Jennifer and her father. She closed her eyes and tried to get her composure, but it was useless. The feeling grew in intensity.

She didn't want the woman to die here. Veronica wasn't known for compassion, but the dad had been adamant. Whatever was in here was horrific, and it was up to her to help. She couldn't move. Her body had betrayed her, and even though she didn't want to call upon her, only one person could save her and maybe save them both.

"Ethel," she called out into the air. She waited a few moments, but the feeling of her grandmother's spirit wasn't there, so she called out again. "Ethel, I need your help. Please."

Veronica had never felt so helpless, and for the life of her, she didn't understand why. She wanted the feeling to dissipate, and she wanted someone with her who could calm her nerves. Veronica had never felt like she needed someone so much in her life. She hoped that Ethel wouldn't be bitter and refuse to come to her. She found herself on the verge of prayer. She hoped Ethel would listen to reason.

Still, there was nothing.

A sob came unbidden to Veronica's throat and she let out a whimper. "Maw Maw?"

The chill came almost instantly; the wind hadn't picked up. Veronica's anxiety instantly waned at the sound of the familiar voice from behind her.

"I told you I was going to stay with the ghost. What do you want?"

Veronica wiped the tear away that was streaming down her cheek and turned around to face her. Ethel's scowl was instantly replaced by a look of concern. Ethel leaned in, and for a brief moment, it seemed as if she might reach for her.

"What's wrong?" Ethel asked forcefully.

Veronica cleared her throat and took a deep breath. "There is a woman in this house named Jennifer. She's in trouble, and I'm here to save her. I need your eyes."

Ethel gave a nervous laugh. "What do you mean?"

"Look, there's no time. Another spirit visited me; it's his daughter in there." Veronica pointed her thumb behind her at the house. "If we don't help her, she's as good as dead."

Ethel stepped forward, her eyes wide in shock. "You can see more than just me?"

"Yeah, and I have no time to get into it, but I don't want to walk in there blind. So I called for you."

Ethel looked over her shoulder and then back into Veronica's eyes. She nodded and strode past her with purpose. Veronica smiled. Her resolve grew stronger by the moment. Somehow, she'd convinced herself she would die, but having her grandmother with her filled her with hope. She had a fighting chance with Ethel by her side. Whatever was in that house didn't stand a chance against them both. Ethel glanced over her shoulder.

"What are we looking for?"

"Not a clue," Veronica admitted.

"Alright. I'll go through—" Ethel started.

The door opened, and a man was standing there. He wasn't

armed as far as she could tell, and was wearing shorts and a shirt that desperately needed to be cleaned.

"Christ, it's Grand Central Station here tonight," he said with a smirk.

Veronica studied his face briefly, and there wasn't an ounce of hostility. He grinned, and she could see by his slight sway that this gentleman had indulged in a few drinks before she arrived. He wasn't three sheets to the wind yet, but he'd probably be out if she returned in an hour. She forced a smile and tried to sound as professional as possible.

"I'm sorry to bother you, but I'm searching for someone."

"You a doc, too?" he asked, his eyebrow raised.

"No, I'm not a doctor," she held up her badge, "I'm Detective Carter."

She's a doctor. Veronica thought to herself. Ghost dad could have mentioned that before. A doctor of what? Medicine?

His face dropped. "This whole Dylan thing is pretty serious, huh?"

Lie, her brain screamed.

"Yes. This is a lot more complicated than we originally thought." She shook her head, wondering if that was a little too much.

Veronica glanced behind him and saw Ethel peering from his left side. They had devised a system when they first started doing cases together so as not to arouse suspicion. Veronica scratched her left arm, a sign to check the surrounding area. Ethel nodded and was gone.

The man sighed. "I should have been there for the boy. I just... I can't look at him. I... I'm sorry." His face turned a deep shade of red and he stepped back from the door. "Come in."

Veronica smiled and strode purposefully into his home, never breaking eye contact.

"Thank you so much." She decided to play it friendly and stall him so Ethel could complete her task. "Hell of a storm earlier. I'm glad it let up so I could find this place."

"I don't mind the rain, just hate it when there's a downpour like that."

"We didn't mean to come up here so late."

"It's alright. But I got a question." His eyes looked upstairs.

"That is?" Veronica felt her nerves jolt. If he asked too many questions, there was a chance she'd slip up. She was a good liar; her entire life recently had been one fib after another, almost to where it was second nature but this wasn't remotely in the same realm as those moments.

"Why now? Dylan killed Beth months ago; this wasn't so important after it happened. What changed?"

The names instantly clicked for Veronica. The case did make national news, after all. This was the boy who attacked his mother in his bedroom and stabbed her repeatedly. She was in that house. This is where the crime was committed. It was all anyone at the station talked about for weeks. There was no explanation for his actions, and through the grapevine and gossip, the wounds were way too deep for a young boy.

She remembered Bradley, another detective in her department, boldly claiming that the boy's sister did it and pinned it all on him. It was her testimony that sent the boy away. Bradley had claimed to have seen the photos of the scene, and the boy couldn't have damaged her in that manner. The media called it another random case of some kid snapping. As usual, the frenzy around the story went pretty quickly, and he was locked away in a state facility. He wouldn't speak to anyone, and even during trial, he was silent. Was Jennifer his doctor?

"Did Jennifer not explain anything to you, sir?"

"She said he spoke today." His voice cracked. The alcohol she could smell probably amplified his emotional responses, but this man was not doing well.

Oh my God. The boy didn't kill his mother. A ghost did, she deduced. *Well, maybe not a ghost, but a curse or whatever Jennifer's dad wrote. We need to get the hell out of here, and fast.*

Ethel appeared through the opening.

"There is nothing down here. He's drinking and watching a dirty movie. The kitchen is a pigsty. I'm so glad I can't smell—"

"He did speak yes, and he said a lot more that I need to relay to the doctor. Where did you say she was?" Veronica needed this over quickly. She didn't like where this was going.

"Upstairs, first door on the right."

Veronica pointed two fingers, her index and middle, in that direction upstairs, giving Ethel a sign.

"I know this is difficult, but do you mind if I ask you some questions?" Veronica asked as Ethel huffed and started for the stairs.

Ethel was already aggravated just being in Veronica's presence. She let her emotions get the best of her when she saw the worry on her granddaughter's face. Ethel still loved that little girl, but Veronica was rotten and nothing resembling the person Ethel envisioned her to grow up to be. Ethel had questioned several times over the past few months if she was angrier about Veronica being the way she was or that she failed as a parent. She had given everything to that girl, and while she felt sorry for the loss of both of Veronica's parents, that wasn't an excuse to be such a heinous human being. Veronica had been loved and never wanted for anything. To see her as she was felt like a slap in the face.

Ethel didn't want to be around her. She needed time away from her, but Veronica could call upon her and Ethel could only ignore it for so long. It was like being yanked through the world by a magnet. Sometimes, when Veronica beckoned, Ethel would stay invisible to her; even though Veronica could see Ethel when no one else could, Ethel still had to want to be seen. It's how she discovered the darkness at the core of the woman she'd raised.

Veronica had asked her for some privacy, which aroused Ethel's suspicion. Ethel had always been nosey. She'd watched several people unawares since her demise and was dismayed at how people acted when they thought they were alone.

The first time she'd been stunned by Veronica's behavior was when she'd appeared only to find Veronica in bed with another woman and cocaine on a mirror beside the bed. She'd watched enough Law and Order to know what it was. She couldn't believe she was involved in sins of the flesh and fornicating with a drug user. Ethel fled the scene and cried for days about it. She never brought it up to Veronica. She was so ashamed that she avoided her for several days until Veronica called her to help on a case.

The second thing she viewed was the tipping point; Ethel watched from the shadows as a man pleaded for his life to Veronica. He begged her to take him to jail. Veronica pulled the trigger, and the bullet went through the back of the man's head and out the front. Ethel had never seen someone murdered before. The violence shown on television and in film is nothing like seeing it happen in front of your eyes. She remembered watching as Veronica stood there emotionless, wiping the gun down and tossing it on the body.

Veronica walked past her, smiling, while Ethel rushed to check on the man. She could still see pieces of his teeth beside where his face used to be. She'd thought Veronica joined the police department to help people, but witnessing that had made Ethel realize that she was dirty. She was a monster in the truest sense of the word. Maybe if Ethel had appeared to her, she could have kept that man alive. It was something she regretted.

Ethel followed her for days after, witnessing her constantly drinking and having sex with multiple people. It was as if her granddaughter was living a double life. She'd be this cartoonish villain at night and this loving friend to other people during the day.

Ethel appeared to her on a Sunday morning and told her she had witnessed everything. Veronica never denied any of it. She only told Ethel that this was her life and she had no business spying on her. As their argument escalated, Veronica said the man she killed deserved to die, and she had no remorse over her actions. Ethel argued for the spiritual side and said that no one but God could take a life. They fought for days as Veronica went out of her way to do things that Ethel found mortifying, as if her granddaughter was taunting her. Her drinking alone was unbearable, as Veronica would get so intoxicated she'd spend the evening telling Ethel she was her own woman and not some miniature version of her, all prim and proper. Ethel had finally had enough and told her she was dead to her. She forbade her from calling her grandma; if she wanted help with anything, she would have to do it alone.

Ethel had wondered if God had left her here to fix Veronica, to save her from herself. She prayed daily for a sign, but nothing was given. The old woman was utterly alone. There were other spirits she could try to talk to, but all of them were too busy feeling sorry for themselves. They complained constantly that they were too young to die or never accomplished what they believed were realistic goals. Everyone was such a crybaby about everything

Ethel hated the whining; she was ready to leave when she passed on. She wanted to see her husband, Martin, her mother and sisters, and to be embraced in the glory she strived to obtain. Yet, here she was, stuck in a world she increasingly felt was lost and wondering if anything she believed was real in the first place.

Ethel walked up the stairs. She had to remind herself to speed up; the pain she felt in life was no longer there and she didn't have to be careful. She peeked back over her shoulder at Veronica; she wanted her little girl back. She wanted the child that called her Maw Maw. They listened to music together and ate sandwiches with the crust removed. There was so much joy between them; now, there was a chasm that neither would cross. There was no way in hell Ethel would reach out to her, and she was sure Veronica's soul was lost. *Thou shalt not kill*, but Veronica had done so brutally.

She reached the top of the stairs, turned, and went through the door. It took time for Ethel to feel comfortable walking through things, especially people. She could see what she was going through, so seeing the inside of an individual was utterly disgusting. She usually closed her eyes but soon developed a habit of avoidance. She would see someone coming and get out of their path to avoid contact.

The room was dark, but some light came in through a window on the far side of the room. It wasn't from the moon; Ethel could tell it was artificial, but it was enough to illuminate the entire bedroom. There was a lot of dust in here; she could see it in the rays of light, covering most of the items on the cheap dresser and nightstand. The walls were adorned with posters of gigantic men in what Ethel thought was their underwear, except for one guy wearing long jean shorts.

Wrestling, she thought and sighed in displeasure. Her son had been into that stuff many years ago, and she couldn't stand watching it on television with him. It was vulgar and violent, and she always thought it negatively influenced him. She hated it with a passion. She fought the urge to walk out of the room.

A woman sat on the bed with her back turned to Ethel. Her hair was a deep shade of red. She couldn't tell if it was natural, but it was pretty, and well past the woman's shoulders and to the middle of her back. Ethel went slowly around the bed, still made.

She circled until she could see the young woman's face. Her face was flushed, and her cheeks were wet. She sniffled every so often and wrung her hands. Ethel scanned the rest of the room and settled her gaze back on the woman on the bed. There was no imminent danger in this room. There was no one in here except the two of them. Ethel felt a hint of anger at the thought that Veronica had brought her here just to toy with her.

That thought went away as quickly as it arose. Veronica's face had been flooded with fear. She couldn't fake that, and with the state of their relationship, she doubted Veronica would call her here for no reason.

"Okay, Jennifer, what's the problem?" Ethel asked as she walked toward the window.

"There's nothing here," Jennifer whispered coldly. "I thought there would be something. Anything."

Ethel stopped in midstride. Could Jennifer hear her?

"Are you talking to me?" Ethel spun around to face Jennifer. She could feel the excitement welling up inside her. She approached her and bent toward Jennifer's face.

"You're going to keep getting away with it," Jennifer continued.

Ethel stood upright. "You aren't talking to me." She was disappointed, but she knew better. The only living person who could see her was Veronica, and Ethel had tried on more than one occasion to make contact with someone else.

"Why did I even come here?" Jennifer wiped her cheeks. "What the hell was I trying to prove?" She hit the bed with her left hand, and a puff of dust rose.

Ethel was at a loss; this house had no spirits. Call it a sixth sense or whatever, but Ethel knew when those of her kind were anywhere in the vicinity. She would have been able to see or at least sense them instantly. There was nothing here.

"I just want to stop you. You've killed so many people."

Ethel studied her face. Her eyes were wide open, and she was sucking in the air as if hyperventilating. Ethel could see the sweat forming on Jennifer's forehead, and when she looked down at her hands, she was clutching them together so hard the knuckles were white.

"Oh, honey." Ethel held her hand out, letting it pass through the girl's cheek. "You're nuts."

Ethel felt bad for this girl. She was pretty confident she was insane. Maybe Veronica thought the girl would harm herself. Ethel figured she'd better wrap this up and fetch Veronica before whatever this poor lady would do transpired. It was apparent to Ethel that she wasn't all there. Jennifer was talking to an empty room. This girl needed professional help in Ethel's eyes, like most of society today.

"I hate this place," Jennifer said. "I'm never coming back. What was I trying to prove?"

"I'm trying to figure that out myself," Ethel responded, knowing she couldn't hear her.

Ethel heard a click from behind her and turned her head. The closet door was ajar, and Ethel was positive when she entered the room that it was closed. She had made a mental note of almost everything in here. Veronica had Ethel convinced they were walking into a bloodbath, so she was meticulous.

The closet door continued to open slowly, and Ethel felt the air around her change. There was a chill, which she found odd because she hadn't felt temperature since her death. A cold was hanging all around her, and the light from the window seemed to dim. Something was happening. Something was coming. Ethel moved back toward Jennifer, whose eyes were now fixed on the closet.

"Maybe you should shut up," Ethel warned, knowing it would fall on deaf ears.

"Come to gloat?" Jennifer turned on the bed to face the closet.

"Don't you be calling no devil. I ain't prepared for—" Ethel began.

It emerged from the closet. Its head was perfectly round, with no eyes. There weren't even sockets for them. Its mouth showed sharp, pointed teeth that seemed to go down to its chin in an overbite. It wasn't overly large, which could have been deceiving considering it was hunched over, but the part that made Ethel gasp was that it lacked skin. It was a bloody mess of muscle and tendon. It seemed like a man, outside of the ghastly face, or what someone would consider one. It had two arms and legs, its fingernails elongated and to a point.

In Ethel's wildest imagination, when she thought of the demons from the Bible, they weren't this disturbing. If she could have fainted, she would have. She reached over and tried to take Jennifer's arm.

"No, no, no," Ethel gasped as her hand passed through Jennifer.

"Haven't you done enough?" Jennifer asked.

Ethel turned and tried again to shush her, forgetting it was for naught. Ethel couldn't believe this woman wasn't in pure panic. She was reasonably sure she couldn't be killed twice, and even armed with that knowledge, Ethel was terrified. Jennifer sat motionless and with a half-smirk on her face.

"You stay away from her," Ethel commanded, swiping her arm toward it, but it paid her no attention. "You hear me!" She stepped forward almost in its path and held her finger out. It never once acknowledged her existence nor paid her any mind.

It can't see or hear me, she concluded, watching as it moved to the corner and sat. Jennifer's eyes didn't follow it. *She can't see it. Oh God, she doesn't see it. She has no idea what she's dealing with.*

Well, look at you, all grown up, it said.

Ethel felt that its voice was almost as unnerving as its appearance. It reminded her of one of the voice boxes people with throat injuries received. It had more inflection, but it still had the disconnect she felt when she'd heard one for the first time. It was deep and artificial. It spoke as if its throat was lined with gravel, and as the words passed through the exposed teeth, there was a quick whistle with certain syllables. Ethel grew more afraid that this thing could talk. Was Hell indeed this ghastly?

"And you still ruin children's lives," Jennifer quipped, finally looking in the direction of the monster.

I thought you'd killed yourself. I lost your feeling long ago.

"You had no right to kill—" Jennifer's lips curled back in a snarl.

I have every right. An eye for an eye, remember? It said.

"That's not your call to make." Jennifer began to cry again. "It was an—"

An accident, you keep telling yourself that. Let me ask you something. Until tonight, had you told anyone you killed Neil?

Even though it had no eyes to read her reactions, Ethel could feel it was taking delight in mocking the young woman.

Jennifer wiped at her tears. "This is about my dad, you bastard."

No, it isn't. Since I collected your debt, have you ever told anyone or confessed your sin?

Jennifer didn't respond. Her lips quivered.

No, you only feel sorry for yourself. Did you ever think of the life you took? What about his mother, his aunt? What if his life had been turned around, and he made something of himself? What of the children he would never have? The wife he could have made happy? Have you ever thought of that instead of your selfishness? It pointed with its clawed left hand, and Ethel could swear the nails were extending.

Jennifer's face lost all color. Her hand came up to her mouth.

Ethel looked over to the thing still crouched in the corner, and even though it had no lips, she could still tell it was smiling. It was in no way sincere.

"It's lying." She put her hands to her forehead because no one could hear her.

Poor pitiful you, right? That boy died alone, in immense pain, and you left him there.

The creature arched its back. It looked like it might pounce at any second; Ethel had seen enough. She rushed for the door and went through it. She stood at the top of the stairs and looked down at Veronica, still conversing with the man. Ethel began touching her arms frantically, trying to remember the code for an emergency, and when she couldn't recall, she called out.

"Get up here before this thing eats her!"

Veronica looked up toward Ethel, her eyes wide open in shock; Quentin, in mid-sentence, paused and followed her gaze. Ethel waved her arms frantically and tried to imitate the monstrosity in the room as best as she could. She held her hands up, swiping at the air and showing her teeth. She knew she looked foolish, but that wasn't the point. If Veronica didn't move, there wouldn't be a Jennifer.

Veronica turned to the man. "Did you hear something?"

"No?" He leaned as if listening.

"I better check on Jennifer. She's been up there a while, and I thought I might have heard her."

"Sure. Sure," he said, backing away. "Just let me know before you all leave."

"Will do." She nodded as she started up the stairs at a brisk pace.

"It's a devil or a demon, or a... I don't know. But it's in there with her, hiding in the corner, and she can't see it!" Ethel cried out as Veronica reached the second floor.

Ethel was sure this thing was dangerous and had come from the darkest pit of Hell. She had spent forever questioning if her faith was genuine. She didn't feel that way anymore. If that thing existed, then the lake of fire and all of it must be real. That meant God was real, and she hoped he'd come and protect them right now. She could accept ghosts, but this was something out of the darkest horror movie. Veronica stared into Ethel's eyes and then turned to open the door.

"Wait!" Ethel cried out. "Maybe you should stay out here. You know what? Don't go in there. Let's just leave. Listen," Ethel pleaded, "we can forget all the bad stuff and start over. Let's just go. You have no idea what's on the other side!"

Veronica froze with her hand on the doorknob, and Ethel was hoping she had reached her. She didn't want to leave Jennifer but also didn't want to see Veronica confront this thing. She still cared for Veronica, and she realized that now. She could get her help, convince her to go to church, listen to her problems, anything but face down the claws of that thing.

To her dismay, Veronica opened the door.

"You're right. I should have told someone," Jennifer admitted.

She had thought about telling someone before. She'd even considered admitting it to the police, but what would be the point now? There would be no punishment, and she doubted that his mother or aunt were still alive. The police would look at it as an accident. Was the Nothing an avenging angel? Was she wrong all this time? Did she deserve what happened? She felt an overwhelming pain and despair and wanted it to disappear.

I can make it go away.

She heard the voice speaking from the corner of the room. Turning toward it, she asked, "What?"

All you have to do is ask. I can feel your torment. You've carried this burden around for so long. Let me end your suffering.

She'd contemplated suicide before. Here, though, was what threw her entire life into disarray, offering her a chance to end it all. The thing she'd searched for most of her adult life was in this room with her, and this wasn't going according to plan in the slightest. Not that she had a plan.

"You want to kill me?" she asked Nothing. Her heart sank further in her chest.

I want to help you, it answered.

Jennifer sat in silence, her body beginning to shake. She couldn't believe the words that came from her mouth, but she recognized her own voice asking, "Will it hurt?"

Before Nothing could answer, the door flew open and Jennifer's gaze jerked in that direction. Standing in the doorway was a woman with a white button-up short-sleeve dress shirt, blue jeans, and sneakers. She was tall and curvy with shoulder-length jet-black hair.

The woman quickly scanned the room before she stopped moving, her eyes landing on Jennifer. In a quiet, steady voice, she said, "Doctor Simmons, I'm Detective Veronica Carter, and I need you to get your belongings,and come with me outside."

"What is this?" Jennifer felt numb. Did someone figure out she had been to the facility already?

"Do not make me come over there and get you, Doctor Simmons. I want to keep this civil," Veronica warned.

"There is no need for hostilities. I have the homeowner's permission to be here, and I have—"

"I could give a shit less whose permission you have. You are coming with me now, or I'm dragging you down these stairs," Veronica said, her voice taking on a sharp edge. Panic flared through Jennifer as she grabbed her purse and stood.

"How dare you? I'll have your badge," she said in an attempt to cover up the way her voice shook.

"Oh no, please don't take my badge," Veronica said as she rolled her eyes. "Hurry up, you've wasted enough time here."

Veronica's eyes darted around the room, never really focusing on her. The detective waved her hand at her to hurry up.

"You better have a damn—"

"Cut the bullshit; I'm not in the mood," Veronica interrupted. "One more word, and this gets violent."

Veronica stepped out of the way, and Jennifer brushed past her.

"Thank you, Doctor," Veronica said as she shut the bedroom door.

They stood at the top of the stairs together, and Jennifer felt her ears ringing as blood rushed through them. She thought it would take days for them to find out, not hours.

"Did it move?" Veronica whispered as she looked off to the side.

"Did what—" Jennifer started.

"Shh. You're going to get the three of us killed. We need to get out of here. Now," Veronica whispered. Jennifer's nerves dissipated immediately. This woman was here over Nothing? How in the world did she know about it?

Veronica tilted her head toward the stairs and mouthed the word *move.*

Jennifer started down the stairs while looking at Quentin, who was waiting patiently at the bottom.

"You ladies finish up?" he asked, still swaying.

"Got everything taken care of. I can't thank you enough." Jennifer smiled. "We'll be on our way."

"You heading back to Baltimore?" He leaned against the railing, probably using it to keep himself from falling over.

"No, this officer," she pointed her thumb behind her, "needs another report written out."

"You all love your paperwork," he snickered.

"You have no idea," Veronica said from behind her.

Jennifer reached the bottom of the stairs and extended her hand to him. His sweaty fingers grasped hers.

"Quentin, if there are any breakthroughs and you want me to keep you up to date on everything, I can do that."

He shook his head. "I just want all of this behind us. But if you hear anything about Dylan's sister, please let me know. I'm worried sick."

"I'm sure Detective Carter can look into it," Jennifer said, looking at her.

"Hmm, oh yeah, sure, Quentin, I will get on that bright and early in the morning," Veronica agreed. She opened the front door and held it for Jennifer. "Doctor, we really need to get back. It's late, and I know you don't want to be stuck with me all night."

A creaking sound made Veronica's eyes widen ever so slightly. Jennifer heard it, too, as everyone paused. There was no mistaking it; at the top of the stairs, the bedroom door opened.

"What the hell?" Quentin spoke up first.

"Let's go," Veronica said while nudging Jennifer. The two of them exited the house together and stood on the porch. Quentin stood in the doorway with his back turned to them, looking upward. He had been distracted by the noise from the above.

"What do you want me to do now?" Jennifer asked Veronica as she noticed the running Nissan parked near her car.

"It's at the top of the stairs. Just get to your car, and you can follow me. We need to get out of here," Veronica whispered.

Jennifer bounded down the porch steps and started toward her car. She reached into her purse and produced her keys. Her mind had not fully grasped everything that had happened. Just moments ago, she was in the worst mental agony she'd ever experienced, and now, she had no idea what this emotion was. She felt numb, as if she'd been shut off from her feelings.

She was glad to be away from Nothing; something happened to her around it. It had a way of reaching into the corners of her mind. It knew what she was thinking and how to exploit that tenfold. It was trying to convince her that she wanted to die. She wanted revenge tonight, not to end herself. To go that far only to take her own life in that room? She was thankful for this woman's interference even though she initially hadn't understood the hostility.

Veronica stayed close to her as they made their way to the vehicles. Veronica kept mumbling to herself, but Jennifer couldn't quite make it out. Was she talking to her or just speaking out loud? Had she had an experience with Nothing before?

"You ladies have a safe trip," Quentin called from the porch.

They both turned, and Jennifer raised her hand to wave back to Quentin. He had been kind to her, and she didn't want to seem rude. She was leaving rather abruptly, despite having every intention of talking to him before she'd left. She was going to try and plant the seeds of reconciliation with Dylan. They needed each other. The family aspect was essential to this man, as in her experience with most people from this state. This man had a lot of sorrow and guilt, and maybe Dylan could convince his uncle he had nothing to do with it. Maybe one day, if Dylan was somehow free from all of this, they could work through those problems together. It was a warming thought.

He stood in the glow of light from the open doorway. Along with the headlights from the detective's car, the house didn't look so imposing from her vantage point now. His hand was up in the air, a smile across his face. He looked utterly ridiculous in his stained shirt and skimpy shorts, but she did interrupt a night of drinking and a movie. She would have been in the same state herself if she had a visitor this late in the evening.

He was about to say something else when blood sprayed from his mouth. Jennifer heard him gurgle as the front of his shirt burst open. It happened so quickly it almost didn't register that something had torn through him. Quentin's hands fired down to his midsection as some of his insides spilled outward from the hole in his stomach and onto the steps.

Jennifer wanted to scream but couldn't find her voice. A look of terror and shock washed across his face as red liquid ran down his chin. Quentin moaned as he lifted into the air. His arms were outstretched one minute, then made their way behind his head as if he was reaching for something on his back the next. The look of confusion turned to a grimace of pain as he hovered there briefly before being entirely torn in half. His lower body slumped straight down on the porch, and his torso fell to the ground below. There was a wet thud as he connected with the earth.

"Jennifer, get in the car!" Veronica yelled.

Jennifer was frozen, still attempting to process what she'd just witnessed.

"Where is it, Ethel? Jennifer, move your ass!" Veronica bellowed.

Jennifer felt her legs moving, but she wasn't registering anything happening around her. She followed Veronica's command, allowing pure instinct to take over. She rushed toward the passenger side of the Sentra at full speed, stumbling for a moment before she regained footing. She tripped again and almost hit the hood of the car, but flung her hand out to stop the collision and dropped the keys to her own vehicle. She paused and was about to turn around to pick them up. Then, she noticed Veronica opening the driver's door from the corner of her eye. Jennifer abandoned the keys and continued toward her goal.

She'd never moved so fast, and her heart felt like it would burst from her chest. Those damned cigarettes. She swore to herself right then that she would give them up. Maybe she could join a gym and start doing high-impact exercises if she survived this. It was such a stupid thing to be at the forefront of her mind, but she'd taught herself to focus on one thing when she was afraid or having a panic attack. Usually, it would be the calming effects of the ocean, but she was in a dead sprint with the sound of her heart ringing in her ears. The memories of the sea would be useless here. She could barely breathe, and felt as if she might pass out. She had just watched a man die, another one, and here she was, lost in thoughts of giving up nicotine.

She grabbed the door handle, pulled it open, and flung herself into the seat. The car was already moving backward before she could spin herself around from her knees to get seated properly. When Veronica hit the brake to stop the vehicle, Jennifer's door slammed shut. Those few seconds of stopping were enough to help Jennifer turn around so she was facing forward and gripping the door handle tight. There was a loud thud, and Jennifer realized she was staring into Quentin's lifeless eyes.

"Holy shit!" Veronica cried out as she spun the wheel and pressed the gas pedal.

Jennifer watched as Quentin slid off to the right as the Nissan gathered speed up the gravel driveway. She was aware that the brain still had some activity after death. Was Quentin still in there when she looked at him? Was he confused and scared? Jennifer felt an acidic taste enter her mouth, and she fought with every fiber of her being to keep from vomiting in her lap. They turned hard onto the pavement, and the tires gave a squelch as they headed to the left, away from the house.

"Ethel, where is it?" Veronica yelled again, looking over her shoulder behind them.

"Who?" Jennifer asked, barely audible.

"Shut up! I need to hear her!" Veronica barked back at her.

Veronica kept looking in the rearview mirror and had almost left the road several times, going into the ditches as she rounded every curve. This strip of pavement was not made for the pace at which they traveled. It certainly wasn't helping Jennifer's stomach, either.

Jennifer hit the button to lower the window; she needed air on her face, even if for a second. The wind was calming, and Jennifer felt relief flow over her. She needed to come to terms with what was happening, and more importantly, she had to figure out how this police officer fit into this equation. However, that would have to wait as they hit a massive dip, and the vehicle left the ground. Jennifer's stomach flipped, and she couldn't hold it anymore. She leaned out the window and let out a loud gag.

"Are you kidding me?" she heard Veronica ask from inside the car.

Jennifer took a deep gasp of air before letting what was left of the food she'd eaten earlier that day spill down the side of the frame. She took in another lungful of the night air and dry heaved. As she finished, she was jerked back into the car by a hard right. She almost slammed into Veronica but grabbed the open window and righted herself, reaching around, Jennifer grabbed the seatbelt, and latched it as fast as possible.

"Why did you provoke it?" Veronica asked, her voice raised.

"Excuse—" Jennifer began while wiping her mouth with her left hand.

"Baby wipes in the glove box. You decided it would be cute to shit-talk a demon? What the hell is wrong with you?"

"No, I was—" she wet-burped and thought she might be sick again, but it passed quickly. "I was confronting it." She pulled the lever to the compartment and grabbed the wipes. "It killed my father," she explained as she pulled one from the top and wiped her mouth and the back of her hand.

"You can't see it, can you?" Veronica questioned as she gave another glance to the mirror.

"No, can you?" Jennifer had hoped she would finally get some mental image of Nothing. For years, she'd envisioned what it could look like. Her mind always went to the fantastic, something like a yeti with black fur or a man dressed in black with thin round glasses holding cartoonishly giant scissors.

"No, but Ethel can."

"Oh," Jennifer muttered, hitting the button to close the passenger window.

They sat mostly in silence for the next few miles as Veronica slowed to a reasonable pace. There were very few lights on the road, and when they did pass by one, Jennifer glimpsed the bloody streaks on the side of the hood. This was her worst-case scenario. Quentin was dead, and she was back to square one. She hadn't thought of what she'd do if Nothing revealed itself.

She could have brought a cross or Holy Water, anything. She didn't even have a firearm on her. What had she planned to do, psychoanalyze Nothing? She should have stayed home in Baltimore. Went to a base-ball game or dialed up one of her friends with benefits. What on earth possessed her to put herself in this position? She sat there feeling sorry for herself and feeling remorse for Quentin. She had no idea what she was going to do next. She finally looked at the woman driving the car.

"So..." Jennifer finally spoke up. "Ethel?"

"She's my grandmother; she's been dead for a few years. I can talk to her," Veronica answered, obviously knowing where this line of questioning was heading.

To any sane person, that would have sounded preposterous, but Jennifer had watched two people die at the hands of an invisible demon. She was more than willing to believe this woman; it was the only thing tonight that seemed plausible.

"So—" Jennifer started again.

"You're welcome," Veronica said condescendingly.

"That's not what I was going to say, but since you brought it up, thank you." Jennifer pulled another wipe from the container and wiped her mouth again.

Veronica stared over at her. Jennifer could tell she was a very impatient woman. She raised her eyebrows and held her fingers out on the steering wheel as if to say *hurry up*.

"What happens now?" Jennifer wondered.

"I promised to get you out of the state," Veronica sighed.

Jennifer leaned forward. "My car? My keys? I can't leave. Are you just going to drive me back to Baltimore?"

"Shit." Veronica tapped the wheel with her hand. "I'll take care of it, but let's get you away from that thing first."

"How did you find me? Did someone from the facility call?" Jennifer asked.

"No, wait what? So, you really were with Dylan tonight? Does that thing have something to do with Dylan's mom?"

"It killed her," Jennifer said.

"You went to see him, and he led you here." Veronica swerved onto a main road, and Jennifer's stomach flipped again.

"I thought you'd come to arrest me," Jennifer added.

"Why would I do that?" Veronica chuckled.

"Because my license is suspended and I lied my way into an interview with him." Jennifer had no idea why she told her. The woman had saved her life, but she was also an officer of the law. Maybe it was her brush with death, but the minute it left her lips she felt a weight being lifted from her.

"What the fuck would you do that for?" Veronica scolded.

"Nothing killed my dad. I had to be sure. I had to know—" Jennifer trailed off, as a realization came over her. "Who did you promise?"

"What?" Veronica asked, but Jennifer could tell she was playing dumb.

"You said you promised to get me out of here. Who asked you to do that?" Jennifer turned her whole body to face Veronica.

Veronica reached down to the cup holder and grabbed a phone. She held it up in her sight and began scrolling with her thumb. "That's not important right now."

"It certainly is," Jennifer assured her.

"Hush a second," Veronica said.

Jennifer folded her arms and watched Veronica scroll through her contacts; she had difficulty trusting this woman. She wasn't likable, and there was no reason to be secretive in this situation unless she was doing so just to be cruel. They drove through the town of Hurricane and onto Interstate 64, heading west as Veronica attempted to call a person three times, each ringing through to voicemail. She sat the phone down in anger and looked over toward Jennifer.

"Tell me," Veronica demanded.

"Tell you what?" Jennifer was confused, but had a good idea of what she wanted.

"What the hell was that thing?" Veronica held up one finger. "How did it kill your father?" She held up a second one. "What is going on?" Holding up a third.

"I'll make a deal with you," Jennifer proposed.

"I don't think you are in a position to make any deals."

"I'll tell you everything you want to know if you tell me why you came to get me. Who told you I'd be there?"

Veronica stared at her. Why not just tell her? What was the big secret? She already told her she could communicate with the de—. Jennifer's breath left her, and her palms began to sweat. Veronica could speak to the dead. Someone who cared about her sent her. Someone didn't want Nothing to hurt her.

"It was my dad, wasn't it?" Jennifer covered her mouth, and she fought every urge to break down and cry.

"Listen," Veronica said, biting her lip before exhaling, "I give you my word, I'll tell you where I come into this if you let me know what the hell I've stepped into."

Jennifer leaned back in her seat and nodded her head. She never looked over toward Veronica; she just stared at the passing signs on the interstate, which was surprisingly empty. There were very few cars coming or going. It seemed as if they were the only ones out in the world.

She started at the beginning, telling Veronica about her childhood and the incident with Neil. She spared no detail as she came to her first confrontation with Nothing. She closed with how Dylan fit into the puzzle.

"Holy shit." Veronica placed a hand on her forehead. "So the kid really is innocent?"

Veronica turned and looked to the backseat.

"Is your grandmother back there?" Jennifer asked curiously. Veronica nodded.

"She's upset by all of this. She gets emotional." Veronica focused on the mirror. "Oh, you do, too." Veronica rolled her eyes. Jennifer slowly glanced into the empty seat and apologized. Veronica smirked.

"It's okay. Be thankful you can't—" The phone buzzed in the cup holder, and Veronica snatched it up and answered it. "Jimmy?"

"'Sup Carter, I saw you called." A man's gruff voice came echoing through the car speakers.

"The apartment in Chesapeake, is it empty?"

Jennifer could see Veronica cross her fingers on her left hand. She found that humorous for some reason.

"Yeah, haven't used it for a month or two. Why? You in trouble?" he asked, sounding concerned.

"Nope, I need to use it for a day or two. I have a visitor that can't stay with me, and I need a favor." Veronica's tone went intense. She wasn't being cordial anymore.

"Don't you still owe me from the last favor?"

"I need a ride. I need you to meet me there and pick me up."

"How far?" Jennifer could hear the hesitation in Jimmy's voice.

"Not far, outside of Hurricane. Just drop me off one way."

"I had some—" Jimmy began.

"Five hundred bucks, no questions asked," Veronica spoke over him.

Jimmy said nothing for a few seconds. "How close are you?"

"Just hit Huntington, almost there."

Another pause. "On my way."

She looked down at the phone and tossed it back in the cup holder.

"I'm taking you to an apartment better than most hotels. You'll wait there while I go back and get your car," Veronica explained slowly, as if she were talking to a child.

"You're going back there after what just happened?" Jennifer was stunned. It was as if what happened to Quentin hadn't phased her.

"Have to. Can't have your car just sitting there beside a dead body," Veronica rationalized.

"I don't want you to get hurt," Jennifer pleaded.

"I'm touched," Veronica mocked. "I'll be fine. Ethel will be with me."

"Still," Jennifer trailed off.

"Look, Doc, I will just get the car and bring it back to you. Then, in the morning, you take the scenic way home through Ohio and never come back here. Do you understand?"

"Was it my dad?" Jennifer blurted the question out. She had to know.

Veronica looked over at her as she turned her blinker on to take the West Huntington exit. "It was."

Jennifer turned away and tried her best to cry in silence.

9

The apartment they were going to hide in was one of two that had been converted from a relatively large home. It was away from the main road by itself, surrounded by trees, with the Ohio River a hundred feet or so in the backyard. Veronica had stayed in both apartments several times with Lacy, or if she was too tired to make it home after long trips.

She had a key to both since it was the same for either door. She had been trusted with them early last year; the only rule was to call Jimmy before using it. Veronica thought it was a good trade-off. It was also a comforting sight because she was somewhere she recognized. Her heart rate was finally normalizing, and she wasn't sweating anymore. Whatever that thing was that had caused such havoc wasn't pursuing them.

She pulled up close to the left side of the brick building, shut her car off, and put her cell phone in her pocket. She let out a triumphant sigh and turned to Jennifer, who hadn't spoken in some time.

"We're here. There isn't a change of clothes, but the shower is nice and hot. The bed is pretty soft. You can get some sleep while I'm out," Veronica said.

"I wouldn't be able to close my eyes," Jennifer sniffled.

"At least you'll be safe," Veronica said.

"You use this place for witnesses?" Jennifer inquired.

Veronica couldn't contain her smile. "Belongs to an old friend. He rents it out sometimes."

"Toothbrush?" Jennifer asked as she opened her door, looking back to Veronica with a hint of hope in her eyes.

"Probably not, but I'll get you one on the way back," Veronica promised as she exited her car.

She walked to the front of her Nissan, balling up her fist at the sight. The hood was smeared in blood, and there was a reasonably significant dent where the body had made an impact. The entire passenger front side was covered in bits of gore. She loved this car, but it wouldn't be cheap to fix given that it was pretty new.

"Shit," she muttered, looking up at the motion light on the side of the duplex. Things kept getting better and better. Veronica wondered if there was a water hose around the back of the complex so she could attempt to wash away some of the worst of it, but there were more pressing matters to attend to.

"Stands out on the white. I'm surprised we didn't get pulled over."

"It's night time, and if someone noticed, I would have said we hit a deer," Veronica responded as she bent down to check her bumper.

"That's a lot of blood," Jennifer said.

"Have you ever hit a deer?" Veronica stared up at Jennifer, who instantly avoided eye contact. If the woman gripped the bottom of her shirt any tighter, it would rip. Veronica's brows furrowed as she asked, "Something you want to tell me?"

"I dropped my keys." Jennifer looked away toward the main road, letting her shirt go.

"Where?" Veronica asked, concerned.

"I tripped right beside where you parked. They should be on the ground."

"Not a problem, don't worry about it," Veronica said, unable to control the sigh that followed. She jerked her thumb over her shoulder. "Come on, let's get you inside. I don't want you out here when Jimmy arrives. He's a little much."

Veronica led the way to the front of the duplex and paused. She chose the apartment on the right and turned the key in the lock. She hadn't exactly lied to Jennifer—a witness had never been stashed in one of these apartments, and it did belong to an old friend—but she hadn't been truthful about the use of the apartments either. It was far more likely that someone *running* from the police had been stashed here; under the bed in each place was a trap door that led to the basement where things were stored, like the stolen car parts Jimmy dealt in. Veronica knew about his dealings, but looked the other way as long as he promised to keep it out of her county.

Veronica wondered if anyone without a criminal record or blood on their hands had ever stayed here, and she was going to assume that would be an emphatic no. She knew some of the people Jimmy called partners that had "rented" this place, and could only imagine the others she didn't know were probably worse.

She walked in, turned on the light switch to her right, and was greeted with the smell of Lysol. *Well, he lied to me,* she thought. The place was always cleaned after someone stayed there. It had to be scrubbed down thoroughly, and the smell was way too fresh for it to have been over a month. Judging by the overpowering chemical scent in the air, she'd say two days at most since someone gave the place a once-over.

The living room and kitchen were one huge room separated by beige carpet and gray tile. Everything in sight was white. The appliances, countertops, cabinets, and furniture all shined in the light from the ceiling fan bulbs in the center of the room. The couch was a white cloth that looked like it had never been sat on, and the loveseat matched. No pictures or anything were hanging on the walls. It gave the room a sterile look, and even though it was comfortable, it was very uninviting. There was no television, and there was no other means of entertainment. She had never realized how boring this place was until now.

Veronica led Jennifer down a tiny hallway and turned on the light to the room on her right. It was a large bathroom with a walk-in shower and an impressive vanity sink combination. Again, however, everything was painted white, with the color scheme to match.

Whoever designed this has no taste, she thought. She went past Jennifer and to the room on her left. She'd stayed in the bedroom with a king-sized bed, a nightstand, and a floor lamp a few times. As before, everything in the room, from the paint on the walls to the bedspread and curtains, was bright white.

"Someone is color blind," Jennifer joked from behind her.

"I was about to say the same thing. I never noticed it before. Christ, this is tacky."

"It's fine. I mean, you can tell everything is clean," Jennifer continued. "I'm taking a shower after you leave."

"Towels are under the sink." Veronica pointed back toward the bathroom.

"I really wish you wouldn't go. What if Nothing is still there?" Jennifer said, rubbing her neck.

"Don't have much choice, but I'll have Ethel with me." Veronica tried to hide her fear by faking a smile and nodding her head confidently.

"Is she here now?" Jennifer leaned in and whispered.

Veronica looked down the hall and toward the bathroom. "Hmm, no."

Veronica tried to recall the last time Ethel spoke up. Was it in the car before or after Jennifer told her everything? She honestly couldn't remember. Veronica walked back into the living room and sat on the couch. She sank instantly and felt her muscles relax. It was so soft, and after how tense she'd been during the drive, she needed a moment to decompress. She thought about everything that had happened tonight and how she would handle going to retrieve Jennifer's car. Veronica had a lot of questions for her, but they didn't have a lot of time, so she decided to get the most pertinent one out of the way.

"Why do you call it Nothing?" Veronica leaned back and ran her fingers through her hair.

"I named it that years ago because you can't see it," Jennifer explained. Veronica nodded at her and went on.

"It killed your dad to get revenge on you over an accident? It did the same with Dylan?"

"I was a kid. I should have gotten help." Jennifer sat down on the loveseat and put her head in her hands, her elbows resting on her knees. "If it did this to Dylan, if it did this to me, how many others are there?" Jennifer's voice cracked.

"Not many police reports are going to mention invisible monsters." Veronica stood and paced back and forth. "You think it only does this to kids?"

"How many kids accidentally kill people, though?" Jennifer fired back.

"I'm sure it happens more often than—" Veronica's mind latched onto a story from her youth. "Holy shit."

"What is it?" Jennifer stiffened.

"When I was a kid—I'm talking maybe seven, hell, I could have been younger—there was this older kid I went to school with. He was twelve or so, and was playing in his apartment with his best friend. They found his dad's gun, and the kid shot his best friend in the face."

"Yeah?" Jennifer held her hands up as if to ask where this was going.

"A day later, the kid's grandfather gets electrocuted. I remember Ethel talking about how terrible it was. *Hadn't the family suffered enough?* You know what I'm saying."

"You don't think...?" Jennifer's eyes widened at the thought.

"I mean, I can't say for sure, but how long has this Nothing been at this?" Veronica questioned.

"I have no idea, but it can't keep getting away with this."

Veronica started laughing, and Jennifer's cheeks instantly turned slightly pink.

"Are you crazy? How do you fight what you can't see? You don't even know what it is."

"We have to do something," Jennifer argued.

"No," Veronica stood and forcefully pointed her finger at her, "you need to understand that sometimes it's best to leave well enough alone. You're going to get yourself killed."

"It can't win. It has to be stopped. Look what happened to me... to Dylan," Jennifer begged.

"My dad died drinking himself to death. Bad shit happens, life isn't fair, I'm not saying it's right, but it is what it is." Headlights shone through the cracks in the curtain, streaking across Veronica's face as she paced. She walked toward the door and said, "My buddy is here. Stay inside and try to relax. I'll be back."

Jimmy was waiting in his truck, an old, beat-up blue and rust-colored Chevy S10 he'd owned for God knew how long. Jimmy was a career criminal who frequented in and out of jail. Veronica had been introduced to him by her girlfriend at the time, Lacy. Veronica remembered how Lacy was terrified to admit he was her brother. There wasn't much he wouldn't do for money; she'd go as far as to say nothing was too far-fetched if the numbers added up for him. She didn't completely trust him; given his felonious history, there was no way she could.

They'd hit it off instantly. Veronica knew he was shady; she knew how often he'd broken the law. He was the complete opposite of her profession, but Jimmy was charming, and beyond all else, he loved his sister. He was highly protective of her, and in turn, he embraced Veronica with open arms. Even after they split up, Veronica and Jimmy stayed in touch. Jimmy even chastised his sister for, as he put it, "letting go of the best thing in her life."

She thought of the night she killed for him, and got revenge for a three-year-old who couldn't defend herself. Even though he wasn't there, and no one would ever find the body, Jimmy brought it up now and then in conversations as casually as if he was thanking her for lighting his cigarette. She could tell that Jimmy still felt like he *owed her one*. So, whenever she asked for favors, his standard fees were much cheaper than they used to be. She probably could have only offered him fifty to seventy-five dollars for this, but she wanted to ensure he couldn't say no. She opened the passenger door, and the smell of motor oil and marijuana almost knocked her over.

"Hurry up, woman," he said hatefully.

"What have you been doing in here?" She waved her hand in front of her face.

"Hey, you're the one that got me out of bed."

"Oh bullshit, you probably just got up." She shook her head at him, sat down, and slammed the door.

"I did! That was you getting me out of bed." He laughed a little at his joke. He turned around in the yard and headed back for the road.

"Who's in the apartment? Someone important?"

"A doctor I'm leaning on for some information. Nothing you should worry about."

"You need my help?" he asked. His *help* usually ended with him in jail, plus she knew he was trying to make more money for God only knew what.

"No, this isn't one of those. It's a personal matter."

Jimmy nodded. Veronica looked over at him. He was wearing a Jack Daniels t-shirt and blue jeans. Not an inch of the skin on his exposed arms wasn't covered in ink. His beard was down to the middle of his chest, showing signs of gray at the edges. She knew he was in his early thirties but looked way older than that. He had gauges in his ears. She had no idea what size, but they weren't enormous. Veronica always associated it with the very young, and on Jimmy, they looked so out of place, like he was trying to hold on to some semblance of youth.

"So, you don't need me to wait on you?" He reached into the ashtray and pulled out a half-smoked marijuana cigarette and a lighter.

"No," she said, twirling her finger around in a circle, telling him to roll his window down, which he obliged. "You're going to drop me off at the front of a gravel driveway and leave."

"That's it? For five-hundred bucks?" He raised one eyebrow.

"That's it," Veronica confirmed.

They crossed the bridge back into West Virginia.

"Your sister doing alright?" Veronica blurted out before her brain could convince her to stop.

"Do you really want to know?" he asked, glancing over uncomfortably.

"I guess," she said as she braced for the bad news.

"She's getting married in a month. Some dickhead that runs a car lot."

Veronica felt the muscles in her neck tighten. *Why did I ask?*

"Sorry. If it makes you feel any better, I hate the fucking guy."

It didn't. She knew Lacy had moved on, but it still stung. She said very little to him for the rest of the trip back to the house. Jimmy took a drag off his joint and blew it out the window. She'd made it awkward by asking about Lacy. Jimmy was always joking and had a lot to say, but he sat silently. She was fond of him, and how much she missed him struck her. She wondered if maybe it was the time with Lacy that she missed, and he was just interconnected with those memories, but she pushed those thoughts aside. Still, she had loved having dinner with him and his wife, Lindsey, at their house on Sundays. The four of them sitting on the back deck with beers, cracking jokes, and thinking things couldn't get any better.

The radio was playing some country station, which, along with the strong smell of cannabis in the cab, had started to give Veronica a headache. She wasn't going to speak up about it. He could have told her no when she called him, but he didn't. He was someone she could rely on. She knew he'd get her where she was going, disappear, and never mention it again. Even when the story of Quentin's body being found broke on the news, and it just happened near the same place he let her off, she was pretty confident he wouldn't give it a second thought.

They were pulling off the Hurricane exit when she finally tried to engage him in small talk to keep herself calm. The closer they got to the house, the more she questioned if Nothing was still there, just waiting for someone else to tear to pieces. She would have sent Jimmy and one of his lackeys to retrieve the car, but they would come across the body, and she didn't want to put that on anyone. Plus, there was a big difference in what she would have to pay to ask someone to ignore a man split in two pieces in his yard rather than to just give her a ride somewhere.

"When are you going to get rid of this hunk of junk?" She asked and tapped the dashboard.

"What? This is a classic," he said as he feigned offense.

"You can afford another truck. This thing is a road hazard." She was already starting to snicker but trying hard to play it seriously.

"I have over three hundred thousand miles on this truck," he said proudly.

"That's a hundred and fifty thousand too many. What year is this?" She held up an empty Marlboro cigarette package from the floorboard and tossed it back.

"2002. I bought it brand new. I'm the only owner."

"There is a reason you're the only owner, Jimmy. No one would buy this piece of shit. Does this death trap have a legal inspection sticker and tags? Jesus, do I even have a seat belt over here?" She felt around but couldn't find one.

"Sticker and tags are completely legal."

"My man," Veronica pointed toward her window, "this thing doesn't have a passenger mirror! Whoever let this pass inspection is really shitty at their job."

"Car prices are way too high right now," he whined playfully.

Veronica dug in her front pocket and pulled out a small wad of bills. She always kept cash on her. It was something Ethel had always instilled in her. She counted out five one hundred dollar bills and laid them on the seat beside her. "Please add this to the 'Get Jimmy a New Truck' fund."

He reached over and snatched it off the seat, leaned up, and stuffed it in his back pocket.

"You aren't going to count it?" she asked.

"If you can't trust the police, who can you trust?"

She dreaded it, but the rest of the drive flew by. She told him where to turn and sat quietly as the country station began to grate on her nerves. The DJ, who would talk occasionally, used an exaggerated accent, which she despised. It made him sound like a caricature and not a natural person. Yes, the people around her had a severe twang in their voices. Jimmy sounded like he crawled out of some backwoods hollow, but it wasn't so pronounced that you couldn't distinguish what he said. The man coming through the speakers sounded like an idiot.

Veronica told him to stop on the side of the road about twenty feet from the turn onto the gravel driveway. The tree line covered the house well, so she couldn't see down into the yard where the car was, and where Quentin lay dead.

"You sure you want me to take off?" he asked while looking around cautiously. "I mean, there isn't anything out here."

"Go on. You need to be up bright and early to buy a new truck. Plus, I'm safer on the side of the road than inside this." She patted the dash with two fingers.

Jimmy laughed and waved as she exited the vehicle, then turned around at the front of the gravel drive, and drove back past her, waving again on his way by.

"Okay, in and out. This won't be bad," Veronica said to herself.

She started toward the driveway. She wanted to be near the yard and have Ethel survey the grounds and the house to ensure it was clear. Veronica felt a flutter in her stomach, and her hands went clammy. She stopped a few feet from the drive, worried she might have another panic attack, but it never transpired. Though she was nervous, she had an ace up her sleeve. Her feet touched the gravel, and she called out to her grandmother.

"Ethel, let's go." The chill hit her instantly as Ethel appeared off to her left. "The car is dead ahead. Jennifer dropped her keys beside where I was parked before, if you could check that they are there. If that thing is still around, come back, and I'll get the hell out of here. If you don't see it, I'll run up the drive, grab the keys, and off we go. Simple."

Ethel nodded her head but was rocking back and forth.

"What's wrong with you?" Veronica grew concerned. She hadn't seen Ethel like this before.

Ethel didn't respond.

"Ethel!" Veronica whispered loudly.

Ethel waved her hand over at her annoyingly. "I'm nervous."

"You're already dead. It can't hurt you," Veronica reminded her, still trying to whisper while becoming more agitated by the second.

"When I was in the room with it, it couldn't see me," Ethel said.

"Then what is the problem?" Veronica shook her hands in front of her. She couldn't believe she was having this conversation right now.

"You didn't see it. It's scary, Veronica!" Ethel answered.

"You are a goddamn ghost—" Veronica was letting her anger get the best of her.

"Watch your mouth! You don't take the Lord's name that way."

Veronica closed her eyes, tilted her head toward the sky, and let out a massive sigh. "I'm sorry."

"They're going to know you were here," Ethel said, ignoring her granddaughter's apology.

"How do you figure that?"

"Well, you aren't taking the body with you, your fingerprints, and that girl—"

Oh shit! What the hell was I thinking? Veronica screamed internally. Ethel was still speaking, but Veronica wasn't paying attention anymore. She couldn't believe she hadn't thought of any of this. This is why criminals get caught. They don't think things through, and she hadn't given any of this a second to roll around in her head. She would need to clean the front door thoroughly, the railing to the stairs, the banister, and the door handle upstairs. She would also need to make sure Jennifer didn't disrupt anything in Dylan's bedroom.

"Okay, change of plans, same as before, then go in the house and look upstairs and down. If there is no sign of it, we can clean up fast and be gone. This won't take more than ten minutes if you hurry."

"I don't know about this, Ronnie," Ethel whined and paced. Ethel hadn't called her Ronnie for a while now. It was Ethel's nickname for her when she was a little girl. It touched her to hear it, and it just solidified that Nothing was something not to be trifled with.

Ethel was terrified of this thing. She wasn't thinking clearly. But the longer they stood in this driveway arguing with one another, or she spent trying to get Ethel's courage up, the chances of getting caught increased considerably.

"We have to do this. They will blame Jennifer for that man's death, and I'll go down in flames with her. Ethel, if you don't move your ass, I'm going to do this myself. I need you. I don't want to die here tonight."

"I don't want that either," Ethel said.

"You got this," Veronica said with a nod. "It can't see you."

Ethel exhaled loudly, started toward the house, stopped, shook her head, and started again. She glanced back a few times, with Veronica motioning her on with both hands each time. The fear in Ethel's eyes saddened Veronica. She didn't like forcing Ethel to do this. She'd rather Ethel not be with her on this at all. Veronica knew she had to hurry. She needed to be on her toes. She'd seen what it had done to Quentin, so there was little doubt that it was incredibly powerful, and the fact that the only one who could see it was Ethel upped the difficulty. She would have to rely on Ethel to tell her if it was around, which put her at a severe disadvantage. It could be watching her right now as Ethel checked out the house. Veronica felt the hairs on her neck stand up at the thought.

Nice going, dipshit. You scared yourself.

She closed her eyes in disgust. Veronica hunkered down and stayed as still as possible. She didn't want anything to see or hear her. She focused on the driveway, which was quite long, and even went around a slight bend. She kept her eyes glued to the bend, waiting for any sign of Ethel. The seconds turned into a minute, which soon led to another. She had already caused herself unease, but the more time ticked away, the worse the feeling became.

"I didn't see anything," Ethel said from right behind her.

Veronica stood straight up, spun around, and slapped Ethel's arm. Her hand went right through her. "What is wrong with you?"

"What?" Ethel asked as she flinched from Veronica's hand.

"You scared the shit out of me!"

"I'm sorry. I thought it would be faster if I poofed."

"Poof" was Ethel's term for when she appeared to Veronica. She'd used it a couple of times, and after a while, it just stuck. Veronica thought it sounded silly but adorable, so she let it go.

"Let's go," Veronica said, giving one final survey before heading up the driveway, crouching low. She looked back to Ethel, who was also bent over.

"Are you sneaking?" Veronica asked her.

"Shut up," Ethel said.

It didn't take long before the car was in view. The door of the house was still open wide and gave decent light that shone across the front yard. Veronica could make out the torso of Quentin off to her right, and it took everything in her power not to look over at him. She didn't want to see his body. She already had the mental image of his death, and seeing him in that state would remind her of the stakes. Besides, she would have to pass by his lower half to get into the house, which would be a challenge.

"I'm going in the house, heading for the kitchen," Veronica said almost inaudibly.

"What for?"

"People keep cleaning supplies under the kitchen sink. I need 409 or bleach."

"I'll go in first. I didn't see it in there, and it's not out here, but I'll check again," Ethel said.

Veronica stood upright, turned, and nodded to Ethel, who went past her, still bent over and moved slowly toward the front porch.

"Speed up. We don't want to be here if that thing comes back," Veronica said through clenched teeth.

Ethel paused at the bottom of the steps and turned around. "Give me a minute. I just need a minute."

"We don't have time. I know it bothered you but we have to move. Listen, I'm gonna look for cleaning supplies. You scream—and I mean *scream*—if you see it."

Veronica set off in a march toward the house. She made sure to step around Quentin's legs and exposed guts at the bottom of the stairs. She kept her eyes on the front door the whole time, trying not to stare at what was left of him. She crossed the threshold of the doorway, went through the archway, and into the living room. The television was still on, and on the coffee table beside a recliner were several empty beer bottles, one still half full. It wasn't as filthy as Ethel had described it, but it could use a cleaning. Dirty clothes were on the couch, and used tissues were overflowing the waste-basket she almost knocked over that sat on the other side of the chair.

There were picture frames all over the wall, none of the Dylan kid Jennifer had mentioned, but some of a young girl and the mother that was killed. She could recall the mother from the newspapers and the internet stories about her death. She didn't have time to take inventory of the room. She reminded herself to focus, walked through another archway, and entered the darkened kitchen. She placed her hand under her shirt and headed straight for the double doors under the sink. She used the hand she covered to open the right side door and peered inside. She couldn't make anything out, so she reached into her front pocket and grabbed her phone.

She shined her camera light into the darkness of the cabinet and almost squealed with delight when she saw the familiar cylinder of Clorox wipes. She snatched them and, without closing the cabinet, walked back into the living room. Ethel met her there with her arms folded.

"What's wrong?" Veronica asked.

"You need to wait for me. We need to be careful," Ethel warned.

"You're going way too slow because you're hunkered down," Veronica explained as she imitated someone sneaking around on their tiptoes. "I'm scared too. I'm about to piss all over myself, but we have to hurry. I'm trying to get us out of here."

"A man is dead, Veronica," Ethel reminded her.

"I know that, and I don't want to join him. I would tell you to breathe but... Now let me finish."

Ethel turned to leave the room, and her hand collided with a cup on the table. It flew sideways and hit the floor with a tink. Ethel stared at her hand before turning and looking back to Veronica, who was too stunned to be upset by the noise.

"How did you do that?" Veronica whispered.

"I have no clue." Ethel rushed over and reached for Veronica, and her hand went completely through her. "I was upset and wasn't think —" Her hand disappeared in Veronica's chest.

It's just like what happened in the trailer. How did Ethel accomplish this feat? How in the hell did the afterlife work? Could she turn this on and off? There was no time to worry about this now. They would discuss it when all of this was over. If Nothing was in the house, it had to hear the plastic cup hit the floor. Veronica shook her head, trying to catch her bearings.

She pulled one of the wipes from the top of the container and started on the inside handle and frame of the front door. "Anything?" Veronica whispered.

"No."

She took several wipes and began scrubbing the railing leading up the stairs. Ethel passed by her and stood at the top. Veronica looked to Ethel now and then, but she shook her head no. Veronica started to relax. Maybe it was gone. What reason did it have to stay? They had left almost two hours ago. It didn't look like it had eaten Quentin, and Jennifer would have brought that up if Nothing had snacked on her dad.

She finally reached Ethel. She started on the handrail, which she couldn't recall if Jennifer had leaned on, and it was better to be safe than sorry. With each passing second, her confidence grew, and she was becoming more sure she would make it out of this whole affair in one piece. She finished up everything on the stairs, meaning she had only one place left to clean. She looked behind her at the room where she'd first met Jennifer, and her mood turned dark.

Something wasn't right. She felt a sickness in her stomach, the hairs on her neck rose again, not so much as in fear, but as if her body was warning her something was wrong. Ethel must have noticed her pause.

"What's wrong?" Ethel asked, her head tilted.

Veronica could barely get the words out. "Before we left, I heard this door open. It spooked me. That's why I rushed Jennifer."

Ethel looked over at the door and gasped.

It was closed.

Veronica took a wipe and cleaned the outside door handle to Dylan's room. "Ethel, you checked this room, right? I have to go in there. I need to clean the other side and take the comforter."

Ethel didn't answer, her eyes fixed on the door.

"Ethel!" Veronica whispered, waving her hand vigorously at her face. Ethel turned slowly.

"I checked this room first, Ronnie."

"And it wasn't in there?" Veronica wanted to be sure.

Ethel shuddered. "This door was open."

The initial wave of fear was almost too much. Veronica instinctively dropped to one knee and put her hand on the butt of her pistol. Nothing was in the house; if not, it was a person. Either one was bad and the last thing she needed. She was moments away from running to Jennifer's car and fleeing, but she'd come this far. If she took off in a sprint, whatever was in the house would hear her. She tried to calm herself by thinking ludicrous things like maybe it was the wind or Ethel was wrong. She knew better.

She counted to three and looked to Ethel. Ethel was rocking back and forth again, much faster this time. Her hands were up by her mouth, and Veronica could swear she was chewing her nails. She didn't want to ask her to go in there. Veronica remembered Ethel hating Halloween and horror movies; she didn't like to be frightened, and even though she was dead, Ethel was still the grandmother she lived with for twenty years.

"Check inside," Veronica whispered.

Ethel did not acknowledge that she'd heard her. She just went through the door quickly.

Veronica was proud of her. She was afraid for a moment that

Ethel might freeze up again. The real question was if Ethel popped back out and told her it was in there, could she get away fast enough? Would it pursue her and take her out? Veronica glanced behind her and then through the bars of the railing. She knew she couldn't see it, but it opened doors, meaning it had weight and could touch her. If she tried hard enough, she might be able to hear it.

She leaned to her right and listened. The house was still. She could barely hear the television; that was the only thing audible besides the ticking of the grandfather clock below her. What was this thing playing at? Why shut the door? What if it wasn't Nothing and someone related to Quentin was hiding? They could be trying to find a safe spot in the house, scared to death that she is the killer. They would have called the police the second they arrived.

Ethel came back through.

"Nothing."

"Oh shit, it's in there?" Veronica felt faint.

"No, no, no!" Ethel shook her head violently. "It's not in the room or the closet. Hurry!"

"We need to work on how you say things, Ethel."

Veronica was on her feet and used one of the wipes to open the door. She left it ajar with enough room for her to pass through. She pulled one more wipe and began polishing the inside handle. She rushed to the bed and pulled the comforter onto the floor. She threw the used wipes and the container in the middle of the bedcover and took the edges up so she could carry it like a sack.

She inspected the room in the few seconds she felt she had. The dust didn't seem disturbed on any action figures or nick-nacks on the dresser. If Jennifer touched something else here, she would have to answer for it. This was the best anyone could expect from her. She was running on an internal timer, hoping that she finished before whatever evil was in this house found her.

"Why do we have the blanket?" Ethel asked.

"She was sitting on it, hands all over it." Veronica was already on her way out of the room with the bedding slung over her shoulder. She slowed her pace for Ethel to take the stairs first. Ethel was taking the steps rather quickly, and for a moment, Veronica was scared she'd fall and hurt herself. She didn't know if that was possible, but the thought was there. She needed to test the limits of what Ethel could and couldn't do in case something so insane ever happened again.

Veronica went behind, doing all she could not to make any noise. Every creak of the wood damn near sent Veronica into a fit. Maybe it didn't know where she was, or maybe it wasn't aware of her being in the house. Perhaps she was thinking all this to try and convince herself that everything would be alright. She was so close; she just had to get to the car, throw this stuff in the trunk, and never look back. Ethel exited through the front door and called back to her.

"I'll stand beside the keys."

This was the final stretch, and Veronica watched from the front door as Ethel started down the steps, taking a wide berth around Quentin's lower extremities. Veronica gave one final look upstairs and then steeled herself for the trip across the yard. She wondered if Nothing was just wandering around the house, and somehow they missed each other. If that was the case, she needed to not stay in one spot very long. She bit her lip and took a deep breath. She only heard the incessant ticking from the clock beside her. Veronica held her free hand up as if to tell someone in the room to hush even though no one else was there, and she listened again.

Oh no. She noticed the hand she held up trembled. She took a few steps to the archway into the living room and went in. It was silent. The television was turned off.

Timer. It was on a timer, she thought. She knew better. She wanted to scream but knew that would be pointless. It knew she was here. What the hell was this thing doing? Was she trapped in some sick game? Was it taunting her or waiting to see if Jennifer was with her?

She scanned every corner of the room for motion, knowing it was futile but more so out of habit. She slowly began backing from the room, trying to be as muted as possible. She couldn't take her eyes off the television. She had attempted to rationalize the entire thing but her brain wasn't having it. Her eyes followed the television's electrical cord to the outlet on the wall. The plug was disconnected; something had pulled it from the socket.

Veronica wheeled around and took off in a trot toward the front door. She ran across the small planks of the porch, and leaped from the top of the wooden steps. She cleared all three of them and what was left of Quentin below, landing on both feet with her knees bent. She looked up and prepared to run toward Ethel, but her heart froze.

Ethel was standing at the back of Jennifer's Ford Focus. She wasn't looking toward Veronica but facing the right with her arm outstretched and finger-pointing. Her other hand was over her mouth. Veronica knew what it meant. Ethel didn't have to say it. Nothing was in the yard with her. It was waiting for her. Veronica wondered why it hadn't attacked her in the house. It knew she was there. Veronica knew her subsequent actions would decide if she lived or died.

She didn't dare look in the direction Ethel was pointing. She wanted this thing to have the impression it had the upper hand. She took her free hand and retrieved her phone. She stared down at it and moved her thumb around as if to be doing something important.

"What are you doing? Run! It's watching you!" Ethel screamed.

Veronica put the phone to her ear, waited a few seconds, and then began speaking. "I got all the evidence cleaned up."

"What's the matter with you?"

Veronica looked back toward Quentin's legs. "He's dead. Well, that's what you get for letting that woman in your house. If he'd told her to piss off, he'd be alive."

Veronica's eyes were locked on Ethel as she started walking toward her. She continued her phantom conversation.

"What do you want me to say? The woman is crazy. She needs to stay up there in Baltimore and leave things alone."

Ethel nodded. "Yes, it's working. It's not moving. It's listening to you."

"I ought to put a bullet in her myself. Blaming others for something that's her fault to begin with."

She continued past the Focus and stopped at the keys lying at

Ethel's feet. Holding the phone with her shoulder she scooped them from the ground. Veronica assumed this thing was evil but intelligent. It had been closing doors and unplugging devices to instill fear. She knew it wanted Jennifer; maybe it even hated her.

Quentin might have just been a consolation prize. If she could convince it that she wasn't a decent person and that there was a chance she'd kill Jennifer herself, maybe it would let her walk. Perhaps it would just listen to the conversation and laugh about what a piece of shit she was later. Or maybe it was animalistic and waiting to strike; she had no idea, but this seemed to be working.

She turned to the back of the Focus and hit the button on the key with the picture of the trunk. It flew open, and she tossed the comforter she'd been holding inside. "Well, I'm about to leave. I don't know what else I could do here."

"Keep going!" Ethel encouraged.

She placed her hand on the trunk, about to close it. "I'll be ther—"

Her phone rang in her hand. She pulled it away from her ear and saw that Jimmy was calling her. The tone played out in the silence of the night air, the default iPhone sound. She closed her eyes and shook her head.

"Fuck," she said to herself.

"IT'S COMING!" Ethel cried out.

Veronica instinctively pitched her phone and the keys inside and jumped in the trunk. She rose and pulled as hard as she could at the tiny metal overhang. It swung down, and the latch clicked as she was encased in the darkness. She was curled up in the fetal position but wasn't hurt.

She was breathing heavily and was seconds away from urinating on herself. She thought earlier that night was the most she'd ever experienced fear. That paled in comparison to what was happening now. She felt tears in her eyes. She would die out in some holler in the trunk of a Ford.

She was jolted by something colliding with the outside of the car. The banging was intense. It was trying to get inside. It wanted to murder her. It was going to kill her, and she could only pull her knees closer to her chest and pray. She could hear Ethel's voice but couldn't understand what she was saying. She would be its victim, and her grandmother would have to watch the horror unfold.

The banging continued, and she could hear Ethel getting louder. Then silence.

What the hell was it doing now? Had it given up? Veronica could feel the tears streaming down her face. She began to whimper. Was her grandmother alright? She couldn't hear her anymore.

"Ethel?" she called.

There was no answer.

"Ethel?!"

The quiet was maddening.

"MAW MAW!"

10

Forty Minutes Later

Jennifer thought it was gross to shower and put on her old clothes, but she didn't have much choice. She tried rinsing her mouth in the sink, but it hadn't done much. It still tasted like she'd sucked on a gym sock. She hoped Veronica was alright and that Ethel would be enough to keep her safe. She kept thinking of how Quentin's life ended as violently and brutally as her father's. She didn't like Veronica much but would have been devastated if something happened to her.

The woman had risked her life to come and save her, and after seeing the way Quentin was dispatched so effortlessly, she had no doubt Nothing would have killed her tonight. She put her socks back on, returned to the living room, and sat on the couch. She was exhausted. She'd driven most of the day and confronted a supernatural being. If it wasn't for the fact she was alone, she might have closed her eyes. She would attempt to get some sleep once Veronica returned and was safe.

She thought about what Veronica had said on the way out the door, how she should accept it and move on with her life. The thing that she failed to realize was that she'd tried that. It didn't work. She couldn't just cut a part of her soul out like that. She didn't know how to live any other way.

She contemplated marrying, having a couple of kids, trying to live an everyday life—surrounding herself with play dates and soccer practices, having unsatisfying sex while the children were in the Walmart brand above-ground pool, and trying to be content. It wouldn't work, and she knew it. How long before she divorced because the husband couldn't handle her mood swings and secrets? She could always tell the man interested in her about Nothing and what happened, see how well that turned out.

She stood and went by the door for her shoes. She needed a cigarette, it would take the edge off, and she didn't give a damn what any medical journal said. It helped her focus. She'd been a tobacco user since she was a teen, and she had tried it all: gum, patches, even hypnosis. None of it worked. She cheated every time, but she finally gave up and accepted that this would be what brought about her end. *Until tonight's events*, she thought as she laced up her white Filas.

She opened the door and walked out into the night air. It was still relatively warm and muggy where it had rained earlier. She straightened the towel she had her hair up in and looked at her surroundings. This place was pretty secluded. It did make her feel safe.

Jennifer had just enjoyed a scorching hot shower and didn't want to stay out in this weather for long. She went around the side of the building to where the Nissan was parked and hoped that Veronica hadn't locked the doors. She was craving her fix and didn't know if she could make it until she returned. She pulled on the passenger door handle and felt relief as it swung open for her. She bent in, grabbed her purse, and closed the door.

The woman who designed the cross-body purse deserves a medal, Jennifer thought. She was able to keep her belongings in all the chaos. She had recently bought a knock-off Michael Kors. She wanted a real one, but she was extremely frugal. She couldn't see herself spending that kind of money on something so frivolous. It always struck her that she was a stickler for appearances but refused to spend money on said look. *Just one more misshapen piece in the Jennifer puzzle*, she told herself. She started digging inside the bag as she walked back toward the open apartment door. She was going to set her purse down in the kitchen and come back outside to enjoy some nicotine to pass the time.

She entered the apartment and laid her purse on the white countertop. She had trouble finding her Winston Lights as she was walking, but with the overhead light, she found them quickly, along with her Zippo. A man she dated a few years back had purchased it for her as a gift. She turned it over in her fingertips, looking at the engraving. *JDS*, her initials. He'd made the joke if they ever married, he'd buy her a new one. She knew it wouldn't last. She didn't feel for him nearly as strongly as he felt for her. So she ran him off, just like all the others.

Jennifer grabbed her phone from the front pouch, and walked back out outside. She lit a cigarette, took a long draw, and placed her lighter in her pocket. Her body instantly thanked her for giving in again. The tension behind her eyes waned and the cramp in her stomach eased. It didn't help the nasty taste in her mouth, but she was learning to accept that nothing was to be done about that one.

She brought her phone up to her face to unlock it, and the background image of the cat she lost a few years ago popped into view. Her phone instantly reminded her that she'd missed eight calls, all within the last seven minutes.

"Hmm," she said to no one. She checked the log; all were from Tina Morgan. "Shit," Jennifer muttered into the night. Corey might have called her, either that or the kids were driving her crazy. She felt uneasy. She hoped Tina didn't know yet. She could go to her house and stay in the guest room, drinking wine and laughing till the sun came up one last time before she cut her out of her life forever.

She couldn't exactly call her and explain what was going on. *Sorry, T, Dylan didn't kill his mom. I used our friendship to get in there, and I was right, turns out the same thing that butchered my dad is responsible.* What would she say to something like that? Tina would have her committed.

Keeping Tina in the dark about everything bothered her. She wanted to trust in her friend, but a friendship could only go so far, no matter how much alcohol got involved.

The phone buzzed in her hand. She was going to have to make something up on the fly. Jennifer took another hit from her Winston and answered. "Hey T, sorry I couldn't pick up earlier."

"What the hell were you doing?"

The level of venom in Tina's voice was enough to cause Jennifer to jerk back in surprise.

She knows.

"What?" Jennifer laughed half-heartedly.

"What. The hell. Were. You. Doing?" Tina asked, punctuating each word.

"What do you mean?" Jennifer asked again, panic seeping into her.

"Did I stutter? What the fuck were you doing at the center?" Tina's voice quaked through the tiny speaker.

"Center?" It was the only thing that sprang to Jennifer's mind.

"Yes, *my facility*. Don't act stupid. We both know you were there; you're on camera!" Tina barked at her.

"I-I was... going to surprise you at work," Jennifer squeaked. She could hear shouting in the background. She couldn't make out if it was Tina's children or not.

"I'LL BE OUT IN A MINUTE!" Tina bellowed. "Bullshit. Jennifer, the police are on their way. What happened while you were there? Do you know how fucking stupid I looked when I got a picture of you going in the building?"

"Why would you get a picture of me going in the building?" Jennifer tensed up.

"Just get your ass here," Tina said angrily. "Where are you?"

"I'm getting food. I was going to surprise you at the house," Jennifer lied. It was the only thing she could come up with under the pressure. "Tina, what is going on?"

"You need to get over here. Stop what you're doing and hurry up!" Tina commanded.

"You aren't making sense," Jennifer said.

"A patient's escaped," Tina howled, "and two people are dead!"

11

Forty Minutes Ago

Ethel backed away from the charging beast. The trunk was closed, and she hoped its claws couldn't tear through the metal and get at Veronica. Nothing slammed into the side of the Ford Focus, and debris from the shattered tail light flew in all directions. The backside of the car moved from the impact of its body.

Nothing raised both arms and brought its fists down on the car's rear panel. Its mouth was wide open, and saliva flew everywhere as it roared in rage. Ethel watched as the muscles contracted and tensed. Now that she was right next to it, she could see the blood flowing through its veins. Its neck flexed and reverberated. This thing should not exist, and yet here it was. It was going to kill her granddaughter, and she was helpless to stop it.

Its hands came up and down again, the car bouncing with the strike. Ethel attempted to keep the creature at bay. She swiped at the monster, but her hand passed through as it had done with everyone else. Ethel stared at her hands. What was it going to take to make it stop? She looked toward the sky and prayed.

Please don't let her die this way, she begged the Lord. She had started to wane in her faith after ending up as a ghost, trapped away from the Heaven she so desperately desired to see. But she had no one else to call upon, and if there was no divine intervention, Veronica was as good as dead. She knew trying to hit Nothing was futile, but she swung anyway. If only she could hurt it or distract it with something. She stepped back as Nothing screamed into the night air and brought its right claw down on the trunk, making puncture marks. The beast was genuinely terrifying.

Ethel could hear Veronica screaming from inside the car. She could feel her despair, and her maternal instincts were on high. She had to save her; she just had no idea how. She kicked at Nothing, but her shoes faded through it. Ethel's mind reeled from all she'd endured these past few years. She remembered the impact that caused her death. She recalled the pain that rocked her entire body as she woke at the accident scene. It felt as if she was burning alive.

They were packing Veronica into an ambulance, and Ethel's remains were zipped in a body bag. She was confused at first, but the realization slowly sunk in, and then the hopelessness of being alone with no one able to see her. She'd tried to talk to every person she encountered, telling them she was right there, but to no avail.

Why am I thinking about this now?

Next was the memory of hearing a crash in the living room and rushing in to find the man she'd dedicated her entire life to dead on the floor from a massive heart attack. She slapped him, she shook him, she tried everything in her power to get Martin to open his eyes, but nothing worked. She held his head until the paramedics arrived. She was lost in knowing she wouldn't see him again till she passed away. Yet, when she did, he wasn't there waiting.

Life wasn't supposed to be this way. Yes, people died, but why had this family endured so much? Why couldn't it just be the way the Almighty intended? Her mother and father died at an early age. All three of her sisters and her brother never lived to see sixty years old. Her husband was barely retired and didn't get to enjoy any of it. She didn't think he got to go fishing once.

Last, she thought of her son, Jamie, Veronica's father, who was ravaged by guilt and tried to drink his pain away until he succeeded. He hadn't spoken to her at all leading up to his death. He had walked out on her and his baby girl. Ethel had lost him twice—once emotionally, and then physically. When was it enough?

Someone help us. Somebody save her.

Why couldn't she have been a better parent to Veronica? Why couldn't she save her from the debauchery and evil that consumed her life? Why did Veronica turn out the way she did? What could she have done differently? She hated herself for letting it get this way, for not intervening and assuming everything was alright. If Veronica died here tonight, Ethel wondered if her spirit would reside here with her or not be here like so many others. They should have never returned here. Ethel should have put her foot down and refused. Why did she think this was a good idea? They didn't need to be here at all. To hell with this car, this doctor, and her problems. Ethel felt for Jennifer's plight, but there was no reason to get everyone killed.

Ethel felt a wave of anger rising in her. The helpless feeling morphed into hate. She despised Nothing, not just for its desire to murder her granddaughter but for what it represented. It was what they warned her about every Sunday. She was livid. The last time she'd been this upset was when she and Veronica fought over her behavior, a feeling she now regretted because there may never be a chance to right that ship. No, this was much worse than hate. She was having trouble concentrating. She could feel her insides trembling. She clenched her fists and stood beside the creature as it put its left hand on the car and raised its right to bash it again.

Leave her alone.

She'd spoken. She was sure of it. She felt the words leave her mouth, but they came from deep inside her chest. Ethel hadn't experienced anything physical since her death. She passed through things and hadn't felt the effects. She'd stood in the sun, rain, and snow, hoping that she could sense the heat or the bitter cold for just one fleeting moment. She never realized how much she missed that until it was taken away. She would touch her body occasionally, but there was no recognition. It was as if her entire body was numb. This was different. She felt the words pass through her throat.

She jerked back and put her hand up to her mouth. It wasn't overly aggressive, and she hadn't screamed. It was as if she'd said it in a normal conversation. The feeling, however, was as if she'd spoken for the first time, and if her reaction to it was shocking, it was insignificant compared to how the beast behaved.

Nothing jumped away from the car, looking in Ethel's direction with its hands in front of it and its mouth wide open. Nothing didn't have eyes or eyebrows, but she could see fear across its face. It went low to the ground and kicked up gravel as it started to move away. There wasn't anything hostile in its posture or movement now.

I don't want to go back! Please don't take me back! it screamed before getting on its knees and putting its hands together. ***Please! I'll do anything! Don't take me!*** Nothing cried out over and over. Ethel stepped forward, and slapped her hand against the side of the car. She felt it connect and heard the *thunk* as her hand made contact. She allowed the anger to well up once more. She had only one thing left to say to Nothing, and she reached inside her and let it out.

Go.

Nothing cowered away from her voice. It held up its hand as if shielding itself from her. It nodded its head frantically, turned, and ran away. Ethel had never seen Nothing standing upright, it was always hunched over with its right shoulder higher up than the left, but here it was running at full speed, standing tall, sprinting away from her, and much more importantly, Veronica.

Ethel followed cautiously around the left side of the house. She didn't want to be caught up in some sort of trick. She was still unsure what was happening but could see Nothing scrambling up into the woods and out of sight. She watched it until she saw no trace, then bent her head, listening until she could no longer hear the rustling as it plowed through the brush.

She'd done it. She'd driven it off. Pride swelled up in Ethel as she began nodding to herself. She'd saved the day. This detestable creature from Hell was no match for this old woman. It was afraid of her, and it damn sure better be. Ethel smirked. She'd never been in a fistfight in her entire life, but she was positive she could take on the world. In her eyes, she'd beaten the devil; she wasn't about to let this thing take her life—*Oh goodness, Veronica!* She hurried back to the front of the house. She turned the corner and rushed toward the car.

She could hear Veronica screaming for her as she got near the trunk. Veronica was yelling, and it sounded as if she was pounding on the inside walls. She could only imagine what was going through her mind trapped in there.

"Veronica!" Ethel yelled out. There was silence, and the night air was still.

"Maw Maw?" Veronica's muffled voice came meekly from below.

Hearing her say that again touched Ethel, and her hand shot up to her chest. She'd asked her not to call her that anymore, but hearing it brought her great joy.

"I'm here. Can you open the trunk?"

"I'm not coming out there! Are you crazy?" Veronica started to panic again.

"It's gone," Ethel yelled in triumph.

There was a long pause.

"What do you mean it's gone?" Veronica's voice asked warily.

"It ran away. I got rid of it," Ethel proclaimed.

"How did you do that?" Veronica whimpered.

"Veronica Carter, you come out of there this instant," Ethel commanded, her tone switching to parental. A few seconds passed, and then the latch clicked and the trunk opened. Veronica was curled up, holding the key in one hand and her legs close with her other arm. She'd been crying; her face was still wet, and her cheeks were beet red. She was drenched in sweat, and her eyes widened in fear.

Ethel bent toward her. "I promise you're safe. I'm the only one here." She tried to use the soothing voice she'd used when Veronica was sick or afraid as a child. Veronica stared at her before nodding and slowly emerged from the trunk. She almost fell over once she made it to her feet. She shook violently but was getting her breathing back on track. She looked around her before she closed the lid and wiped her forehead with the back of her hand.

"See? It's gone." Ethel smiled as she held out her arms and, in a spectacle, twirled around in a circle.

"I can't see it anyway," Veronica responded quite rudely.

"Well, I watched it run away. I scared it off," Ethel said.

Veronica's face said it all. She wasn't buying it. "Why would it be afraid of you?"

Ethel recalled the entire story from the moment Veronica went into the vehicle. She tried her best to stay composed but couldn't help herself. Her voice swelled as she explained how she'd spoken and practically scared the life out of Nothing. It ran out of there as if she was an actual threat and begged the entire time not to be taken back.

"Take it back where?" Veronica thought aloud.

"Hell, the closet, Kentucky," Ethel joked. "Who cares, it's gone."

Veronica looked at the back of the Focus. "It really did a number on this."

Ethel looked at the damage. It had shattered the tail light, and six large dents were all over the back driver's side and across the trunk. Nothing had also left three puncture holes trying to claw into her.

"At least you're safe," Ethel comforted.

"Wonder if the doctor will feel that way." Veronica wiped more sweat from her brow and rubbed her hand on her shirt.

"She'd better," Ethel answered. "You could've been killed."

Veronica clicked the button to open the trunk back up.

"Are you getting back in?" Ethel giggled.

Veronica frowned at her, bent, and retrieved as many pieces of the tail light as she could before pitching them in the trunk and slamming it shut.

"Do me a favor?" Veronica asked without looking back at Ethel. She went around to the driver's side door and opened it.

"What's that?" Ethel asked, concerned.

"Can I ride back alone? Please?" Veronica still hadn't made eye contact.

"You're gonna cry, aren't you?" Ethel probed.

Veronica entered the car and leaned out, finally glancing back at Ethel. "Probably."

12

Nothing slammed into the tree in front of it. It wasn't looking; all its attention was focused behind it for any sign of pursuit. It stumbled to the ground on its backside and hurried to its feet, reaching out to regain its balance. It could run for hours if need be. It had to. It wasn't going back into the dark. It would not. It had tasted freedom for far too long. It would fight, but that would be pointless. It knew this day would come, that it was inevitable, but it wanted to prolong it for as long as possible.

It craned its neck, listened for any movement in the leaves, and heard no noises. Nothing rushed behind the tree its hand was on, and peered out from behind it and into the woods, hoping it was alone.

Nothing knew it shouldn't have killed the man on the stairs. It had been following its rules to the letter to avoid detection. It had never played fast and loose. It had broken its own set of guidelines. It tried its best over the decades to convince itself that it punished and did not murder anyone outright. It knew somewhere inside its mind that it was a silly thought, but Nothing believed it would be safe if it stayed the course in those convictions. It had been that way since the late 40s.

Nothing shuddered at the thought of going back into the black. Hell's image had been depicted as fire and brimstone for as long as it could remember. That wasn't what it was in the slightest. It was something far worse. Hell was tailor-made for your life, but there was hardly any light. It was dark, it was cold, and worst of all, it was painful.

There was nothing like the pain inside the dark. Just touching the ground itself hurt, and the air burned to breathe. The things in the dark inflicted unspeakable horrors; you could try and hide, but they always found you.

Maybe all that pain was where the idea of hellfire came from, but as far as Nothing knew, no one had ever escaped from its walls. So, the image of the fiery lake had to be conceived somewhere. Maybe the Master himself had given it to Man.

Nothing had no idea how long it had been trapped inside the dark. All it knew was that it was one too many years. When it was roaming the Appalachian countryside, it never thought about what it was before it came to the shadows. Inside the dark, however, it was treated as something less than human. But it *had* been a man, it remembered that much. It had lived a man's life and had a man's name, though it couldn't recall what that name was. Jennifer had called it *Nothing,* and that suited what it was now far better than any human name could.

Nothing punched the tree, cracking it around its base and watching it fall. It was a man once. He could recall entering the dark, his wife waiting for him because of his sins, and then the workers peeling his flesh away, as one would skin an animal. He remembered them nailing his claws onto his fingertips and how they laughed at his pleading to stop. Next, they removed his eyes, and filed his teeth. He could still see everything awash in a red haze. It made everything look sickly and unnatural.

The Master would come and collect one of them every so often and send them to hunt a newcomer into the dark. Nothing enjoyed these excursions; it was the only time pain wasn't ravaging his body, and he got to inflict all his anger on someone else. The second he caught them, however, it was back to his room where his wife ridiculed him for being such a rotten man. He couldn't recall what he'd done. His mind didn't put things together correctly the way it did when he was alive.

The day he was pulled from the dark was the happiest of his recent existence. A woman in Braxton County had called upon a curse to punish a man who'd killed her sister. The whole town knew he was in the vehicle, but they couldn't prove it. His wife and sister-in-law had given him an airtight alibi. So, the woman tried her hand at a curse to make him pay. Curses usually don't come from the dark. Not that he had ever heard. The only thing that made sense was that this woman had no idea what she was doing and called him instead. She'd used an evil power to summon him, and he was back on the mortal plane.

He was free in West Virginia, a place Nothing had never heard of before. He knew of Virginia; how long had he been in the dark? It didn't matter. He was here now, and this woman was asking him to kill, something he had perfected throughout the years. Nothing tried to do the task he was summoned for, but the man had passed from a stroke a day beforehand, so Nothing decided to slaughter the wife instead.

He'd caught her outside her home, in the backyard, and made her suffer. He did it slowly, ensuring she felt every ounce of pain he could inflict. Looking back now, he'd thought of his wife and the hellish torture he was enduring. It added to his brutality. Once he'd finished, he returned to the lady who'd conjured him with the trophy of his victim's heart.

"I didn't want her. I wanted him," she'd complained.

Do you think she was innocent? That she was unaware of his crime?

"You've made your point. I release you," she said.

Nothing had been pleased with what he'd done, and secretly he'd wished the man would have been alive to see him kill his wife. That would have been fitting in his mind. Nothing hadn't thought of that woman who called him forth in a long time, and he could barely recall what she looked like. He was fairly sure she was dead now.

When she told him she released him, Nothing tensed and was

ready to be whisked back to the dark. He wasn't thrilled about returning to the suffering and the torment, but as the minutes grew, he realized no one was coming. Maybe the Master had been pleased by what he'd done? He left the woman and roamed for days. All the while, he observed and watched a world that was very different from what the spots in his memory could pull to the surface. Nothing wondered why he'd been forgotten, and as time passed, he believed it was because of his actions that the Master had left him there.

Nothing heard movement off in the distance, and his attention returned to the present. He practically got on his belly to try to hide. He held his breath and gazed at the sound, only to see a deer emerge behind the brush. He stood, frustrated with himself, questioning why he was given this existence. He remembered being a man, but his face was lost to time, and that thought enraged him. Was he so heinous that he deserved to be made into this? Nothing took off into the woodlands again, attempting to distance himself from the voice that had told him to stop. He had been happy with the way his second life had gone. He'd punished people by taking those they cared about. It was a fair trade for their crimes.

Bloodlust was inside him; he had to kill, and the rules he laid down were the ones he modified for his original calling. He believed that as time went on and the numbers grew, the dark approved of what he was doing. Why else would he be allowed to stay? Plus, the violence filled the void inside him and brought him peace after every kill.

Everything was fine until Jennifer reappeared. He'd had her in his grasp. He was going to kill her in that room. He'd even asked for her permission. He'd felt someone calling out to him, and he answered. He was shocked to see her. It had been ages. Every so often, Nothing would visit the ones he passed judgment on. He would pop in on her from time to time and relish in her misery. He'd thought of her a few years ago but couldn't sense her. He'd hoped she'd taken her life, and he'd not thought of her since.

When he saw her tonight, he fed on her loathing and grief. He would end her and bathe in her sorrow as the light went out in her eyes. It warmed him to know that she'd not forgotten what he was nor what he did. He was flattered, if he was being honest. He would have murdered her in the same room as his last kill. It was almost poetic.

Who was the woman who intervened? The one who tried to trick him? He wanted to kill her too, though his desire for her death was nowhere near as severe as his wish to murder Jennifer. Still, it would happen if he got the chance. He was going to settle for this new woman, but the voice called out. They had found him and wanted to take him back to the dark. Jennifer had made him so angry when she was leaving that he killed the man on the steps. He'd broken his own rules. Jennifer had brought them to him.

This is all your fault, he thought as Jennifer's face filled his mind. She was just another of those who made the same excuse: *it was an accident.* Nothing didn't care. Jennifer was just another in a long line of those who refused to take responsibility for bringing him into their lives. She was weak, and he would enjoy watching her leave this world. The question now was how he would get close to her while he was being pursued. Nothing hit himself in the head with his fist a few times.

Stupid, so stupid. He sat down in the dirt to think. He needed to concentrate and come up with a plan. He knew he had to hide. He needed to be away from the eyes that could see him. He tapped his head with his claws and tried to calm himself. He needed a way not to be found but to continue the hunt. He knew he couldn't run far enough that they would never find him. It was only a matter of time before he would be dragged back into the depths.

He thought back to his time in the dark when he was called away to do the Master's bidding. In some instances, those hunts involved more than one person. Sometimes, he would enter the bodies of one of them and chase the others down. They would die at the hands of the people they cared for the most. Could he possibly do that here? Could he occupy someone? He'd never attempted it. It worked in the dark, but here, a lot of the rules were different. He'd need someone who wouldn't fight him, someone who would give in to him and let him try to push their soul out.

He felt excited at the prospect as he racked his brain, trying to think of who would be a perfect candidate. He would have loved for it to have been Jennifer, but he couldn't feel her anymore; she'd passed beyond the threshold, and he feared he'd lost his chance with her forever. He needed someone easy to control, and he needed them now. Who could he convince? His mind went to his victims, and suddenly, Nothing stood upright as the name crossed his mind.

The boy, Nothing answered himself as he grinned. Nothing started walking again, and he let his mind drift to Dylan. He could feel him; he could practically see him. The last thing Nothing thought about before he faded to his destination was what if he'd fallen through the cracks? What if he wasn't supposed to be here at all? Was this some giant mistake? What if, all these years, he'd been following these stupid rules for no reason whatsoever?

A cruel smile played across his features as he said, ***I could kill as many as I like. I'll make up for all that lost time.***

Dylan had finally finished crying, his head pounding from the tension. He was right; his mother was dead, and it was his fault. If he'd just shut up and taken the abuse from Miss Addis, his mother would still be alive, and he wouldn't be here. Trapped and alone with just the walls to keep him company.

Dylan wondered what day of the week it was. He thought it was Monday and missed the wrestling show he watched. His mother sat with him and cheered on his favorites while his sister complained that she was on the phone. It was the only night of the week Dylan was allowed to stay up late. Of all the things he'd lost, he missed those Monday nights with his family the most.

The room he was stuck in was painted in the same awful green as the hallway. He'd grown to dislike the color and wished they'd paint it a different color just to give him something else to look at. His bed was the most uncomfortable thing he'd ever felt, and it made a terrible squeaking sound when he rolled over. He always tried not to move whenever he lay down because it reminded him of nails on a chalk-board, which was awful. After all, there was nothing to do in this room but lay in bed. He only had the meshed window to look out of, and it only had a view of the other side of the building. There was barely any light coming in at all.

After nine, the lights in his room shut off, and the black would envelop him. He hated that; ever since what happened, he didn't like anything to do with the night. He grew anxious as his internal clock would start to tell him the sun was going down. He was always afraid it would come back for him, that it was always in the shadows waiting for him. He told himself repeatedly that it was only a matter of time. The other doctor he saw had told him that if he spoke to her, she would get him toys or books. But he didn't dare say a word.

The voice had warned him to keep his mouth shut, and he had. He never fought back, even when they said he'd killed his mother. He never denied it. He just sat there and let them say all those lies about him. Even when his sister called him scum in the courtroom, he never made a peep. The voice had told him it would do the same to him. It was livid that he'd tried to hurt it. He ran, got the knife from the kitchen, and stabbed the air around his mother's body. He just wanted it to stop; he'd known she was already dead, and enough was enough.

The voice had reminded Dylan that this was his doing. If he had behaved, none of this would have happened. The new doctor, that honest lady, confirmed it to him tonight. Nothing had killed her father for her being bad too. She let the little boy die, and Dylan did the same to his teacher. He'd hoped the doctor was right and she could kill Nothing, but he knew better. You can't kill a voice. He looked toward the window, and a little light shone through. He wished for rain again. The sound always put him to sleep.

Trouble sleeping? Nothing called from the corner.

Dylan moved away from the voice and into the upper corner of the bed against the wall. He wanted to scream, and he clutched the sides of his head. It was here to kill him for talking to the doctor. She'd failed, it had snuffed her out, and now it was his turn.

Don't be afraid, Nothing chuckled from the corner.

"I'm sorry. I didn't want to talk about you. She knew things," Dylan whispered with his hand outstretched as if he could stop it.

It's alright, Dylan. I'm not angry.

"What... what do you want?" Dylan cried.

I was wrong about you.

Dylan lowered his hand. He was confused. Nothing's voice wasn't as before when they'd first met. There was no glee this time around. The metallic grating was still present, but the tone was softer, not a hint of threat.

"I didn't want her to die."

The teacher? You should have. She was a rotten woman. I had no idea the horrible things she'd done. Once I found out, I was angry at what I'd done to you. You didn't deserve it. I can't take it back, and I am not asking you to forgive me.

Dylan didn't know what to say. Nothing was apologizing? Dylan's fear was giving away to anger. Nothing had killed his mother for no reason at all. Why had it come here? To gloat over him being a prisoner? It was too late to do anything about it now. He looked down at his waistline, he had urinated himself in fright. He wrapped his arms around himself tightly, and the words came out between gasps for air.

"You ruined everything."

I did... I was wrong. There is nothing to be done about that and believe me, I will be punished for it, but I have come to make it up to you.

Dylan couldn't scoot back any further. He was already against the corner. But the voice had grown closer, and he knew it was approaching him. Even though it was talking to him in a friendly way, he'd seen what this thing could do firsthand. He didn't want to die that way.

"You can't fix this."

Oh, but I can. I don't want you to rot in this place. You don't belong here. You didn't do any of this.

Dylan thought back to his trial; he was told he would reside in this place under the care of his current doctors until he was eighteen. That seemed like a lifetime away; the last school year he was in seemed to drag out forever. How would the next seven years feel? The woman doctor he saw every other day told him that once he reached that milestone, there was a chance he would go to a prison cell. He didn't know if that was true; many people had been trying to scare him since the incident.

Dylan certainly didn't know anything about the law; they thought he murdered his mother with a knife, and when you killed people, he thought you went to jail for life. He could have sworn he'd heard that in a movie somewhere. Nothing's words made sense, but Dylan knew he was responsible for the death of Miss Addis.

"But the pills..." Dylan began.

You've done wrong, you admit that much, and you've paid the price. But she was evil, a bully who took delight in watching you hurt. Plus, there are things about her no one knew about.

"Still, why'd I do that?" Dylan whined.

Do you think she would be upset if you'd died? I can guarantee you that she wouldn't, not in the slightest.

"So, what happens now? Everyone hates me." Dylan lowered his head.

I am going to protect you. I will make sure no one ever hurts you again. I want you to be free from all of this. I want you not to have to worry. I want you out of this prison.

Dylan didn't want to be in his cell anymore. He wanted to be outside, to see his friends again. His mind went to tacos; he missed them. All the things he used to do before he came to only know this room. Video games, television, stupid YouTube videos, and food that didn't taste the same. He yearned for those things.

"How? If I leave, they'll come for me."

Dylan wasn't pressed against the wall anymore and wasn't near the level of panic as when Nothing came in. If it planned to murder Dylan, it would have already done so, and it sounded as if it was trying to make amends for what had happened. Dylan thought about getting away from here and finding his sister. Telling her he never meant for any of this to happen. Maybe he could find Uncle Quentin, and he would listen to him. All Dylan knew was that he wanted to be free of his cage.

They won't find you. I promise.

"How can I trust you? I'm here 'cause of you!"

Then tell me no, and I will be on my way. You will sit here and be forgotten. You will be brought in front of doctors, and when you tell them about me, they'll think you're insane. You'll never leave this room.

Dylan sat in silence, already knowing the answer, but he still let the last thing Nothing said hang in the air.

"What do I have to do?"

Just repeat the words I say exactly as I say them.

"That's all?" Dylan asked.

That's all.

"Alright then." Dylan leaned forward on the bed, onto his hands and knees.

Nothing began saying words to Dylan that sounded like complete gibberish. He almost started to laugh but kept it in. They didn't sound like anything at all. Dylan wondered what language this was. He'd heard a man speaking Spanish in the past, and this wasn't anything like that either. The words were long and drawn out and felt more like sounds than anything else.

Nothing enunciated everything, and Dylan repeated it exactly. Just when Dylan thought they'd finished, Nothing had another set for him to do. Dylan had hoped he was doing it right, but since Nothing hadn't stopped him, he went from unsure to confident as he spoke. He felt excitement tingling in his fingers and toes. He would be able to make all of these things right. Maybe he could find the doctor who came to see him and tell her that Nothing freed him. Perhaps, for once, everything might work out in the end.

Dylan finished another set that Nothing spoke aloud, but then Nothing laughed. The tone of it was different. The hatefulness and malice were back. Dylan felt fear come over him again, and he started back toward the corner. His breathing became labored. He clutched at his chest and tried to ask out loud what was happening. Dylan's mind raced, it reminded him of a year ago when he choked on a chicken nugget and couldn't breathe.

He had clawed at his throat and tried to get air into his lungs with all his might. It wasn't until his mom's boyfriend turned him upside down and began pounding on his back that he felt it dislodge. He'd told that story at school the next day, and Mr. Floyd told him how lucky he was since what was done to him could have made it worse. What was he choking on now? He wasn't eating anything, but the sensation was the same. Something was blocking him from getting his breath.

There was no one in here to help him, however. He was alone except for Nothing, and if he couldn't see it, could it see him? Dylan reached before him and tried to gasp again, but his body wasn't listening. He fell forward on the bed, rolled off, and crashed onto the floor, sending a shockwave of pain through his body. He rolled over again into the wall on the farthest side away from the bed and kicked at it. He was trying to get someone to hear so they could come help him. Dylan could hear his heartbeat ringing in his ears; it was loud, and he noticed it was slowing.

Oh my God, I'm dying. I'm dying, ain't I?

Dylan closed his eyes and tried to pull in anything one last time. His strength was gone, and he was losing consciousness. He couldn't kick the wall anymore; his body had stopped listening to his commands. He was going to die. Nothing had tricked him. It lied to him. Dylan looked toward the door and saw it open. He could see a pair of white shoes running toward him as his vision blurred and faded to black.

At least I will see Mommy.

"DYLAN!" Corey screamed in his face as Dylan slowly opened his eyes. Dylan reached up and wiped his mouth. Dylan felt as if he was going to be sick as a wave of nausea came across him. "Oh, Jesus! Dylan, look at me!"

Dylan looked up at Corey, then turned his head to survey the room. His door was open, and on both knees beside him was the orderly who always brought his dinner. Dylan would see him every evening, and in the mornings, it was a woman named Pam. He knew his name from the tag that hung from his pocket. Corey had always been overly friendly to Dylan. He always spoke to him even though he'd never answer.

Dylan sat up, leaning back on the palms of his hands.

"You weren't breathing. What happened? Are you alright? Nod if you can hear me." Corey's face was white, and he placed his hand on Dylan's shoulder. His voice was shaky. Dylan could feel his fear.

Dylan looked up at Corey and nodded, and then Dylan slowly rose to his feet.

"No, no, lie down, okay? I just gave you CPR. You need to lie down while I get a doctor to check on you," Corey said while trying to keep his voice kind but firm.

Dylan was on his feet, while Corey was still on his knees and had both hands on his shoulders. Dylan nodded again and leaned forward slightly. Why were all these images flashing through his mind? Why did he remember the orderly's name? Why did he remember the things about dinner?

"Dylan, why don't you lie in bed so I can—" Corey began.

Dylan gripped the sides of Corey's head and thrust his fingers into his eyes. Even though this body was tiny, Nothing could command much power from it. He felt them go in easily, pushing the eyes backward and down. Corey tried to move away, but Dylan leaped forward and shoved him to the ground, using all the weight his body could muster. With his hands still holding on, Nothing took Corey's head and drove it hard into the floor five times while letting out a primal roar.

After the final time and being satisfied with the audible crack Corey's skull made, Nothing let go and pulled his thumbs back. Blood spilled out from under Corey onto the linoleum. Nothing sat atop the fallen orderly, proud of his actions. This man was much bigger than Nothing, and he had dispatched him quickly. The boy's soul was gone, and Nothing delighted in the thought. A stupid little hillbilly who killed his teacher because he was weak and couldn't take the abuse. All the things Nothing had endured in the dark? That was a thousand times worse, and he hoped that Dylan's soul was on its way there so he could understand what the meaning of real hurt was.

Nothing stood, bent, and wiped his hands on the shirt of the man he'd just killed. He knew his name and had memories of him. It must be a residual effect of the possession. Nothing couldn't believe it worked. He was in total control, and besides being able to recall some of Dylan's thoughts, this body was his to do with as he pleased. It was difficult taking that first step. This didn't suit him at all. His hellish form had much more weight, and now he felt light as a feather. He still slumped slightly with his right shoulder raised for some reason. He never understood why that was. It hurt him to straighten it out, and it was easier to slouch sideways. He was small, and Nothing remembered being taller when he was alive. He almost tripped and fell as he stepped around the convulsing body on the floor.

"Are you still in there?" Nothing said as he brought his foot up over Corey's head before bringing it down several times across the bridge of his nose. Nothing leaped backward in fright after the third strike and reached down toward his new ankle.

"Pain!" he cried.

It had startled him, he hadn't felt that in quite a while, and it made him chuckle. He reached down again, took the keyring off Corey's belt loop, and took a few steps around the room to gather a feel for his new stride. He bent at the knees and hopped a few times. He felt alive again. His previous form felt dull, but this was electric. He could taste, feel the air moving through his lungs, and most of all, that old familiar copper smell of blood.

Nothing exited the room and into the hallway. He was hoping there would be more people. He wanted to inflict more punishment. He yearned to make his presence known to the world. He was shaking with anticipation at the havoc he could wreak. He felt invincible.

Calm yourself. Figure out your limitations. Things were much different from when he was a man. His memories came much easier now. He was no longer a perversion but a whole. His thoughts weren't jumbled or a mess of images anymore. He started down the hallway, and for a fleeting moment, he thought of opening all the other doors and ending the lives of those who dwelled inside.

When he was alive, he was a man of the cloth. Sure, he had proclivities; yes, they weren't of his wife. Men had died at his hands in the war, but he saved souls. He was there on Sunday speaking of the Lord, and for his service, he was forsaken and cast into that awful place where his wife broke him, where the things she did were the truest form of evil.

How much of my power have I lost? he wondered. His soul now occupied this body. Gone were the teeth and the claws. He knew he couldn't think of someone and go to them anymore. He was a physical being now, back in the land of the living as one of them. Would he age? He could feel pain; he'd learned that the hard way. Could he be killed? His mind was filled with images of his former life. He was an older man before; he died early in the 1800s and had sat in a room much like Dylan until he was sent into the dark.

He held the keyring up and looked at all the shiny metal objects dangling in the light. Nothing had been watching Man for decades. He knew of technology and how most things worked. He had always been curious when he was alive, and once he returned as an abomination, he was even worse. He knew the world was different from when he was alive, and he was eager to learn it.

He gripped the keys tightly and stopped walking to try and collect himself. He was about to succumb to the anger but needed to get out. He needed to find Jennifer and take care of her. He needed to find a place to hide and—

"Hungry..." He smiled. He wanted food. He hadn't felt hunger in over two hundred years. What else awaited him? He hurried forward with purpose. He reached a large metal door and began trying the keys one by one until a smaller one made of brass slid in the lock and turned. He pulled on the handle and was surprised by how heavy it was. Once he had enough clearance, he walked through, and it slammed with a bang. He held his ground briefly to ensure no one rushed to the sound. He found himself in another room, as drab and dreary as the place he'd just exited. No one was on the other side of the glass, and the chairs he noticed looked seriously worn and ready to fall apart.

I'd have given my soul to get out of here, too, he snickered as he exited through the only other door and out into another hall. He looked down the darkened hallway and saw no one. The elevator in front of him was roped off and had yellow stickers across it telling all it was out of order. The stairs to his right led in both directions and were very dimly lit.

This is almost too easy, Nothing thought. He descended the stairs, listening for any sounds of someone coming his way. He continued until he reached a locked door at the bottom and used the same keyring until a large silver one opened it. He peered around the frame and slowly went through, exiting at the end of a much larger hallway. This time, he could hear voices off in the distance, so he zig-zagged to open doors as he went, trying his best to stay out of sight. The rooms were primarily tiny offices; quick scans revealed nothing of interest, and he moved on. It wasn't until he reached one that looked like a kitchen that he finally saw something that could help him escape. There was a countertop with a coffee maker and a microwave, but to the left was an open toolbox.

He eased himself over to it and took a screwdriver that felt comfortable in his hand. He didn't like the fact that he was so short, and he didn't want to climb on top of the counters. He had to stand on his tiptoes. The less noise he made, the better. He examined his find. It had a filthy brown handle, and the metal was five or so inches long. He ran his finger across it and relished how cold it felt. He could use it in a pinch if needed, so he exited the room and sneaked toward the sounds of conversation. He passed vending machines and a few closed office doors until he reached an opening. He glanced around the corner and saw a desk with two men talking to each other and, beyond them, the glass door to the outside.

Nothing entered the room unnoticed and hid between two massive plants before going under a bench against the back wall. The room had an odor, one he couldn't place, and as he lay against the cold tile, he noted how dirty it was. He kept quiet and stayed under the bench, for he knew that he could be seen now, and the best thing was to keep out of sight and strike from the shadows.

He felt uneasy after feeling the pain in his ankle when he used his foot to stomp on the orderly. He could still feel it, and after the initial rush of being in a new body, he was starting to realize that the drawbacks of having it were there too. He worried that these men he found himself staring at could overpower him, and there wasn't much he could do.

The men were dressed in white, like Corey. One had a brownish-yellow beard with long, unkempt hair, while the other man was portly with glasses. He was so close; he just had to bide his time, and he could make his escape. How long before they found Corey and actively searched for him? He had the element of surprise and needed to use it, but he doubted he could conquer these two men in this tiny frame, even armed with his screwdriver.

"I'm telling you she's not into you," the man with the beard said.

"We're going out Friday," the heavier-set man responded.

"I don't give a shit what you're doing. It's because you've aggravated her for a year. Your ass is lucky she didn't go to HR." The man with the beard walked around the desk and picked up a soda can. "Do you realize she used to date Jamie on sixth?"

"So what?" the heavier man asked, annoyed.

"So what? He's cut like a brick shit house. He's the perfect man. Hell, I've thought about fucking him," the bearded man teased.

They both laughed for a moment before the heavier one said, "Well, they aren't together now."

"Right, but holy shit Chuck, that's like going from a Porsche to a tricycle. They're two totally different rides."

The bearded man threw the empty can toward a trash container beside the bench where Nothing was hiding. It missed and landed a few feet away from Nothing's face. They both broke out laughing again.

"Can't you be happy for me?" Chuck asked.

"No, no, I can't."

The bearded man walked right in front of Nothing and bent down to pick up the can, causing Nothing to tense, ready to pounce.

He threw it in the trash and paid no mind to Nothing, who remained motionless.

He had not seen him, and Nothing smiled, relieved at his luck.

"But listen, I'm going on my rounds on two. When I get back, I'm gonna tell you how sleeping with you after Jamie is pointless."

"Fuck you, Tyler," Chuck scoffed.

Tyler started away and toward the direction Nothing had entered from. Nothing was glad the taller one was leaving. He had no idea what he'd have done if he had to go one-on-one with him, much less both these men. Tyler disappeared around the corner.

"She's getting drinks and a free meal out of you!" the bearded man yelled out to him as he left.

"I don't know why I bother with that asshole," Chuck grunted.

Nothing needed to be careful. He slid out from under the bench and backtracked to the opening of the hallway that Tyler had gone into. He watched silently as he went from room to room and into the stairwell Nothing had exited from earlier. That only left Chuck between himself and freedom.

Chuck was now seated and watching something on his phone, chuckling to himself. Nothing wasn't paying attention to the sounds. He just needed it to keep him distracted. He walked to the trash bin, retrieved the soda can, and, staying low, went around the front of the desk to the other side. Chuck was lost in whatever he was viewing.

Nothing sat the can down. He planned to use it as a distraction but wouldn't need it. He slowly approached the man with the screwdriver firmly clutched in both hands. He stood directly behind his prey, brought the screwdriver overhead, and swung it down hard at the base of the man's neck with all his might.

It went in several inches and made barely any noise. The man's hands grasped the back of his head, and he spilled out of the chair sideways onto the floor. He thrashed around and reached behind him for the screwdriver protruding from his nape. He wasn't dead, far from it, and Nothing knew he had to do something quickly. The chair collided with the floor. The gurgling voice and the violent noises from him writhing around would eventually bring someone running. Nothing tried to go for his eyes, but the man flailed and knocked his hands away. The man kept trying to get to his feet but slipped.

Their eyes met, and Nothing could see the shock and horror across Chuck's face. He wouldn't have the advantage much longer, so he gripped the man as if hugging him and bit down as hard as he could on the front of his neck. He could feel his teeth go in, and the taste of blood entered his mouth. The man gave a strong push at Nothing, but he was on him at an awkward angle. It was enough. The man went down on his side and was attempting to turn away. Nothing grabbed the screwdriver's handle and began to pull with all his might.

He felt it give, and then it slid out of the man's neck, and Nothing brought it down again, this time into the man's abdomen off slightly to the right. Everywhere the man's hands were, Nothing would stab somewhere else. He didn't have the power to drive it deep, but he was fast and stabbed several times in rapid succession. It wasn't long before the man slowed in his motions, but Nothing kept swinging ferociously. He felt a burn in his throat, and his arm ached, but he kept bringing it down repeatedly. It wasn't until Chuck had stopped moving that Nothing finally paused. He could hear the man breathing and whimpering, but it was shallow and had a rattle to it.

I did it! He won't last much longer. Nothing stood, and he realized he was drenched in the man's blood. He would need a change of clothing from somewhere or at least to get cleaned up. Anyone who saw him would be terrified. He looked at the desk and saw a half-eaten sandwich atop a wrapper. He gathered it with his hand still covered in blood, which left prints all over the food.

"Thank you." He held the sandwich out toward the man dying at his feet. He took a bite of the sandwich and closed his eyes at its taste.

It was the greatest thing he'd ever eaten. He nodded to the man and took off in a sprint toward the glass doors.

Please be open.

When he collided with the left door, it swung open, and Nothing escaped into the night. He was free.

13

Veronica could tell something was wrong as she pulled in. Jennifer rushed to the driver's side door, and her face looked like she had been crying. Veronica turned the key and opened the door.

"What's the matter?"

"We have to go back!"

"Are you crazy? I just had a near-death experience with Nothing. I'll be damned if I ever go back to that house."

"Not that house. I have to go to Charleston. A patient has escaped, I'm on camera, and the police are at my friend's house."

Veronica exited the vehicle. Jennifer was frantic and on the edge of hysterics. She was in worse shape now than when Nothing killed Quentin. She had to think this through: how did she know these things, and what had happened while she was gone?

"Jennifer," Veronica gripped her shoulders, "stop. Listen to me. Slow down; explain what is going on so I can figure out our next steps."

Jennifer nodded and closed her eyes, breathing in and out slowly.

"There you go." Veronica feigned an encouraging tone. "Keep breathing and talk to me. What happened?"

Jennifer told Veronica about the phone call, how angry Tina was, and that the police were on the way there.

"Dylan?" Veronica asked.

"I mean he's just a boy, you don't think—"

Veronica knew there was more to it. He would have needed to have a tremendous growth spurt to fight his way out mano a mano. This whole mess just kept getting dirtier. Maybe she should call Jimmy and have Jennifer dumped in a river somewhere. The thought crossed Veronica's mind about ending this and going back to her life. Just pull her gun out and fire; it would quickly put this whole thing in the rearview mirror.

But Veronica didn't want to hurt Jennifer. She felt sorry for her. She shuddered at the thoughts she had just kicked around. This woman had honestly been concerned for her when she went off to get her car. She had put her blind trust in her, and cared for the little boy who didn't kill his mother. Veronica felt her cheeks heat up. Veronica thought of Ethel and her disappointment. She was ashamed.

There was very little wiggle room in any of this, and with one screw-up, she could have people watching her like a hawk, which could cause her to wind up in jail or worse. No one alive would believe that a monster was responsible for this carnage. They had to do something.

"Hey, are you still in there?" Jennifer broke the silence, causing Veronica to come back to reality.

"Tell me about Tina."

She didn't want to walk into a situation she had no control over, and she needed Jennifer to be as relaxed as possible. This was already a terrible night, and it seemed like it would worsen. Jennifer explained they were college friends who stayed close, that they were in the same profession before Jennifer lost her license. She gave Veronica a summary of Tina's children and spouse and mentioned several times that Tina went to bat for her when her hearings came up for her suspension. Someone's head would roll, and Jennifer feared it would be Tina's.

"Alright, I got this. Let me talk to the police; keep your mouth shut."

Jennifer nodded before looking over and noticing the damage to the back of the Focus. "What happened?"

"Nothing chased me into the trunk." Veronica rubbed the back of her neck as she thought of being crammed inside the tiny space. Jennifer placed her index finger in the puncture holes, then moved to look down inside one.

"How did you get away?"

"Ethel somehow ran it off. It's terrified of her." Veronica smiled and looked around for Ethel. She slowly turned in a complete circle, but Ethel wasn't anywhere to be seen. "Ethel..."

Jennifer came back to where Veronica was standing. "I'm glad you're okay. I was worried."

Veronica felt worse about the thought that crossed her mind a moment ago. "Sorry about the car," Veronica apologized.

"It can be fixed," Jennifer responded, dismissing it with her hand. "I guess I should thank Ethel, though."

Veronica turned around in a circle again. "Huh," she said out loud.

"What is it?" Jennifer asked curiously, looking around herself.

"She's not here," Veronica confessed. They stood momentarily, peering back and forth, which amused Veronica since Jennifer couldn't see Ethel.

"So, what's the plan?" Jennifer interrupted the search.

"We're going to take my car. You drive," Veronica stated as she tossed her the keys. "I need to relax a little. We need to hit the car wash off the Nitro exit to wash this blood off. Then you drive us to Tina's. Remember, let me—"

"Do all the talking. Got it," Jennifer said and walked toward the car.

Veronica kept her phone hooked to the USB charger and let her 80s music playlist shuffle. She glanced over her shoulder into the back once and saw Ethel making faces. She was relieved the old woman was back. She wanted to ask her where she went, but she knew Ethel would get defensive, and she wasn't in the mood to fight. She was gearing up for what would probably be a confrontation with some officers from Charleston. Anytime she'd dealt with them, they acted like complete pricks.

She knew Ethel hated her music, and that brought her a little joy. Ethel had always listened to this God-awful, twangy 60s country, singing along in the car while Veronica rolled her eyes. Veronica would ask to listen to anything else, practically begged, and Ethel's answer was always the same: "When you get your own car, you can listen to whatever you want."

Enjoy "Hold Me Now," Maw Maw.

"I'm sorry," Veronica said as the song ended. Jennifer turned to her gaze. "For your father to die from that... thing, and for you to see it."

"Yeah, Nothing has followed me my entire life. Every decision I've made, all of it seems to go back to it." Jennifer's voice cracked.

"No child deserves to go through that. We'll figure it all out. You just have to trust me okay?"

Ethel scoffed from the backseat, and Veronica pivoted and wrinkled her nose in her direction.

"Hey," Jennifer said as she changed lanes. "What happened between you and Ethel? I know I can't see her, but the tension in this car is unreal. Are you guys fighting?"

"Yes, Veronica," Ethel said. "Go on, tell her."

Veronica was ashamed, but the sharpness of Ethel's words bore under her skin. "I took a man out somewhere secluded and shot him."

Jennifer's hand went to her mouth. "Why?"

"Because he was a pedophile and hurt someone I cared about, and I couldn't do anything else about it."

"It wasn't you're—" Ethel began.

"My place... I shouldn't have done it. I've heard you, Ethel." Veronica turned around to face Ethel.

"There had to be another way. You just took the devil's way out, the easiest."

"We're never going to agree on this. Let's go back to not talking about it, like usual," Veronica said.

They continued the drive in silence. Veronica was thankful not to be behind the wheel. She felt like she'd driven all day and was glad to pass the wheel to Jennifer. It was just after midnight when they pulled off the Nitro exit, and Veronica guided Jennifer to the all-night car wash. She left Jennifer inside as she paid the quarters and used the pressure hose to get as much blood as possible off the car. It took much more money than she thought, and she still wasn't delighted with the results. She would get it into a shop quickly to fix the dent.

When Veronica returned to the passenger seat, Jennifer leaned over before turning the ignition. "I get it, I worked with a lot of children that went through, well, you know. There are a lot of people out there that deserve to die for some of the things they've done."

"And I'd do it again, but damn do I miss my Maw Maw," Veronica sighed.

Ethel rolled her eyes and huffed. "You're both wicked," she hissed.

Veronica sat silently, listening to a Duran Duran song she couldn't recall the title of as they entered the Charleston city limits. Veronica noticed Jennifer gripping the wheel tighter, and every time they passed a street light, she could see the worry on her face.

"It will be fine, just remember what I said," Veronica said.

"You don't know Tina. She can be... a little much," Jennifer warned.

"How are you going to handle this?" Ethel asked from the backseat.

Veronica turned to look at her.

Ethel took one look at her expression and said, "Oh no."

Veronica nodded and smirked.

An exit and a few turns later, they were on Ruffner Avenue near the river, and Jennifer stopped in front of a two-story home with brick and white panels and a stone porch. There were two Charleston police cruisers parked in front of them, along with another that Veronica knew to be an unmarked police car. The officers were probably already irritated by how long they'd had to wait.

The yard was immaculate; there were bushes everywhere of all shapes and sizes. In the front yard was a sign for the landscapers that worked on it. She couldn't make out the name, but a tiny bird was over the lettering. It was in the University colors like most small businesses in the state used.

"I need to mow my yard," Veronica remembered. She turned to her left and smiled at Jennifer. "The boy I used to pay has discovered girls, and well, let's just say he's unreliable."

Jennifer gave a nervous laugh.

"Well, I'll see you inside," Veronica said as she exited the car quickly and started up the walkway. She heard Jennifer let out an audible "Wha—?" as she shut the door. She hurried toward the door and pulled her badge from her pocket.

"Veronica, this is Jennifer's friend. Don't do it," Ethel called out, trying to keep up beside her.

"I got this," Veronica whispered.

"That's what I'm afraid of," Ethel finished.

Veronica went directly up the steps and, without hesitation, opened the door. She started down the hallway and into a living room where a petite woman with short platinum blonde hair stood with three men. One was in a cheap suit and the other two officers were in black uniforms. All eyes in the room turned on her at once.

"Excuse me, but can you—" the woman turned and started toward her, her face red and her eyes wild with anger.

That's got to be Tina, Veronica thought to herself as she flashed her badge to everyone in the room.

"Veronica Carter, Parkersburg PD."

"Parkersburg?" one of the officers said out loud.

Jennifer came trotting in behind her, huffing where she'd run to catch up.

"Where the fuck have you been?" Tina yelled and started in her direction.

Veronica instantly cut her off, her finger pointing in Tina's face.

"Don't," Veronica warned her with as much grit as she could muster.

Tina jerked back. "Jennifer, who is this?"

"What did I just say to you? You've already upset her enough," Veronica barked.

Tina backed away slowly and in the direction of the officers. Her eyes darted back and forth from Veronica to Jennifer. She was making stuttering noises as if trying to find the words to speak.

The man in the suit held his hand out. "Let's relax, okay? Detective Carter, can we calm down for a moment?"

"Calm down? She was screaming at Jenn," Veronica pointed at Tina before addressing her. "She's just as upset as you are. Do you know how awful the ride over here was?"

The man stepped forward and shook his head. "Listen, I know this is a shock, but the last thing we need here is everyone cranked up to eleven. Can we all try and sort this thing out?"

Jennifer stepped around Veronica and spoke up. "I'm Jennifer Simmons. I'm sorry I'm late. We were an hour or so away."

"Jennifer, who is this woman?" Tina demanded.

"This is Veronica, she's a friend of mine. We were together when you called," Jennifer explained, her voice shaky.

"I've never heard of a friend of yours named Veronica, much less a police officer," Tina said.

"Can someone tell us what the hell is going on?" Veronica interjected, trying her best to seem confused by the whole situation.

"Sure," the man in the suit came forward with his hand extended to Veronica. "I'm Detective Mike Green from the Charleston Police Department. Back there," he nodded his head toward the officers, "is Officers Mays and Oakley."

Veronica ignored which was which. She took the detective's hand and gave it a firm shake. It didn't matter what happened now; she had control of the room and knew it. She had to keep everyone uncomfortable and uneasy. That way, everybody would be in a hurry, and there would be fewer questions.

"Green, Mays, Oakley," Veronica repeated, nodding after each one. "So, Tina called Jennifer a little while ago and said a patient escaped? That's all I got out of this mess so far. She used to deal with kids; was it one of her old patients?"

Green's face went cold, and he looked over at Jennifer.

"This isn't just any patient, it's Dylan Jeffrey. You know who that is?"

Veronica opened her mouth slightly and nodded. She had to play this off perfectly, or they would spend their night at the station in North Charleston, and Veronica didn't want that.

"I... I do." Veronica glanced over at Jennifer, trying to maintain the stunned look on her face.

"Exactly," Green continued. "He didn't just kill one person. He killed two. One was Corey Thompson, and the other was Chuck Ferguson. There's actual video of the second murder from the security cameras. So there's no denying what happened."

"Wait," Veronica shook her head for effect, "what was he, nine?"

"Eleven," Green answered.

"An eleven-year-old boy killed two grown men? With what, his bare hands?" Veronica kept eye contact. She even curled her lip up in disbelief.

Green seemed as if he was going to answer her but turned his attention away instead.

Jennifer stumbled over and sat down on a tacky, purple loveseat. "Corey was so nice to me," she placed her head in her hands. She groaned softly and ran her fingers through her hair as she looked at the floor.

"This is your fault!" Tina screamed.

"Can you please...?" Detective Green waved a dismissive hand at Tina.

"Excuse me a moment," one of the officers said and walked past Veronica out the front door. Veronica looked down at his nameplate.

This one was Oakley; she made a quick mental note of that. He smiled at her on his way out the door.

Jennifer looked up, brows furrowed, as she watched him leave the room, and then Veronica's way. "Where's he going?"

"It's no big deal, Jenn. He'll run my name to see if I'm who I say I am. I'd do the same if it were me," Veronica said.

"Yes," Green scratched his neck. "I just want to know why Ms. Simmons went to the hospital. I have video of her arriving and going up the stairs. The cameras on that floor are spotty, so I don't have footage of her up there, but she was inside the building for a long time, over an hour and a half, then I got her on that same camera leaving in a hurry, like a bat out of hell. What happened while you were there?"

Jennifer leaned back. She looked to be on the edge of crying again. "I wanted to surprise Tina at work, and when I got there, it reminded me of my old job. It was heartbreaking thinking of all I've lost, and the road I need to take to get back to it. Corey was a saint, listening to me whine and try to work my way through what I want to do. I talked to him the whole time I was there." Jennifer turned to Tina. "I know you work late, sometimes till eight or so. I was just going to pop in and catch up. I'm sorry."

She's really bad at this. I wouldn't buy this, Veronica thought as she moved beside Jennifer.

"Did you and the deceased talk about anything else? Anything related to the escaped kid?" Green asked, making his way over to them both.

Keep it short and sweet, Veronica said to herself.

"We talked about Tina. He made jokes about how she was hard to work for. He was flirting with me, but I wasn't there for that. He was sweet, though. He told me he was leaving soon and hiking the Appalachian Trail."

Green looked at Tina, his eyes narrowing at her tomato-red face.

"Anything else?" Green asked, writing something in a tiny hardcover pocket notebook.

"He let me inside to leave a note on her desk, but I couldn't find a pen. Her office is pretty bare. He went on about how he couldn't wait to be done with the place."

"He let you in the wing?" Tina seethed. "Are you kidding me? You know better. Or you should, anyway. There are protocols."

"Anything else?" Green tapped his finger on his notebook.

Jennifer leaned forward, and Veronica panicked. *No, for the love of God, tell him no,* she echoed in her mind repeatedly, hoping Jennifer would somehow pick up on her words.

"Dylan's file was open on her desk," Jennifer said, rubbing her palms on her pants. For a psychiatrist she certainly didn't know how to disguise a lie.

Shit. This just got complicated. Veronica was going to have to use a different approach.

"Who was in my files?" Tina's voice practically shook the house.

Detective Green held his hand up at Tina. "One more, and I'll have to do this without you present."

Tina folded her arms across her chest and gave a terse nod.

The detective knelt on one knee to be at eye level with Jennifer. "It was just the two of you? And you didn't see Dylan? Do you know why Corey would have that folder out?"

"No, I saw the folder and caught the name, and Corey tried to steer me away from it. I even went to pick it up, but he stepped in front of me," Jennifer lied. Her voice was very shaky and sounded unsure. If Veronica were conducting this interview, she'd have pounced on her by now.

Oakley entered the room and nodded his head at Green.

"See, told you," Veronica smirked, trying to draw attention away from Jennifer, who seemed like she might crack at any second.

Green stood up and closed his notebook. "Well, this is all interesting. But I have something that's bothering me here." He stood up and started approaching Veronica.

Oh, here it comes. Veronica had done this many times before. The tone of this entire questioning was about to change. He was going to try and get a contradiction or a mistake. Veronica was young and had quickly made detective in her department, but she was seasoned. She wasn't naive, and she certainly wasn't stupid. She played on both sides of the line.

He stopped a foot away from her, and she sized him up. A tall, athletic man who was balding on the crown of his head and wore a cheap suit that looked disheveled. He was clean-shaven across his jawline but had one of those chevron mustaches. It was thick and colored in. He didn't want to be here, she was sure of it, and Tina had probably had this man at his wit's end, but she'd be damned if he was going to slip her up.

"Where do you come in?" he asked her with a smile.

Don't play with me, you smug son of a bitch, Veronica thought.

"So, Ms. Simmons comes down to visit her friend, talks to the orderly, then leaves. Dylan rampages like Michael Myers and brutally murders two people. The odd one out here is you," he pointed at Veronica. "Why is there a detective from Parkersburg here?"

Veronica stepped forward, getting closer to him and smelling some cheap cologne. "I can tell you for a fact that she was with me after she left the hospital."

"Why is that?" Green pressured, his tone becoming harsh.

Veronica pursed her lips and said, "We were fucking. Are you happy with that answer now that you just had me out her to her friend? Would you like me to call her other friends in Baltimore and let them know, too?"

Green's face flushed. Jennifer could be heard audibly sucking in air, and everyone else grew deadly silent. *Gotcha.*

"Oh, Veronica, for heaven's sake!" Ethel said from the corner.

Tina looked at Jennifer in shock. "I... I didn't know."

No one said anything else. They just exchanged glances out of the corners of their eyes. Veronica had accomplished what she'd set out to do. She had made everyone extremely uncomfortable, and Jennifer probably wouldn't utter another word till they left. The focus had shifted, and now anything Veronica said would drive the narrative. She knew the police would have to be easy with her. She was one of them. But now? They had to tread extremely carefully. If he pushed too hard, Veronica could act offended and lose her shit.

She still needed to exercise caution; she certainly didn't want this man looking at her too closely, but she didn't want to be overly friendly; that would make him suspicious too. So her following words had to be the ones that shut this entire thing down.

"We met," Veronica paused and rubbed her forehead, "on a dating app. She was from here originally."

"Um, Charleston?"

"Oak Hill, if I'm not mistaken." Veronica knew she wasn't mistaken. Jennifer had told her that on the way to the apartment. "She lost her dad early on in life, and we clicked over that. We've talked almost every day for the past couple of weeks. She was going to visit her friend and see me in the morning, but she called, and we met up." Veronica looked away from him. "This was our first time face-to-face. We planned on spending the evening together, and I was going to show her around Parkersburg tomorrow. It's what took us so long to get here, we were..." She let it hang for a moment. "Busy."

Green looked over at Tina, who was speechless and ghastly white.

"Aunt J is a lez bean?" came a voice from off to the left.

"I said *lesbian*, dummy," came another.

Veronica looked over to the hallway that led to the bedrooms, if she had to guess, and standing there were two young boys. The one in the pajamas looked to be around seven, and the tall one in shorts and no shirt had to be twelve or so. The older one was smirking, and they were both staring at Veronica.

"Boys! What did I say?" Tina roared and stormed at them. "Terry, can you watch the fucking kids like I asked!" she shouted around the corner as the boys jetted away from her. She turned back around and held her hands up. "I'm sorry about that," she said in Veronica's direction.

Veronica shook her head and grinned as if to tell her it was all right. She was practically doing cartwheels in her mind. She'd won. She pointed to the corner away from everyone, and Green followed her. She wanted to be out of earshot.

"Officer Oakley, could you take Ms. Simmons and Doctor Morgan outside and get all their contact information for me, please?"

"Can do, Detective," Oakley acknowledged and led the ladies back down the hall, leaving Veronica, Green, and Mays in the room alone.

Ethel stayed within earshot of Veronica, but Mays caught her attention. He had his hands on his hips, but she could swear that his eyes were following Ethel. That was ridiculous, but she was almost positive it was the case.

She turned back to Green and whispered, "Listen, you have a long night ahead of you. You've got paperwork and forensics to deal with, but Jenn and I are both tired. The place we are staying at is across the river in Ohio. We have a hell of a drive ahead of us. I will give you my card, and you should call me tomorrow afternoon. Both of us will be right there when you need us. She can stay at my place for a couple of days."

"You know I'll need a formal statement, maybe a couple of follow-up questions. I won't need to put anything in there about the two of you after if you need that kept quiet." He pinched the bridge of his nose.

"The media is gonna have a field day with this," Veronica stated.

"This will go national. We have everyone in two counties looking for the kid. It's gonna make us look bad. Especially if we can't find him." He shook his head in disbelief. "I sure as hell don't want to be on 20/20."

"How bad is it?" Veronica whispered to Green. She decided to fish for information, to see if he'd offer her anything. They were starting to be pretty friendly, after all.

"He's a psychopath. He snuck around like a ninja and killed the Ferguson guy at the door. Never seen anything like it. I'd say he stabbed him forty times." Green tilted his head, and his eyes narrowed. "Guess this isn't how you wanted your first date to go, huh?"

Veronica smiled and stalled as she thought over how to respond. She'd been around enough people to get a pretty decent read on them, and she felt like she could play this up by watching Detective Green in case she needed more information from him. They would find

Quentin's body, opening up an entirely new level of problems, so she needed to be on his good side.

She scanned him up and down one last time, and noticed he wasn't wearing a wedding ring. Given his age and the fact he went so far as to dye his mustache, she thought he had loved and lost. She would try to find a way in with that.

"I use that app mostly for booty calls. I don't have the time or patience for love." She laughed. "Had a serious relationship once, and she couldn't stand me being a shield. The long hours, court dates... Ran off with a girl she met at work."

"Oh," he sucked in air. "That's rough. I know that feeling."

"Had the wedding planned out and everything. Left me a few weeks before our trip to Vegas."

"Be thankful you didn't go through with it. I was stupid enough to do it twice," he admitted.

"Being honest with you here, I mean, this girl's great and all, but she has a lot of baggage. I was gonna spend the night with her, maybe tomorrow, and then I was planning on losing her number. I mean, I can't now until this whole thing blows over, but this woman complains about losing her job constantly. It's annoying."

"WHAT IN THE WORLD ARE YOU DOING!" Ethel yelled beside her.

"You talked to her. Does she seem like the most stable person to you? I want this one out of my life as soon as possible," Veronica continued.

"YOU'RE AWFUL, VERONICA LYNN CARTER!" Ethel screamed, pausing after each word.

"I get it," Green said, nodding.

Ethel pointed at Detective Green. "AND YOU'RE AWFUL TOO!"

Officer Mays chuckled before pretending to cough. Veronica had noticed it; he could see Ethel, and hear her, too. She was almost positive. He was looking right at her.

"How many more people have to die? Jennifer's dad, Dylan's mom, his uncle, and you know somehow that monster is responsible for those men dying. We need to get out of here!" Ethel threw her hands up. "I'm going outside!"

Veronica watched Officer Mays out of the corner of her eye. He took his hands off his hips, and his eyes widened. It was laid to rest right there if she had any inkling of a doubt.

"Do you need anything else tonight?" she asked Green. Her anxiety spiked knowing Officer Mays could see her grandmother's spirit.

"Nah, I'll talk to Doctor Morgan and get out of here. I need to get back to the facility and wait for the officers who went and told the families." Green took his little notebook and tapped Veronica's shoulder. "Good to meet you, Carter."

"Likewise," she smiled.

Green strolled out of the room, and Veronica stood with Mays, who was walking over to her. He was a young man, short and stocky, with a faded haircut. He stopped right beside her and whispered.

"I have no idea what happened tonight, but what kind of monster was she talking about?"

Veronica was going to play dumb; she was going to pretend not to know what he was talking about, but it would be pointless. He'd heard Ethel, and he knew, and if he wanted to, he could probably convince Green she was lying.

"I have no idea. I couldn't see it."

"Couldn't or didn't?" He scratched his cheek and raised an eyebrow. His steel blue eyes barely blinked.

"Couldn't. It tried to get at me and I hid in the trunk of a car. The spirit is my grandmother. She scared it off." Veronica folded her arms and leaned against the lavender-colored wall.

"I've never heard of anything like that." Mays looked away as if he was trying to figure out what she was talking about.

Veronica shoved his shoulder to snap him out of it. She whispered, "How can you see her?"

"Who?" Mays seemed at a loss.

"Ethel, my grandmother," Veronica asked, irritated.

"I got the broach from Wallace. You?" Mays responded nonchalantly.

"Who the hell is Wallace?" Veronica had never heard the name before.

Mays looked stunned. "How do you not know Wallace?"

"I don't know shit," Veronica confessed, her hands outstretched.

"Listen, check out the website West Virginia Weird," Mays leaned in and whispered.

"What is that?"

"We need to get outside, or they're going to wonder what's going on. Check the site. You can contact Wallace there." Mays moved away from her.

"Wait, I don't—" Veronica started.

"You can catch me later, but you need to talk to Wallace right now. Find out what kind of monster that is."

And just like that, he was in the hallway heading for the door.

Veronica said goodbye to the officers and leaned on the hood of her Nissan. She watched as Jennifer told Tina she would call her later. They hugged, and Jennifer started her slow walk back toward the car, a scowl on her face when she looked at Veronica. Veronica smiled at her, but Jennifer's face turned a deeper scarlet.

"Nice to meet you, Tina!" Veronica called out, waving, but Tina shut the door without responding.

"Do you want me to drive?" Jennifer asked hatefully as she approached.

"I think I can handle it," Veronica said as she got in the car. Veronica started the engine and pulled away from the house. She rubbed her hand over her tired eyes and said, "I thought that went well."

14

They were on the interstate for a few miles before Veronica spoke. "Do either of you have something you want to say?"

Jennifer had been sitting in the passenger seat, slumped with her knees against the dash and arms folded. Her brow was practically against her eyes. Veronica wanted Jennifer to talk to her so she didn't fall asleep. She was exhausted. Veronica had been up since the night before and hadn't slept well then, and her body was telling her that it was heading for a shutdown.

"No, I don't," Jennifer huffed.

"Seems like you do," Veronica teased.

After a brief moment, she blurted, "I can't believe you said that about me."

"What? I had to make sure no one suspected you. You want to go to jail?"

"You told everyone there I was a lesbian, and we were fooling around, and... and... Do you know what you've done?" Jennifer waved her arms frantically.

"I'm sure you're going to tell me," Veronica said.

"Tina will text me and call me a thousand times a day now asking what happened, how we met, how is it being with a woman? I can't lie like this. I'm not good at it." Jennifer looked out the window and flicked her wrist at Veronica as if she wanted her to disappear.

"You did great back there. You looked like a lesbian that had just been outed to the world. I, for one, was proud of you," Veronica said, placing a hand over her heart.

"I'm glad you can just joke about this, but I'm going to screw up somewhere, and she will know. I'm gonna get caught."

There was legitimate panic in Jennifer's voice. Veronica would have to calm her down before telling her the great news. "Didn't you go to college? What did you do there?" Veronica hit the rumble strips and jerked the wheel.

"I studied and graduated." Jennifer tried to express pride in that statement, but her voice cracked and made her sound silly.

"So, you were boring," Veronica joked. "Listen, in your profession, you talk to people and help them with trauma; in mine, I deal with people all day and learn how to manipulate a situation."

"That's not your job at all. You solve crimes and help people. Well, at least that's what you are supposed to do."

"Right, but one of the tools in my kit is the ability to read the room and the people in it," Veronica explained, winking at her. This was the most fun she'd had. She didn't mean to taunt her the way she was, but she needed an outlet with everything that had happened tonight, and driving Jennifer crazy was helping.

"Jesus Christ," Jennifer slapped her leg in distaste.

Ethel huffed from the backseat.

"Don't do that," Veronica said.

"Don't do what?" Jennifer asked, bewildered.

"Say the Lord's name in vain; Ethel hates it." Veronica shook her head.

Jennifer stared at Veronica, her mouth open in shock. "Are you serious right now?"

"I am. If she knew you could hear her, she'd be all over your ass right now." Veronica clicked on her turn signal and took the Cross Lanes exit.

"Where are we going?"

Veronica pointed at the dash. "I need gas."

"I just don't understand how you can be so happy about all this."

"It all worked out." Veronica turned toward the nearest station, a deserted-looking BP.

"For you, sure, but for me?" Jennifer exited the car once they stopped by the pumps.

"Look," Veronica taunted, getting out with her, "if it bothers you that badly, wait about three days and tell her I was too rough with you or said really crazy shit in bed. Who cares as long as I gave you an alibi? Where are you going?"

"I have to pee." Jennifer turned and stormed away.

Veronica smiled, walked to the pump, and put her debit card in. She selected the middle grade and grabbed the hose. She sighed as Ethel approached. Veronica squeezed the handle and began fueling the car.

"Quit picking on her," she ordered. "You're acting like a schoolgirl."

"Can you actually remember that far back?" Veronica nudged at her, her arm going through.

"Oh, now it's my turn. What in the world has gotten into you? You're acting a fool."

"I know you're upset, but you don't deal with people like that daily. I learned how to play this game. Jennifer would crack under interrogation. I needed to keep that man away from her." Veronica turned around in a circle to make sure no one was in earshot to hear her talking to Ethel.

"It was tacky, and rude." Ethel folded her arms.

"I did what needed to be done, I didn't mean it," Veronica assured her.

Ethel looked away with concern. "Does your job..."

"Does my job what?" Veronica gave a fake laugh trying to lighten the mood.

"Do you have to lie like that with your work?" Ethel asked.

Veronica knew where this was going, she'd known Ethel all her life, and could read her better than anyone. She was wondering if her job had made her into the heinous person she felt she was.

"Don't be like that. I'm happy," Veronica proclaimed, pulling the hose out and placing it back.

"Why?" Jennifer asked as she neared.

"Because I got us a lead on figuring out Nothing, and whenever you stop acting like a whiny shit, we're gonna get to work." Veronica took the receipt from the front of the pump and smiled. Jennifer's eyes lit up.

"What happened?"

"Are we still dating?" Veronica smirked.

"Will you stop?" Ethel barked.

Veronica felt utter glee from watching Jennifer grind her teeth. It was time, though. It had gone on long enough, and she was pleased with the annoyances she'd caused them both.

"Alright, I'm done. So, you remember the officer in the room with us?"

"The one that went outside with me," Jennifer asked, getting back in the Nissan.

"The other one," Veronica said as she put her seatbelt on.

"What about him? He didn't say anything."

"He could see Ethel," Veronica announced.

"What?" Ethel and Jennifer shouted at the same time.

"He heard her too, and asked what monster attacked me." Veronica headed back toward the interstate.

"How is that possible?" Jennifer asked while looking in the backseat.

"How should I know? He got tickled when Ethel called me awful. He was staring right at her. He wasn't even hiding it. I at least try to pretend she isn't there, you know?" Veronica admitted. Jennifer nodded in agreement. "If I'm staring off into the distance or talking to myself, who knows what people would think? He saw me glaring at him, so he approached me after you guys left the room." Veronica realized how hard it was to ignore Ethel. It took time to hone that skill, especially if Ethel was loud or angry.

"Wait," Jennifer held up her hand, "why did she call you awful?"

"I told Detective Green that I was using you for sex." Veronica glanced over and then slapped Jennifer's leg. She recoiled slightly.

"What the hell is wrong with you?" Jennifer's hateful tone reemerged.

"Well if it would keep you both safe," Ethel said from behind Veronica.

"Thank you, but something about Dylan is really bothering me. I can tell you right now this whole thing stinks. All this time, he stays dormant, and then," Veronica snapped her fingers, "the night you show up?"

Jennifer leaned against the armrest, her hand on her chin.

"So," Veronica continued, "Dylan sneaks around the hospital like an assassin and kills two grown men? Green told me he massacred them. Does that sound like the little boy that you talked to yesterday? The one who confessed to killing his teacher and watching his mother die? No. You know who that sounds like?"

"Nothing," Jennifer answered, her eyebrows lowered. "You don't think...?"

"This whole time, we have been running around and taking loss after loss, and I hate to lose. Now I know I can see other ghosts. I know other people can see them too. I'm not alone. Mays didn't know what Nothing was, but he knew someone who might. Maybe he'd know how to stop it."

"So what's the plan?" Jennifer asked, her smile returning.

"Do you have your phone on you?" Veronica asked.

Jennifer looked at her perplexed and reached down in the center console to retrieve her phone.

"Go to the website West Virginia Weird."

Jennifer pulled up her browser and typed it in the address bar. Veronica hadn't turned her music on, so the clicking of her typing and the hum of the road were the only sounds.

The page came up instantly, a dull brown color with a few old photos and a white menu bar on the side. It looked like a page created back in the America Online days.

"This is archaic. It's hideous. I can barely read any of this." Veronica saw out of the corner of her eye that Jennifer had brought her phone practically to her face. "West Virginia Weird, it says here *everything that goes bump in the night in the Mountain State could kill you.*" She looked up to Veronica. "No shit."

She went to the very bottom of the page, and beside a copyright of 2008 was the phrase, "*There are no such things as coincidences.*"

"That's cute," Veronica said as she shook her head.

"It looks like one of those travel fan pages but with ghosts," Jennifer said.

"Anything stand out?" Veronica asked, trying to glance over.

Jennifer narrated everything she read. "The menus have all sorts of weird selections. There are ones for ghosts, vampires, the undead, and werewolves. What the hell is a *Snipe*?" Jennifer shrugged.

"Just keep reading off the menu; maybe something will click."

Jennifer nodded and kept going. "Seer, muck, snallygaster—any of this mean anything to you?"

Veronica shook her head.

"I'm going to skip to the bottom. Maybe there is a help section?" Veronica glanced in the rearview at Ethel, watching over Jennifer's shoulder.

"The last thing on the menu is *reward*. It's in yellow text instead of white."

"Yeah, click that."

"Wealth beyond your wildest dreams if you can bring about the demise of Nadine." Jennifer laughed. "Is this some kind of joke? I think Mays was playing with you."

Veronica chilled at Jennifer's words. She glanced over and caught eyes with the doctor, and something on her face must've given away exactly how serious the moment had become.

"What's wrong? Someone, you know?" Jennifer asked.

Ethel's eyes had grown large, too. Veronica looked at her and said, "I know, Ethel."

"Who is Nadine?" Jennifer pressed.

"*There are no such things as coincidences,*" Veronica responded. "Can you contact anyone on there?"

"There's an email address right here beside the rhyme."

"Send them a message," Veronica said.

"What do you want me to say?" Jennifer brought the phone up to her face and clicked the blue link to bring up her email client.

"We have information on Nadine." Veronica nodded, but she didn't look confident in the slightest.

"Do we?" Jennifer asked doubtfully.

"Maybe, but I need to meet up with Wallace."

Jennifer nodded and began typing, reciting as she went. "We have information about Nadine. Need to meet." She looked at Veronica for approval, and when she nodded, Jennifer hit send.

The rest of the trip back to the apartment could have been more exciting. Veronica turned her 80s music on and didn't speak. What the hell were they getting into? This day had started with an age sucking woman, and was ending with her too. This had to be connected. Jennifer hadn't spoken, just played with her phone, and that was fine by Veronica. She needed to think. It wasn't long before they had crossed the river back into Ohio.

"Bed or couch?" Veronica asked her when they finally pulled into the apartment.

"Couch is fine," Jennifer responded sleepily.

"You got a change of clothes?"

"No, I keep some at Tina's, but I forgot to get them."

"There's a Walmart three miles away. In the morning, I'll grab some stuff," Veronica said.

Jennifer nodded and exited the car. She pulled out a cigarette, lit it, and stood by the doorway. As Veronica passed by her to enter, she stopped.

"I'll grab the extra blanket and pillow, and they'll be on the couch. I'm going to bed. I'll see you in the morning."

"Night," Jennifer called out to her.

Veronica didn't respond. The whole Nadine situation had thrown her for a complete loop. She'd told Jennifer that it was *another monster*, but hadn't elaborated. Surprisingly, Jennifer hasn't asked further.

She went back into the living room and tossed the extra blanket and pillow on the couch. Veronica went to the bedroom and threw herself onto the mattress, not bothering to disrobe. She had no time for reflection on Nadine, Nothing, or anything else. She was exhausted and almost instantly drifted off to sleep.

Jennifer could smell coffee when she opened her eyes. She sat up quickly and started to panic because the place was unrecognizable. It was a few seconds before she recalled the events that led her here. She bent forward, picked up her Ravens shirt, and put it on. She rubbed the sleep from her eyes, stood, and stretched. The couch had been comfortable, but she missed her bed. It had taken her years to find the perfect mattress. She was very particular about the lack of firmness in a mattress. She had to sink into a bed before she was happy.

She folded the blanket, sat it back on the edge of one of the cushions, and followed the smell that had brought her out of slumber into the kitchen. A pot was being warmed in a coffee maker, and mugs were sitting beside the pot. The mugs hadn't been there the day before; Veronica must have laid them out for her. She couldn't turn down coffee, so she snatched one up and poured herself a cup. She walked over to the refrigerator and opened it. There weren't many things inside: beer, some condiments, and a carton of milk. She pulled it out and checked the date. It was two weeks out, so this had been purchased recently.

She added some to her coffee, put the milk away, and began to drink. Her stomach wasn't pleased; she was hungry and couldn't recall when she ate last. She would fetch Veronica and ask if they could get food together. Somewhere they could sit and talk. To say she was concerned about Veronica was an understatement. It was a morbid professional curiosity. Veronica seemed to thrive in chaotic situations. She was ruthless in her teasing last night after a stressful situation with the police. Jennifer found that alarming. She was concerned Veronica might have a narcissistic personality disorder.

Don't do that, she told herself. *You do this every time with friends, boyfriends, and anyone you meet. Don't analyze her, just be her friend.*

They could have breakfast together, and Jennifer could keep the prying questions out of the conversation. Let Veronica offer up things if she wanted to. She was, after all, trying to help her. They needed to sit down and plan whatever was next on the agenda. She went to the hall to see if Veronica's door was open. It was, but she wasn't in there, and she wasn't in the bathroom. Jennifer walked to the living room and peered out from behind the blinds. Veronica's car was gone, so she figured she'd gone to purchase a change of clothes for the two of them.

She took another drink of her coffee and went over to the counter to retrieve her phone. She held it up to her face to unlock it and noticed it was 10:50 AM. She'd way overslept, as she was usually up at the crack of dawn. She must have been worn completely down.

"She should have woken me up," Jennifer said to herself.

Her notifications said she'd missed two calls from a Charleston number, four calls from Tina, and three texts from Tina. Of course, she was going to blow her phone up. Tina loved her unconditionally; she was the only friend who stayed with Jennifer throughout the years. Tina was a decent child psychologist, but she was a massive drama queen in her personal life. She would want to know everything about her newfound relationship.

It was the last thing listed that caught her eye, though. She even held her breath when she saw it. She had an email from West Virginia Weird. It was received at seven that morning, so they responded fairly quickly. She tapped on it.

We have to meet today. You need to be here before 5:30. I know what it is. Included below was an address; she long-pressed and copied it and opened her map application. It was an address in the small town of Fairlea, a few minutes from White Sulphur Springs. Veronica wasn't going to like this at all. The travel distance was three hours, and if she'd learned anything from these ETAs, you must add to that quite a bit. She wondered if they would be able to go today. Could they possibly make it before six with everything they had to do? Jennifer sat back on the couch, returned to her coffee, and waited for Veronica.

Jennifer wondered what Ethel thought about the whole situation. She wished she could talk to her. She wished she could see her. The gift that Veronica was given was special. Jennifer would give anything to see her mother and father again, to talk to the ones she'd lost throughout the years. Jennifer was an atheist, but after last night, she knew there was an afterlife, and her entire perception of reality had changed.

Jennifer worried for Dylan; could Nothing be guiding him? Could they be coming for her? She was hoping they could get some answers.

It wasn't long before she heard the car pull up, and she sat her empty cup on the coffee table. Veronica opened the door with some bags in her hand and laid them on the counter.

"Got some cheap underwear, socks, a Marshall t-shirt, and some pants. I looked at your clothes before I left. The sizes should be the same," Veronica stated.

"Thanks, you didn't have to do that," Jennifer said.

"It's no problem. We can't go around stinking," Veronica sneered.

"Wallace emailed back, said he could help, and we needed to meet up with him," Jennifer said with much less enthusiasm than she meant to.

Veronica's eyes lit up. "Oh, yeah? You don't sound overjoyed."

"We have to drive to Fairlea," Jennifer told her as she shook her head.

Veronica's shoulders dropped. "That's in Greenbrier, isn't it?"

"Yup, three hours away, and he said we had to be there by 5:30." Jennifer could feel the heaviness in the air after she said it. They would have to hurry and be in the car all day. And who knew if it would be worth their time?

"This day just keeps getting better and better," Veronica sighed.

"What happened?" Jennifer didn't like where this was going.

"Green called me; they found Quentin," Veronica told her, getting some things out of one of the bags on the counter.

"Is that bad?" Jennifer knew what was coming couldn't be good by the look on Veronica's face.

"I have a bad feeling. I figured he would think Dylan did it, but there was something about how he talked to me. I think he may have pinged your phone. He's hiding something," Veronica admitted.

Jennifer stood. "Okay, so that's bad?"

"Very. I had your car taken out of here this morning," Veronica said.

Jennifer started to panic. "Why?"

"Relax, I had Jimmy pick it up; he's taking it to get the damage fixed. It will look good as new," Veronica dismissed.

"Yeah, but why?"

"Nothing busted the taillight, and there's no way I got all the pieces picked up off that driveway. I need to start covering our asses here. This could get bad," Veronica told her as she started removing tags off the clothes she bought.

"Veronica," Jennifer paused, she kept her tone serious.

Veronica widened her eyes, then smiled and said, "Jennifer...?"

"What do you do?" Jennifer asked.

Veronica looked at her with her eyebrows lowered. "What do you mean? I'm a detective."

"No," Jennifer walked toward her. "What do you do?"

"I don't understand—" Veronica laughed.

"Here we are in an apartment, away from prying eyes. You can get a person to come out in the middle of the night to retrieve a car from a murder scene, and you can get that same person to fix that car under the radar." Jennifer stopped short of her. "What do you do?"

Veronica's smile faded and was replaced by a frown. "Jennifer, I don't know you very well."

"No, you don't."

"That isn't a question you should be asking me," Veronica

warned. She stepped forward, inches from Jennifer's face. "I'm going to take a shower, then you are. Then we will meet up with Wallace or whoever runs that shitty website."

Jennifer looked away. She didn't understand if this was a threat, but it felt like one. She knew better than to challenge her, so Jennifer stepped back.

"Can we get food on the way?"

Veronica walked past her. "I was going to suggest it."

They both took their showers and left in Veronica's car with their hair still wet. They stopped and got some burgers before hitting the interstate, and Jennifer indulged in a strawberry milkshake.

Veronica hardly spoke on the trip; the only thing she asked from Jennifer was the address. She punched it into her phone and then put on her 80s music. Jennifer sat silently and read the West Virginia Weird website, going from menu selection to menu selection. The wording in each description was littered with spelling errors. She had no idea who wrote any of this, but when they got there, she honestly thought about offering to fix it for them.

She was going to read the seer entry to Veronica, but when she looked over at her, she thought better of it. Veronica looked angry, and the furrowing of her brow convinced Jennifer not to bother. A seer, according to the website, was someone who could communicate with the dead. Some spirits never take their doors to the afterlife, or aren't offered, if the ghost still has unfinished business to attend to. The door part confused Jennifer. Did they mean an actual door? The seer's level of power grows as they get older. Some are just gifted and need a trinket to see a spirit; some can see them and not communicate, and very few can see them and speak to them. Jennifer found that fascinating. Veronica was somewhat unique; if what she read was true, not many could do what she could.

Jennifer scoured every entry, but there were no invisible mass murderers mentioned in any passages. She felt disheartened; first, because Veronica seemed increasingly irritated as they drove, and second, what if there was no way to stop it? Jennifer sat her phone down and leaned the passenger seat back. She wondered if she had bothered Ethel by tilting back and then dismissed it. She closed her eyes, and the next thing she knew, Veronica was poking her.

"We're here," she said grimly.

Jennifer pulled the seat upright and looked out. They were coming up a dirt road. The only thing in front of her was a house coming into view.

"Is this house out here by itself?"

"We're a few miles outside of Fairlea. This is the first house I've seen in about a mile."

Jennifer rubbed her eyes and shivered slightly. The car was cold, and "Purple Rain" was blaring from the speakers. She could see two figures off in the distance, coming off a porch and moving through a yard, but she couldn't make heads or tails of them. She turned to Veronica.

"How do you want to handle this?"

"I haven't thought that far ahead," Veronica whispered.

There was a bitterness to her words. Jennifer wondered if confronting her had anything to do with it. It shouldn't have. There was no confrontation, and there was no argument. Jennifer conceded all ground the second Veronica became even slightly hostile. Surely she wasn't still mad about it?

They passed a no trespassing sign and then a no solicitation sign before reaching the end of the road. Veronica pulled the car up in front of the house. It was like something out of an old movie, with a sweeping white wooden porch, and two stories. The massive yard stretched for what seemed like forever back to a treeline off in the distance. In the front yard was a clothesline, but there was nothing on it, and Jennifer could make out an old Chevrolet 3100 truck, rusted, with weeds growing out of it, under the shade of one of the largest oak trees she'd ever seen.

"Wow, I think that's a '53," Jennifer exclaimed excitedly.

"How would you know that?" Veronica scoffed.

"I dated a guy years ago, a real antique car freak. I tried to get into it so we would have something to do together," Jennifer explained as she pressed up against her window, looking attentively.

"How'd that go?"

"He was so grateful, when his ex got a divorce he dumped me to go back to her," Jennifer said.

"Wow. Sounds like a real winner."

Jennifer nodded. "I know how to pick 'em."

Veronica smiled, but her tone was serious when she said, "Listen, I see rocking chairs on the porch. If I hear the Deliverance banjo when I get out of this car, we are getting the hell out of here."

They shared a laugh, even if Veronica's seemed forced, and exited the vehicle. Two men stood off to the side of the house, and Jennifer could finally get a good look at them once she approached. One was an elderly black man, and a much younger white man, younger than Jennifer by the looks of it. The old man looked in their direction as Jennifer waved nervously.

"Well, it took you long enough. It's almost six!" the old man complained as he took his fedora off and wiped the sweat from his brow with a cloth.

"It's a long trip," Veronica retorted. "Are you Wallace?"

He nodded.

"Well, we should hurry. We ain't got long; follow me," the old man called back, already walking away from them. He shuffled slowly around the right side of the house, the younger man in tow.

"Where are we going?" Jennifer asked as she and Veronica followed close behind them.

"Somewhere we can talk," the old man said, continuing along the house. "I have just the place."

"I read your entire site," Jennifer called out to him.

"I didn't make it." He pointed in the direction of the younger man. "He did."

Jennifer looked over at him. He couldn't have been more than twenty. He had a light brown goatee, a shade darker than his hair, which instantly caught her attention. It was short on the front and sides but dangerously flirting with becoming a mullet if he let it keep going. He wasn't muscular; he was chubby and tall. He wore dried, mud-encrusted work boots, jeans, and a West Virginia Mountaineer shirt.

He looked over at her and nodded. "Actually, my brother made it years ago. I don't update it. We just use it to try and find Nadine."

"Quiet," the old man ordered as they went around the corner. "We'll get to her later."

On the side of the house was an open double door into the cellar; Jennifer could see the steps descending into the darkness. Her anxiety was starting to rise. What had they gotten into? Did he want them to go into the basement?

"Well, in you go. Like I said, we have to hurry," the old man commanded as he waved his hand at the stairs.

Veronica started laughing. "Are you crazy? I'm not going in there."

"Why's that?" the old man questioned, a hint of offense in his voice.

"Because I don't know you. I don't know what's down there. I don't know what any of this is."

Wallace started laughing, and a little spit came from his mouth. He was wearing a top denture, Jennifer could tell. His teeth were too straight and too white. He didn't have a bottom in. His lip curled under, and his chin was too high. He wiped his mouth with the cuff of his shirt.

"Are you serious, woman? I have to sit down to pee 'cause it takes 30 minutes or so till I'm finished. Even then, when I stand up, there's a good chance I'll still piss all over the place." He pointed to the other man who was standing with his hands on his hips. "And the boy, well, he's a pussy. The other day, he fell off the porch and started crying that he thought he'd broke his leg."

There was an audible "Uh" from the young man, who looked away nervously.

"What?" The old man continued. "Ain't no reason to be embarrassed; they ain't here looking to court. They want answers, and I got 'em. Now, are we going to stand out here and waste the little time we got, or are we going to get this show on the road?"

Jennifer watched as eyes darted between the four of them. They'd come a long way, and there was no reason to stop now.

"I'll go first," she told the group, and descended the stairs. She could hear Wallace say, "That a girl," behind her. It wasn't long before she reached the concrete floor. Her eyes took a second to adjust.

Her heart sank. There was no great library, no maps of the state, and no trap waiting for them. It was one of the biggest disappointments of her life. She had no idea what she expected when she descended those stairs, but this was far from it. She looked back to Wallace.

"Well, let's get started," the old man said.

15

"You can call me Wally. I don't like when folks call me Wallace," he said as he made his way slowly to the chair in the middle of the room. He paused momentarily, then pointed to the young man leaning against the wall. "That's Cliff, he hates his name too. Goes by Allen; that's his middle name. I think they're both shit, and he should have just picked a new one altogether."

Allen chuckled and shook his head. Jennifer watched as the old man made his way across the room. His posture was terrible. He was bent forward to the point he probably needed a cane. She envisioned he'd taken a header a time or two and wondered if it was from years of hard labor or a medical condition. His clothes were baggy; he was thin and frail. He couldn't have weighed more than one hundred and fifty pounds, which looked highly unhealthy for a man of his height. Jennifer started forward to help him, and Allen waved his hand back and forth at her as if to tell her no.

He shuffled along slowly and Jennifer glanced at Veronica and smiled. Veronica had been irritable on the way over, and Jennifer could feel the tension. She kept her arms folded defensively and tapped her foot slowly. She had a scowl, and everything about her

203

screamed that she would rather be anywhere else. Veronica didn't smile back; she just slowly looked away and back toward Wally.

The chair Wally was walking around and the wood around the base were covered in reddish-brown spots. Jennifer couldn't make it out from the lack of light, but she could swear it was dried blood. There were no fixtures on the cellar's walls, just the small cabinet beside Allen and the sun coming in from the open hatch they came down. They hadn't turned the light above on, so Jennifer guessed it didn't work, or no one thought about it.

The room was bare except for the single chair, and she couldn't be sure but thought that the legs were bolted into the concrete. She wanted to step forward and take a closer look at the stains, but she didn't want to offend her hosts. Allen had already waved her back once.

Wally stopped and turned back toward Jennifer. "You the seer?"

Jennifer pointed to Veronica.

"How powerful?" he asked.

"What do you mean?" Veronica shifted as she answered.

"How many can you see, can you mess with 'em? Do you need to be holding something to see 'em?"

"I can see my grandmother and one other. I can talk to them, and I don't need any items." Veronica answered shortly. Jennifer worried that Veronica would walk away from this situation. She kept eyeballing the stairs.

His eyes widened. "Woo, you big time, ain'tcha girl?"

"So I hear," Veronica said.

Wally started back toward the chair and began to pull down his suspenders. He had a bit of trouble pulling them from his shoulders. Once he got both sides removed, his pants fell to his ankles. He looked back and motioned Allen forward.

Allen walked over to him, and Wally put his hand on his arm and stepped out of one leg of his pants and then the other. He was barefoot, so the only clothes he had left on were his boxers, a button-up blue shirt, and his hat. Jennifer couldn't tell how old his outfit was, but it needed to be replaced at least a decade ago.

"Why are you taking off your clothes? I can't speak for her," Veronica pointed a thumb at Jennifer, "but I don't swing that way, old man."

"Don't want 'em ruined," Wally replied as he patted Allen on the back.

Allen walked back to the spot he had occupied before and leaned against the wall.

Jennifer leaned over to Veronica and whispered, "Is he going to get—"

Wally bent and removed his boxers with his back to them, exposing his buttocks.

"Yes, he's getting naked," Jennifer finished.

"Old Timer, while I appreciate your... confidence, I don't think Jennifer's heart can take the—Whoa!" Veronica turned her head slightly as Wally turned around, exposing himself to them both.

"Stop, it ain't like you haven't seen a naked man before. And the only woman to lay her hand on me was Nora, and you ain't Nora." Wally was getting winded, and his voice was resentful at Veronica's suggestion.

"I've seen a few before, and I am not a fan." Veronica glared at Jennifer, who couldn't tear her eyes away from the man unbuttoning his shirt and staring back at them.

"You one of those?" Wally chuckled, his eyebrow raised curiously.

"I am. That gonna be a problem?" Veronica stated and looked back at him.

"Not at all. Someone gave me a videotape back in the 80s of two women together." He let the shirt fall at his feet, reached behind him to the arm of the wooden chair, and guided himself into a seated position. The last thing he removed was his fedora, which he threw on the pile before him.

"How'd that go?" Veronica's words dripped with contempt.

"Bad. Scared the shit out of me if I'm being honest." Wally scratched his chest; the hair was almost white, with flecks of gray. "Are we gonna talk about our funny parts, or are we getting to business?"

"You do all your business in the nude?" Jennifer finally found her voice.

"I brought you here to show you I ain't playing," Wally proclaimed.

"Well, pulling your dick out sure proves it to me," Veronica scoffed.

"Give me twenty minutes, and you'll see how serious I am," he said, his tone darkening. His eyes glazed over as if lost in thought.

"Fifteen," Allen said from his spot. Jennifer watched as Allen put his phone back in his pocket.

Wally nodded. "Oh, I better get started."

Wally leaned forward, and Jennifer was thankful that no light was shining directly on him. She didn't want to stare at this man's penis for the next half hour.

"Now, ladies, I need you to understand you aren't in danger here. Nothing will harm you."

"Goddamn right nothing will harm us." Veronica unfolded her arms.

Wally shook his head. "Seer, you need to let that anger go. There are people in a hell of a bigger fix than you. I need your help, and in return, I'll help you both."

"What could we do for the man with all the answers? I've seen the website," Veronica mocked.

Jennifer elbowed Veronica in the side.

Veronica instantly turned to her. Her eyes were wide, and she bared her teeth. "What?" She held her hand out, pointing to him. "We drive all this way on nothing but cryptic messages, and now I'm staring at some eighty-year-old man's dick!"

"Ninety-one. Just had a birthday last week." Wally smiled.

"Congratulations," Veronica said.

"Hear me out, and if you think I can't help, you leave, and that'll be that. I'll find someone else."

Jennifer nodded.

Wally looked saddened, but then his face relaxed.

Jennifer glanced into Veronica's eyes. Why was she so angry? What if he could solve their problems? What if he knew how to defeat Nothing and give Veronica whatever the hell it was she wanted? Jennifer felt a small glimmer of guilt for never asking Veronica what she hoped to get out of all this. She made a mental note to take the time to find out once they finished.

"Can I go on? I don't have much longer," he pleaded.

Veronica sighed. "Whatever."

"I was born in 1932 in Lewisburg. We had some land down a holler out there. I'm the last one standing. My Ma, my Pa, and nine brothers —even my brother's kids—are gone. The only thing close to family I got left is Allen over there." He pointed a bony finger in the young man's direction. "I left at fourteen. Didn't have a choice. Ma and Pa went back to back, so I was out on my ass. I got a job in White Sulphur Springs at a gas station owned by a family whose last name was Taylor."

"Are you writing this down?" Veronica leaned in and asked Jennifer without any subtlety.

Wally continued without hesitation. "I made friends with Mr. Taylor's son, Bill. He was a hell of a mechanic and taught me to be a hell of a mechanic too. When Mr. Taylor passed, Bill sold the gas station and bought a car lot. I was the head mechanic."

Jennifer almost jumped as something scurried past her right foot. It was a spider and wasn't small by any stretch of the imagination. It went right up to where Wally was seated and stopped a foot short of the chair. He noticed it, and his lip curled slightly, but he continued.

"I met Nora in 1949. She worked at the Greenbrier Hotel in the laundry room. Her daddy left her momma, so she was sent up from New Orleans a few years before. Her momma didn't have money to keep her fed, so she stayed with her aunt."

"This is a charming story, but—" Veronica began.

"Shhh," Jennifer quieted her.

"We were married that year. She was everything to me," he paused.

"My wife had a curiosity with the odd, so to say. Said she could see ghosts. Collected all kinds of weird things, stuff a person shouldn't play with. Said it was her mission to keep that stuff out of the wrong hands. I never talked much to her about it. Didn't want to. I thought it was a bunch of silliness."

Another spider passed by, this time from Veronica's side, and went up to where the other spider was stopped. It was much smaller, but that didn't matter to Jennifer. She feared spiders; the thought of them always gave her goosebumps. She was starting to feel unnerved.

"I was working the day of the fire. She was six months pregnant. They didn't make it." He took another long pause and rubbed his bald head. "That was 1951. Bill owned some property and let me have a house: this one, matter of fact. I worked for him up until he passed in 1982. Allen is his great-grandson." Wally pointed the same finger again.

"So your wife taught you everything about what happens here? The curses, the ghosts? Was she a witch?" Jennifer asked.

Wally started laughing, and Jennifer looked over at Allen, who was also trying to hide the fact that he was chuckling.

"Mays was right, you two really don't know shit, do you? A witch? My wife was more of a dabbler. Honey, the last thing you ever want to run into is a witch. You're thinking of those that play with the cards, and live out in the woods. Those people are dabblers, they're happy folk, with happy lives. I'm talking those that feed on babies and'll kill you as soon as look at you."

"That's why we came here. We don't know anything. I don't understand how to fight this thing. I don't even understand why any of this exists," Jennifer said.

"You could always leave," Wally stated. "Once you cross the state line, all the bad stays here."

"Why?" Veronica's voice was different. She was curious, and Jennifer felt relief knowing there was a break in the tension.

"This is how it is, this place," he patted his chest. "They can't cross the line, and there are always three hundred and four. The things you hear stories about, the devils, the monsters, all of it is real. It becomes legend to the outside world, like the Mothman or the vampire. But they're not fairy tales. It's been that way for a long time. Few know, and they fight back every day." His smile warmed. "Joe is one of them."

"Joe?" Jennifer asked.

"Mays. The cop, like you." Wally pointed to Veronica.

"I thought what happened to me was an isolated incident."

"You'll learn a lot today, young lady." He shifted his weight in his chair. "Where was I? Right, Bill had two sons, Travis and Tyler. Tyler is Allen's granddaddy. Tyler worked with me on the car lot; really nice boy, helpful as all get out, a spitting image of his daddy."

"And Travis?" Jennifer couldn't help but interject.

"That boy was a handful. He lived a ruckus lifestyle: girls, grass, and whiskey. He wasn't a criminal, no. He just lived loose, if you follow me."

Jennifer nodded.

"He met a girl and fell hard for her. She was the prettiest thing you've ever seen, and charming as all get out. Have mercy, Lord; she was the vision of an angel. To this day, I've never seen a woman so lovely, save for my sweet Nora of course."

He leaned forward, and Jennifer noticed several spiders near the chair. Jennifer gasped and felt woozy.

"What are they doing?" Jennifer asked.

"You have a problem with spiders?" Allen asked from off to her side.

"A little." Jennifer felt her cheeks warm.

"You might want to leave, and I mean right now," Allen warned.

"You won't be harmed. I give you my word," Wally emphasized. Jennifer looked at the spiders, barely moving like an invisible barrier froze them.

"You promise?"

"I promise." He tapped the arm of the chair as he said it before crossing his heart with his finger.

"I'll stay."

"So, that pretty girl? Her name was Nadine," Wally said.

"Oh shit," Veronica said.

"Travis was smitten to the point it was damn near crazy. He followed her around like a lost puppy. That boy had it bad. Bill had made a name for himself, and the family had money. Travis bought that girl everything. He'd even let her use cars from the lot."

"Five minutes," Allen spoke up.

Wally thumbed his nose. "Running low on time... so, when Travis comes to him with plans to move away with the girl, Bill got tired of seeing his boy acting the fool and cut him off. And when Nadine's honey pot ran dry, let's just say she wandered."

"She left him," Veronica deduced.

"Yup, a month later, I went to work, and when I opened the garage, I found the boy hanging." Wally slumped.

"That's awful," Jennifer said.

"It was. Bill was beside himself. He blamed himself a bit, but mostly he blamed Nadine. I lost my child before I got to see it, but Bill had raised his. The man was never the same."

"I'm investigating a woman who killed a man by making him older. Is this the same woman?" Veronica took a step forward.

"I'm sure of it," Wally said softly.

"How in the hell can that be possible?" Veronica held her arms out in disbelief.

"Folks would come to my Nora when a problem would crop up, and she would handle it. See, we kept all the things she collected in a big shed behind that house that burned down. I couldn't let any of it go. So I moved it here: the books, the trinkets, I kept it all. She never allowed them in our home. Nora said they could corrupt a man." He looked down into his lap.

There were more spiders at the foot of the chair now. All sitting there, almost motionless, with different shapes and sizes practically on top of each other. Was he calling them to him? Jennifer remembered what he'd promised her, yet she inched toward Veronica.

"Bill came to me some time after Travis died. He knew I kept Nora's things, and he asked me to help him avenge his boy. Bill had always been a good friend, I couldn't tell him no." Wally looked up toward the ceiling and continued. "So, I got in my wife's things and found some books."

"You aren't about to tell me you put a spell on her," Veronica said.

Wally looked over at Veronica, his eyes wet. "I put a curse on her, for vanity. I didn't think anyone would get hurt."

"What did the curse do?" Veronica asked.

"Bill said the girl was all about being pretty. Said she loved herself more than any man ever could. I wanted her to age fast. I wanted her to lose it all." Wally closed his eyes.

"So what happened?" Jennifer asked.

"She found a loophole. She has to eat. If she doesn't, she'll fade away in days, dust and bones. She takes people's lives, and it's my fault. She's been doing it since the '70s. I don't know how she figured it out."

"How do we stop her?" Jennifer cried.

The room went quiet at the question.

Allen's phone alarm broke the silence. He reached down, opened the small cabinet, and removed a roll of surgical tape. He closed the door and walked around the spiders to the backside of the chair. He pulled off a strip and stood there.

"That ain't the worst of it," Wally said as he looked at Allen. "When you wish bad on someone, there's always a price."

Allen reached over Wally's head, taped his mouth shut, and hurried around the chair, avoiding the spiders a second time to stand with Veronica and Jennifer.

"Are you kidding me?" Veronica whispered.

Jennifer had been watching the fear grow in Wally's eyes. She glanced over at Veronica, who had her phone out and the camera light shining toward the cellar's ceiling. Jennifer followed the beam and saw the spiders. Hundreds of them gathered above Wally. Jennifer gripped Veronica's arm to keep herself from falling over. She felt faint. It was something out of her worst nightmares.

Wally rocked back and forth and made a low guttural noise. Spiders were at the base of the chair, all crawling atop one another now. Jennifer could finally hear them, their legs hitting the wood above. How many were there? What was about to happen in this room?

"Just stay where you are. It doesn't last long," Allen told them.

"What doesn't—" Jennifer started.

The spiders at the chair's base and on the ceiling moved as one. Every inch of Wally's skin was covered instantly. It was as if he was swallowed whole by them. He twisted and writhed in the chair, and Jennifer could hear him moaning through the tape. They skittered across his body, and she saw him jerk violently every so often. Jennifer felt her stomach flip. She wanted to look away; she needed to, but her eyes betrayed her. Veronica shone the flashlight on Wally's blanketed body; the spiders were shiny in the light. They were covered in his blood.

"They... Oh Jesus, they're biting him." Veronica's hand covered her mouth.

"Since 1972. Every day since he cursed her." Allen turned away, walked to the cabinet, removed a small basket from inside, and returned beside Jennifer. She looked down, and several different ointments were tucked away in the basket.

"Every day?" Jennifer asked.

"Six o'clock on the dot. He heals for the next hour, and then the countdown starts again." Allen lowered his head. "I've been taking care of him for years. My dad before me."

The spiders moved away from him, albeit slower than when they attacked. He was covered in marks, and his brown skin was soaked in blood. He trembled and whimpered. Jennifer suddenly thought of Quentin and how his life ended quickly. But this? This was the cruelest thing she'd ever seen. She watched as the spiders paid her no mind and traveled past her.

"Where do they go?" Veronica questioned as she, too, watched them fleeing.

"Don't know. I wish I could kill every last one of them." Allen sat the basket down and pulled out a bottle. Allen walked over to Wally, who was about to fall out of the chair. He pushed the old man back into it and slowly peeled the tape from his mouth. "I tape his mouth so they don't get in there. That used to happen a lot back in the day because he'd scream."

"You said your dad did this for him too?" Veronica stepped over the basket toward Allen.

Allen seemed to ignore the question. "He'll start to clot in a few minutes, and then I put salve on his skin. It soothes the itching."

"This doesn't kill him?" Veronica's voice cracked.

"I just... I just want to die... Help me die," Wally muttered.

Veronica turned to Jennifer. Her face had lost all its color. "I'm going outside to talk to Ethel. Will you stay with him?"

"Of course," Jennifer said. She watched as Veronica ascended the stairs. She finally turned to Allen and asked, "Is there anything I can do to help?"

16

Veronica stood beside the entrance to the cellar, and she kept Ethel's gaze.

"That was awful," Veronica began as she pinched the bridge of her nose.

Ethel nodded.

"I mean, spiders? The man gets munched on every day." Veronica placed her hands on the top of her head as Ethel nodded again. "Is that all you have to say?" Veronica complained.

"What do you want me to say to that, Ronnie?" Ethel shrugged at her. "That was as bad as Nothing."

Veronica wanted out of there more than anything. She couldn't believe what had just transpired. A few days prior, she knew of the existence of ghosts, but a new fear crept over her. What else wandered the shadows of West Virginia? She turned to the sound of the cellar steps creaking, and Jennifer emerged.

"I don't..." Jennifer started.

"I know. What the hell was that?" Veronica agreed.

The three of them stood there, each visibly shaken. The sun was going down, and the humidity was high. Veronica wanted to speak, but she had no idea what to say. She figured the same could be said for her companions. It wasn't long before Allen came up with Wally holding onto his arm. Wally stepped over to the house and leaned against it. The bites on his skin were slowly closing, and the blood began to dry. He was still in pain, but he managed a shaky smile.

"You ladies okay?" he asked, catching his breath.

"Not really," Jennifer said.

"I needed you to see that. I needed you to understand. A curse ain't nothing to mess with, but as long as Nadine is free, well you seen it. " His face contorted. He was still in pain as he reached up and scratched his shoulder.

"Well, thanks for the show," Veronica said. "I might have believed you. I've seen some shit over the last couple of days."

"I heard. Mays called us. That's why I believe you can help."

Wally kept digging at places on his body. Veronica thought he must itch something fierce. He was still slightly out of breath and looked like he would fall over, but he slowly gained strength with each passing second.

"What is it you want?" Jennifer asked.

"What I want is to finally rest. Which one of you is dealing with the invisible?" Wally pulled his hand away and wobbled left to right before he stood upright again.

"Me," Jennifer said, raising her hand.

"Got yourself a demon," Wally nodded at Allen as he said it, who, without a word, went around the house and out of sight. "That's a rare thing. It found its way here. It's stuck between worlds. *Son of—*" Wally jerked and pulled his fingers back from an apparent tender spot he'd scratched under his arm. He shuddered, then continued. "That's why you can't see it, don't know the ins and outs of how that works. But neither of you ladies are nuns, and I doubt you know a priest. So you're gonna have to put it down yourselves."

"How the hell do you expect us to do that?" Veronica shook her head and looked over at Ethel in disbelief.

"Silver." Wally patted Jennifer's shoulder. "I'm gonna give her some silver."

"I thought silver was for werewolves," Veronica spoke up. She was sure the old man was wrong, wouldn't they need something like crosses or holy water? Wally started to laugh and held his side.

"Don't make me laugh... it hurts."

"No, she's right, werewolves—" Jennifer began.

"Are some of the dumbest people I know," Wally interrupted, still snickering.

Allen returned with a small leather book under his arm, a closed container that looked like it might house foundation makeup, and a six-inch spike with a handle that shined in the last of the sun.

"What's so funny?" he asked as he handed the items over to Jennifer individually.

"They thought silver was for werewolves." Wally started chuckling again and Allen tried to hide a smile before they both broke out in hysterics.

"Are we missing something?" Veronica couldn't hide her annoyance.

"When you think of werewolves, you think of them movies. A man turns into a giant wolf then snacks on people on a full moon," Wally said, wiping tears from his left eye.

"Is that not what happens?" Jennifer asked.

Veronica hated to admit it, but she was more than curious about what the old man knew that she didn't.

"Hell no, they actually turn into a wolf, look like a scraggly ass coyote. They have the smarts of one too. Werewolves are damn near extinct. Think about it... Most of them change, then go raid a chicken coup and get shot by a farmer."

"Remember Danny Biddle?" Allen interjected.

Wally started bellowing again.

"Always bragging about being one with nature. Dumb sumbitch changed one night and got run over on the highway near his house." Wally was still snickering as he spoke to Jennifer. "You take that book and flip through it. Be careful, it's old. It'll tell you how to call the demon. Inside that little jar there," he pointed to the tiny case, "a mixture of salt and silver, it's ground up. You throw that on the bastard, and you can see it. Sprinkle it on the ground around you. It steps in and it'll burn like the dickens."

"I think it possessed a little boy. We can already see it," Jennifer explained.

"Do it anyway; it'll hurt, make it weak." Wally started scratching himself all over again. "That tickler there?" Wally pointed with the same finger at the spike in Jennifer's other hand. "Pure silver, blessed too, only have to nick him with it, then get the hell away. The sickness will spread through him, and it'll die."

"What if I put it through its heart?" Jennifer asked coldly.

Wally's eyes widened at the question. "Then it'll probably die faster."

Jennifer gripped the handle tightly and turned it end over end. "It's light; the problem will be getting close to Dylan." She put her finger on the tip. "That's sharp. I'm sure I'll figure something out. Thank you." Jennifer gave a slight bow, which Veronica thought looked ridiculous.

"No problem. Now, it's your turn." Wally turned to Veronica and stretched a finger in her direction. "I need you to bring me, Nadine."

"Do you have any idea how I can find her?" Veronica was excited. If he had gifts for Jennifer, she could only imagine what he had in store for her. Allen reached into his pocket and pulled out a slip of paper. He handed it to Veronica.

"Why do I have an address for a Kelsey Skaggs?" she asked, trying to hide her disappointment. She thought she would have received a magic bullet or nunchucks, something cool.

"Nadine's great niece. We think she's helping her. If you stop by and ask questions, Nadine should come for you," Allen answered.

"How can you be so sure?" Veronica pocketed the paper and put her hands on her hips.

"Because she's killed everyone who got too close," Wally said sadly.

"Why not send Mays after her?" Veronica asked.

"We like Mays. We don't really know you." Wally smiled.

Veronica should have been insulted, but she was starting to warm up to him. He was a straight shooter, and she admired that.

"So, I put myself in her crosshairs, draw her out, and then what? Kill her?" Veronica didn't like using herself as bait, but he was helping Jennifer with Nothing and kept his word. So maybe there was more to Wally's plan.

"Can't kill her that way. You can hurt her for sure. She ain't nothing special, just have to avoid her mouth. Only way to end her is to starve her." Wally rubbed his chin and glared at Veronica.

She could tell he was deadly serious; he thought she could pull this off. She could see the desperation in his eyes.

"Capture her alive and...?"

"Bring her here. We'll put her down below, and in a few days, I'm free," Wally said. "When she comes for you, and I'm sure she will if you start poking around, she won't see your guardian angel."

"I think he means me," Ethel spoke up.

"That's exactly what he means," Veronica called back to her.

Wally started walking away from everyone. "Well, go on. Get to work. Make the world a better place and all that shit." He waved his hand at them as he passed the corner.

Allen handed Veronica another slip of paper. "This here is my phone number. Once you have her, I'll come get her no matter the time of night."

Veronica looked down at the digits, and when she glanced back up he was already off after Wally. Veronica placed the number in the same pocket as the address.

"Well, it's a start," she said to herself.

"So, what do we do now?" Jennifer came around to face her.

"On the way back to the apartment, I'm going to stop by this address," Veronica said as she patted the pocket. "Get the ball rolling. It's the next town over, so not too far from here."

"Then what?" Jennifer was bouncing up and down like a child.

Veronica was about to burst her bubble. "You are going back to your car and waiting in Baltimore while I deal with Nadine."

"But—"

"No. I can't deal with both right now. Let me handle Nadine, then *together* we take down Nothing or Dylan… or whatever." Veronica started back to the car with Jennifer in tow.

"Veronica—" Jennifer whined.

"Promise me you'll go back to Baltimore. I don't want to be worried that you're off doing something stupid. You almost died in that bedroom. *We* need a plan. Ethel and I have the first part covered." She didn't want Jennifer to get hurt, and she didn't want her to be in the way, either.

Jennifer didn't say anything once they got in the car. She'd put the items Wally had given her in the backseat. Ethel was oddly quiet, but Veronica was sure she was still processing the day's events. Ethel hated spiders; Veronica remembered that from her childhood. So, she was positive, either living or dead, she was still rattled. Veronica felt around in her pocket and produced both pieces of paper. She entered the address into her phone, and they departed.

It was barely fifteen minutes before they were outside a small town named Fort Springs. The GPS took them to a little yellow house with a dirty picket fence; the place was run down, but still tidy, and there was a swing in the front yard. Veronica opened the center console and grabbed two cards. She also took a pen from inside and wrote on the back of one.

"Before I forget, this is my cell number. You make sure you call me when you get home," Veronica ordered.

"Yes, Mother." Jennifer took the card and rolled her eyes.

"I mean it." Veronica stared at her.

She wanted to tell her that this wasn't a game, that she had her best interests at heart. She didn't want her to die. She knew Jennifer wasn't stupid, so she left it at that, opened the door, and started up the walkway with Ethel right behind her.

"You know the drill?" Veronica slowed down just to make sure Ethel was on the same page.

"I do. You're going to play dumb, and then I'll stick around and see how she reacts," Ethel said.

"Exactly."

She knocked on the door, and a woman answered it seconds later. She had to have been by the door, watching. Veronica saw a Ring camera doorbell off to the left. *Even better, if she contacts Nadine, she can show her what I look like.* The overpowering smell of incense seeped out from behind the tiny woman. If she was over five feet it wasn't by much. She was wearing a tie-dyed shirt and ripped-up jeans. Veronica could hear music from within but couldn't make it out from the loud voices.

"Can I help you?" the woman asked, brushing her blonde hair away from her eyes.

"I sure hope so," Veronica grinned. "I'm at a loss here."

The woman stepped out on the porch and shut the door. "I'm sorry. I don't know you."

"My name is Detective Veronica Carter from the Parkersburg Police Department." Veronica patted her jeans until she felt and produced her shield. "I just need to ask you a question or two, and then I'll be on my way."

"Parkersburg? Where is that?" the woman said as she laughed uncomfortably.

"Other side of the state. I know I'm way out of my jurisdiction, but I'm investigating a murder. I wouldn't have come all this way if it wasn't important." Veronica didn't meet her eyes; she glanced around the yard. She wanted the woman to be uneasy.

"Murder?" The woman's face started to lose color. "Sure, ask away."

"You wouldn't happen to know a Jeff Browning, would you, Miss...?" Veronica asked, pointing her hand out to her.

"Skaggs," she smiled. "No, I've never heard that name before."

Veronica feigned disappointment. "Miss Skaggs, I'm sorry I bothered you. It's just that I have a man that's turned up in a trailer park dead; his body was moved there. I lucked onto the original crime scene."

"Out here?" Miss Skaggs pointed toward the ground.

"Oh, no. Parkersburg," Veronica chuckled.

"So," the woman asked as her eyes narrowed in confusion, "why are you here?"

"Well, the suspect didn't expect me to find where the man was killed, so many personal effects were there. Including this address written down on an envelope, of all things." Veronica stepped back, turning her head left and right to look at the house.

The woman's eyes widened. "That certainly is... strange." She brushed her long hair out of her face again.

"I mean, there were a lot of oddities in there. I wouldn't have driven a few hours if I wasn't stumped," Veronica continued as if she hadn't heard her, still pretending to examine the house.

The woman was fidgeting already; if pressed hard enough, she would probably break down in a heap. Veronica knew precisely how to handle this.

"So, my address was on an envelope?" She folded her arms defensively.

"Yes. May I ask if it's just you here?" Veronica asked, her tone serious.

"Well, I have a few friends over right now. Normally it's just me and my daughter."

Miss Skaggs started to sweat.

"I don't know why the suspect wrote this place down, but what happened to Mr. Browning was..." Veronica shook her head.

"I'm sorry to hear that," Miss Skaggs said tightly.

"I see you got a Ring." Veronica pointed at it. "Do you own a firearm?"

"No," the woman answered unconvincingly.

"I'd go purchase one," Veronica told her.

Miss Skaggs glanced around before leaning in. "Can I be honest with you?"

Veronica also looked all over, playing along. "Of course."

"I... I sell weed to make ends meet. I don't get child support, so maybe they buy from me?" Miss Skaggs was as white as snow.

Veronica nodded. She had seen this too many times to count. A criminal or suspect often confessed to something minor to make themselves look trustworthy. What Miss Skaggs was doing was simple: deflect any suspicion by admitting to something else.

"I don't care about that." Veronica waved her hand and grinned. "People gotta eat. All I care about is Mr. Browning, and finding his killer so he can rest easy." Veronica let the silence go on till it became unbearable. "Well, I hate wasting my time and yours."

"Me too," Miss Skaggs said, visibly relaxing. Veronica held out her card.

"Here is the Parkersburg office number. If any of your customers or someone comes around here that you find suspicious, call 9-1-1 and then call me immediately. I wouldn't wish what happened to Mr. Browning on my worst enemy."

Miss Skaggs took it without making eye contact and stared at it; Veronica started walking away.

"You have a safe trip back, officer," Miss Skaggs called out to her.

Veronica turned around and held up her hand. "Oh, one last thing."

"Yes?" Miss Skaggs was smiling.

I love this part, Veronica thought.

"Does the name Nadine mean anything to you?" she asked.

There was a pause from Miss Skaggs; her smile instantly faded, and her brow dropped. It took a second for her to acknowledge what Veronica had said to her.

"No... No, I don't know that name either," she stuttered.

Got you.

"Well, sorry again. You have a nice day." Veronica turned around, not looking back as she entered the car and pulled away, leaving Ethel behind.

"How did it go?" Jennifer asked after a few moments.

"Do you gamble?" Veronica stopped at the light and chuckled.

"No," Jennifer stated.

"She won't be long. Our girl Kelsey is calling Nadine right now," Veronica said.

"You think so?" Jennifer asked.

Veronica turned to Jennifer and smiled. "Oh, yeah."

They had just started making small talk when Ethel appeared in the backseat. Veronica nudged Jennifer, then pointed her thumb back in her direction.

Ethel didn't wait for Veronica to say anything before starting in. "You started a war. She ran to the bathroom and called Nadine, screaming her head off. The girl was shaking so bad she couldn't hold the phone."

"What did she say?" Veronica slipped effortlessly into business mode.

"Kelsey screamed at Nadine for leaving her address out, and Nadine told her she wasn't that stupid. She wanted to know how you got the address then. There was a lot of swearing."

"I'm sure," Veronica nodded in agreement.

"Everything changed when she told her you asked for Nadine by name. She told her you were on to her. Then she read off the card you handed her." Ethel moved over to the center of the seat.

"Anything else?" Veronica asked.

"Nadine told her you would be dead by tomorrow," Ethel said.

Veronica suppressed the urge to laugh. "Well, thank God I have you watching my back, huh?" Veronica glanced in the rearview at the old woman. "Unless you have plans?"

"I think I'm free."

Veronica relayed the conversation to Jennifer, who seemed more concerned than Veronica. It wasn't that Veronica wasn't cautious about the entire situation, it was just that everything was going exactly how she wanted it to, and she was confident it would *keep* going her way.

"I'm worried about you..." Jennifer began.

Veronica held up a hand to stop her. "She won't be a problem."

"You can drop the tough girl act. It's okay to be scared," Jennifer said. Veronica could see the concern on her face.

"Scared? I have Ethel with me. I'm untouchable," Veronica said, tapping the steering wheel.

"That's right!" Ethel cried, even though Jennifer couldn't hear it.

Veronica gave a thumbs up and nodded in her direction.

"Will you be serious for a minute? How are you going to handle her?" Jennifer threw her hands up, her voice shockingly firm.

Veronica grinned at Jennifer. "I'm touched, seriously. But Ethel doesn't sleep and can see into rooms I'm not in. She can walk through walls, so if someone is sneaking around, they have no idea she's watching them. When I was trapped inside the trunk, she chased Nothing away, she *yelled* at it, and it ran like its ass was on fire."

"I don't know if I can do that again," Ethel admitted.

"You won't need to," Veronica said to Ethel before continuing: "Besides Jen, I have to stop her. Wally helped you, and we have a deal. I might need him some time. Plus, you're forgetting something."

"What's that?" Jennifer asked, bewildered.

Veronica latched eyes in the mirror with Ethel. "It's my job."

Jennifer shook her head and sighed, but Veronica could tell she had won. That round, at least.

<hr>

The rest of the trip was spent reminiscing about the last two days and stories from their life. Veronica would shoot Jennifer down every time she tried to get too personal. She wanted Jennifer to steer the conversation into her own life. She enjoyed listening to her. She was intelligent, quick-witted, and funny when she wanted to be.

As they got closer to crossing into Ohio, Jennifer opened up and told horror stories from her love life. She said, "It was the greatest date I've ever been on. He opened doors for me. He was charming. I mean, everything he said was clever. Men shouldn't look the way he did; he was *pretty*."

"Oh, this should be good." Veronica braced for the catch. She knew it was coming; she just had no idea what.

"He was extremely successful, no ex-wives, no kids. I thought I'd hit the lottery." Jennifer adjusted her seatbelt. "I'm rambling all through dinner, and he's listening. I could have quizzed him later, and I guarantee you he'd have gotten an A. He was practically perfect."

Veronica nodded.

"So he takes me home and gives me a peck on the cheek. I mean, who in 2021 does that? He was just so sweet."

"Hmm, sounds perfect." Veronica rolled her eyes.

"So, I get a text message from him about thirty minutes later. Telling me he had a great time and hoped we could see each other again." Jennifer placed her palm on her forehead. "I start talking flirty to him. I mean, I'm not tired, and I *really* wanted a second date."

"Okay, so where does this fall apart?" Veronica peeked over and could see Jennifer's face beginning to redden.

"I mean, I'm not saying anything too graphic, but teasing. You know? I just wanted to make sure he knew I was interested. But then, out of the blue, he asks for pictures of my feet."

Veronica almost choked. "He. Did. Not. What did you do?"

Jennifer sat in silence, biting her bottom lip.

"You didn't," Veronica gasped.

"I had ankle socks on. I didn't think much of it. I thought he'd ask for pictures of my legs next. You know, playful stuff. He asks for the socks off, and I'm getting worried." Jennifer's voice was low; Veronica could hear the embarrassment in her tone.

"Please tell me—" Veronica began.

"I thought it was a strange thing to ask for, but what the hell. Then he asks me to get them dirty and send them again."

Veronica should have been paying attention to the road but couldn't help herself. She stared at Jennifer with her mouth agape.

"I blocked his number and took a shower." Jennifer sighed and put her face into her hands. The car was still; the only sound was the hum of the road. Ethel snorted, and Veronica glimpsed into the mirror. Ethel had her hands over her mouth.

"Are you okay back there?" Veronica asked.

Ethel cackled wildly and fell to her side. In all her years alive or dead, Veronica had never heard Ethel in stitches this way. She was mesmerized by the reflection of the old woman having a fit. It didn't take long before it became infectious, and Veronica started to chuckle before she was roaring along with Ethel.

"Stop laughing, it was traumatizing," Jennifer pleaded.

But it wasn't long before she started in with the other two, even if she couldn't hear one of them. It took several minutes for any of them to regain their composure.

They arrived back at the apartment around eleven. Jennifer's car was parked on the side of the building. It was immaculate. Jimmy had outdone himself. Veronica could find no trace of the damage Nothing had inflicted. Jennifer argued to let her pay for the damage, but Veronica insisted that Jimmy had done this as a favor. This was somewhat true; she would owe him for the replacement trunk and panels, but Jimmy would let the labor cost slide. There was no way they patched this and painted. He would still have the car if that were the case. She wouldn't ask Jimmy where he got the parts as long as it was done.

Neither felt like driving home; they were exhausted from driving for so long. So, they agreed to stay the night again with the same arrangements. Veronica was confident Nadine couldn't travel across the state line to pursue her, and even if she could, how would she know where she was? She wanted to return to West Virginia; she missed her grandmother, but at least now she understood why she couldn't come to Ohio with her.

Before turning down for the night, she double-checked all the door locks and windows. She worried her mind might start racing, and she wouldn't be able to fall asleep, but that was far from the case. When Veronica rolled over the following morning at a little after nine, she entered the living room, and Jennifer was already gone. She'd left a note on the kitchen countertop beside the coffee pot.

Thanks for everything
Call me the second you catch Nadine
Stay safe
Jennifer

Veronica fixed herself a cup of coffee and took a quick shower. She was on the road before ten thirty, heading back toward Parkersburg and home. She called Jimmy, who was asleep and irritated that she woke him so early. She'd wanted to thank him for the repair work, and he assured her it wasn't any hassle. He informed her it would run her twelve hundred dollars, which was a steal in Veronica's mind. She told him she had some work to finish at her office and would get it to him when she found herself in Huntington. Ethel appeared shortly after crossing the state line back into West Virginia. She'd asked about Jennifer, but the conversation quickly turned to what they would do about Nadine. Veronica repeated the plan several times to etch it in Ethel's mind.

"If she wants me, she will have to come for me. I'll be mostly at work and home for the next few days. You are my eyes. You'll check every corner constantly. I'm keeping my Taser X2 on me at all times. We need her unconscious; it's a long drive to Wally's," Veronica said.

"Where are we heading now?" Ethel asked.

"The office. I need to check on something."

Veronica headed to the station while she and Ethel continued to go over the plan for Nadine. They hadn't argued about anything and had stayed pleasant with one another. It was a decent change of pace from the previous months, and Veronica was thankful for it. Veronica stopped at a Tudor's Biscuit World and had a very late breakfast. She sat silently as she ate her biscuit with ham, egg, and cheese. She decided to wash it down with another coffee. The stress of the last few days had wreaked havoc on her, and she felt beaten down.

She was curious if Detective Green had contacted her superiors. They had several people dead and a young boy still on the loose.. Not to mention the crazed youth eater from the 1970s wanting to kill her. She didn't need anyone poking around in her life. She needed to keep her stories straight and make sure no one suspected her of anything.

The drive home became irksome. The interstate was so tedious. Ethel kept her somewhat sane by talking about the fleeting moments she lived in Baltimore with Veronica's grandfather. Ethel only complained about how she would have loved to have a bite of Veronica's food, but outside of that, she kept Veronica in good spirits.

Veronica was euphoric when she pulled into the lot beside the familiar brick building. It was nice to be back in her element. She wasted no time entering and using her keycard to get through the locked door. It was surprisingly empty for a Friday. Only Brian was at the front desk, and he was half asleep.

"Where have you been?" He sat up, genuinely surprised to see her.

"Greatest date ever," she smirked, stealing the line from her conversation with Jennifer.

"Anyone I know?" Brian asked. He was easily one of Veronica's favorites here in the precinct. The guy joked about everything. He would always run up on Veronica with vulgar jokes or outlandish stories. Brian was one of the few people that could honestly brighten her day.

"Nah, she'd hate your guts. Most women do," Veronica teased.

"That burns Carter," he put his head down on his desk in defeat. "My girlfriend doesn't hate me."

She sat on the edge of the desk. "Yeah? How does your wife feel about that one?"

"Damn, you aren't playing around, are you?" Brian looked up, his eyes enormous in shock.

"You know I'm fucking with you. I actually like your girlfriend." She patted his shoulder. "The Cap' in?"

"He is; he told me earlier he needed to call you today. What's going on?" Brian perked up.

Shit, Veronica thought. This wasn't off to a good start.

"I have no clue." She hopped down. "Guess I'll go find out."

"I hope you're getting fired," Brian said with a chuckle.

"Eat shit, Brian," Veronica fired back.

Veronica walked toward Captain Aaron's office. She peered inside, and he was writing something at his desk. "Hey, Cap'."

He waved his beefy arm at her. His sleeves were rolled up as always, and she could see he was sweating profusely. Veronica felt that Captain Aaron needed to retire. His diabetes had gotten out of control, and he was constantly sick. He had missed numerous weeks this year and looked worse every time she saw him. He refused to take proper care of himself, and he'd taken a turn for the worse.

He finally looked up from his work. "Carter. Come in and shut the door."

She did as told and sat at the desk across from him. He tossed his pen down, and Veronica noticed he was breathing heavily. His face and hands looked swollen, and he had dark circles under his blue eyes. He adjusted his tie and arched back, the chair squeaked under his massive frame.

"I normally don't give two shits about what my people do on their personal days. But my phone has been lit up by a Charleston detective."

"Green?" She already knew but asked anyway.

Captain Aaron nodded.

"What did you do to this guy?"

"I went on a date with this great girl out of Baltimore. Problem is Green thinks she interviewed Dylan Jeffrey a few hours before he broke out. So this sack of shit calls us over from a few hours away. We get there, and he's all in her face, wondering what she did to set him off. He thinks he's clever."

Veronica had a fantastic rapport with her coworkers. She did her job and cut up with them when she got the chance. She was one of them. They had no suspicions of her bending the rules or, in the case of her murdering the pervy asshole for Jimmy, ignoring them completely. She was the last person anyone would suspect of wrongdoing. She'd had several commendations, and there had been no complaints outside of a man who attacked her when she confronted him about embezzling from his work.

She didn't hang out with any other officers in her private life. She kept most of that to herself. She would buy them and their families birthday gifts, attend weddings, and go to their big cookouts in the summer. But she didn't feel like seeing them most of the time after the workday. She didn't dislike any of the people that she worked with—she respected most of them—and as far as she knew, the feeling was mutual.

"He claims you haven't been straight with him," Captain Aaron said.

"He was accusing a woman I'd been with all evening of God knows what. Guy's a prick." Veronica shook her head.

"I agree. But he wanted a lot of information about you, arrest records, personnel file," Captain Aaron warned.

Veronica balled her fist. She'd not expected this. What set him off? He couldn't have pinged the phone without a warrant, and this didn't fall under the exigent circumstances umbrella. "You didn't give him any of that shit, did you?"

"Nah, I told him to call his rep and that you were one of my best." Captain Aaron smiled. "Plus, he made an enemy out of me anyway."

"How so?" Veronica was doing her best, but she was livid. How dare this man pull a stunt like this. He may have suspected something fishy, but there was no reason to go from zero to one hundred the way he had. Plus, the last thing she wanted was anyone suspicious of her at the precinct. Green would be a problem, and she needed to handle it somehow.

"After I told him no, he had his Captain call and ask for it; absolutely unprofessional." Captain Aaron's eyes narrowed. "Just keep me in the loop and stay away from him."

"Anything else?" Veronica asked.

"Nah, you took what, a week off?" Captain Aaron leaned on his armrest.

"Two," she said.

"Hell's bells, Carter. This lady must be something special. You got big plans with her?"

You have no idea, Veronica thought. She said, "Lots of dirty things you don't wanna hear about."

"Get out of here." He smiled and waved his hand back and forth.

"Later, Cap'." She smirked and left with a wave. She stopped by her desk and retrieved her Taser X2 from the bottom drawer.

"What'cha need that for?" Brian asked, hovering behind her.

"Just want to have it around the house, you know?" she answered.

He nodded, but she could tell he was confused by it.

"Hey," Brian called out as she approached the door.

"What's up?"

"You really like my girlfriend?"

"She's nice. I get coffee at her shop all the time," Veronica said.

"What about my wife?" Brian pressed. Veronica grimaced at him as she backed out the door.

Veronica decided to hit the gym on the way home. She hadn't worked out in a while, which always helped her blow off steam. She needed it right now, too; she was concerned about Green looking into her so aggressively. He hadn't contacted her on the phone, and Jennifer hadn't mentioned any messages from him either. Maybe he didn't believe the little show she'd put on at Tina's. She could always try contacting Mays to see if he could dig up anything.

She pulled into the Dawghouse gym and went inside. Veronica had been boxing since she was eighteen. She loved the smell of the canvas and the sound of the gloves as they collided with the heavy bag. It was far and away her favorite exercise, and she couldn't wait to get some time in.

She changed in the dressing room and took a bag off in the corner by itself. The staff and regulars knew her, and they left her alone to do her own thing. Maybe it was because they knew she was in law enforcement, or she gave off a vibe that she didn't want to be spoken to. But it was one of the perks of coming to this place; she felt alone, which was satisfying.

It wasn't long before she was sweating a storm and dancing around in a semicircle hitting her combinations. She let the rhythm of her fists take over. She always envisioned it as music, and was lost again in the beat. Veronica had her breathing down and had hit her zone. She was leveling all her power into each shot. She used to wear headphones when she worked out, but the sound of her fists striking was so satisfying that she stopped.

She'd never fought professionally; she had no desire to. She'd sparred with a few women and men here and there, but nothing serious. She'd done this to stay in shape and train for when she needed to use her fists. She didn't stay too long today, just enough to feel a slight burn in her shoulders and take a little aggression out. When she felt her arms tiring, she called it a day. She didn't want to push herself too much.

She went into the back to shower and change before heading home. The water at the gym was boiling, which was another reason she loved this place. She knew it wasn't good for her skin, but she didn't care. She relished the heat. The spray at her house never got near this scalding.

It had only been a few days, but It felt like she hadn't been home in forever. She was delighted when she pulled into her driveway. At least tonight, she'd get to sleep in her bed, under her massive comforter and all her pillows.

Her house was small, with the most horrific color of brown siding she'd ever seen, but it was still hers. She'd bought it before she started making money as a detective, back when she was a patrolwoman. She'd always planned on getting the brown replaced with something brighter, but she never had a free moment anymore. She loved her home; it was quaint and cozy, a place where she never brought the outside world.

"Ethel, check the house," she whispered as she exited the car.

"You think she might be in there? Already?" Ethel asked.

"You can never be too sure. Check everywhere, up and down," Veronica said as she walked to her mailbox and retrieved a few envelopes. She shuffled through them; nothing was significant, just some monthly bills. Veronica looked over at her neighbor's house. She was the last one on the street, so she only had the couple off to the right. They were elderly and didn't talk to her much. The woman, Rachel, was friendly enough, but the husband would grunt when he saw her. She found it amusing that, for the life of her, she couldn't remember their last names.

"Ronnie?" Ethel's voice was shaky from behind her.

Veronica wheeled around and could tell right away that something was wrong. Ethel's eyes were wide, and her eyebrows were raised in fear.

"She's in there, isn't she?" Veronica confirmed.

"Yes. She's in the double-door closet in your bedroom. It's dark, but I'm certain she has a needle in her hand." Ethel put her hands up near her face.

"Like a sewing needle?" Veronica asked, not fully understanding.

"Looks like a shot," Ethel corrected.

"Wonder how she got in," Veronica said. Sure, it had been over a day, but Nadine had moved fast. To be lying in wait for her already? How long had she been here?

"That's what you're worried about?" Ethel asked, annoyed.

"You go stand beside her and call out if she moves. And by calling out, I mean yell."

Veronica returned to her car and retrieved her Taser X2. She loved this model because it had a double load. She could fire it twice. It could come in handy if she missed her first shot. She tucked it in the back of the sweatpants she'd put on after cleaning up at the gym.

"Are you serious? You're going in there now?" Ethel backed away as Veronica passed by her.

"Go on, I need your eyes," Veronica growled without looking back.

Veronica turned the key and walked into her living room. She'd kept a clean home, and nothing seemed out of place. Without pausing, she headed past her couch and down the hall to her bedroom. She passed by pictures of Ethel when she was very much alive, holding a younger Veronica. She passed her graduation certificates from the academy and her degree from West Virginia University in criminal justice. She heard Ethel cry out from the bedroom.

"She's tensed. She heard you come in, but she hasn't moved!"

Nadine was hiding inside the closet on the far wall, near the other side of the bed. She didn't want her bursting out and surprising her, so she stood away from the double doors. She moved her hand toward her back and her taser, then paused. An idea came to her mind.

"Nadine, I know you're in there. I also know you're armed with a hypodermic needle. Come on out, I just want to talk."

"What are you doing?" Ethel yelled.

"Nadine, I can pull my pistol and put two shots into the closet door, but I don't want to do that. I'm serious. I need to speak to you."

The closet door opened slowly, and Nadine stepped out. Wally hadn't exaggerated in the least. Nadine was beautiful. Her hair was a shade of red she'd never seen before, and her eyes a piercing green. She was wearing a long-sleeved Led Zepplin shirt and jeans. Veronica had seen attractive women before, but something about Nadine was hypnotic. This had to be part of her curse. How could she draw someone's attention so easily? Nadine had a syringe in her right hand, and she moved slowly around the bed in Veronica's direction.

"Stop, Nadine. I'll put two in your leg. I swear to God. Right in your kneecaps."

Nadine stopped. Veronica twisted slightly to ensure she saw the handle in the back of her pants. From that distance, it probably did look like a pistol. Nadine nodded and tossed the syringe on the bed.

"Happy?" she muttered.

"Not yet." Veronica shook her head. "You didn't waste any time did you?"

"Why are you looking for me?" Nadine replied in outrage, balling up her fists. "What do you want?"

"I want you to come back to White Sulphur with me. You need to answer for what you've done," Veronica said.

"For what *I've* done? I didn't ask for any of this." Nadine pointed at Veronica. "Who the fuck do you think you are?"

"I'm not arguing with you. You broke into my house."

"I'm protecting myself. Maybe if I could leave this shit-hole state, I wouldn't have to always be looking over my shoulder."

"And what about Travis Taylor? Or Jeff Browning? Or any of your other victims? Were you 'protecting' yourself from them, too?"

"Victims?" Nadine laughed. "Oh honey, those boys were anything *but* victims. I've never so much as raised a finger against anyone that didn't deserve it. How in the hell do you know about Travis? That was before you were born."

"And Jeff Browning? He deserve it?"

"Who the hell is that?"

"Let me give you a refresher. Nice guy in his thirties. Found him dead and withered in some meth den bathtub in Parkersburg a few days ago."

Nadine paused. "Are you fucking kidding me? His wife had left him, and he was on the verge of suicide. He was a pathetic man, if you can even call him one. He'd given up on life, and thought he hit the jackpot with me. We went back to where I was staying and he went on and on about how he couldn't stop thinking of this ex-wife, and that he was sorry. I did the world a favor."

"So someone who's sad deserves to suffer and die?" Veronica asked.

"He admitted to me that he fantasied about killing her, I can't remember her name."

"Does it matter to you?"

"No, but I know the type. He'd have killed her. Don't tell me you haven't stepped over the line. Look at the shit you're pulling right now with me."

"I'm facing the consequences for it every day."

Nadine was trying to be sneaky and had inched forward. Veronica let it happen. She needed her to move around the edge of her bed. As soon as she did, Veronica moved as she'd been taught. She lunged forward off her right foot and stepped with her left. She threw an overhand right with all her might, and it connected flush against Nadine's eye socket. Veronica howled as she drew back to swing again but realized there was no reason to. Nadine was unconscious in a heap on the floor. Veronica stood there panting in fury.

"Oh, Ronnie," Ethel said.

"No," Veronica vented. "Not now. We don't have time now."

"It's okay. Calm down, you got her," Ethel said. "You didn't even have to shoot her."

Veronica pulled out her Taser and stared down at the prone body.

"Ronnie..." Ethel said. "Don't."

"But I *really* want to." Ethel gave her a stern look, and Veronica pursed her lips. "Fine. But if she tries anything, It's her ass."

Veronica stomped out of the room and headed outside to her car.

She took a moment to gather her senses before she retrieved her phone and the paper with Allen's number on it. Good reasoning or not, she had promised Wally that she would bring Nadine back to look him in the eye, and she didn't have the luxury to be soft now. She unlocked her phone, and dialed the number.

"Hello?" Allen answered warily.

"It's Veronica Carter," she said.

"Hey, what's—" he began.

"I got her," she said.

"Are you serious?" he yelled.

She held the phone away from her ear. "I am. I can't remember. Is there a hardware store near you?"

"Yeah, why?"

"Go get me a padlock for the cellar, a shit-ton of rope, and duct tape. I'm bringing her in."

"It'll be waiting for you when you get here." He hung up without saying goodbye.

She tossed her phone on the bed and stared down at Nadine. Veronica would back her car in the driveway once the sun was down, which shouldn't be much longer. She would tie Nadine up, gag her, and throw her in her trunk. She walked over to the bed, picked up the syringe, and held it in the light.

"What do you think it is?" Ethel asked.

Veronica shrugged before walking over and jabbing it into Nadine's neck and pushing the plunger.

17

adine's eyelid opened; the other was swollen shut and a disgusting shade of black. She tried to move, and her eye narrowed as she realized she couldn't. She looked down at the rope around her chest and then attempted to glance behind her at her arms.

"Don't bother. I've gotten really good at that over the years," Veronica said.

Nadine's gaze slowly matched Veronica's. Her lip curled back in a snarl. "Untie me, bitch."

"That's not happening." Veronica stood and pushed the hanging light bulb above her so it swayed, illuminating the hot, dry cellar and casting strange shadows over the tiny cabinet and one other chair. The first step in any interrogation is to confuse the suspect. She wanted her to have a feeling of emptiness, to understand there was no way out. She wanted her to know she was caught.

There was no way she would get free. Veronica had used so much rope, with layers of duct tape underneath. She made sure she couldn't move. The chair had metal legs and was bolted to the floor. Even if she attempted to tip over, she would just be wearing herself out.

Veronica felt herself flipping an internal switch off. The one where she shut her emotions down and did the job at hand—she

237

learned that trick early in her career. She taught herself to close off a piece of herself. To allow the event to unfold and throw it away. These last few months with Ethel, and especially the last few days with Jennifer, made it harder to withdraw from the situation.

Veronica knew this would be rough. She would have to put on a callous exterior. This wasn't an ordinary criminal in this chair. This was a monster, one with countless victims over fifty-plus years. Veronica had booked three days at the Greenbrier Hotel; she would stay at night and most of the day before visiting this room with Nadine when the sun started its descent. She was going to make sure that the job got done, and no others could be hurt. She'd made the deal for a way for Jennifer to stop Nothing. Nadine didn't look threatening at all. She looked helpless and broken. Her eye darted around the room.

"Why are you doing this?" Nadine asked, her voice filled with hate.

Veronica started to chuckle. "You're some kind of age-eating vampire. I mean, do they even have a word for it?"

"So you're going to torture me? Is that it?" Nadine growled.

"No," Veronica smirked. You're going to sit in that chair until you die. I'm treating you like you did your *meals*."

"Ugh," Ethel uttered from behind Veronica in revulsion.

"You know," Nadine let out a phony laugh. " A lot of people say the phrase 'nice guy.' They don't exist. We call a guy *nice* if he pays for a movie and tries not to jam his fingers in us on the way home," Nadine spat. "The first were accidents I couldn't control it, but I had a system. Pedos, rapists, murderers—real murderers—have kept me alive all these years. I've done more good for this state than you ever could, *officer*." Nadine looked away.

The second step for a successful interrogation, especially if no one was watching, was to intimidate them.

"You look away again, I start breaking fingers, and if that doesn't work I'll take teeth," Veronica said, grabbing Nadine by the chin and forcing the monster to look her in the eyes. Veronica too had done terrible things, not unlike what Nadine had done. Veronica wondered for a brief moment what she would do in the same situation. Was it all about survival? Would she enjoy it? Would she feel sorry for anyone whose life she took?

"How many?" Veronica asked.

"What do you mean?" Nadine asked.

Veronica slapped her. Nadine couldn't get away, but she wasn't looking at Veronica with contempt anymore; her eyes widened in fear.

"How many people have you killed?" Veronica never raised her voice. She would grill Nadine for information, maybe close some missing person cases, send anonymous letters to the families, and give them closure. She also was curious about how Nadine's body worked. Veronica had only dealt with the spirits of the dead, nothing anywhere close to this.

"I try to keep them for as long as I can, usually one a month." Nadine's voice was loud and shaky. "I stretch them out."

"You've been at this for fifty-one years..." Veronica could almost see the numbers floating through her mind as she did the math. "Oh my God, that's over six hundred... *Six hundred fucking people,*" Veronica whispered.

She was thinking of all the bodies lined up end to end. How many families did she destroy? Fathers that never came home to their children? She had to be lying; it wasn't feasible. There were towns in West Virginia that had less population.

"I would have died without them," Nadine said.

"How in the hell did you get away with six hundred? How did no one notice?" Veronica tried to keep her tone firm but was failing.

Nadine looked down at her bound body again. "I had a warden from Moundsville in the 80s, a police officer in Wheeling in the 90s. Do you realize the things I had to do to stay alive?"

"Holy shit, are you kidding me?"

She looked back at Veronica, her one open eye red and filled with tears of anger.

"Did you stop once to think about what you were doing, the lives lost?" Veronica stood and pushed her chair violently away from her.

"You didn't give a damn about anyone but yourself. You're a murderer, Nadine, this isn't about surviving—"

"Like I told you, I had a system, " Nadine screamed. "Would you let yourself die? No, you wouldn't! The hunger, it feels like my guts are eating away at themselves. There's no pain like it. The only way to get it to stop... Oh, fuck you. Nothing I say will make a difference."

Veronica paced around the room. She would try to justify this no matter what Veronica threw at her. "You stopped seeing them as people?" Veronica asked.

"After a while, they all start to seem the same. For so many years, I tried to only take criminals or the worst of the worst. Maybe one or two good ones slipped through the cracks, but a girl's gotta eat."

If steps one and two aren't getting the point across, there is always a third: Up the physical violence.

Veronica swung around and landed a solid jab, blood spurting around her knuckles as Nadine's nose cracked. Nadine screamed.

"I want names, places, everything you can remember!" Veronica shook out her hand. "I don't buy your 'bad guys' bullshit for one minute."

Nadine turned her head and spit; it was mostly blood. "I ain't giving you a goddamn thing. You're no better than me. If you were, we wouldn't be down here in this shithole basement."

Veronica stood and pulled her hand back again. Nadine closed her eye tight and braced for impact.

"Ronnie," Ethel popped in behind her. "Maybe you should take a break."

Veronica looked over her shoulder and shook her head. "I'm fine."

"Is something wrong with you?" Nadine was staring in the same direction. "Who are you talking to?"

"I'm a seer. It's how I caught you. I showed up at your niece's house, and my spirit waited to see if she'd reach out. I knew where you were every step of the way. You didn't have a chance. You're sitting here telling me this is about surviving? You're a piece of a shit." Veronica felt her anger rising at the thought of Nadine breaking into her sanctuary.

"What did you expect me to do?" Nadine responded with resentment.

"You know what? You almost had me feeling sorry for you. *Tell your sad story and maybe I'll let you go.* Maybe some of the people you killed deserved to die, but what you have done affects more than just the dead." Veronica said.

"And *that* is what I have been trying to tell you. Practice what you preach." Ethel fussed from the corner.

Veronica paused and glanced over. "Not right now."

She heard someone coming down the steps and could tell by the pace it was Wally. She didn't look back at him; she held Nadine's gaze. Nadine finally craned her neck to look, her brows pinched together, and she squinted. Veronica stepped aside to let Nadine see him finally.

"Been a long time, girl," Wally said, shuffling in. Veronica held out her arm so she could guide him into the seat.

"I don't know you," Nadine replied.

"You do; I'm the man that found Travis Taylor hanging in the garage." Wally put his hands on his knees. He was winded and breathing rapidly. "You killed him."

"I didn't kill him. He hung himself," Nadine said.

"Girl, I have the sight; don't lie to me," Wally said.

Nadine stared at him, her face contorting in anger. "I told you. He. Hung. Himself. I had nothing to do with it."

There was silence. Veronica went over to the cabinet and got the roll of surgical tape.

"I didn't know you had the *sight,* Wally."

Wally started to laugh. "I don't, but she don't know that."

Nadine roared at him. Veronica walked over to Nadine and tore a piece off. "Well, she does now. Wait till she finds out you're the one that put the curse on her."

"WHAT? YOU MOTHER—" Nadine thundered before Veronica forcefully put a strip over her mouth.

"That's enough out of you," she told her, wagging her finger. "What time did you come down here, Wally?" Veronica asked, keeping her eyes locked on Nadine.

"About 5:30," he answered.

"Then she's in for a real treat."

It wasn't long before the spiders descended. Veronica didn't feel much sympathy for Wally; he shouldn't have played in things he didn't understand. If she were being honest, he'd brought this plague onto the world, and he needed to be punished.

Veronica knew he'd wanted this for a long time; it would be over. Once this was done, she'd call Jennifer and get her back down here, and they would take care of the Nothing next.

The spiders had gathered in mass, and Nadine struggled to no avail.

Veronica leaned toward her and whispered, "You think you got it bad? Watch this."

She slowly backed away from Nadine and walked around the spiders to Wally, who had begun disrobing. She tore off another piece of tape and handed it to him. His lip quivered.

"I didn't want this for either of us, girl. I'm sorry." He reached up, taped his mouth shut, and sat back down.

Veronica tip-toed around the spiders directly behind Nadine and placed her hands on her shoulders. "This is the price he has to pay."

The spiders had their evening feast on Wally while Nadine tried to look away. Veronica gripped her head and turned it back toward him. She didn't know if Nadine closed her eyes part way through, but she wanted her to know everything that happened. She wanted her to see all of it.

As the spiders went on their merry way after having their fill, Allen came down the steps with his basket of salves and went to work on Wally's wounds. Veronica stood before Nadine, saying nothing. She had won this round; the next day, when the begging began, she knew she would handle that too.

"Allen, make sure after you take Wally out of here, you chain this cellar up just as I told you."

"Will do, detective," Allen said.

"I'll be back at the same time tomorrow to unlock it. I'm keeping the key."

"Sure thing," Allen responded.

"Nadine, I'll see you later." Veronica turned to leave.

"Mmm, mmm." Nadine tried to speak behind the tape.

"Oh yeah, right." Veronica removed a long strip of the tape, threw the roll to the ground, and placed the fresh one over the first. "I doubt they'd want to hear a peep out of you tonight."

Veronica said nothing to Wally or Allen as she ascended the stairs. Ethel was already waiting at the top.

"A tad over dramatic." Ethel shook her head.

"You used to watch Mama's Family." Veronica walked past her.

"So, are you going back to the room?" Ethel asked, trying to keep up.

"Yeah, it's too late for the spa. I might hit the casino and lose some money."

"Gambling? Really?" Ethel complained.

Veronica turned around and held out her arms. "I'm thinking of trying my luck. I just happened to catch a notorious serial killer."

Veronica went straight to the Greenbrier and decided to turn in for the night. She was tired, so she headed to her room instead of the blackjack table. The bed was soft, the room smelled flowery, and her head had barely touched the pillow before she was sound asleep.

The following day, she went to the main dining room, ate from the breakfast buffet, and nursed a morning mimosa. She was a little embarrassed by having a drink so early, but later that day she would be dealing with Wally and a monster, so she decided it was worth it.

She returned to her room to find Ethel waiting for her.

"What time are we going over to Wally's?" Ethel asked.

"You don't have to go, Ethel. I know it makes you uncomfortable."

Ethel didn't endure those things when she was alive, and Veronica was sure Ethel didn't like seeing her granddaughter torturing another living being, no matter what they'd done.

"No, she has to be stopped. It's what I always pictured you doing in your job," Ethel admitted.

"What, starve the unholy to death?" Veronica found that hilarious but kept herself from laughing.

"No," she frowned, "I always thought you saved people."

So much had changed over the last few days. Since she entered that godforsaken trailer, she'd gone from being the occasional ghosthunter to fighting demons and whatever Nadine was. Veronica was conflicted. What if this was what she was meant to do? What if Ethel didn't get to move on because there was a plan, a higher calling? It sounded ridiculous, but then again, a hellspawn was running around in the guise of an eleven-year-old. Anything was possible.

She got to Wally's home right after five, and as she passed by the porch she waved to Wally and Allen who were eating dinner. She pulled the key out to the padlock she'd given Allen, walked around the house, and released the lock from the latch on the door to the cellar. She descended the stairs and felt around for the light switch on the wall. After stumbling for a moment, she heard the audible click and looked at the chair.

She tried to keep her composure, but she couldn't. Nadine had undeniably aged. Her hair had grayed around the temples with streaks throughout the rest. Her skin was wrinkled and didn't have any of the glow or vibrancy it did the day before. Veronica strode over and ripped the tape off her mouth, trying to keep the hardened cop facade intact.

"Don't... Don't," Nadine muttered.

"Don't what?" Veronica asked.

"Don't tape my mouth again," Nadine pleaded. "I can't breathe."

Veronica grabbed a chair, placed it in front of Nadine, and sat down.

"You don't look so good," Veronica observed.

"It hurts... I'm so hungry. I'm going to die here." Nadine was out of it. She had two black eyes, and her nose was crooked, obviously broken. Most of the skin on her face was a nasty purple.

"You are. It won't be much longer."

"Just let me go. I don't want to go out in a basement. We could work together. You bring me the worst of the worst. I can make sure they get what—"

Veronica shook her head.

"This wasn't my fault. There are *real* monsters out there," Nadine gasped.

Veronica knew she would try to talk her way out of it on the second day. She still wasn't prepared. Veronica *was* killing her; she was aware of what she was doing. She'd have shot her in the head if she thought it would work, maybe finish this off mercifully, but Wally told her the night Veronica arrived with Nadine that it had to be this way. She had to finish the curse out. It had to run its course, like a virus.

Nadine struggled against her restraints. She was running out of energy. It was a sad attempt. She was starving and in pain. The woman she was yesterday still had fight left in her and was unruly. She'd made every attempt to justify her existence. This was someone desperate and broken, someone pleading for Veronica to remove her binds so she could live. Veronica had called Nadine a monster, but Veronica felt like one.

"I'm not a good person. I know that, Nadine. I haven't been for a long time. I killed a man a while back. I thought I was doing the right thing. I did something that, in my line of work, I'm supposed to stop." Veronica paused, wondering if she should finish; there was no need to talk to Nadine this way. She didn't owe her an explanation but she needed an outlet.

Veronica continued. "I've made a complete mess of my life. I make terrible decisions for all the wrong reasons. If it's revenge you want against me, you might not have to wait too long." Veronica rubbed her neck and thought of Jennifer. "There's a woman I've been with for the last few days. Someone who cares about me and worries if I could be hurt. She barely knows me, but she's the closest thing to a friend I've had in years." Veronica shook her head. "You know, there was a moment I was going to kill her just because I didn't want to be bothered with her problems. I'm almost as bad as you."

Nadine watched her, listening.

"My grandparents raised me. My grandmother, she's the ghost I can see. She gave me everything in the world and tried to be a parent and my best friend. She wanted me to change the world. My grandfather, on the other hand, was a judgmental prick who hated my guts and couldn't be bothered. I always wondered how my life would have been if it would have only been the two of us."

Veronica could see Ethel from the corner of her eye but didn't dare look her way. She wanted to confess. She wanted this woman tied to the chair to be her witness.

"The only person that believed in me doesn't anymore; she thinks I'm awful." Veronica chuckled at the thought of Ethel calling her that in front of Detective Green. "I don't know if this is my attempt at making something right. I've shit the bed so bad there's no cleaning it up, but you're not killing anyone else. I'm making sure of it."

Veronica leaned back as she heard creaking coming down the stairs. She stood up and moved the chair back to the corner. She waited until Wally came into view. "Hey Wally, how are things?"

Wally looked over at Nadine. "She don't look good."

Wally started to take his clothes off, and Veronica walked over and grabbed the tape roll she'd thrown on the floor yesterday. She waited patiently as he sat back down and taped his mouth shut. She patted his shoulder and nodded at him. She turned toward Nadine.

"No tape. I won't say a word. Please," Nadine begged, turning her head away. The cellar was silent as the spiders came into view. They stopped in front of the chair. Something was different. They had always been different sizes, but now they looked abnormally large. At least as large as her hand, and more frenzied. They skittered back and forth, excited for their meal. She tried to press the fear down, but it stayed there just under the surface.

"Are they bigger?" Nadine observed.

"You said you wouldn't say a word," Veronica reminded her.

It wasn't long before they were on him. There were fewer of them, but Veronica found their new-found girth more than made up for it. Wally groaned a lot louder than the previous times and recoiled more often. Veronica wished it would end. She found herself hoping that he would die right then. As they left his body, he reached up and tore the bloody tape off himself. He was soaked, and she couldn't see a dry spot on his skin. The bite marks were more pronounced this time, too. She could see them easily in the dimly lit room.

A few moments later, Allen descended the steps slowly, his face white with fear.

"Those ain't brown recluses or black widows. What types were those?"

"Don't know," Veronica shrugged, "I don't collect bugs."

"Don't you get it?" Nadine laughed coldly from her seat as Veronica glanced down at her. Nadine met her stare. "We're connected." Her laughter grew. "Can you imagine what tomorrow will be like, Wally?"

Veronica slapped the tape over Nadine's mouth as she'd done yesterday.

"You don't get to enjoy this. " Veronica checked the ropes to make sure they were still tight, and Nadine couldn't get free; it was apparent she had lost weight, and there was slack in them. She pulled and knotted until Nadine cried out in pain. Then she bent to eye level with her, and Nadine's eyes were filled with detestation.

"See you soon," Veronica mocked as she blew her a kiss. Veronica started toward the stairs. "Lock up on your way out," she said in Allen's direction.

"Detective, what if she's right?" Allen stood from tending to Wally.

"About?" Veronica stopped mid-stride and looked his way.

"What if tomorrow it is worse on him?" Allen asked with a sense of dread in his voice. Veronica paused and dwelled on it for a moment.

"It will be over soon."

"He didn't hate you," Ethel said on Veronica's way back to the car. She sounded as if she was trying to convince herself.

Veronica kept walking and opened the door before she looked back at Ethel, whose head was down, her hands clasped in front of her. "Could have fooled me."

"Your grandfather loved your dad. They did everything together. I was jealous of it, honestly. They had something special, just the two of them, and nothing else in the world compared." Ethel stepped forward; Veronica could swear for a brief moment Ethel looked as if she would cry. "And then you came along, his little mini-me. You talk like him, you walk like him—everything about you reminded your grandfather of the love he'd lost. He didn't hate you, sugar. You were a painful reminder of the best thing he had."

Veronica turned away from her grandmother and swallowed back the lump that had formed in her throat. *Sugar.* The familiarity was a comfort and a curse. Veronica couldn't afford the feelings that Ethel's sudden outpouring was dredging up. Not here, not now.

"I'm sorry he hurt you. I'm sorry *we* hurt you."

"I don't think hearing him talk about how much he loved my dad and how much he hated me would have done much good," Veronica said bitterly.

"Sugar, that man loved you, even if he never figured out how to show it. Just a week before he died, he went on and on about how proud he was of you for graduating the academy. He told me there were things he should have done differently. I told him to call you. He was just so damn stubborn." Ethel tried smiling, but Veronica could tell it was forced.

Veronica felt the wave of sadness overwhelm her. She didn't want to break down in front of Ethel. These were conversations that they should have had when they were alive. She turned as the wind picked up, letting it blow in her face. She closed her eyes and thought of this whole situation. She could walk a fine line; she'd been used to it these last few years, but now she just wanted to escape everything. She didn't want to deal with any of this anymore. The wind gave another hard gust. She opened her eyes and grinned at Ethel.

"I wish you could still feel the wind," she said.

"I do, too." After a pause, Ethel whispered, "I just need to know you're okay."

"I just... I thought I had everything figured out, you know?" Veronica started.

"What do you mean?"

"The man I killed? You know why I did that, right?"

"It doesn't matter—"

"He hurt children, Ethel. Little kids. He was the biggest monster of all. You kept shutting me down every time I tried to tell you."

"I saw how proud you were after it was over," Ethel said. "You *enjoyed* it. But it is not our place to do something like that, Ronnie. The Bible tells us not to take vengeance; he would have gotten what he deserved. If not in this life, then in the next. You could have found another way."

"I know it was wrong. I had convinced myself I was doing the right thing, and it took a long time to understand why I did it. I've been broken for a long time now." Veronica paused, wincing at the memory that came unbidden to her. "Remember the little boy that died? The one where I had to shoot the man in his living room?"

"How could I forget? You cried all night. The boy was already hurt. There was nothing you could have done," Ethel said.

"That was the night I knew the world had lost its mind. Since then, my whole life has been one mess after another. This job does something to you. You have no idea, and now, with all the stuff I've learned, I wish I could take it back. I really do."

Ethel nodded but didn't say anything in response.

"I have no idea how this thing is going to end. We've got invisible monsters, witches, and curses. Those spiders are getting bigger. A woman is aging overnight in front of me. I'm talking to my dead grandmother. I can't tell how crazy this is going to get. I just think you and I need to get some things off our chests, just in case. Maybe we can talk some more if we make it through this."

"You're not going to die," Ethel scoffed.

"You don't know that. I was trapped in the trunk of a car, and if you hadn't been there, I'd be in pieces right now. It's still out there, inside the body of a little boy." Veronica rubbed her face with both hands. "We still haven't dealt with that yet. And then there's the whole Detective Green thing. I just don't know what to do next."

"You'll figure it out." Ethel's gaze fell away momentarily as if she was working up the nerve for something. Finally, she took a step toward Veronica, lifted her hand, and cupped Veronica's cheek.

Veronica's eyes went wide. "Ethel," she whispered, "I can *feel* you."

Ethel gave a small nod as if saying, *Of course you can.*

Veronica closed her eyes and leaned into the touch. It had been *so long* since she'd felt her grandmother's touch, but the way it eased the ache in her heart was the same as it had always been.

"Maw Maw," Ethel said, her voice barely more than a whisper.

Veronica smiled and said, "Okay, Maw Maw."

"I'm proud of you. Despite everything that has happened. You're still my sweet girl."

With that, Ethel's touch fell away.

Veronica opened her eyes with a sigh. "I want to be alone tonight. Can you do that for me?"

"You're going to cry, aren't you?" Ethel smiled feebly.

"Yes," Veronica said as she got in and shut the door.

She told the truth. She went straight to her room at the hotel, crawled into the bed, and cried herself to sleep.

The next morning, she had breakfast in her room. She wondered what would be in that cellar when she returned to Wally's. How many more days would this take? She wanted to see this through, but she was drained. She wanted to go back home and surround herself with her work. What surprised her, though, was that she found herself missing Jennifer. Veronica didn't make friends; she had acquaintances, and

Jennifer was the most she'd wanted to be around any one person in years.

She thought about getting something small from the gift shop. She hadn't realized how lonely her life was. Jimmy wasn't a friend; he was a connection to the only person in her life who she thought understood her. She thought of work and how none of her coworkers fit that bill either. The only person she'd even remotely been able to consider was Ethel, and Veronica had ruined that.

When four o'clock rolled around, she felt nervous. Yesterday was rough, and she knew today would be worse. She dressed, and as she was putting on her shoes, she called out to Ethel to have someone to talk to on the ride over. She also was curious as to what she did during the night. It wasn't as if Ethel needed sleep.

Seconds passed, and the feeling never came. So she called out again. She watched the digital clock beside the bed, and as a minute passed, Ethel still hadn't appeared. Veronica had dealt with this before. Sometimes, Ethel wouldn't come right away if she was busy talking to another ghost, but a feeling of unease came ebbing in. Veronica grabbed her phone and her keys. She looked back over the room to see if she missed anything. She told herself that the old woman would be there at Wally's. No way she'd miss today. She wanted to end this curse as much as Veronica did.

She left the hotel and arrived at Wally's shortly after. When she pulled up, Allen came trotting off the porch and over to her car. She got out quickly. She could see the worry on his face from across the yard.

"Everything alright?" she asked.

"Some of his wounds didn't close last night," Allen told her nervously.

"Has that ever happened before?" Veronica asked, concerned. Allen shook his head. "Where is he?" Veronica gazed up to the porch, looking for him.

"On the couch resting. I'm—" Allen started.

"It's going to be alright," Veronica lied, "we will get through this. Go keep him company while I go check on Nadine." Veronica put her hand on his shoulder. He nodded, and off he went. She descended the stairs and turned on the light. Nadine was unrecognizable. Her eyes were glassed over, and she looked sickly. Her hair was white, and her skin was covered in dark spots. Her wrinkles were profound, and she shook as she looked up at Veronica. Nadine was nearing the finish line, and Veronica could feel anticipation replace the fear.

"I don't think I have to comment on how you look today," Veronica said as she walked over and took the tape from Nadine's mouth.

"I don't hurt. The hunger is gone. That's good, right? I keep thinking of my mom. I keep thinking of Travis. He told me he was going to take me away from here." Nadine's voice was raspy.

Veronica nodded; she didn't know what to say to that.

"I just want it to be over." Nadine's lips quivered as she smiled. "You aren't going to hit me again, are you?"

Veronica shook her head. Nadine chuckled before having a coughing fit.

"Thank you," she attempted to smile, but her jaw shook.

Veronica walked behind her and loosened some of the knots she'd tied. She didn't say anything as she did it. This wasn't out of pity; it was out of compassion. Nadine would not make it through the night.

"You think I'm going to heaven?" Nadine asked.

Veronica laughed as she came back around to face her. "Probably not."

"I don't think so either. You know, I was gonna drain you dry the night I came to your house. I hadn't eaten in two days." Nadine paused and smacked her lips. "I would have done anything to live."

"I think most of us would." Veronica heard the steps creaking, and she turned to see Allen helping Wally down the stairs. Allen was practically walking for the old man, his feet dragged across the ground. The man looked as if he would pass out at any moment. His face and arms were still covered in bite marks. The color had all but drained from his face. His eyes weren't looking at anything in particular, and he had saliva at the corners of his mouth. He looked as bad as Nadine; she had been right. They were connected. Allen guided him and placed him in the seat. Veronica could see the blood soaking through spots in his clothes and could hear him breathing heavily.

"You look awful," Nadine remarked as she broke into a cough.

Wally nodded, took the handkerchief out of his pocket, and wiped his head before throwing it on the floor.

He took a second to catch his breath and looked at Nadine. "I'm sorry. I did you wrong."

Nadine snorted. "It's a little too late, old man."

Allen looked at his phone. "Almost time, you gonna undress?"

"Oh, to hell with 'em; if they want it, they gonna have to bite through." He waved his bony hand scornfully. Nadine started to laugh, but her eyes widened. Her right eye began to twitch, and she groaned between quick intakes of air.

Wally placed his hands on his knees. "I'll meet you there shortly."

Veronica watched Nadine shudder, and her breaths came further apart. Phlegm flew from her mouth, and she craned her neck. She blinked a few times before she gasped, and then she was still. Allen rushed over to her and placed his finger on her neck. Veronica didn't need reassurance; she already knew. The curse had been broken. Nadine was dead.

"You okay?" Veronica asked the old man, who was crying softly, his eyes fixed on Nadine.

Allen's alarm went off in his pocket. Veronica glanced around the room. The spiders had not come early this time, and none were waiting by his chair. The walls were bare, and they weren't on the ceiling. Allen took his phone out and silenced it.

"It's over? He's free?"

"I guess so," Veronica said. Wally shook his head and wiped his tears.

"You forgot, we are connected," he whispered.

Allen backed against the wall and slid down it. Veronica hadn't noticed before, but her eyes darted back to the stairs. Three spiders faced her, black as night and as large as the beagle she owned as a child. They were terrifying. They slowly descended the stairs and stopped. It was as if they let the two of them take in their presence. Veronica stepped back and joined Allen against the wall.

"Did you bring your gun?" he whispered

"No," Veronica mumbled.

"They ain't here for you," Wally snorted. "Well, don't tease me, you sons of—"

The first one turned and rushed him, knocking him from the chair and onto the floor. It had a hold of his left leg as he kicked and let out a yell of pain. He was bleeding instantly, and Veronica could hear the sounds of its legs against the concrete and the tearing of Wally's clothing.

"I HOPE YOU CHOKE!" he screamed, swinging his fists down at it.

The second one skittered across the room and latched onto his stomach as he cried out. He was trying with all his might to get them off of him. Veronica stepped forward, but the third one by the stairs raised its legs threateningly. She put her hands up and returned to where she'd been. She could hear them biting him. Her stomach turned violently, and she swallowed hard to avoid vomiting. She glanced over at Allen, who had curled up into a ball and began to whimper.

The third one was on the move, and it went for his face. She could no longer hear Wally screaming, only the nasty wet sounds of them feasting on the poor man. She wanted to help him; she knew this was his punishment, but she prayed for it to end. *Just let the man die.*

But there would be no compassion for Wally. His blood spread over the floor, and the spray from a particularly gruesome bite to Wally's neck had coated the nearby wall. Veronica kept wondering when they would stop, but they just kept going. Wally wasn't visible anymore, just the spiders, feasting and convulsing. Veronica couldn't take it anymore. She closed her eyes and leaned against the wall. She found herself wishing her grandmother was here to make her feel safe. Where was she?

The sounds would haunt her for the rest of her life. As they slowed, she opened her eyes and saw the first spider leaving the basement. Wally was nowhere to be seen.

There's no trace of him; they took him, bones and all.

The second spider slowly followed the first, leaving a trail of blood. Veronica put her hand over her mouth and held her breath. Even his clothes were gone, eaten. He had been erased. There would be nothing to bury, nothing to remember him by. The only thing left was a thick, red goop.

The third spider went over to Nadine's chair and froze in place. Veronica was hoping it wouldn't consume her, too. She just wanted it to go away. She knew she'd never be the same around spiders again. She had never had arachnophobia before, but now she wished death upon the entire species. It raised its front legs and lowered them slowly, close to the ground.

Did that thing just bow?

It spun around and quickly bolted up the stairs and out of sight.

Veronica was afraid to move. Even after Allen finally stood up and walked over to where Wally had been, she kept motionless. She didn't want them to come back. She tried to calm her trembling by taking deep breaths and holding her hands together, but it had no effect. She kept telling herself over and over to move, and after a while, her left leg responded. She took another step and almost went down. She headed over to Allen, who turned and looked at Nadine.

"Whoa."

Nadine turned to dust before Veronica's eyes. Her face collapsed inward and poured into the collar of her shirt. Veronica stared as the grains drained from the opening of her pants legs and piled up on the floor. Veronica nudged Allen as Nadine's body continued to wither away.

"Let's get out of here."

"You need to follow me up on the porch." Allen sniffled.

"Why?" Veronica asked as the last bit of Nadine spilled out. The ropes sagged, and all that remained were her clothes.

"Wally left you something," Allen said.

<h1 style="text-align:center">18</h1>

Veronica stood on the porch and admired how it wrapped around the left side of the house. She hadn't been up here yet and wished she had before. It was a fantastic view. The sun was setting, and all she could see was green. The wood looked great, and she wondered if Wally had it recently built. There were two rocking chairs and a fairly large glass table to the side of the steps. Allen made a straight line for it. He picked up a large manilla envelope and held it out for her.

"Inside is the business card for the attorney and the paperwork you need to sign." Allen nodded at the envelope in his hand.

Veronica took it without hesitation. "What am I signing?"

"I'll have the couch and chair out of there tonight. I'm leaving the rockers and this table." He tapped the glass with his knuckle. "I'm also supposed to remove his body and hers, but that won't be much of a problem. Other than that, the house is already empty. The building out back has a numbered keypad lock; code is 0327, the date Wally and Nora got married. All of his collection is stored there."

"Wait," Veronica laid the envelope on the table. "What the hell are you talking about?"

"The house, the land—everything—it's all yours. He left it to

256

you." Allen explained, looking confused. "Did we not tell you that? The reward for stopping Nadine?"

Veronica shook her head. "It never came up."

"Oh, well, congratulations." Allen gave her a half-assed thumbs up. "There are four keys in the pack there. Two for the front and two for the back—"

"What am I supposed to do with all of this?" Veronica interrupted.

Allen looked at her and smiled. "I don't care, detective. My job is done when I get the couch and chair out of there and clean the cellar. I'm already packed. I'm on my way to Florida. I'll never step foot in this state again."

"Yeah, but why not leave it to you?" Veronica made a sweeping gesture with her hand at everything she could see.

"I don't want it, and I don't need it. I promised my father and grandfather to help Wally until the day he died. I was so scared that I was gonna pass this down to my baby girl. You did it. It's over. I'm as grateful as he was." Allen's smile widened.

She thought about it for a moment. How long had he been watching all of this happen? He probably was afraid he would be trapped here, miserable with a man who couldn't die. She picked up the sealed envelope from the table and held it against her chest.

"When you say that his collection is stored there? You mean…"

"All the books, crosses, weird carvings, the lot of it. Do with it what you will. Sell it off, burn it, I don't give two shits." He went to the front door and put his hand on the handle. "You want to take a look inside?"

Veronica shook her head. "No, you finish up and get out of here. I need to call Jennifer, and I'm worried about Ethel. I'll come first thing in the morning and look around myself."

She *was* worried about Ethel. She had not shown up during the entire sequence of events and wasn't here now. This whole house situation and Wally leaving everything to her was astonishing, but she had more pressing matters.

"Suit yourself. No offense, but I hope I never see you again, detective. I don't ever want to come back here," Allen said as he went through the front door.

Veronica started down the steps, still shocked from being given everything the dead man owned. They'd known each other for less than a week. She looked down at the envelope. The only thing written on it was *Nora 0327*. She recalled how his eyes lit up as he mentioned Nora. She found herself hoping they were reunited in the afterlife.

She called Ethel's name as she made it to the yard. She paused, hoping this time would be the one. She finally reached her car, and panic had set in once she closed the door. Ethel was still nowhere to be seen. What was going on? Why was she ignoring her?

"ETHEL!" She gripped the steering wheel tight and held her breath. She felt as if she was going to hyperventilate. Her grandmother never materialized. What if something had happened to her? Was she in trouble?

"Maw Maw?" Veronica whispered as she saw Allen come out on the porch. Veronica started the car and waved at him. She didn't want him to ask questions, so she turned around in the yard and headed back toward the hotel.

She turned on some music. It helped her relax when she felt overwhelmed. She couldn't pinpoint where her love for the 80s genre came from but couldn't get enough of it. Maybe it was the positivity or hidden sexual innuendos in most songs. She also had a love for 80s television and film. A lot of the media she consumed was from that decade. She always joked to herself that she was born too late. She tapped her fingers along the steering wheel, trying not to think about Wally's passing or that Ethel had snubbed her. She started to crave a drink, something to take the edge off.

She had one more night at the Greenbrier and contemplated leaving and heading home. She could call Jennifer on the way, and they could meet at her house. She was excited to tell her about being given Wally's possessions, most of all, though, she wanted to be somewhere familiar. This whole Nadine affair had been enough, and she was exhausted. The clock on her dash showed 6:40 PM. She could make it back to her house by eleven if she left shortly.

I just want away from here, she thought. She was about to turn into the Greenbrier parking lot when her phone started ringing. It had interrupted her singalong of Sledgehammer by Peter Gabriel, and that irritated her. She'd always been a fan of that one. She noted the number, which she didn't recognize, but the ID told her it was a call from Oak Hill, West Virginia.

That's where Jennifer's from, she remembered. She slid her finger across the phone to answer and put it up to her ear.

"Yello."

"May I speak to Detective Veronica Carter?" a man's voice asked professionally.

Oh no. A sense of dread came rushing forward. Something set off alarm bells in her head.

"This is her."

"This is Officer Valerius from the Fayette County Sheriff's Office."

Oh, God, please, no. Veronica pulled over to the side of the road.

"What can I do for you, Officer?"

"I got your card out of a woman's pocket. I'm hoping you can help me?" His tone was almost impossible to read, but she knew he didn't have to tell her.

Please don't, please don't do this. She wiped the tears that were already rolling down her cheek. "I'll do what I can."

"I have a woman with me, in her early thirties; she's cut up pretty good at the bottom of an embankment. Only thing in her pockets was your card, this number on the back. Would you happen to know who I'm looking at here?"

"She's dead?" Veronica knew the answer before it left her lips.

"Yes, ma'am."

NO. She started to sob.

"Is her hair dark... Reddish... Shoulder length?"

"Yes, ma'am."

"Check your local hotels to see if there is a registration for a Jennifer Simmons. That's the last person I gave my card to." Veronica wiped her tears again. "And, officer?"

"Yes?"

"If you find out if it's her, can you call and let me know? She's a friend of mine." Veronica closed her eyes.

"I can do that, sure. I hope it isn't your friend, ma'am." Officer Valerius said with sincerity.

"Me too." Veronica flung the phone at Wally's envelope on the passenger seat. She bawled for several minutes and called out for her grandmother several times. Veronica was alone. Ethel never came. She leaned over, reached into the glove compartment, got some napkins, and blew her nose.

As the passenger door opened, she jumped in her seat, and a teenage girl entered her car. Veronica threw the napkin down and raised her fists, shocked.

The girl had light brown hair and wore too much makeup. She matched Veronica's gaze and smiled at her. Her jeans had more holes than fabric, and she wore a Type O Negative t-shirt. Her ears were pierced multiple times, and she had a strong scent that reminded Veronica of burning wood.

"KID!" Veronica barked, wiping her tears away with her left hand. "You picked the wrong fucking car to jack."

"It's okay, Veronica. I just want to talk." She patted her pockets. "I'm sorry I don't have my tissues, or I'd offer."

"HOLY SHIT!" Veronica cried out as her left hand began to burn. She started digging at it as the pain intensified and caused her fingers to lock up. Veronica felt faint as memories of the night Chris died washed over her. Then, as quickly as it had set upon her, it dissipated, and she leaned back, clutching her hand and trying to catch her breath.

"I wish that could have been easier on you, but..." the teenager confessed.

"Grace," Veronica whispered. "It's you, isn't it?"

Grace nodded and turned sideways to face her. She smiled, and her brown eyes lit up. "I have wanted to come see you for so long."

"What the hell do you want?" Veronica whimpered, still dizzy from the effects of what had happened.

"I came to apologize and try to make things right," Grace responded cheerfully.

"How so?" Veronica looked at her left hand, terrified the pain would return.

"I was supposed to die that day, you know that? My aunts were trying to get to me; Ariel had a vision of me dying on that porch, and she's never wrong. Somehow, you ended up there and stopped it. You defied fate, and none of us can figure out how." Grace fidgeted in her seat.

"What did you do to that family? You didn't belong there."

"I was there to drive them mad, and then Chris was to come home with me. It was my first real job. I'd never been on my own before."

"You targeted them?" Veronica asked, confused.

"Yes. Bruce was a member of the flock and ran away. He thought he could hide from us. It was up to me to see him punished," Grace said with pride.

"Jesus," Veronica leaned against the steering wheel. "You're a witch, aren't you?"

Grace didn't respond to her question but continued recalling her side of the events. "Ariel wanted to kill you and the other cop. Babby wanted to wipe your memory and leave you both on the couch naked and ashamed."

"That wouldn't have worked." Veronica laughed nervously.

Grace chuckled along with her. "You'd be surprised what she can do."

"So why couldn't I remember you until now?" Veronica changed the subject.

"I gave you the best of both worlds. I was just starting, like I said. I gave you your sight while Babby hexed you both to forget."

"You're the reason..." Veronica began.

"You can see the dead, yup, that's all me, ancient spell I shouldn't have been playing around with. My dumb ass thought that would be handy for you." Grace shrugged. "I was young."

"It helped me; I could talk to my grandmother," Veronica said. She had been thankful for the extra time they'd had together.

"I know. But look at the mess you are in now and all the damage I've done. Ariel calls you my biggest screw-up." Grace's face turned a light red; Veronica could see it embarrassed her to admit that. Veronica didn't like being called a screw-up, but she sat silently, waiting for Grace to finish.

"So here's how I'm going to fix all this." Grace held out her hand. "I'll undo my spell, and you'll fall asleep. When you wake up, you will be in your bed, no memory of me, dead grandma, Wally, Nadine, Jennifer, none of it. I'll take care of Green and make sure Jennifer gets taken and buried properly with her family."

My God, how much does this kid know about me?

"More than you think," Grace responded.

Veronica was afraid now; this was something worse than Nadine and Nothing combined. Grace could erase someone from existence if she wanted. No one to mourn, no one to even remember. She had allowed her to communicate with the other side and saw it as a gigantic fuck up. Just exactly how powerful were witches?

"In a few hours, Lacy will come to your home and be smitten and enthralled with you as if your ass was made of gold. You can live out your days with her, and we're even. I'll give her back."

"How would I get home?" Veronica stalled.

Grace glanced behind them, and Veronica looked into the rearview mirror at the familiar black car parked behind her. The one from the day they met.

"So, do we have a deal?" Grace looked at her hand and held it out a little further.

Veronica stared at it and bit her lip. She thought of her grand-mother and Jennifer. She just learned of her death, and she was contemplating forgetting her. It was almost as disgusting as when she thought about killing her. The only person Jennifer would have grieving her was Tina, which bothered her.

"Grace, don't take this the wrong way, but get the fuck out of my car."

Grace's smile widened as she pulled back her hand. "Have to say I didn't expect that."

"I'm full of surprises. I appreciate the gift you already gave me, and I think I'll keep it," Veronica said as she stared forward out the windshield.

"Well," Grace said, bringing both hands down her thighs and making an audible slap. "I hope you understand this will only get tougher for you."

"I'm full of—" Veronica began.

"Surprises," Grace finished. "I heard you." Grace opened the passenger door and exited the Sentra. She leaned back in and said, "Before I go, I want to warn you: I don't ever want to see you again. If you have the urge to go to Weirton, don't. We aren't friends, we aren't buddies, and you sure as hell ain't family. Are we clear?"

Veronica couldn't let that slide. She turned to face her. "Same goes for you and Parkersburg." It was a stupid and meaningless threat, but she wouldn't let this kid intimidate her.

Grace's face couldn't hide the shock before she smirked. "Fair enough."

Veronica jumped again as she slammed the door and watched as she walked back to the classic automobile and entered. She heard the engine fire, and they zoomed past her. Ariel in the driver seat and Grace in the passenger, both staring at her menacingly. Veronica waved, retrieved her phone, set a destination for Oak Hill, and took off.

19

The Day Before

When the phone rang early that morning, Jennifer almost let it go to voicemail. The tinny ringing sent her groggy brain into a tailspin, and as she moved to make the ringing stop, everything that had happened over the last few days came rushing into her sleep-addled mind.

Jennifer pressed the button to answer before checking to see who was calling. She expected to hear Veronica's voice on the other end, though she hoped she was mistaken. If Veronica was calling her already, something had gone wrong.

But it wasn't Veronica. It was Tina.

"Are you ready to tell me what the fuck is going on?"

Jennifer blinked back her surprise. "Good morning to you, too."

"Good morning?" she huffed. "Are you kidding me?"

"Tina, what's wrong?"

"You know damn well what's wrong," she said, her tone going high through the receiver. "You broke into my facility, went into my office, showed up at my house with your new lover... You're a lesbian now? When did—no, nevermind, not important."

"Tina, that's not—" Jennifer began.

"No, absolutely not. After all that shit you pulled, abusing my friendship, endangering my career, and behaving like a goddamn criminal, you have the nerve to ignore my calls? You owe me an explanation."

"You're right, I do."

When Jennifer paused a few seconds too long, Tina said, "And? Are you going to give me one?"

"I wish I could. I definitely owe you one, and I will figure out a way to make things right between us, but the things that are happening right now…"

"Unbelievable," Tina said.

Jennifer sighed. "Okay, okay. I will tell you but you have to promise, you have to *swear* you won't freak out."

"What the hell have you gotten into?" Tina asked.

"Promise me." Jennifer ran her fingers through her hair.

Tina sighed. "Fine. I promise."

"The thing that killed my father—"

"Oh fuck, we're back to this? It was a bear, Jenn. A fucking bear."

"No," Jennifer said, shaking her head even though Tina couldn't see her. "It was the same thing that killed Dylan's mom."

"Jenn," Tina said, putting on the voice she used when trying to calm her patients. "We've been through this multiple times. We had this same conversation when that other girl—"

"Michelle. Her name was Michelle."

"When *Michelle* lost her boyfriend, you thought the same thing. Look where that got you. You pushed too hard and ended up losing your license."

"You think I'm crazy."

"I think you've been through a traumatic loss, and you relate to these kids who have dealt with something similar. You can use it for good once you get things squared away and you're reinstated. But that's never going to happen if you're talking to patients when you shouldn't be."

"I never said I talked to Dylan," Jennifer breathed.

"Your fingerprints were all over his file."

Jennifer's stomach dropped. The police knew she'd been looking at his file, and Tina knew she'd talked to him, despite her best efforts to hide it.

"We talked about the monster," Jennifer admitted. "It's dangerous."

"Uh, yeah, you think I don't know that? That kid just happened to escape after you talked to him, murdered some of my employees, and is on the lam. I think I understand how dangerous the situation is. What I don't understand is how you got so involved after one conversation."

"I don't know what to tell you; Dylan opened up to me."

"Well, thank Christ for that, since you're going to help me set things right."

"How can I do that?"

Tina sighed. "He called me at work."

"Who? Dylan?"

"Yes, Jennifer, keep up. The kid called me an hour ago from a gas station in Harvey. He said he'll turn himself in if I meet him tomorrow morning. Alone."

"You can't meet him alone." Jennifer felt her stomach knot. *What was Nothing planning?*

"No shit. But I can't meet him at all unless you tell me where to go. He said if I sent the police to the place he was calling from, the deal was off."

"I don't know where he is."

"I don't need you to know where he is. I need you to figure out where he's going. Jenn, the voice on the phone... It was him, but it wasn't. He's had a complete psychotic break. He kept asking how my children and husband were *by name*. I'm terrified. I asked him where he was, and he said you would know."

Jennifer momentarily let the words hang in the air as what Tina said rolled through her mind. *He's going to kill her. He wants me, and if he doesn't get his way, he'll kill that whole family.*

He could be anywhere in West Virginia for all she knew. He could be... Then it hit her: of all the places Nothing could go, only one meant something to both of them.

"He's going to the bridge," Jennifer lied.

"New River Gorge?"

"Yes," Jennifer said. "He kept going on and on about it. That he wanted to see it when he got out."

"Okay, Fayetteville it is. I gave him my cell number. I'm expecting his call. He asked for yours, but I refused."

"You're not calling the police?"

"I can't risk it," Tina said. "Listen, before you say anything else, I know this is a bad idea. I know I'm walking into trouble. But if there's a chance I can bring Dylan in safely, I have to take it. No matter what he's done, he's still just a kid who needs my help."

"I'll meet you there," Jennifer said.

"No. He told me to come alone. I need to do this on my own. Tell me you understand."

"I do," Jennifer said.

She truly did. She told Tina to go to Fayetteville, not Oak Hill, where he really was. Nothing wanted to finish the story in the place where it all began. She couldn't let it hurt her friend and Tina's children.

"I love you," Tina said. "You're a terrible friend and I'm still pissed, but I love you."

Jennifer smiled. "I love you, too. Talk soon."

She disconnected the call and began to pack.

Jennifer leaned down and plucked a weed from her father's grave. She tossed it to the side and knelt with her hand on the tombstone. She smiled as she read the etching in the stone.

Patrick David Simmons
May 14th, 1961 - June 12th, 1994
Father, Husband, Man

The last word bothered her, but her mother insisted on it. She always thought it was weird. Her mother wasn't in her right mind when she asked for that inscription and, to be honest, never regained her sanity fully after his death. Everyone lost a piece of themselves that day.

"I'm sorry I haven't come to visit." A group of people walking in the distance momentarily caught her eye. "It was too painful. I hated being reminded of what happened here." She stood and watched as the people walked out of sight. "I'm sure you were lonely. Without Mom to visit, I should have made an effort to see you once in a while."

Jennifer wouldn't cry; she'd done that enough in her lifetime. She wanted to put on a brave face for her father. She knew she shouldn't be here. She should have waited like she'd promised Veronica. They were supposed to take down Nothing together, with Ethel as the backup plan. She wanted to honor that vow, but she couldn't. Not with Tina in danger. Besides, this was Jennifer's fight; it was unfair for Veronica to put her life on the line like that. She'd done enough for Jennifer already.

"I think I can beat it, Dad. I read the book. I know what I'm dealing with. It won't be easy. I can feel it coming. It won't be long." She looked down at the nail on her index finger that she'd chewed to the quick. "Thank you for sending Veronica to save me. I couldn't have gotten here without her."

Jennifer felt a strong breeze coming from behind her. She could swear she felt his presence. Maybe he was there with her. It wasn't too far-fetched after all the things she'd learned.

"I know she's a bitch, but she could have let me die in that room, and she didn't."

As the wind came and went, her mind raced with memories of her dad: him showing her how to make eggs, helping her with her homework, teaching her to ride a bike. She remembered his aftershave and his laugh; she placed her hand back on the marker.

"I hope I made you proud. I know I didn't turn out to be perfect, but I will try to live up to the standard I think you wanted, and it starts tonight."

She rubbed the stone gently and turned away. She had one more person to visit. She walked past the rows of headstones and over to a slight incline. There was a small path that went through the entire graveyard. She headed around a slight bend until she reached a row near the back. Her destination was the last one on the left. She stood there, barely able to look down on it.

"Hey, Neil." She tried to smile but couldn't. "Listen, I don't know if you're still here like Ethel is, but if you are, Christ, I'm sorry. I never meant for you to die. I should have gotten someone. I should have said something, and I didn't. I left you all alone. There's no excuse for it." The wind blew in her face, and she envisioned him calling her every name in the book. "I know. You're right. You deserved better." She placed her hand on his monument and rubbed it too. "I hope you can forgive me, and I hope you're rooting for me tonight."

It was a slow walk back to her car. Being back home was a strange feeling; she had spent more of her life in other places, but this was home. The place she last remembered being happy. It had changed a great deal since she'd last set foot in the town. The Kmart her mother worked at didn't exist anymore. Neither did the pizza place that her dad loved so much. She'd driven by where her house used to be, and it was gone. She was surprised to see the Pullen family name on the mailbox next to where her home once sat. It looked as if it was now an extended part of the Pullen's yard. It was as if everything that defined her as a child was gone. There were more houses and different businesses. Her school had been rebuilt and consolidated. It was all so familiar and alien at once.

She went back to her room at the Comfort Inn. She lay on the bed and opened Wally's book to see if she missed any minor details. The book had a slight musty odor to it, and it didn't feel sturdy at all. It was as if the pages were brittle and might crack in her hands. She was careful, though; she had been warned. She wondered if Wally or Nora had acquired it. The book discussed demons and possessions and how to deal with them. If the text was to be believed, Wally was correct. Blessed silver was the weapon of choice against them. It never explained why, but the salt and the silver dust would make the demon visible and cause it pain. With the spike he had lent her, all she had to do was nick the monster.

She wanted to drive it through its heart. If it had taken Dylan over, he was gone. The tome did say once a person was possessed, they were dead. It selfishly took control of that boy; imprisoning him wasn't enough. She flipped from page to page, looking at the crude drawings and footnotes left by whoever had owned the book before. Once she killed it, it would instantly return to where it spawned, making her happy. It was afraid to go home and had begged Ethel not to send it there. She'd remembered Veronica telling her that.

Dylan escaped a few days ago and was all over the news. Well, not Dylan, Nothing, but it killed two people in its escape. How many had fallen victim since then? What atrocities had it committed in the body of an innocent boy? She shivered at the thought of Nothing roaming free.

She pulled up the sleeve of her shirt. The symbol on her wrist was still there. The book had said she could compel the demon to come to her if she marked her skin in her blood. All she had to do was think of it when she did it. It seemed like something out of a terrible horror movie as she stuck her finger with a stick pin several times, but the more she dwelled on it, the more it made sense. It was drawn to blood and violence, and it was obvious that she and Nothing were connected. It would come. It wanted to kill her. One thing she was sure of—it was going to die tonight, or she was.

She picked up her phone and thought about calling Veronica. She was going to ask her how the hunt for Nadine was going. She had the card with her number in her pocket. If she called her, though, she'd ask her what she was doing and see right through her. Veronica was trained to know when someone was hiding something. She didn't want the headache of Veronica trying to talk her out of what she was about to do.

The tingling on her wrist became more intense. Nothing was getting closer. Soon, she would confront her past, and one way or another, she'd be free. The time on her phone told her it was after six, meaning Wally just endured another round with the spiders. Jennifer shuddered at the thought. She would rather die than have that happen to her. She put on an Oak Hill Red Devils t-shirt she'd picked up in town, which she found ironic. She grabbed the small bag she had bought and put the powder container and spike inside. Her phone started buzzing from the bedside table, and she saw that Tina was calling her again. She was probably in Fayetteville close by, and Dylan was nowhere to be seen. If she made it out of this alive, they would have a long talk, and Jennifer would tell her everything. Whether she believed her or not, she had been her friend through thick and thin, and Jennifer needed to come clean instead of hiding the truth.

She left her phone there, ringing, and went to her car. She drove silently to a blue mailbox in the corner of town and, using a prepaid envelope, mailed the book Wally had given her back to his address. If something happened to her, she wanted someone to find it and start down this path. Then she drove to where the house she grew up in used to be. She parked in front of the waist-high fence on the side of the road. She took the bag with the belongings she brought and exited the Focus. She stepped onto the sidewalk and stared at the man-made pond where her bedroom used to be.

"Can I help you?" called a woman's voice from the front of the house off to the right.

Jennifer looked in that direction, and a younger woman was coming her way cautiously. Jennifer smiled and shook her head.

"Then do you need something?"

The woman's tone wasn't friendly at all. But that was to be expected when an unknown person had just pulled up in front of your house and looked longingly at your possessions.

"My house used to be right here." Jennifer pointed toward the yard. "My bedroom, I'm fairly certain, was where your little fish pond is."

The woman's face changed instantly.

"You're Patrick Simmons' daughter!" Her hands shot up to her mouth in shock. Jennifer was a tad confused.

"I'm sorry, have we met?"

"No, I apologize. I'm Gloria Pullen. My husband and I own my mom and dad's old house." She held out her hand. Jennifer took it and gave it a shake.

"I didn't mean to startle you. I haven't been in town for decades, and I came to visit my father's grave and see some old friends."

"No, it's alright. Dad used to go on and on about how great your dad was." Gloria smiled. She was a fairly tall woman with short-cut, light brown hair. When she'd shaken Jennifer's hand, Jennifer noticed how calloused Gloria's was. She didn't know what she did for a living, but it had to be rough. Gloria was stocky. Her shoulders and forearms were thick with muscle. Jennifer was happy this woman wasn't as belligerent as she initially thought.

"They were pretty close. They used to have a beer and watch baseball together," Jennifer said.

"Just one beer?" Gloria joked.

"Well, they got together and drank beers. The baseball game was an excuse." Jennifer giggled at the memory.

Gloria laughed along and looked at her yard. "They couldn't sell your house after what happened, so Dad bought the lot. After I was born, he wanted to build me a house there."

"Is he...?" Jennifer hoped he wasn't, but it would be rude not to ask.

"Dead?" Gloria scoffed. "Oh no, Mom and Dad are in Florida bitching about the heat and playing shuffleboard all day."

"That's great. They were so good to me." Jennifer told the truth. They were so friendly and loving to her. Gwen always made Matt cookies but would make him bring some to Jennifer. When the incident happened, they constantly checked on her and apologized a thousand times. She had forgotten them, and it embarrassed her.

"Dad always wondered what happened to you. He used to have me scour social media for you. He said you were the sweetest thing."

Gloria was fishing for information; she wasn't hiding it. She probably loved to gossip, but Jennifer didn't mind. This was Matt's daughter, and it made her feel good to know that he was still alive.

"You wouldn't believe me if I told you," Jennifer teased.

"I just might," Gloria answered excitedly.

"I went to the University of Maryland and became a psychologist specializing in children," Jennifer said. "I'm Doctor Jennifer Simmons."

"No shit! I can't wait to call him and tell him. He'll be over the moon." Gloria squealed as if someone told her that her high school crush liked her, too.

"Can I ask a favor of you?" Jennifer asked, holding her wrist as it was starting to burn.

"What's that?" Gloria leaned in.

"I'm going to walk my old stomping grounds and see some people I stayed in touch with. Is it okay if I leave my car parked here? I might even have a few drinks at their house, so it might be late before I come back, but I don't want to be a bother."

"No problem at all. I'm just glad I finally got to meet you! Dad was always heartbroken over what happened to you guys. He had a picture of the six of you on the mantle above the fireplace, your family and mine."

That one stung Jennifer a little. She should have kept in touch with the family. Matt and Patrick were inseparable; maybe it was too painful for her to see him. Once this was over, she'd get his number and call them. If she felt brazen enough, she'd make the trip down and have Gwen make her cookies.

"That means a lot to me. I'll tell you what, I am already late, so I will get going, but tomorrow is my last day here. I'll stop by if that's okay; I'd love to talk to him on the phone."

"That would be great. I see you got the Red Devils on." Gloria pointed to her shirt. "I'm the phys ed teacher there."

"Oh, I picked one up for the hell of it. I would have gone to Fayetteville if we'd stayed around, but I wanted something to remind me of here. No place like home, you know?" Jennifer started to walk away.

"Don't I know it! Have a good night!" Gloria said and waved.

Jennifer followed the same route she took that day. She thought of the purple bike she'd gotten for Christmas and the vacation they never got to take. She passed a few people out for strolls on the warm summer evening. Each one nodded or said hello; it was the one thing she missed about West Virginia. She'd been to a lot of places, from DC to LA. The people here were the friendliest in the country. Maybe it was how they were raised or the dark secrets Wally told her existed. Did the people here act that way to try and weed out the evil that lurks beneath the surface? She was cautious of everyone now. What if one of them was a wolf or a witch? Wally had said witches were practically the worst creatures ever to exist. How many had she interacted with in her lifetime? How many were they in total?

She was lost in thoughts of everything she'd believed to be fictitious from films and novels and wondered how many resided in the little town she now found herself in. She turned onto Old Minden Road as the sun disappeared behind the horizon. It was supposed to be a clear night, right around seventy degrees—a perfect night for a fight with a demon from the depths of the abyss.

She almost turned around as the corner where Uncle Joe had crashed through the railing, and Neil fell to his death, came into view. She stopped as the images of Neil lying motionless played out in her mind. This is where her world changed, the birth of her monster. What happened to her led to the death of her father, Quentin, and poor Dylan. She felt the hopelessness start ebbing its way in again, but she shoved it down and walked with purpose. She unzipped the bag she was carrying and removed the container and spike. She flung the bag over the hillside and continued to the curve.

She laid the spike down in the grass below the guardrail, opened the container, and set it down at her feet. She pulled her pack of Winston Lights from her pocket; she only had two left. When she finished them, she was going to quit. For real this time. She lit one and took a long draw. She rested against the rail and exhaled. The metal was warm and uncomfortable, but as badly as her wrist was burning, she knew it wouldn't be long now.

"I got this, Dad," she said as she looked up at the stars. She wished she brought her phone, but she knew if she did, she'd just end up calling Veronica or Tina and losing her nerve. She had to stay angry;

inside, she was, but underneath were the what-could-have-been questions that had plagued her for years.

She looked down the road and saw movement; someone was coming her way. She didn't need to squint. She didn't need to take a second glance. She knew who it was. Her wrist felt as if it was her heartbeat. It thumped along in rhythm with the figure's steps. She kept her eyes glued to it as it got closer, and when he came into view, she felt nothing but rage. She took another long drag from her cigarette and glared.

He wasn't wearing a shirt, and his jeans and black sneakers were caked in mud. He was filthy. The grin on his face showed too much teeth. She shook her head and scoffed. There wasn't anything left of the broken child she visited a few days before.

"Found you," he taunted.

"Cut the bullshit," she hissed.

He put his right hand to his chest. "How dare you? Didn't your daddy teach you manners?"

"That's cute. Where did you get the jeans?" She was scared to ask but was compelled to know. She was sure the story would be awful and regretted it once it left her lips.

"Killed a kid on the way here. You'd be surprised how many people come running when they think a child is in trouble." Nothing laughed. It wasn't from amusement either; it was dripping with cruelty.

Jennifer reached down, picked up the small circular container of salt and silver flakes, and removed the lid. She was taken aback by how steady her hand was. There were no nerves; she wasn't experiencing fear. She was furious, of course, but she was in control and gaining confidence every second.

"Are you ready to die?" Nothing questioned.

"You first," she answered.

He kept his distance on the other side of the road, pacing back and forth. She could see he was excited. She placed the cigarette to her lips and inhaled.

"I'm going to kill you with my bare hands," she said as the smoke poured out of her. Nothing stopped moving, and stared. There was a look of disbelief in his eyes, his mouth slightly open.

"Have you lost your mind?"

"No, I've been fantasizing about how I will do it. I'm thinking of beating you to death. Just fists to the face, over and over till you stop moving, then I'm going to keep going. Make sure you're gone."

She took one final pull from her Winston before she flicked it at him. It flew across the road and hit him square in the chest. Nothing looked down and then slowly back up at her. His eyes narrowed, and his mouth curled into a snarl. She waited for him to move. She had played this over in her mind a thousand times since yesterday, and it was going exactly as planned.

"Do you know what I am? You don't have a chance. Get on your knees. I'll make it quick, and you can finally have the closure you want. Go see Poppa."

"I've got a better idea. You get on your knees, and I'll finish *you* off, send you back to where you came from," she said. Nothing winced. For something so evil and vile to fear Hell, it must be worse than her imagination could fathom. "What's wrong? Don't like that? Tough shit, you made a mistake coming here. You've already lost and are too stupid to realize it." She poured some of the mixture into her left hand. It was fine, almost as if she had a small handful of sand.

He growled like an animal, his eyes maddened.

"I have killed a lot of people in my day, but you, I'm going to savor. You are going to beg to die," he spat. A car came into view from the top of the hill coming down. Neither of them moved. They just stood staring at each other as the headlights came closer. As the yellow Chevy Blazer passed, Jennifer nodded at the man who waved. Nothing looked nervously as it went on down the hill.

"No one is with me; it's just the two of us. I'm handling this on my own," Jennifer reassured him.

Nothing reached behind his back and produced a small knife. He breathed heavily, his body shaking in anger. "I gave you a chance. I can't believe you came back here. You stupid bitch!"

"Are you going to keep talking?" She chuckled. "You've lost your nerve. That's it, isn't it? You can't sneak attack from the shadows; have to face things head-on. Come on, Nothing. I came alone and unarmed. You keep telling me what you're gonna do. How about you shut the fuck up and do it?"

Nothing wailed and charged her; he raised the knife in his left hand and closed the gap quickly. Jennifer flung the powder directly into Nothing's face as he got close. He dropped the knife and backed up a step. His hands shot to his eyes, and he cried out in pain. She took the rest of the container and gave it a flip; the dust went all over his stolen body.

Jennifer tossed the container behind her and reached into the grass for the spike. She held it in her right hand and started toward Nothing. He writhed in the road, screaming at the top of his lungs. He rolled to the high grass on the other side, and Jennifer smiled.

I got you, ya bastard.

At first, she thought he'd caught his jeans on something. There was a loud tearing sound. Blood flowed everywhere, then another rip, then another. She could see the slits forming on Dylan's skin. The wounds opened, becoming larger until they were huge gashes along his stomach and arms. He rolled over and looked up at her.

"WHAT DID YOU DO TO ME?" he cried, but Dylan's voice was gone. This was the one she recognized.

His face split open, and soon he was tearing down the middle. It was coming out of Dylan. She saw the clawed hands hit the ground first as it slowly rose. It was worse than when Veronica described it. Ethel had not done this thing justice. It had long, sharp teeth, no eyes or skin, and hunched over. It was covered in leftover pieces of Dylan, drenched in his blood. She almost froze in place. It was one thing to face something human. This was a monster.

"WHAT HAVE YOU DONE?" It rushed her as she backed away out of instinct. When she reached the guardrail, Nothing descended upon her, and its clawed hand entered her side. She cried out in pain as she felt the warmth of her blood pouring from her waist and down her leg. It had gone in deep, and she was sure it went all the way through.

Fight back!

Jennifer stabbed Nothing in the side with the spike. It howled, a low, metallic, guttural scream. She pulled the weapon back and stabbed it again into its stomach. Through her tears, she could see a black web oozing across the surface of its muscles from each puncture mark she made.

Nothing bit down into her shoulder, tearing a large chuck from her flesh. She fell backward over the railing and onto the ground. Nothing still had its claw in her side, and she held fast to the handle of the spike in its gut. They rolled over, and Jennifer was on top of it. She pulled the instrument back once more and drove it under its rib. Nothing gargled and pulled its claw from her side, only to plunge it into her shoulder and neck.

The pain was excruciating. Jennifer attempted to escape, pulling herself backward, but its claws were buried deep. She could feel herself losing consciousness. She could feel herself bleeding out. The wound it had left in her side was fatal; she could see how much of her life gushed away. Jennifer hugged Nothing tight and rolled hard to the right with all her strength. Together, they went over the edge and off the curb, falling below.

20

"Jennifer!" she heard someone scream.

There was a burning sensation across her body as if it were on fire. She opened her eyes wide and tried to gasp.

"Give it a second. It'll stop," Jennifer heard from above her. Her vision was blurry and out of focus. She couldn't concentrate; every nerve ending felt like fire. She tried to speak but could only muster a low "uh" sound.

"Quit squirming and just lie still," the voice commanded. Jennifer decided the unknown voice knew better than she did and followed the command. After a minute, the feeling subsided and was replaced by numbness. She opened her eyes again to see the sky and a woman staring directly down at her. Her gray hair contrasted against her blue dress.

"God?" Jennifer asked.

"No, stupid," the woman said sarcastically. "Can you stand?"

Jennifer raised her hand, and the older woman helped her to her feet. Jennifer could see that the woman was not happy just by her expression. Her arms were folded, and her eyebrows were down in obvious disapproval.

"I was—" Jennifer started.

"Stupid. That should be the next thing out of your mouth."

Jennifer swayed. Her body didn't feel right; it was as if she'd fallen asleep on her arm but all over.

"I don't feel good."

The woman placed her hands on Jennifer's shoulders. "It takes a few minutes."

Jennifer looked at the woman again, but this time, there was a hint of sadness behind her eyes. Jennifer concentrated and thought of the last few minutes.

"Shit," she muttered. "I lost."

"Well," the woman nodded, "it was a tie."

Jennifer started to turn, and the woman grabbed her face and forced her back toward her.

"Don't. You can't unsee something like that."

"I have to…" Jennifer stepped back and wheeled around.

They were lying side by side at the bottom of the ravine. Jennifer's body was doused in blood; she hardly recognized herself. She put her hands to her mouth. She didn't even look human anymore. She'd have sworn it was fake if she'd seen this in a film. She approached slowly, overcome by the emotions of seeing her dead body. The corpse was on its back, arms outstretched like a grotesque snow angel. The wound in the side exposed the innards, and the collar bone was exposed from the shoulder Nothing had bit through.

It repulsed her, and she was about to look away, but the thing beside her stole her attention. She'd expected to see the monstrosity that was Nothing. Instead, it was a heavy-set, older man lying face down. His hair was bushy gray, and she saw a white beard covering his cheeks. The suit he wore was from an era long gone; she wasn't an expert by any means, but it wasn't from this century, maybe not even the one before. Jennifer looked back at the old woman, bewildered.

"Who is this?" She pointed at him.

"I have no idea. But Nothing turned into that when you both hit the ground."

"Nothing is… an old man?"

The old woman shrugged. Jennifer walked to him and leaned down to see his face. His right eye was covered with an eyepatch;

outside of that, he looked like an off-duty mall Santa. He seemed harmless. Where did Nothing go? This couldn't be it, could it? She knelt to look closer and was startled as he opened his eye.

"Holy shit!" Jennifer shouted as she backed away quickly. He groaned and brought his hand to his head. Jennifer stuck her fists up. The man looked over at her and then down at himself before sitting up suddenly. He stared at his hands and then over to her.

"I'm..." He patted his chest and his legs. "I'm me."

"Nothing?" Jennifer scowled. He rubbed his chin. He sighed whimsically and began to feel his face.

"I'm me," he repeated.

"This is Nothing?" the old woman asked as she came forward.

The man smiled at them both. "You went to all that trouble," he chuckled, "just to kill me." He slapped his stomach as the chuckle turned into laughter. "You made me whole again." He lay back on the ground, snickering. "Jennifer, you might just be the unluckiest woman I've ever met."

Jennifer took a step forward, ready to fist-fight him. She couldn't believe the gall of this man. All the lives he ruined, all the pain inflicted on others, and he got to be happy? He got to be human and not the animal he was? Where was the justice in that? He must have been able to read her reaction.

"Don't try it, girl; I'll bounce your head off these rocks. You can't grab your fancy knife." He waved his hand around. It took two attempts, but he stood and dusted himself off despite no dirt to remove.

Jennifer was speechless; she had given her life to kill him, and an outcome she couldn't have foreseen was playing out before her eyes. He was free. Every action she'd taken with Nothing had ended in complete disaster.

"Well then," he bowed. "I will take my leave. I thank you again, Jennifer."

Jennifer was about to attack him; what was the worst he could do? Kill her again? Could that even happen? As she contemplated how she would take him down, she noticed the ground darkening beneath his feet, swirling with thick smoke. Her eyes went straight to it, and he followed her gaze.

"NO!" he screamed.

She watched as he twisted, trying to escape it, but his legs weren't moving. The smoke grew dense and enveloped his ankles. He began to thrash left and right, his eyes filled with terror.

"I DON'T DESERVE THIS!"

The smoke climbed up his legs and around his waist before wrapping around his throat. It pulled him down, the inky cloud at his feet consuming him. Jennifer imitated his bow from earlier, and the old woman beside her giggled.

"GODDAMN, YOU!" he yelled at Jennifer. "I SWEAR TO GOD I'LL GET YOU! YOU WHORE! IF IT TAKES ME DECADES TO GET BACK YOU'LL—" He was down to his waist and reached out, clawing at the ground in front of him. The smoke wrapped around his arms, and another finger-like portion gripped the top of his head. "NO! PLEASE NO!" He sank into the haze and was gone. The smoke swirled a few moments longer before dissipating, leaving no trace.

The air was still. She hoped whatever awaited him would be a thousand times worse this time.

"Such language," the old woman said, breaking the stillness.

It dawned on Jennifer. "Ethel?"

"Yes?" Ethel answered.

Jennifer held out her arms in excitement. "ETHEL?!"

"What?" Ethel looked confused. Jennifer grabbed her in an embrace. After a few seconds, Ethel's arms wrapped around her.

"It's you! I can't believe it!"

"It's me," Ethel smiled.

"Why aren't you with Veronica?"

"Well, Veronica is busy with Nadine," Ethel said.

"She caught her? Already?" Jennifer grabbed Ethel's shoulders with excitement before realizing it and letting go.

Ethel nodded. "She's in the basement at Wally's right now."

Jennifer clasped her hands together. "And she's safe?"

"She is."

"That's great. So, what happens now?" Jennifer was thrilled by the news. It would only be a matter of time before Wally was free, and Nadine would be dead.

"Well," Ethel got in her face. Her smile faded, and her nostrils flared. "You tell me what you were thinking, doing this on your own."

"I—" The shift in Ethel's demeanor took Jennifer aback.

"I don't want to hear it, Jennifer! Veronica told you to stay home!" Ethel pointed her finger violently in Jennifer's face. "You were supposed to do this together! Do you know how awful this is? You're dead. DEAD! You didn't win anything! You lost! How could you do this?"

Jennifer's joy at stopping Nothing was instantly siphoned away. She felt ashamed and held her head low. She knew her actions would have repercussions, but she was expecting them from Veronica, not Ethel.

"Your father wanted you to live, young lady. He contacted Ronnie so you could go on!" Ethel's lower jaw was thrust outward. "Now you're stuck here like I am, just wishing for someone to take you home."

Jennifer felt like weeping. It hadn't sunk in that she was no longer living and couldn't interact with people in her day-to-day life. She was no longer Doctor Jennifer Simmons. She was now a footnote in history. Ethel was right. Jennifer should have held onto the plan, and maybe the three of them could have done it without casualties. She wouldn't enjoy another cigarette or steak again. She'd never drive her car or talk to Tina.

"I didn't want it to hurt anyone else..." Jennifer muttered.

"It didn't just hurt you! It KILLED you!" Ethel exclaimed.

"It was going after Tina, I had to... I had to stop it." Jennifer attempted to explain herself, but she couldn't find her voice.

"I know, I know." Ethel took a small step back and put her hands up. "I tried to use my voice and scare it, but I couldn't." She ran her fingers through her hair. "I wasn't prepared for all this. I thought you were out for a stroll when I showed up." Ethel threw her hands up.

"How is Veronica going to feel? She did everything to keep you alive!"

Jennifer was going to beg for Ethel's forgiveness. She didn't mean to hurt her this way. She thought she was protecting Veronica, but actually, she'd let the group down. They were supposed to work together, and Jennifer was less resourceful than Veronica. She was lucky Nothing wasn't dancing on her corpse right now. Her beating back the devil was a fluke.

She glanced up at Ethel, but what was behind her took focus. She thought she was hallucinating at first, but she could see it plain as day after blinking hard. A door, along with a frame, stood off in the distance at the bottom of the embankment with them.

"Are you even listening to me?" Ethel shouted before seeing what held her attention. "Oh," Ethel's hand went to her chest. "Oh, Jennifer!"

"Is this what I think it is?" Jennifer asked as she approached. It was just a plain wooden door with a gold handle.

"It's your door," Ethel whispered.

"This was on the website, but I had no idea it was a *literal* door."

Ethel shook her head as if she was snapping out of a trance. "Yes, I've seen a few of these. The door appears for some of us. It's their way out of here."

Jennifer walked to the other side, awestruck that it was held up by nothing. "So, is it the way to... Heaven?"

"I assume so," Ethel's voice cracked.

"This is amazing," Jennifer said aloud.

"Yes," Ethel paused. "I'm sorry I snapped at you."

"It's alright, you don't—" Jennifer began. She placed her hands on the wood, and even though the rest of her body had no feeling, she could sense a warmth coming from within. What could be on the other side? She let her mind wander, thinking of all the stories she'd heard as a child. She hadn't been to church in decades, and she rarely, if ever, prayed. Was this a reward for stopping Nothing?

This was the opposite of what had happened to him. There was no thick Darkness that came for her, so she was safe on that front.

Jennifer looked over to Ethel and saw her lower lip was slightly protruding. Veronica had told her that Ethel had lived an honest life and didn't particularly enjoy being a spirit. She expected that Ethel had been waiting on her door since the day she died.

"Hey, are you okay?" Jennifer asked.

"I just wanted you to know I was sorry. Some things... Some things were said while Ronnie and I were alone. I think you had something to do with that. You were a good influence on her, and the last thing I wanted was for you to die." Ethel stared at the ground as she spoke.

Jennifer felt terrible. She could tell what was going through this woman's mind. She was a part of all of this, too. Ethel was instrumental in stopping Nothing; she probably helped capture Nadine. Veronica and Ethel had a tumultuous relationship now; she likely took no joy in any of this.

"Will you do me a favor? I know we just met, but on the other side, if you can find my Martin, tell him... tell him..." Ethel stumbled over her words.

"I promise." Jennifer nodded as she placed her hand on the handle. "Will you tell Veronica I'm going to miss her and to behave?"

Ethel snorted with laughter but never glanced up. "I can do that."

Jennifer turned back to the door and took a deep breath. There was nothing but silence all around her. This was the end of her existence and the beginning of a new life somewhere else. What could be on the other side? She looked at Ethel, who was still staring at her feet, her hands clasped together in front of her. Jennifer pushed on the door and frowned. There was a loud noise as she jiggled the handle. She tried again, but it wouldn't budge.

"Huh," she said loudly as she backed away from it.

"What?" Ethel asked from behind her.

"I can't..." Jennifer shook the handle again. "I can't get it to open."

"That's not possible. Did you turn the doorknob?" Ethel scoffed.

Jennifer looked back at her, shocked. "Seriously?"

"Well, I don't know. I've never heard of one not opening," Ethel said.

"Maybe..." Even though she couldn't, Jennifer could swear she felt her heart in her throat. "Maybe it's not here for me?"

Ethel's hands dropped to her sides. Her mouth opened and closed several times, but nothing came out. Jennifer motioned at her and then to the door. Ethel's eyes grew wide, and she shook her head. Jennifer repeated the same gestures. Ethel tilted her head and approached skittishly, her hand outstretched. She paused a few times before getting to her destination and stood motionless with her fingertips on the handle.

"I'm scared." Ethel forced a laugh. "I've dreamt of this moment. I don't know what to do if it doesn't open."

"Just try," Jennifer encouraged. Ethel closed her eyes and turned her hand. She gasped as the door opened, and a blinding light poured out from beyond. Jennifer had felt something beyond the door, but it was nothing compared to the heat that emanated from the radiance. She smiled and stepped up beside Ethel. "I guess you can tell him yourself."

Ethel put her hands on her cheeks in dismay. "What about Ronnie, who will watch her after—"

"I will. I got this. You go," Jennifer said softly.

"I haven't said goodbye. I don't know—" Ethel stammered.

"You don't know how long this will be here." Jennifer pointed toward the illumination. Go!" She told her again.

"You have to want her to see you. You have to—" Ethel took a step back.

"Ethel," Jennifer tried to be as forceful as possible. "If you don't go, I will push you through."

Ethel looked into the light, returned to Jennifer, and touched her cheek. Her eyes softened, and she smiled.

"Thank you. I wish we had more time together."

Jennifer put her hand up to hers. "Me too. I'll watch after her. I promise."

Ethel entered the Brilliance.

The door closed and faded from view.

Jennifer stood still, hoping the door wouldn't come back. She owed Ethel almost as much as she owed Veronica. Even though she couldn't see her most of the time, she was there watching over her, too.

She hoped Ethel was a part of the light now; it was so warm and inviting that Jennifer almost stepped through herself. She envisioned Ethel being reunited with her husband and the rest of her loved ones. She was happy to be there to see her off. Ethel deserved it, and it was time she got it.

Jennifer stood there for what seemed like forever. The door never reappeared. She was alone with her dead body in the small ravine that had changed her life before and ended it now.

"I've spent so long avoiding this place. Now I'm stuck here," she said to no one. She glanced down the hillside toward the town with the rolling hills behind them. "Not so bad."

She smiled, knowing that Ethel had gone to the other side, and was pleased that her plan worked. Jennifer never turned the handle, just rattled it in her hand for the noise. She hadn't a clue if the door would have opened for Ethel, and she certainly had no idea if she could pass through. Something inside her had told her this needed to be done. A test of some kind. What if she never got another chance to get out of here? Jennifer felt fear for a fleeting moment.

No, it was the right thing to do, she told herself.

She'd given Ethel her afterlife.

The sun rose over the horizon, and Veronica stared over the guard rail and police tape. Her friend, if you could even call her that, was found dead yesterday evening by local police. She'd felt like they had become more than acquaintances, and with as many tears as she'd shed on the trip here, someone might have thought they were sisters.

They didn't tell her much. She'd rented a room at the Comfort Inn and went into town. She'd parked at her old house, telling the neighbor she was going for a walk to meet someone, and then somehow ended up here. Veronica knew the significance of this place.

The police were glad she'd made the trip, and they asked her to identify the body. They had trouble with their computer systems and couldn't get a fingerprint match. Veronica had been on the other side of those moments. This was the first time she had to affirm someone she knew. Jennifer had been torn to bits. She'd been stabbed through the neck and side, and half of her shoulder was missing. The back of her head was split open from the fall, and most of her bones were shattered. At least her eyes were closed. It was bad enough to see her in the state she was in; she doubted she could handle it if they'd been open.

A police officer had found her; he'd stopped because of the blood all over the road. He thought someone had hit an animal. He just happened to look over the railing and saw her. Veronica was glad he did. Who knew how long her body would have sat alone before being found. No one should just decompose in the brush. Veronica prayed she had an insurance policy to be laid beside her father. Jennifer would have wanted that.

Nothing had won. At least, it seemed that way. There was no sign of Dylan alongside Jennifer, but there had clearly been a confrontation. Veronica doubted that Jennifer had punctured herself, removed some of her shoulder, and then jumped into the ravine. She hoped that Jennifer at least cut him as Wally had instructed. That somewhere right now, Nothing was in agonizing pain and rotting away.

It didn't matter, though. Jennifer was gone and Ethel was still missing. Where was she? Why had she left her alone? She needed her right now, even if it was just for argument's sake. Veronica was hurting and needed someone to assure her that things would be alright, even if they would be lying through their teeth.

"Ethel..." she called out, but she knew it was pointless. She hadn't come the last fifty times she'd said her name, and she doubted this would be the one that brought her forth. Something had happened between them, and Veronica regretted everything she'd said to Nadine. Maybe the talk about her grandfather had been the last straw for Ethel. Maybe Ethel was ashamed for divulging the way she had. Veronica felt it may have been in her best interest to keep those thoughts to herself.

The sun had cleared the mountains, and she could feel the warmth on her face. She would have a long, lonely trip back to Parkersburg. She was dreading it already. Her pocket began to vibrate. She'd put her phone on silent on the way here and forgotten to turn the ringer back on. She reached in and extracted it. It was a Charleston number. She had no idea who'd call her this early in the morning, but the number seemed familiar. She just couldn't place it.

She answered and put it on speaker. No one was around listening; even if there were, she wouldn't have cared. She had the luxury of being all alone on the side of the road.

"Yello." She tried her best to sound pleasant.

"Detective Carter?" The voice asked back. *Green.* She knew instantly, and her blood began to boil.

"What?" She was itching for a fight.

"This is Detective Green. I'm going to need you and Ms. Simmons to come in and speak to me." She could hear the contempt in his voice; he was trying his hardest to be cordial.

"I'm afraid that's not happening," she snapped.

"Now you listen to me—" he began.

"No, you sack of shit, you listen to me," she lashed out. "I'm in Oak Hill, Jennifer's dead. Just saw the body myself."

There was silence on the other end.

"Her body is with their M.E. right now. Someone ripped her apart. So, she can't *come speak* to you," Veronica fumed.

"You have my condolences," he said.

"Really?" Veronica laughed. "Do I now? Listen, Green, my captain called me in and told me what you pulled. You've been digging into my life and had zero reasons to do that."

"I had several reasons," he retorted.

"Is that so? I would have cooperated in any way I could have if it helped you out. Instead, you went behind my back without cause."

"You lied to me," Green hissed.

"No, I didn't. We were together the entire time. What she and I were doing was none of your goddamn business. But since you've been looking into me, you must know the kind of woman I am." Veronica bent and clutched the guardrail.

"What are you trying to say?"

"I'll tell you plainly: if you ever call me again, call my Captain again, get your captain to call my captain again, write my name on a piece of paper, talk about me in passing, mention my name to your dog, if you even think of my name, I'll make you pay." He didn't respond. She gave him a few seconds to mull that over. "I'll make it my mission to humiliate you, to ruin you, and that's a promise. So, try me." She smiled. She meant every word.

"You have a nice day," his voice was low, almost grumbling. He'd probably had a partner recording the call. He would have to if he was trying to build a case against a fellow officer. She decided to throw one last insult on top.

"Fuck you, I hope you get hit by a bus," she chirped.

She hung up and stared at her phone. She knew that he'd never stop until he found something. She didn't care. Things were going to change when she got home. If Green needed to be dealt with, she would handle it, but a chill hit her, and she perked up instantly.

"That was rude," Jennifer called from behind her.

Veronica jumped, her phone flew out of her hand and over the railing, falling into the grass below. She'd tried to catch it, but she pushed it further away when her fingertips touched it. She watched it tumble before spinning around to see Jennifer. She was standing on the side of the road in a Red Devils t-shirt and jeans, smiling at her. Veronica couldn't believe it. Jennifer was a spirit. She was one of the ones left behind. She would have never wished this upon her. She felt tears coming, and then rage.

"What happened?!"

Jennifer shrugged. "A big epic fight, like something out of a movie; sorry you missed it," she joked.

Her nonchalant attitude angered Veronica even more. "You're dead!"

"I know. It was my fight. If something would've happened to you..." Jennifer shook her head slightly.

Veronica swung, her arm passed through Jennifer's midsection, and then she swung again. Jennifer flinched and backed away, but Veronica gave chase. She swung wildly. A car slowed as it passed by them both, and the driver stared out the window in disbelief.

"You're acting crazy," Jennifer observed.

"Do you know what you've done?" Veronica asked her, tears streaming down her face, her fists still passing through their target.

"I stopped a monster that was rampaging across the state, killing everything in its path?"

Jennifer was trying to reason with her, and Veronica knew it. She just wasn't having any of it. She needed to vent, and trying to fistfight a ghost was a great place to start.

"You got killed, and Ethel is missing!" Veronica roared before swinging at a wide arch and almost falling. Jennifer looked away, and Veronica could tell instantly that Jennifer knew something about her. She stopped punching and stood there panting. "Jennifer, where is Ethel?"

"Listen," Jennifer stepped back. "I can come back later after you've calmed down to discuss it. I don't think you're—"

"Where is she?!" Veronica hadn't been this upset in her life.

"She... gone," Jennifer winced.

"What do you mean?" Veronica raised her fists again as she shouted at the top of her lungs.

Jennifer held her hands up. "Ethel got her door."

"She's moved on?" Veronica put her hand to her forehead. "Now?"

Veronica felt like she might vomit. She turned and kicked the guardrail as hard as she could. She started bawling again. Veronica had never had a chance to mourn the loss of her grandmother because she was never truly gone. Now she was, and she could feel herself breaking down. There was a loud buzzing in her ears, and for a fleeting moment, she felt faint.

"Goddamn it. We were... We were getting somewhere. She was listening to me!" She paced around in a circle before kicking the metal again. "Mother fucker!"

Ethel abandoned her and went through the door just when they started bridging the gap. It wasn't fair. It was like she'd died all over again. Veronica sat down against the railing, put her head in her hands, and wept.

"Don't you dare disappear too," she whispered between wails.

"Me?" Jennifer asked.

Veronica nodded without looking up. "Everyone always leaves."

"I won't, I'm right here. I'll stay here as long as you want," Jennifer said.

Veronica looked up, reached out her hand, and it went through Jennifer, making her cry harder.

"I'll have to get used to that," Jennifer joked.

"Ethel," Veronica tried to catch her breath, "was with me for years and never got used to it."

"I finally got to see her, though. She was a beautiful woman," Jennifer remarked, sitting beside Veronica.

"I'm glad you were there for her." Veronica placed her hands on her forehead and ran her fingers back through her hair.

Jennifer finally broke the silence that followed. "She wanted me to tell you she was sorry, and she forgave you."

Veronica shot her an angry look, her voice dropping to a threatening tone. "Don't lie to me."

"Alright," Jennifer put a hand up. "She asked me to look after you and to tell you goodbye."

"This is such bullshit. Ethel moved on, you're dead." Veronica held her hands out.

"I'm sorry," Jennifer said.

"That's not all," Veronica continued. "Wally is gone, and we didn't save Dylan. We lost."

"That's not true," Jennifer said. "Nadine is gone, right?"

Veronica nodded.

"And Nothing is gone. Think of how many people we saved."

"I'm not sure it is worth it." Veronica picked up a tiny rock and threw it.

Jennifer waited until Veronica looked her in the eyes. "Did you tell that other officer that you hoped he got hit by a bus?" Jennifer asked.

"Yeah, I guess I did."

They broke out in uncomfortable laughter, and Veronica looked over the edge. She was still gasping every few breaths.

"I lost my phone." Veronica glanced over the railing.

"You can have mine. I don't need it."

"I have to find mine. I have some nudes on there," Veronica added while wiping her tears, her voice hoarse from crying.

"Tasteful stuff?" Jennifer asked.

"Not in the slightest." Veronica shook her head. They laughed as they started down the road to get to the ravine.

"I can't wait to tell you about Nothing," Jennifer said.

"You know a witch gave me the ability to see you?" Veronica asked, desperate to talk about anything that would take her mind off Ethel.

"Really?" Jennifer flinched playfully. "I thought witches were evil incarnate."

"So did I," Veronica rubbed her chin. "And Wally left me his house and the *collection* out back."

"Hmm. What will you do with all that?" Jennifer trotted in front of her excitedly.

"Well, Nothing and Nadine were pretty fucking awful, but I kinda want to see what else goes *bump in the night*." Veronica sniffled, recalling the phrase for West Virginia Weird. "You in?"

"I've got nothing going on at the moment. And who knows,maybe there is all kinds of stuff about ghosts? Like a handbook or something in Wally's stuff?"

"Hey," Veronica said.

Jennifer turned to face her.

"Thank you, you're a good friend. You're the only one I have." Veronica wiped what was left of the tears from her face.

Jennifer wheeled back around, starting down the hill once more, and quipped, "It's because you're a bitch."

ABOUT THE AUTHOR

Stephen Bias was born and raised in Barboursville, West Virginia. His first novel, Afterwords, whetted his appetite for writing. Now, he spends his later years coming up with terrible idea after terrible idea before choosing one he thinks is the best of the bunch. His days that are not spent with his children or wife are wasted away pecking at a keyboard in hopes of making someone somewhere smile.

f X

The Dictionary Game
by Mike Hornyak